A Kiss Across a Millennium

Swirling the wine in the bright blue glass, Nils regarded her closely as he lowered his voice.

"I also recall you saying that Ethelred is no longer king of England."

"Not for almost a thousand years." Linnea stiffened, and he knew she was as uneasy with this turn of the conversation as he was. "It is 1817."

"That term means nothing to me." Nils looked away from the abrupt compassion on her face. He did not want to be pitied. He was a warrior. Draining the goblet, he set it on the windowsill beside him.

"Ethelred was king of England around the year we would have called 990."

He clenched the fingers on his right hand into a fist. Slamming them into the arm of the bench, he ignored the shock on Linnea's face and how her servant whirled in her seat to stare at him, her eyes wide with terror.

"I know Ethelred is king of England."

"But I told you —"

He snarled a curse at her. Heaving himself to his feet, he hopped to where a window opened on the seaside of this building. Ignoring the pain raging in his head, he fumbled as he tried to open the shutters on the window with a single hand. Several of the slats hung, broken. When Linnea's slender fingers reached to unhook the stubborn latch, he caught her wrist. Her servant shouted a warning, but Linnea did not make a sound as he tugged her closer, keeping her from undoing the latch.

Had Olive's warning been for Linnea or for him? he wondered when the soft scent of whatever she used to clean her hair drifted toward him, as luscious as the first blossoms after a long winter. Her curves pressed against him were as seductive as the allure of the sea.

His lips were on hers before she had a chance to protest. They tasted sweet, just as he had imagined.

For Debra Dixon
vice president extraordinaire and good friend
Enjoy your "retirement!"

My Lord Viking

***

J. A. Ferguson

MY LORD VIKING
Published by ImaJinn Books, a division of ImaJinn

ISBN: 1-893896-18-8

10 9 8 7 6 5 4 3 2 1

PUBLISHER'S NOTE:
This book is a work of fiction. Names, characters, places and
incidents are products of the author's imagination or are used
fictitiously. Any resemblance to actual events or locales or persons,
living or dead, is entirely coincidental.

Books are available at quantity discounts when used to promote
products or services. For information please write to: Marketing
Division, ImaJinn Books, P.O. Box 162, Hickory Corners, MI
49060-0162, or call toll free 1-877-625-3592.

Cover design by Patricia Lazarus

ImaJinn Books, a division of ImaJinn
P.O. Box 162, Hickory Corners, MI 49060-0162
Toll Free: 1-877-625-3592
http://www.imajinnbooks.com

Prologue

So this was death.

He had not thought it would be like this. Where was the *Valkyrja* to carry him to *Valhalla* so he might spend the rest of eternity among brave warriors, trading tales of spectacular deeds and of enemies slain in vengeance and for glory?

He was so alone.

That was worse than the pain. The pain would soon be gone when his last breath sifted from his body. But would he spend all of eternity alone?

He had fought valiantly. He should have earned a warrior's death. Those enemies who had fallen around him would never again raise their swords against his chieftain.

Salt flavored the gulps of air he tried to pull into his broken body. Where was death? A seat at the table in *Valhalla* should be his reward, but how could he aspire to that when his blood-oath remained unfilled?

"Freya!" he called with what strength he had left. His voice was as raw as the wounds sending his blood to mix with his enemies' and the sand. "Freya, send your handmaiden to me! Help me complete my quest for my chieftain. Bring me strength to complete my quest, or bring me death."

There was no answer but the sound of the waves on the shore and the sea birds.

He was alone. His prayer had not been heard. Now he would die, his vow incomplete. Maybe that was why he had been denied *Valhalla*.

"No!" he cried into the merciless sunshine that seared his skin.

There was no answer.

He was alone...with death.

One

Sunlight teased the waves, glittering them with jewels before they dashed themselves into oblivion on the sand. Above the water, gulls spun the clouds together like a spinster at her wheel. The last signs of winter had been banished, for gorse flowered on the low hill rising from the shore.

Linnea Sutherland pushed back her straw bonnet to let it hang by its pink ribbons over her shoulders. Mama would be dismayed to see her youngest child letting the sun paint color on her face, but Linnea did not care. Not today. Loosening her hair, she let it fall in waves along her shoulders. The dark strands blew into her face, but she simply shoved them aside. She wanted to be as free as each droplet within the sea, free to wander from one shore to another to discover what might be waiting there. As free as her cocker spaniel puppy Scamp, who was barking at each wave and snapping at the water.

She raised her hands to embrace the fresh air and the sunshine. Mayhap they would wash away the consternation inside her that even Scamp's antics could not dispel. She should be happy. How many times had she told herself that in the past week since Randolph had asked her to marry him? Randolph Denner had asked her nicely, and no one in the shire would be astonished that Lord Sutherland's youngest was making a match with Randolph Denner who had recently inherited the title of Lord Tuthill along with his father's holdings farther inland. She should be happy, so filled with joy that she could not walk to the beach. She should be dancing about like her sister Dinah had when she had become betrothed.

But she was not. She did not understand why not. She had known Randolph for a long time, and she had imagined many times getting married in one of the gardens with a view of the sea. She should be happy.

"Blast and perdition!" she called to the sea. Then she laughed. Mama would be even more distressed by Linnea using such language than by leaving off her bonnet. Yet the truth was simply that Linnea could not understand why she had not given Randolph an enthusiastic yes when he proposed, or why she was not as elated as she had dreamed she would be.

Pulling off her slippers and stockings, she curled her toes in the warm sand. The sea would be deadly cold at this time of year, but the sun had heated the strand, luring her from the heavy walls of Sutherland Park to this quiet cove. With the preparations for Dinah's wedding in two weeks, all the talk was of betrothals and wedding guests. That was too unsettling when she was so torn.

She balanced her slippers in her hands as she looked across the sea. There were so many places she had read about, so many things she had dreamed of. If she married Randolph, she would see no more than his fusty house and London. The one time she had broached the subject of going to Italy for their honeymoon, he had acted as shocked as if she had suggested they live together without the benefit of the clergy's blessing. Was that what was bothering her? No, for this uneasiness had begun before they had discussed that.

"I wish I knew what was wrong," she said to Scamp

as he ran about her feet, threatening to trip her. She smiled as he raced back to the soft rush of the waves. "Everything is going just as I had expected, so mayhap it is time to do something unexpected."

She arched a single brow at her own thought. Papa and Mama would not force her to wed Randolph. She could not imagine Papa forcing anyone to do anything, even though he was a capable businessman who, rumor suggested, could wring every shilling out of a deal. Papa had told Mama over and over that he had worked so hard to bring wealth back to the family for the benefit of Mama and the children. He wanted each of his six sons and six daughters to be happy. And he had succeeded...until now when Linnea could not sort out in her mind what she wanted. Even a few days ago, she would have laughed if anyone had spoken of how she would feel once plans for her own wedding were about to get underway as soon as Dinah's was over.

What was wrong with her? It must be her, for there was nothing amiss with Randolph. He was the fourth viscount in his line. He was well-favored, if one ignored his chin that jutted out and his ears that turned red each time someone spoke to him. Tall, he carried no spare flesh. He could ride well and oversaw his father's lands with a cautious wisdom that bordered on parsimony. That was to be respected when his father had left him little coin. Never had she heard of him drinking more or gambling more than a gentleman ought. He was the perfect husband for his nearest neighbor's youngest daughter.

Linnea sighed as she continued along the sand. She should be grateful that Randolph had approached her father to ask for her hand. Papa had said yes, if she agreed. While growing up, she had longed for this chance to have a man propose to her as sweetly as her other sisters had been proposed to. Then when Randolph had, she had surprised herself as much as anyone when she had asked for time to think it over.

She smiled.   Randolph had thought her overmastered by his proposal, and she had let him hold onto his misconception. It was simpler than the truth, although she must own to the truth soon. How could she tell him that she seemed to like the idea of marriage more than the idea of marriage to him? It would hurt him, when he had done nothing but try to make her silly dream of being in love come true.

"Egad! How do you expect him to understand what you want when you do not know yourself?" She chuckled at her own outspokenness, even though no one was near enough to heed her, save for Scamp and the birds turning overhead.

A frown lowered her brows as she shaded her eyes with her hand. The birds were acting most peculiarly. They were circling, as if a storm had scoured the sea bottom and the waves were tossing a feast onto the shore. Her nose wrinkled. Dying fish and drying seaweed always created such a noxious scent.

She almost turned to walk in the other direction, but her curiosity refused to let her resist the temptation of discovering what had the birds so excited. Once she and her brother Alfred had chanced upon a case of smuggled French brandy on the beach. Papa had been furious with them for bringing a single bottle to the house, and he had ordered such froggish drink destroyed. Who could guess what she might find today? Mayhap it would something to help her deal with her dilemma.

Laughing at her silly thought, she called to Scamp to follow, but did not need to worry, for he was eager to chase every wave. The puppy's fur, which was usually the shade of honey, had become the dreary color of wet sand. Barking, he sped toward her.

With her hand on the boulders to keep herself from slipping into the water, she eased around the edge of the cove. She winced when she scratched her toe. Blood dripped from the torn skin, but she paid it no mind save to dip her toe in the icy water. The salt would help heal the small cut.

Linnea flinched again as she stepped on a sharp shell, but did not slow. This was as close to an adventure as she might find today, so she wanted to enjoy it. She did not doubt that Randolph would not look kindly upon his future wife cavorting upon the shore with her bonnet, shoes, and stockings off. He would surely—

She froze and stared at a body lying on the beach. The man did not move. Was he asleep? She did not want to disturb anyone who might wish to be alone. The puppy ran, barking, up to the man, but he did not move. Not even when Scamp licked his face.

"Oh, my dear heavens!" she whispered as she saw blood on the sand. 'Twas much more blood than from her scraped toe.

She must get help! She must do something. She must...

Taking a deep breath, she warned herself to be calm. She could do nothing to help this man—if, indeed, he was in need of help—while acting like a want-witted chucklehead.

"Sir?" Her voice cracked on the single word. She inched forward and tried again. "Sir, do you need assistance?"

A groan answered her.

Linnea rushed to his side. She pressed her hand over the ribbons laced through her bodice as she stared down at him. What sort of man was this?

Blood was caked on his forehead, in his tawny hair, and through his beard which was a shade darker. By his left side, his arm lay at an angle that was impossible unless it was broken. His clothes were unlike anything she had ever seen. He wore a woolen shirt that was longer than Papa's nightshirt. Embroidery in colors that once might have been as bright as the flowers in Sutherland Park's water garden accented the neckline and ran down its front. Around his neck was a gold chain. On it, an odd triangular ornament hung. A belt, holding a pouch and an empty scabbard, at his waist was made of the same cracking leather as the bands lashing his stockings below his knees. He wore only one shoe, and his other foot was covered with dried blood.

"Sir?" she whispered. She pushed Scamp's curious nose aside. Until she was sure where the blood was coming from, she did not want the puppy causing the man more injury. "Sir, can you hear me?"

Only the waves sliding up onto the sand answered her.

Squatting next to him, she put out her hand to shake him gently, then drew it back. There was so much blood! She should get help. The cry of a gull halted her from jumping to her feet. She could not leave this man here, unprotected from the sun and wounded. If only he could speak...

She dipped her stocking in a wave and dabbed it against his forehead. He muttered something she could not understand. She hoped his wits had not been rattled from his skull in the blow that had raised a lump.

Carefully she washed the crimson line from his forehead. She frowned when she saw the wound that was surrounded by a lump nearly the size of one of Scamp's paws. The bruise was still red. The man had been struck not long ago. Her hand clenched the ruined stocking. Mayhap the man who had landed him this facer was still close by.

Her heart thudded against her breast as she glanced both ways along the beach. It was empty, but... A glint on the sand caught her eye. She nearly cried out her relief when she saw a knife lying beside the man's left hand. A weapon! A scoundrel would think twice before attacking her if he saw this knife. Horrified, she realized that this broad-shouldered man who was lying on the sand may have wielded it first against the one who had laid him so low.

Stretching across the unconscious man, she realized

those shoulders and his chest were even wider than she had guessed. She balanced herself carefully as she reached for the knife. To tumble atop him might be dangerous for him and would be unquestionably embarrassing for her. She smiled when she grasped the blade's engraved haft. Holding her breath, she lifted it from the sand and sat back on her heels.

Linnea squinted to look at the pattern on the knife's pommel, for the sun shimmered off the metal. It was engraved with a series of circles and figures. Mayhap human figures, and she bent to determine what they might be.

Fingers closed around her wrist. She gasped and tried to pull away. Her arm was jerked toward the ground. She stared in disbelief into eyes as purple as the first glow of dawn. The man was awake!

"How are you faring?" She winced as his grip on her wrist tightened. "That hurts! Please let me go."

"*Feila*?" Bafflement threaded his brow, and a flash of pain swept his face. His incredible eyes did not release her, nor did his strong fingers.

"I don't understand," she whispered. She tried to tug her arm away. "Let me go!"

Linnea gasped as he slowly forced the point of the dagger up toward her chin. She released the knife. The blade struck the sand between them. He shoved her back and reached for the knife. She moaned as her bottom landed hard on the sand.

Scamp rushed, barking, to her side. She pushed the excited puppy off her lap. Rising to her knees, she cried out in horror as the man gripped the ribbons holding her bonnet around her neck.

"Release me!" she cried.

He pulled her toward him, the sharp edge of her bonnet cutting into her nape. A smile spread through his shaggy beard, and his eyes narrowed to amethyst slits. He said something, but she could not understand a single word.

Fury strengthened her. She tugged at the ribbons, and the bow untied. Again she rocked back onto the sand. Jumping to her feet, she ran toward the other cove. Over her shoulder, she called, "Scamp, come!"

The puppy yelped.

Linnea looked back. The man was leaning on his right elbow and held Scamp by the scruff. The puppy was wiggling in a futile attempt to flee. Knowing she should go for assistance, but fearing the man would hurt her puppy, she faltered. She could see his smile glimmering even from where she stood as she took a single step, then another back toward him.

"Let Scamp go. Please," she whispered when she stood beside the man again. She pointed to the puppy. "Scamp. Let him go."

"Scamp?"

She flinched as he repeated the name back to her. The odd accent his deep voice put on the single word was one she could not place. But what did she know of the ways of low folk who would threaten a woman wanting only to help? "Yes, that is Scamp. My dog."

"*Rakki*," he said as he held the pup off the ground.

"*Rakki*? Dog?" She nodded. "Yes, that is my dog. Please do not hurt Scamp."

Satisfaction widened his smile. He released the dog, which darted beyond his reach. "*Britannia*?"

"Are you asking if this is England?" She never had met such a peculiar man. Even though the wound was still oozing on his forehead and his left arm had not moved, he acted as if nothing were amiss. "Who are you?"

Nils Bjornsson continued to smile at the lovely woman. That was one question he did not intend to answer until he discovered what was happening here. He could understand this woman, even though he had never heard any of the gutless Anglo-Saxons use some of the words she did.

Pain scored his skull as he shifted and tried to sit.

His left arm hung at his side, useless. It was his
misfortune that he preferred to hold his knife in that
hand when he drove it into an enemy. His left ankle
burned as if it were a torch. If his ribs were not broken,
the agony of every breath made them seem so. Blood
trickled along his side, and he knew his foe had gotten
in one successful strike before Nils saw him dead. Then
he had been hit again by his blood-enemy. Where was
Kortsson now?

Fighting to clear his blurred eyesight, he looked up
at the woman who was edging away. He grasped the
sax, and she halted, an expression of fear on her face
as she stared at the blade. Good! She was not as witless
as others he had met during his previous journeys to
this island.

Nor was she without other attributes that appealed
to him. Although she wore her ebony hair shamelessly
uncovered about her shoulders and a white gown that
was as gossamer as a fair weather cloud, her face was
finely boned. Eyes as dark as her hair did not lower
before his steady gaze. She possessed a brave spirit he
had not seen here. Yet it was not her spirit that drew
his eyes to the intriguing curves which were revealed
so delightfully by her damp dress.

His eyes narrowed as something glistened just above
her breasts. He could see well enough to determine the
necklace she wore around her neck was of fine gold
and gems. He doubted if such a young, wealthy woman
would wander far from her home. There might be a
treasure waiting there for the daring man who sought
it.

But that man could not be Nils Bjornsson. He had
his duty, the sworn oath that had brought him to this
desolate place. He could not forsake it to fill his pouch
with gold.

"*Feila!*" he called. When she did not move, he
repeated in her language, "Woman. *Aa-sjaa.*"

"What?"

Nils sought in his slow mind for the English word. "*Aa-sjaa*. Help."

He was astonished when she folded her arms in front of her and said, "You have your gall asking me for help when you have threatened me with a knife and nearly choked me to death."

Trying to decipher her peculiar accent, he smiled as he said, "I did not kill you."

"You tried."

"If I had tried, you would be dead."

"Do you expect me to be grateful for your clemency?"

Nils gave up all attempt to comprehend what she meant by that question. His mind was clearing, and he could recall more and more of the language of Britannia. Lowering the *sax*, he said, "I need help. Bring some."

He watched as she hesitated. Her dog ran about her, but he ignored it. The pup had no more sense than the birds above, and he saw no use for such a puny creature. It was too small to herd or to hunt.

Slowly she nodded. "I will get some help, but you must give me the knife."

"So you may kill me?"

"If I wanted to kill you," she said in the same superior tone he had used, "you would never have wakened. You were as helpless as a babe."

In spite of himself, Nils smiled again. This *was* a dangerous woman, for she used words with the skill of a *skald*.

"Will you bring help?" he asked.

"Will you give me the dagger?"

He flipped the *sax* into the air. The blade drove into the sand only an inch from her toes. "That is your answer."

Taking a deep breath, she bent to pick up the knife. "Rest. I will bring others to help." She frowned as she looked at his left arm. "That will need to be set. It looks broken."

"It feels broken."

Her eyes grew wide. She took a step toward him.

He tensed. Did she mean to slay him now that he had been a *daari* and given her the dagger? Maybe she had guessed how weak he was.

When she knelt beside him, she said, "Rest here. I will leave Scamp with you. He will keep the birds and any other curious creatures away until I can return."

"He will do nothing but make noise."

"Exactly."

"I need no more noise when my head is as heavy as a *drakkar*."

"What?"

Could she be so sheltered she did not know of the large ships which could slip in and out of every bay and estuary on this island? "Take the beast with you, and bring help."

She picked up the thing she had tied around her neck. "This will shield you from the sun."

He took the basket-shaped thing and stared at it. What was he to do with it?

Her laugh startled him, and he looked from the straw basket to her face which was pleasingly close to his. The sunshine had scored her cheeks with the same color as the laces on the basket.

She lifted the basket out of his hand and, up-ending it, set it on his head. "I know 'tis a lady's bonnet, but it will keep you from turning as red as—" She gulped and suddenly looked away.

Red as what? Blood? He smiled as he stared at the sand. His enemies had...Where were their bodies? He scanned the beach in both directions. Had they been sucked out to sea? If so, there was no explanation why he had been left behind.

"Rest," she said, yet again.

He caught her hand before she could rise to her feet. "What is your name?"

"Linnea."

"Daughter of whom?"

She regarded him with bafflement, but said, "Lord Sutherland."

He smiled. *Suthrland!* A name he recognized. All might not be as bizarre as he had begun to think. The chieftain was sometimes called Suthrland. This woman must be part of his family. He might be closer to the completion of his quest than he had guessed. If he...He swayed and fought to hold onto his senses.

"Careful," Linnea warned needlessly, for he was certain his head had been laced with a demon's fire.

When she put her hand on his right shoulder, he let her lean him back against the embrace of the sand. He hated being as frail as a nurseling, but the ethereal caress of her fingers on his skin through his ripped tunic was an unexpected diversion on this journey. Her skin was as soft as freshly carded wool.

"I shall return as soon as I can with help," she whispered. "With *aa-s*—"

"*Aa-sjaa,*" he supplied, although speaking even the single word sapped him as if he had rowed from Jutland to this accursed island.

Nils watched as she gracefully rose. She held the *sax* close to the diaphanous fabric of her gown, and she backed away as if she suspected he might give chase even now. Clearly she no idea how feeble he was.

With her puppy at her heels, she rounded the pile of rocks at the edge of the headland. She glanced back once.

He wondered if she would return.

Two

How was she going to explain *this*?

Linnea hurried along the path leading from the shore as Scamp sniffed in the hedgerows edging either side. Her efforts to persuade the pup to remain with the stranger had been futile. He continued to tag along at her heels.

Pulling her hair back, she tied it in place with a ribbon from her bodice. She hoped no one noticed she wore no stockings beneath her gown. If she walked quickly enough, nobody might ask for the truth. How could she explain finding a man on the beach?

And such a strange man. Even if she could have guessed the source of his accent, the words he muttered in some other language were totally incomprehensible. She had seen his eyes narrow in concentration each time she spoke, as if he understood her and yet still did not.

Those eyes...She shivered, although the sun was still warm. She had seen such eyes in one of the foxes prowling through the gardens. Cold as a snake's, but with wit that could bamblusterate the master of the hounds. Yes, he had the look of the hunted in his eyes. Dampening her lips, she glanced back at the narrow strip of strand she could see from here. She could not see the man, but his eyes haunted her.

The thought added speed to her feet. In the distance, beyond a copse in the shape of a crescent moon, the roofs of Sutherland Park rose like a beacon. Chimneys sprouted as wildly as weeds, and windows twinkled in the stone dormers. The first house on this site had been raised centuries before the Conquest. Papa had found Roman coins and tools in a barrow beyond the stables.

She wondered if, in all that time, anyone had found a castaway like the man on the beach.

Dash it! He had never even told her his name. She paused, mid-step. He might have a good reason not to reveal his name, a reason that could explain his injuries. If he were a gentleman of the pad, those wounds could have come when the coachman fought off his attempt to heave the purses of the carriage's passengers.

That made no sense. No highwayman would be riding out in such an outlandish outfit, and only an addled fool would go out to rob someone with a knife as his sole weapon. None of this made any sense.

The scents of the stable grew stronger as she neared. When Scamp bolted off toward the house, yipping wildly, she was tempted to follow. It would be so simple just to pretend she never had met the man on beach. She sighed. She could not leave him there alone when he was in such dire condition.

"'Morning!" came a cheery voice from behind her.

Linnea whirled. Resisting the temptation to throw her arms around the short, thickset lad who held a currying brush in one hand and, in the other, a bucket, she said, "I need your assistance, Jack."

Jack Wetherell dropped the brush into the bucket. Setting them on the cobbles in front of the stable door, he pulled his cap off his red hair and wiped his full sleeve across his freckled forehead. His breeches were stained, and he wore heavy boots, warning that she had arrived while he was busy getting the horses ready for Papa, who must be expecting guests to arrive soon for

Dinah's wedding. Oh, dear heavens, could it get more complicated?

"'Course, Lady Linnea," he answered. "How can I help?"

She was grateful for Jack's friendship and loyalty. She had first met him when he was just a youngster in the kitchens where his grandmother was the cook. "Come with me."

"All right. Soon as I put away this bucket." He gave her a ragged-tooth grin. "If we have time."

"Of course." Again she wanted to hug him. If she had gone to her brother, he would have peppered her with so many questions, the man on the beach could have died of old age before she finished answering all of them. "Bring some of those rags."

"Yes, Lady Linnea."

"And, Jack?" She held out the knife the stranger had given her. "Please put this somewhere safe until I can decide what to do with it."

His eyes widened, and she knew he had taken note of the strange engraving on the pommel. "Safe?"

"Where no one will find it."

He grinned. "Know just the place."

Jack hung the wooden bucket on a brad inside the door and went somewhere into the shadows to hide the dagger, and Linnea motioned to another of the stablemen. She gave him a quick message and turned back to Jack before the other stableman could ask the questions she saw in his eyes. Just now she did not have any explanation of why she wanted her maid Olive to meet her at the fishing pavilion in the water garden. She had no explanation save the truth, and, right now, she wanted to be careful who was privy to that. The pavilion was the building closest to the sea path, so they could tend to the man's wounds there to ease his pain before taking him the rest of the way up to the house. His odd words and strange actions worried her. He might have some appalling fever. If so, she must discern that before taking him into the house.

As Jack walked with her back to the beach, he whistled a merry tune and his boots stamped against the road, sending the pebbles skittering ahead of them. Linnea was glad Scamp had found something to amuse himself. She did not need him getting in the way. With luck, Cook would give him some scraps by the kitchen door or a bone which would keep his attention until they could get the man off the beach.

"So you found something right interesting," Jack said as they stepped out onto the sand.

"Yes."

"Always interesting to see what washes up after a storm." He began to whistle again.

Linnea doubted she could have displayed his lack of curiosity. As she climbed over the rocks separating the coves, her shoes slipped on the moss-covered boulders.

"Careful there, Lady Linnea," Jack said, putting his hand under her elbow. "You could break your neck doing this."

"I was barefoot before."

"Right wise of you." He glanced at her feet, and his forehead furrowed.

Again Linnea was grateful for his lack of curiosity, for he did not ask why she was out without stockings as well as without a bonnet. As before, she shielded her eyes with her hand and looked along the beach.

The man was gone!

Linnea jumped down off the rocks and ran to where the man had been lying. When she saw indentations in the sand to mark where she had knelt beside him, she was relieved. At least, she knew she had not imagined the whole of it. How could she imagine a man like *him*? And where was he now?

"Where to now, Lady Linnea?" asked Jack.

Linnea motioned for him to follow as she saw more impressions in the sand. Deep holes where a hand or a foot would have pushed against the beach. Shallow ones, too.

"Someone dragged something away from here." Jack's smile disappeared as he scanned the cliffs above them. "Someone might have come and taken what you found, my lady. Let me check to make sure no one is up there." He turned and loped back toward the stones.

A faint motion had caught her eye. Raising her voice, she shouted, "Not that way, Jack! This way! There he is!"

"He?" called Jack back to her.

Linnea ignored the disbelief in the stableman's voice. She rushed forward to where, in the shadow of the cliffs, the man had wedged himself into a cleft. He would not have been seen once the tide rose to wash away the marks in the sand. The man waved his unbroken arm and shouted something she could not understand.

"Are you mad?" she asked as she ran up to him. "You could have hurt yourself worse by—"

He grabbed her arm and jerked her down to the sand. As she shrieked, he clamped his gritty arm over her mouth. Jack cried out a warning and came running as the man growled in her ear, "*Uraad*. Quiet!"

Jack skidded to a stop, spraying them with more sand. Linnea realized why he stared in horror at them when the glitter of the sun off something metallic seared her eyes. The man was holding another knife in the hand directly in front of her.

"Whoa, friend," Jack said, raising his empty hands. "There is no need to be waving that blade around. Lady Linnea and I are here to help you."

"*Uraad!*" The man muttered something else, then said, "Danger! There is danger here. For you. For the woman. Hide!"

Jack flattened himself against the stone an arm's length from them. The glance he gave Linnea warned that he was certain this man was out of his mind.

Slowly Linnea reached up and put her hands on the man's arm. She gave a slight tug, and he lowered his arm from her mouth. "You are mistaken. There is no danger here, except that you will injure yourself worse."

"I saw him!" the man exclaimed, his eyes narrow with fury. "I thought I had slain him, but he is here."

"Who?" asked Linnea and Jack at the same time.

"Wyborn Kortsson."

Nils saw the woman named Linnea and the lad exchange another glance. Even though he spoke their language with difficulty, he could easily understand what went unspoken between them. They thought he was seeing things that did not exist.

That was confirmed when Linnea said, "You have been struck hard in the head. You must let us tend your injuries."

"I know what I saw. He is here. You are in great danger!"

"If he was, he is no longer," she replied quietly. "The sand is empty save for us."

Looking past her, he saw she was being honest. Kortsson was not in sight. Had her arrival with the lad sent Kortsson into hiding? That made no sense. Kortsson always fought to be the first ashore so he might have his choice of the maidens.

"Please release me," Linnea continued.

He fought to focus his eyes on her face. No, Kortsson would not have left if he had chanced to see this pretty woman. He gritted his teeth. Was he mad with pain? They should have seen his blood-enemy as soon as they reached the rocks at the edge of the beach. He must get all of them away from here. He could not confront Kortsson while in this condition. Kortsson would give him and the lad death with quick slashes, then make Linnea rue that she had ever been born.

"Go," he ordered.

"The knife—"

He looked down at the small blade he had hidden in his gartered stockings. "You will not have this one! While Kortsson lives, I will not be left unarmed." He did not add that he feared that, if he moved his arm any farther, he would topple on his face in the sand.

When she slid from beneath his arm, he had to clench his teeth harder. Her slow sinuous motions while she eased away contrasted with her expression that revealed she did not trust him not to slice into her with the *sax*. How could he think of anything but her touch, which sent a sensation through him that was as powerful as the blow of a broadsword? Her soft curves made him rue his injuries that kept him from pulling her back into his arms and persuading her to caress him even more intimately.

He cursed under his breath, and she froze. He was tempted to tell her that she need not worry. His obligations to his chieftain must come first, so, even if he was hale, he would have had to ignore her obvious charms.

The lad edged away from the wall and took her arm, pulling her away from Nils. Linnea had called him "Jack." The lad was frightened. Good! Jack was wise to be fearful when Kortsson was nearby.

Trying to push away from the cliff, Nils collapsed to the sand. By Odin's beard! He was too weak. He tried to stand, but pain riveted him. Something struck the sand. The hat Linnea had given him to protect the wounds on his face. He heard a snicker.

"Hush, Jack," Linnea said, bending to pick up the bonnet. She shuddered when she saw the blood on its rim. Jack would learn soon enough that, even though the bearded man wore her bonnet like some weird badge of honor, only a fool would fail to look past it to discover the inherent power in the blond man's gaze.

"You came back." The man's deep voice crashed on her ears like waves in the midst of a tempest, sweeping through her.

"I told you I would," she said as she knelt beside him again. His face was a paler gray than it had been before.

His gaze swept past her to scan the beach. He must truly believe someone dangerous was close. "Only a *daari* believes someone of this island."

"*Daari?*" She noticed Jack's frown of concentration. She wished him better luck than she had had in figuring out what place had spawned the man's accent.

He smiled. "A man without wits."

Deciding the best answer to that was none, she asked, "Do you need help to get back to your feet so we can take you where we can tend your wounds?"

He pointed to his shoeless foot. "I doubt I can walk. That may be broken as well."

"Rough use," Jack muttered.

The blond man glanced at him. "Yes. Kortsson thought to leave me dead."

"Who is this Kortsson?" the lad asked.

"My blood-enemy."

Linnea held out her hand, and Jack handed her the ball of rags he carried. Peeling off the top one, she said, "While we are asking such questions of names, I would appreciate you answering the same one."

The blond man's purple eyes crinkled with amusement she doubted she could feel if she were as battered. "Your words confuse me, Linnea."

Jack cleared his throat, and Linnea saw a rare anger on his face. Quietly he said, "*Lady* Linnea would like the courtesy of your name."

"Lady Linnea is it? A most unusual lady you are," the blond man said. His fingers once more reached for his knife, so she knew he had seen Jack's fury. "I am Nils Bjornsson."

"Are you Swedish?" she asked.

He started to shake his head, then winced. "*Norrfoolk.*"

"You're from Norfolk?" This was the first worthwhile bit of information she had gotten from him. The city was no more than a week's journey north from Sutherland Park.

"No. I am—"

Jack caught the man's shoulders as he sagged back toward the ground, senseless. "Lord-a-mercy on us!" he breathed. "This cunning shaver has been smashed by someone who took a mighty disliking to him. The arm looks broken, it does, as well as his foot. By all that's blue, he must have a reason to fear this Kortsson chap if he crawled all the way to this cliff with two broken limbs."

"Can you set it?" she asked.

"'Course." He looked up at her, concern on his face. "Best if you walk a little ways along the shore. Setting bones is no spectacle for ladies."

"I can help if—"

"Set Old Calvin's leg for him last winter. This chap cannot be half as cantankerous."

Linnea was not so sure of that, but she recognized the stubborn tone in Jack's voice. He had not changed one smidgen in the years she had known him. He was as pliable as satin until he dug in his toes. Then nothing could or would budge him.

But she could be stubborn, too. She bit her lip as she looked at Mr. Bjornsson's face. The only color there was the blood still dried on his cheek, but she had seen how swiftly he could use what strength he had left to get what he wanted. "I should stay. I found him."

Jack nodded. "Mayhap 'tis a good idea for you to help. Keep the sun out of his eyes."

Linnea saw Jack looking both ways along the beach, and she understood why he truly had acquiesced. He did not want to send her into the path of this Kortsson...If the man even existed. With a shiver, she wished she could dismiss Mr. Bjornsson's warning as just an injury to his head, but *someone* had left him for dead here.

Would that someone follow him to Sutherland Park? That could endanger her whole family.

She sat cross-legged on the sand and cupped Mr. Bjornsson's head on her lap. His golden hair sifted through her fingers, warm and coarse, yet silken. The scent of salt and wood smoke teased her as she bent to shield his closed eyes with her other hand. This man must have spent much time near the sea, for only that way could he have gained such a deep bronzing on his skin. Looking out at the water, she wondered if he had been washed up upon this shore. If his injuries were from surviving the sinking of a ship, the man he spoke of might be just his imagination.

She recoiled when she heard words that were spoken with the intensity of curses. Mr. Bjornsson jerked his head out of her hand. He growled something up at her when his cheek struck her elbow. Tingles exploded down her elbow.

"Take care!" she cried.

He snapped something at her. She could not fault him for his language. She closed her eyes and shuddered when Jack said his prayers backward as loudly as Mr. Bjornsson had. *Those* maledictions she understood quite well, even though Mama would be shocked to discover any of her daughters knew such words.

"Lady Linnea, it is set," Jack said.

"His other injuries?"

He flushed, surprising her. "Won't take no for an answer this time, my lady. The man needs privacy for me to bandage him."

"Jack will take care of you," Linnea said, slipping Mr. Bjornsson's head off her lap.

She yelped when he grasped her arm. It still stung from his head striking her. "What is wrong *now*?" she asked.

Mr. Bjornsson's eyes widened at her testy question, then he chuckled. When she stared at him, wondering if she would ever guess what he might do or say next, he murmured, "Do not go far, milady. Kortsson is as wily as a snake."

Linnea's gaze was caught anew by his. There was no mistaking the course of his thoughts, for there was a heat in his eyes that had nothing to do with his enemy. That warmth surged over her, more potent than the sun upon the sea. She was shocked. How could he be thinking of anything save his injuries? Slowly she drew her arm out of his grasp and turned away so he did not see the fire that was climbing her cheeks. Rising, she fought not to flee from his bold summons to delve deeper into the passions that his smile promised would be as sweet as the first berries of spring.

Her fingers trembled when she clasped them in front of her while she stared out at the dance of the waves. Getting him well and on his way would be the smartest thing she could do.

At Jack's call a few minutes later, she turned to look at the men. She was astonished to see Mr. Bjornsson on his feet—or, to own the truth, on his foot. His left ankle was wrapped in rags to match the ones crowning his head. A sling supported his left arm which was tightly tied in more rags.

She rushed to them, but Jack waved her aside. "Can't help when he don't have another arm for you to hold onto."

"How can you get him over the rocks by yourself?"

Mr. Bjornsson said, in a voice taut with pain, "At the other end of the cove, there are no rocks."

Jack frowned. "Got your head struck right hard, Mr. Bjornsson, didn't you?"

"You can call me Nils."

"No matter what I call you, truth is rocks aplenty at both ends of this cove."

Linnea took an involuntary step back as Nils Bjornsson's eyes narrowed in a flash of fury. Even with his wounds, his stance warned he was a man not to be trifled with.

"'Tis true. Rocks came down in a storm during my grandsire's time," Jack said almost defensively, and she knew he had noted her reaction.

If Nils had not seen the rocks, then he may not have seen this man he warned them about. Foolishly she looked at the man whose shoulder was even with Jack's brow. That hint of a smile peered through his thick beard. Again she had the uneasy feeling he could sense what she was thinking even when she was silent.

Do not be silly! Just because he acted as mysterious as a highwayman stopping a carriage on a moonless night was no reason to become fanciful.

"Let us get going," she said, raising her chin in defiance of Nils's smile. "The longer Olive waits for us, the more vexed she will be. You know how she likes to read quietly during the afternoon."

Linnea was sure there could be no more absurd parade than the three of them walking toward Sutherland Park. Nils Bjornsson was more able to help himself than she had expected. He must have extraordinary wells of strength he could draw upon. Although he spoke with frequency what she was certain were curses, she pretended not to hear. If she were as hurt, she suspected she would find it impossible to stay mum. What disturbed her even more was how he continuously scanned the shore and the road ahead of them. His knife remained in his hand that was draped over Jack's shoulder. Again and again, his fingers tightened on it as if he feared an ambush.

She breathed a sigh of relief when they reached the fishing pavilion was at the side of the water garden closest to the sea. The stone building which rose from the largest pond had storage for rowboats at the water level and a clean room above with a shuttered window. The shutters could be opened if any ladies wished to enjoy some fishing without worrying about sunshine or mud or water ruining their day.

"What is this place?" asked Nils. "Do you live

here?"

"No, I live in the house there." She pointed to where the chimneys were visible above the trees.

"How many others live within its walls?"

Hearing Jack grumble at the interrogation, Linnea answered quietly, "My family and our servants."

"How many armed warriors?"

"None."

Nils stared at Linnea and her companion in disbelief. Did she honestly expect him to believe that there were no warriors in an English house this close to the sea? When he saw the amazement on their faces, he knew they considered that he was the one whose mind could not be trusted.

"Then I will stay here," he said.

"But it is damp here, and the house is—"

He pulled his arm from around the lad and put the knife in his belt. Gripping Linnea's chin, he tilted her face toward him. "The house is indefensible if you have no warriors within its walls. Here there is a view of the shore. I shall stay here where I can keep watch for my blood-enemy."

Her face was as easy to read as the moods of the sea. Fear and skepticism and pity flew through her eyes. "My family prides itself on our hospitality. Having you stay here in the garden pavilion—"

"Your family will be dead if Kortsson learns that you have given me a haven beneath your roof."

"Nonsense!"

Before he could reply, the lad Jack said, "Mayhap not, my lady. I have heard of such tales among the low taverns in London."

"This is not London," Linnea retorted, furious that Jack would take Nils's side against her. "Do not give him further reasons not to heed good sense."

She was surprised when Jack took her arm and drew her away from where Nils was leaning against the stone wall of the pavilion. When Jack bent toward her, he whispered, "You did not hear what he said while I was bandaging him, my lady. This chap truly believes that Kortsson is determined to kill him and anyone who helps him. Suggested that we should leave him on the sand, so you were not caught up in this blood feud between him and Kortsson, he did. I persuaded him to come with us because if he was found anywhere on Sutherland Park, Kortsson could turn his fury on you and your family. He agreed, saying that he believed you were safer if he was alive and watching for Kortsson."

"This is all silly."

"He don't think so, my lady."

Linnea shivered. Something that Nils had said, something that Jack was not repeating, although she could see the truth in his tight expression, had convinced Jack that Nils was not lying about his blood-enemy. She would find a way to get Jack to tell her all the truth. That must wait for later. Now, they must tend to Nils.

"If he intends to be stupid and insist on staying here, my one concern is the steep stairs to the upper floor. The ground floor is awash with water from the pool."

"We shall get him up there, my lady." Jack's face brightened in a smile. "Olive will help."

She turned to see Olive waiting for them at the arched door. The maid was no taller than Jack and almost as wide. Older than he by nearly two decades, she wore her gray hair in a conservative bun. Not a hint of dust clung to her simple gown. Olive always looked as if she had just finished her *toilette*, a skill Linnea was certain she would never master.

Olive clucked her tongue as she gave Linnea the stern stare that suggested Linnea was still her young charge and Olive remained her governess. "No bonnet, my lady? Your mother shall be displeased." She looked past Linnea. "And what is this to-do? Where did you find this man? What will your father think?"

"Chide me later," Linnea replied as she motioned toward the stairs. "For now, we need to get Mr. Bjornsson to where he can recover from his injuries."

"Here? Why not up at the house?"

"I will explain later."

"But this is silly. There are medicines in the house. This pavilion is damp, and—"

"Olive," Linnea said in a tone she had never used before with her maid, "I said I would explain later."

Olive stared at her in disbelief, then slowly nodded. "I brought pillows and blankets and water." She pointed to the pile of blankets and canisters at the foot of the stairs. "If you will take them upstairs, my lady, we can help this man." She put her arm around Nils's waist and guided him toward the stairs.

"I do not need your help, woman," he said, sternly, but his voice was growing fainter as she and Jack assisted him into the pavilion.

"Is that so? I think it is quite to the contrary. Now help us help you."

Linnea was glad all of them had their backs to her as they struggled up the stairs. She was not sure if Nils or Olive would be more upset at her smile. It should not take Nils long to discover he had met his match in her maid. Olive never backed down—not ever.

Taking an armful of blankets and a pillow, Linnea went up the stairs after them. The high ceiling, which was laced with thick rafters, was flushed with sunshine, and the dust had been chased to the corners. Muddy scents from the pond flushed through the room. A pallet was set on the stone floor near the oval window overlooking the pond, and she wondered who else had used this place as a sanctuary. Jack rushed back down the stairs and brought up a canister of water and fresh bandaging. He set them on a bench by one of the shuttered windows that ringed the room.

Olive helped Nils stretch out on the pallet, which was too short for him. Linnea rolled an extra blanket

and propped it under his hurt ankle. As she knelt by
the pallet and looked at her friends, she was unsure
what to say. The sound of frogs in the mud below
filled the room as the silence smothered them.

"*Vatn*," Nils whispered.

The raspy sound of the single word needed no
translation. He wanted water. Linnea jumped to her
feet.

"Let me, my lady," Olive said. She filled a tin cup
and handed it to Linnea.

Bringing it back to him, Linnea smiled as Jack
helped Nils sit up enough to drink it. "More?" she
asked softly.

"Later," Nils murmured.

Olive held out a container of salve and a clean cloth.
Before Linnea could take them, Jack reached in front
of her. He said nothing, but she understood. Slowly
she rose and left him to tend to the rest of Nils's wounds.

Going to the window, she folded her hands on the
thick sill. The light breeze off the sea tugged at the hair
that would not stay pulled back. When fingers pushed
it over her shoulder, she tried to smile at Olive.

Her maid did not smile back. "This is not like you,
my lady."

"No, it isn't."

"Your father would be distressed to see you
wandering around the estate in such a state of undress."

"I needed my stockings to stop Mr. Bjornsson's
bleeding."

Olive opened her mouth, then scowled when Nils
hissed something at Jack. "That is a very bold man. I
don't recognize him."

"Nor do I."

"Strangers can present a danger to young ladies."

Linnea patted her maid on the arm, trying to keep
her voice light as she recalled how Nils had gazed at
her when she was pressed against him by the cliff.
"When it was clear Mr. Bjornsson was not enjoying

excellent health, I did not fret about my virtue."

"Lady Linnea!"

She was startled when she realized Jack had called to her at the same moment as Olive's scold. Deciding she would rather see what the stableman had accomplished than listen to another of Olive's admonishments, she went back to the pallet.

Nils appeared worse for the attention they had given him. Every golden hair in his beard was bright against his face which was as bleached as the cloths tied around his head. The side of his smock was ripped enough to reveal more bandaging.

"How do you fare?" she asked as she squatted beside him.

Nils closed his eyes and motioned her away in a clear dismissal. "*Sofn.*"

"What?"

"*Sofn.*" He opened one eye and glared at her. "I want to sleep." Suddenly he seized her wrist.

"Hey!" shouted Jack. "She is your ally, not your enemy."

Linnea waved him back, swallowing her irritation. She should have pity for Nils, but it was hard to foster sympathy for him when he was so dashed arrogant. Staring at him, she said, quietly, "You might find it easier to get to sleep if you don't grab me every time I speak with you."

"I wish to wake again."

She tried to stifle the shudder racing along her shoulders. From anyone else, she would have dismissed the words as fear about the state of his injuries. "We have not spent all this time tending to your injuries so we can let you die the first time you close your eyes."

"Where is my other *sax*?"

"You have one knife."

"I wish to have my *sax* that yearns to taste Kortsson's blood."

"Jack has put the other dagger where it shan't be

found." She looked over her shoulder when Nils re-aimed his glower at the man behind her.

Jack squared his thick shoulders and nodded. "Won't be found until you need it... sir."

Linnea stared, wide-eyed, at the stableman. What had Nils told him to persuade him to speak with such grudging respect?

Slowly Nils's fingers loosened on her wrist. They slid along her arm to curl around her elbow. Her breath caught in her throat while a warmth as potent and perilous as the sunshine oozed outward from his fingertips to flood through her.

"*Engill*," he whispered in the moment before his eyes closed again.

"What did he say?" Olive's lips were pursed with disapproval.

Linnea stood and chafed her wrist where his fingers had dug into her skin. She did not dare to touch her elbow where he had caressed her with such surprising tenderness. "I have no idea."

Jack gave her a wry smile. "Won't be a good patient. Worse than Old Calvin, I would wager. Did you slip something into his water, Olive?"

"Just a bit of tincture of opium." Olive shook her head. "His lordship isn't going to like this."

Linnea returned to the window as Jack went down the stairs to collect the other supplies Olive had brought. "I want no one save for the three of us to know he is here."

"Why?"

She faced her maid. "Someone attacked him, and Mr. Bjornsson believes that man might be about waiting for another chance. Mr. Bjornsson needs time to recover."

"If someone set upon him," argued Olive, "then we should take him to the house."

"He will not go."

"There are three of us and but one of him."

Linnea kneaded her hands together. "I suspect he would try to flee if we take him there, for he believes he will endanger us all if he goes to the house. I fear he will hurt himself worse trying to escape the sanctuary we offer."

"We should at least warn the authorities."

"You are right, and I shall speak to Papa about it as soon as I can, even though I do not believe we are in any danger from his enemies." She wrapped her arms around herself as if a sudden chill had brushed her. "I believe he will come to see that, too, as his head heals."

"I pray you are right." Squaring her shoulders, Olive added, "If you intend for him to stay here, I need to find him some decent clothes. What he is wearing is threadbare and filthy as well as torn in dozens of places."

"Ask Mrs. Gerber to get some clothing from the attics. There may be something stored up there, although he is taller than Papa or any of my brothers. If anyone would know, Mrs. Gerber shall. If she asks why you need it, tell her a vagabond came begging, and I asked you to get these clothes."

Olive nodded. "I will check with her. Lady Sutherland has many items in storage in case guests require them, so she is sure to have something that fits Mr. Bjornsson. That is a very odd name, my lady."

"Scandinavian, I would guess, although he said he is of Norfolk." Linnea turned as the door at the top of the stairs reopened. With a relieved smile, she motioned for Jack to enter.

He edged into the room, carefully balancing his armload of horse blankets. Olive scooped several off the top.

As the rest tumbled to the floor, Linnea caught one and rolled it tightly. She knelt and put it beneath Nils's other foot. He mumbled something in his sleep, but did not wake.

"Lady Linnea," Jack said quietly.

"Yes?"

"Saw a carriage going toward the house." He shuffled his toe against the floor. "Looked like Lord Tuthill's."

Linnea's eyes widened. Randolph? Dear heavens, why was he calling this afternoon? She looked from her friends to the man sleeping in the middle of the floor. How was she going to explain looking disheveled like this to *Randolph*?

Three

Nils heard Lady Linnea's footsteps vanishing into the distance. The old woman and the lad were talking quietly in a corner, and he suspected they believed he was asleep. Maybe he had surrendered to sleep for a few moments, but the pain was too strong for whatever the old woman had put in his water. He had tasted something strange in the cup. Although he had considered the idea that they might be poisoning him, he doubted Lady Linnea would have had him brought from the strand simply to slay him here. That made no sense, and he had seen that she was, surprisingly for an Englishwoman, very sensible.

He fought to open his eyes. Lying here as helpless as a baby would not get him closer to slaying Kortsson before his blood-enemy could attack again, or to accomplishing the vow he had made to Freya.

"You are right to worry. She does become impatient with those who make promises and never do as they pledged."

Who was that?

Nils opened his eyes, glanced around, and frowned. Was this the place he had been brought to? If so, the people who had helped him were nowhere to be seen. He could not remember much about this haven. His pain had blinded him to so much, save for the loveliness of his rescuer. So readily he was able to recreate the image of her glistening black hair and her earth-brown eyes filled with strong passions that intrigued even a half-dead man. His dreams would be flavored with the memory of her pliant body against him. The lilt of her voice was like a bard's song in his ears, and he wondered how it would whisper with delight to him if he had put his thoughts of seduction into action.

He groaned with frustration. He could not seduce her when he was swathed in bandages and his arm and ankle were immobilized.

"I do not have much patience, either."

He turned his head toward the voice. His eyes widened. Never had he seen the short man sitting on the deep-set stone windowsill, but he recognized him immediately. The sharp features and wiry hair were images he had seen on carvings and engraved in jewelry. His right hand closed into a fist. The knife that he sought for his chieftain had an image of Loki raised on its haft.

But what was Loki doing here in this English building so far from the halls of *Asgard* where the gods of the *Norrfoolk* resided? And where were those who had rescued him? Was this even where he had been, or had Loki taken him somewhere else?

Nils frowned. Any mortal or any god who dared to trust Loki soon found himself suffering from one of his oft-times deadly pranks. The wizard dared to challenge even the great Odin himself with his tricks. The old tales spoke of Loki's lies. As a child, Nils had asked why the gods endured his tormenting them, why they had not destroyed Loki. No one had been able to explain it to Nils, replying only that Loki was part of the gods' plans for all the Nine Worlds.

"Why are you here with me, Loki?" he asked, not sure if the wizard could read his thoughts.

"Freya has others to escort to *Valhalla*, so I thought to watch your attempts to complete your quest and report them back to her."

"So you sent the Englishwoman to help me escape from death at the hands of my blood-enemy. All of this madness is your work," he replied to Loki's taunting smile.

"Madness? The madness comes from your vow, Nils Bjornsson." Rubbing his hand against the tip of his long nose, Loki laughed. "Freya was amused that so brave a warrior would deny himself the glories of *Valhalla* in order to try to regain the honor of another. She agreed to let me teach you a lesson for turning down the great reward you should have accepted as your due."

"By abandoning me in this strange place?"

"It is Britannia. You have been here before while far from your home a-viking."

"But Britannia never has been as it is on this voyage. I have never seen a building like this one in Britannia, nor an Englishwoman who dresses as Lady Linnea does." Nils considered trying to sit, but the thought was enough to sap him.

"What is now and what was and what will be are much the same until the day *Ragnarok* ends it all."

Nils did not want to discuss the last day of the world, when the powers of good and evil clashed. Not even with Loki who, legend said, looked forward to that day so he could gain vengeance on the gods for the many slights they had served him since the beginning of the nine worlds. Nils's troubles were here and now.

"I have my pledge to my chieftain to complete," Nils argued, hoping that Loki would continue to be in a benevolent mood. If not, the god who delighted in lying could banish him to the depths of the god Hel's icy realm of Niflheim to live all eternity in torment. Why was Loki taunting him like this? A single word from the wizard, and Nils would be dead. There must be something about all of this that Nils did not understand...yet.

"So you do." Loki laughed wildly. "You have gambled your honor in making this vow. Die now, and *Valhalla* is denied to you forever."

"My wounds should not be fatal."

"But your task may be deadly." Loki jumped to the floor and stared down at him. "You have no allies here, for you are among your enemies."

"You speak of Kortsson. I have faced him before and sent him fleeing. If I had not been injured already, he would not have been able to give what he thought was a fatal blow."

Loki laughed. "You have enemies here other than the son of Kort."

"That I know."

"Do you? Do you know who here is your true enemy? Do you know who may be your ally?" Again Loki laughed. "Know the difference, Nils Bjornsson, or else your quest to bring honor back to your family is doomed."

Four

Randolph Denner, 4th Viscount Tuthill, smiled as he entered Sutherland Park's massive foyer. Already he could seen the signs that preceded every wedding in this grand house. On the stairs that curved upward from the foyer before dividing to reach the three wings of the house, footmen were helping maids take down the portraits of family ancestors. Dust was being banished from the frames.

He watched with interest as the butler supervised the lowering of the oldest portrait. It was of a tall, blond woman with a regal mien. She wore loose robes that were unadorned except for a length of embroidery at her throat and at the gown's hem. The gold bands around her arms matched the ornate necklace that fell over her breasts. A set of simple iron keys were held to a chain that encircled her waist. In her hand, she held a primitive spindle. She was not a young woman, but her beauty had not diminished.

Randolph had been told that this woman was supposed to be one of the earliest progenitors of the Sutherland family. No one knew who she was, and Randolph suspected the portrait was kept here for sentimental reasons. Or mayhap because it had incredible value due to its age.

On the upper floor, where a gallery connected the wings of the house at the staircase's first landing, more servants were carrying furniture from one room to another. He could see, even from where he stood, that the huge ballroom to the left on the floor above was being aired. The double set of double doors had been thrown open.

His nose wrinkled. This house might be the finest in this section of England, but there was an odor that bespoke its age. Mayhap it was the remnants of countless years of ashes burned on the hearths, or it might be the memories left by all the storms that had come out of the sea and slashed this house for centuries.

He squared his shoulders as a familiar shadow crossed from the upper gallery and came toward the stairs. Failing to make a good impression on his soon-to-be father-in-law would be silly. Lord Sutherland respected him enough to agree that Randolph might ask his daughter to marry. But Randolph could never forget the cloud of his spendthrift ancestors that had followed him when he had made inquiries about marrying Lord Murray's daughter and when he had wished to court Sir Anston Grainger's daughter.

Linnea Sutherland might be too much of an air-dreamer, but she could be taught to be a good wife. All she needed to do was accept his offer to wed. She had been so intrigued with the idea when he first had started to call on her. He must be certain that her maidenly concerns did not halt this match which would solve so many problems.

"Tuthill, I had not guessed you were calling today." Lord Sutherland motioned for him to come up the stairs. "Linnea said nothing of expecting you."

Randolph hastened to obey. The earl always was busy with one thing or another. As he took the steps two at a time, he saw Sutherland smile. By all that's blue, he always did something to make a jumble of every meeting with Linnea's father, who resembled his daughter only in coloring, for his face could have been carved from the same rough rock as the house's foundation.

"I had thought to surprise her," Randolph said, hoping the earl would take his eagerness as more of a desire to see Linnea than to impress his prospective father-in-law.

"I fear the surprise is on you, my boy. She apparently has gone out to take the air."

Randolph fought to hide his frown. Linnea should be more like her sister Dinah, for the young woman looked up from her embroidery in the parlor to the right of the landing and gave him a welcoming smile. Dinah Sutherland might not have hair as lustrous as Linnea's, and she was a bit plump, but she knew that Lord Sutherland's daughter's place was not rushing about the downs like a hoyden.

Not for the first time did he curse his ill-fortune in failing to see that Dinah Sutherland would have made a good match for him. Now she was marrying Simmons in the next fortnight. The baron had courted Lady Dinah while Randolph was busy settling the matters of his late father's estate. That had left Linnea without a match.

A smile curved along Randolph's mouth. Mayhap he had gotten the better of the deal after all, because Linnea was beautiful and possessed all the graces of the lady who should oversee the estate he intended to bring back to its former glory with the help of her dowry. She would be an exquisite addition to the collection of—

The yelping of a dog and light-hearted laughter struck him fiercely. He looked over the carved railing to see a footman chasing a very dirty pup. In their wake, Linnea followed, her dark hair flowing over her shoulders and down her back where her bonnet bounced, hanging by its ribbons. She carried a shoe in one hand and a heavy book in the other. Where her matching slipper might be, he could not guess.

He started to frown, then heard Sutherland's boom of laughter. The earl spoiled his youngest daughter, which was why she too often forgot her place in society here at Sutherland Park.

Linnea noticed Randolph's taut face. She gave up the chase to catch Scamp and climbed the stairs. Randolph's dour expression added to the length of his already long features. It was a decidedly vexing countenance, but one she had seen too often lately. Avoiding his eyes, for she did not want to distress him, she forced a smile onto her face as she stepped up beside them. She must find a way to speak alone with Papa.

In spite of her determination to act as if nothing out of the ordinary had happened, she stiffened. She needed to keep from thinking about that stranger. But how could she when she had so many questions whirling through her head? How had he gotten onto the strand, and who had beaten him so mercilessly? And, the most compelling question of all, why did the steady stare of his purple eyes unsettle her so? He had the appearance of a vagabond. Yet she could not deny there seemed more to him than just a land-loper.

She kissed her father on the cheek, and her smile became genuine when he picked a piece of seaweed from her hair. She could not guess how it had come to be there, although she suspected it had fallen into her bonnet when she left it with Nils Bjornsson while she was getting Jack.

"Papa, may I discuss something important with you?"

He chuckled. "I suspect you should allow Tuthill to speak with you first. He seems about to burst with impatience from waiting to talk with you."

When her father looked past her, she turned to Randolph and kept her smile in place. It was not easy. She wished he had delayed calling. She wanted to talk to him about her uncertainty about marrying him, but not now. If someone really was trying to kill Nils, the authorities must be forewarned posthaste. Even though she had reassured Olive, she was not so certain that Nils had been mistaken about seeing his blood-enemy on the beach just before she and Jack arrived.

"Randolph, forgive how I look," she said. "I was taking a walk with Scamp, and I am afraid he quite earned his name."

"Were you walking along the shore?"

She followed his eyes to the hem of her dress that was glazed with sand. "The walk was supposed to be in the water garden, but I am afraid Scamp led me on quite a chase." She hated lying, but she knew how easy it would have been for so many of the household to notice her near the pavilion in the water garden. "If you will excuse me, I shall tend to Scamp and change into something more presentable." Again she looked at her father. "Papa, are you bound for your office?"

"After I ride into town to speak with Mr. Norman about the repairs to the church steeple." His smile showed he was clearly puzzled that she seemed more anxious to spend time with him than with Randolph.

"If I could talk with you about..."

"*I* can stay just a few minutes," Randolph said, his impatience as obvious as her father's bafflement.

Her father patted her shoulder. "Come to my office later, Linnea. On my way out of the house, I shall make sure that Scamp is taken down to the stable to be cleaned. That will give you a chance to speak with Tuthill during the few minutes of his call."

"Thank you, Papa," she said, wishing she could sound more grateful. Surely there was a way to persuade Papa that she must speak with him *now* without offending Randolph. When Randolph's lips grew rigid, she wondered what he had heard that she had not intended. Or had it been Papa's words? Nothing in them or his tone had been amiss, but Randolph seemed irritated. She sighed. A vexed Randolph was sure to prove to be a most disagreeable caller when she was anxious for him to be gone so she could talk with her father.

Linnea did not see what message passed between Papa and Dinah, but her sister gathered up her needlework and excused herself as Linnea and Randolph walked into the parlor. When Dinah winked at her, Linnea wanted to urge her sister to stay in the light blue room. No one would heed Linnea's assertion that she did not want to be alone with Randolph so they could steal a few of the precious moments all lovers craved.

"Would you like some lemonade?" Linnea asked when she saw a tray with pitcher and glasses sitting on the cherry sideboard.

"I said I had very little time." Randolph's tone had taken on that arrogance that meant his annoyance was with her. She could not fault him. His coat and breeches were as clean as if he had just donned them, and his shoes were impeccably polished. "I wished to see how you were faring in the midst of the plans for Lady Dinah's wedding."

"As you must have seen for yourself, the whole house is being turned inside out in anticipation of the guests. Mama is having a glorious time."

"And you?" His full lips pursed. "Are you having such a glorious time that you have finally given thought to our own wedding plans?"

"My thoughts at this time must all be focused on Dinah's wedding." What a lie that was! She had not thought of it since finding Nils on the shore.

He clasped his hands behind his back in a pose better suited to the long-suffering tutor who had let her sneak into the classroom while he taught her brothers. "You are a kind sister to care so much for her, but you must think of yourself as well."

"I am." She set her shoe on the floor. The other had come off while she pursued Scamp through the kitchen. She must go and retrieve it as soon as she finished this conversation with Randolph. Placing the book on a nearby table, she reached for the pitcher and poured herself a glass of lemonade. "Are you sure I cannot offer you some?"

"What have you given thought to?"

Linnea sighed into her glass. Randolph could be so single-minded in his determination to get an answer.

Just as Nils was.

Dash it! She did not want to think of Nils Bjornsson now. Those unanswered questions crowded her head along with the irritating memory of his superior smile...and his brawny muscles that had strained to help Jack get him off the beach and to the water garden pavilion. Nils might be hurt badly, but his pride had refused to allow him to reveal anything save for the most fierce agony. And if he was not mistaken, he had an enemy who was stalking him. Olive's warning echoed in her head. She should have insisted that Papa heed her and contact the authorities now.

She had delayed too long in her answer, she discovered, when Randolph reached past her and picked up the book. His frown became amazement as he asked, "*History of Norfolk*? I had no idea you were interested in Norfolk."

"I am interested in all sorts of things."

He paged through the book. "This appears to be dry reading for a young woman."

Linnea bristled, but said nothing. It would be just a waste of her words. Randolph believed she was like his sister who never had bothered her mind with anything that would not assist her in the pursuit of a titled husband with plump pockets. Even if she had not chanced upon Nils and wanted to learn more about the city he was from, she often wandered through Papa's book-room to find something to read. As her father shared her eclectic interests, she usually found something intriguing to peruse.

"I have never been to Norfolk," she replied when

he glanced up from the book. "I thought I might learn more about it, so I will enjoy it more when I visit it."

"You are planning a trip there?"

"Not just now, but it would be nice to go there some day."

His nose wrinkled. "I have been to Norfolk. There is nothing there that would interest you."

"I would like to determine that for myself."

He opened his mouth, then closed it. His dark eyes snapped with fury. She could not blame him, for she had been less than polite since the beginning of his call. If she could explain why she was so at odds with herself, he might understand. But she must stay mum about Nils until she was sure that he was out of danger from those who had hurt him.

"Randolph, I—"

"You must excuse me now. I said I could stay but a short time." He set the book on the table and walked toward the door, then looked back at her. "Do think more about our plans, Linnea. The announcement has been delayed too long already."

Taking a deep breath, she knew she must be honest with him...at least about his desire to marry her. Randolph deserved that. "Before you go, there is something we need to speak of."

"Of our wedding?"

"No...yes...I mean, we need to speak of your offer for me." Flinging out her hands, she said, "You can see how the house is all in an uproar over Dinah's wedding. It is all any of us have been thinking about. I do so love to see Dinah and Lord Simmons together. They are so happy."

"Yes. That is quite obvious."

"One could only wish that everyone was that happy. Love is most contagious, infecting those around us like a sickness." She hesitated, gauging his face. Did he guess what she was finding difficult to say?

He laughed. "I have seen some men who look as if

they need to recover from some hideous plague when they fall in love."

"But so often a sickness passes quickly, and it is as if it never had been." She waited, holding her breath.

When his eyes grew wide with consternation, he grasped her hands. "Linnea, do not even jest about such a thing. My heart remains constant, and I hope that yours will as well."

"Randolph—" It was the last word she had a chance to speak as he spoke on and on about his hopes for their future.

When he finished with, "And our match will heal so many of the wounds left by my father's death," Linnea knew she could not break his heart anew. Not today. Not when she had been left so bewildered after discovering Nils Bjornsson on the shore that her words might be unthinking or downright callous.

As he took his leave, along with her reassurances that she would take more time to think their plans over, she sat on the closest chair and ran her fingers back and forth on the navy satin. Randolph should be everything she wanted in a husband. He was intelligent and hard-working. He respected his own family heritage and hers, for both families had been long settled here by the time of William the Conqueror. She had seen his kindness to her when he did not take her to task for her lack of manners during their brief conversation.

But he was not the man of her dreams! How ironic that her dreams of falling in love had apparently led her to fall in love with the wrong man!

He could not understand her longing to go beyond Sutherland Park and London. Her love of reading baffled him. His favorite topics of conversation were his investments and his country estate. If she had to endure another long explanation on how he was so unlike his spendthrift father, she was certain she would have to leave the room. He had not changed. Only her silly dreams of being in love had. It was as if she were waking from what had seemed to be a dream come true to discover it was not.

"Another thing..."

At Randolph's voice, Linnea looked up, astonished. She came quickly to her feet and hoped that her face revealed her amazement rather than her dismay that he had returned. "Yes?" she asked.

"I did not want you to believe I was distressed with you."

Was his smile as insincere as hers? She could not ask that. Instead she said, "Of course not, Randolph."

"You know I have much affection for this family and you. I do understand your reluctance to do anything that you believe will detract from your sister's nuptials, and I know as well that..."

Linnea stopped listening as she heard a soft hiss. Looking past Randolph, who was continuing with his long-winded attempt to smooth any mistakes he might have made by being honest with her—a fact that was more irritating than his words—she struggled to keep her face even. Jack was in the doorway, motioning to her.

She waved him away. Smiling, although she was sure Randolph would sense that her expression was even more feigned than before, she clasped her hands in front of her as Randolph kissed her cheek. She saw Randolph's amazement—and Jack's—that she was allowing Randolph such a liberty when she had followed Society's dictates and kept him at arm's length until now, but she would do just about anything to get Randolph to take his leave when Jack looked so frantic.

What could be wrong?

She did not worry that Randolph would take notice of Jack loitering in the hall. Since she had known him, she had discovered how Jack had slipped in and out of too many other places with ease. He would not be caught now. Waiting impatiently for the stableman, she sat on the very edge of a chair. She did not want to appear as if anything were amiss if someone passed by.

"My lady?" Jack's voice was little more than a whisper.

"Come in. Come in."

He shook his head. "Not here. We need to speak...We need to speak elsewhere."

Linnea did not have to ask if someone was nearby. Jack must have seen someone approaching. "I need to retrieve my slipper from where I lost it in the kitchen," she said.

"I believe I saw it in the stillroom." His eyes twinkled for a moment, then grew serious again.

"Then I shall retrieve it from there right away."

"Yes, my lady." He scurried out of the room.

She wondered how he failed to run headlong into one of the footmen who seemed to appear in the doorway at the exact second Jack rushed out. Keeping her curiosity to herself, she nodded when the footman told her that Lord Sutherland had asked him to arrange for Scamp to be cleaned. She thanked him.

Linnea tried to keep her own steps to a sedate pace as she walked out of the parlor and toward the stairs. Her hopes of reaching the kitchen without delay vanished, however, when her sister burst out of a room on the other side of the gallery.

Dinah rushed to her and clasped her hands. "Can I congratulate you *now*, Linnea?"

"Not yet."

Rolling her eyes, Dinah sighed. "Linnea, Lord Tuthill is clearly devoted to you. Anyone can see that he simply adores you. How can you let him linger on and on without giving him your answer?"

"I believe Mama has enough to fret about with *your* wedding. She might have apoplexy if she had to plan two at the same time." She edged toward the stairs before her sister guessed that her thoughts were not on Randolph but on another man. Her hand clenched on the railing along the edge of the gallery. Thinking so much of Nils Bjornsson was absurd. Certainly once her curiosity was soothed about him and how he had come to be here in such poor condition, she would be able to put him from her mind.

Dinah frowned. "Linnea, you know that is not the reason you delay."

"And what do you believe is the reason?"

"Linnea!" her sister gasped.

Realizing that her tone had been too harsh with her impatience, Linnea let her shoulders ease from their inflexible line. "Forgive me, Dinah. I did not mean to put the question to you like that. I am a bit disconcerted."

"By Randolph?"

"Yes." That was not false, for Randolph's call had led to this uncomfortable conversation.

"If you do not wish for him to court you—"

"I did not say that."

"No, but I suspect you wish to. Once you were so excited each time he came to call. Are you having second thoughts about this match?"

Linnea wanted to focus on one problem at a time. "You are right that I am having second thoughts." She did not admit that they were the same as her first thoughts. Wishing she could take her sister into her confidence now, but fearing what might be amiss in the water garden pavilion, she soothed her sister's disquiet quickly.

She went down the stairs at the swiftest pace that would not call attention to her. Hearing barking as she neared the kitchen at the far left wing of the house, she was not surprised when Scamp came running toward her. She smiled weakly when she bent and took her missing slipper from his mouth.

"Thank you, Scamp," she said, patting his silken head. She raised her head and saw Jack watching from the stillroom door. She came to her feet, her smile gone, because his face was somber.

The collection of aromas from within the small room reached out to draw her past the door. When Jack closed it behind her, she was not surprised. The tension that tightened every motion he made warned that something was terribly wrong. Leaning back on the table where Cook made preserves and distilled potions and possets from the herbs in the kitchen garden, she asked, "What is it, Jack?"

"'Tis him, Lady Linnea."

"Mr. Bjornsson?" There would be no other reason for Jack to wear such a grim expression.

"Aye, he was thrashing something terrible in his sleep. Olive is worried that he would hurt himself or go mad. Then—"

"I shall go right out there." She glanced toward the door. "Thank you for saying nothing in front of Randolph."

Jack scratched the side of his nose. "I did not know if you had told his lordship about what you had found, so I did not want to say anything in his hearing."

"That was a good decision."

He cleared his throat. "Begging your pardon, my lady, but there is more."

"More?"

"Olive and I both had to leave him alone—"

"I thought you understood that you should not leave him by himself."

"Aye, but 'twas just a moment, and he was asleep and..." He motioned for her to come closer. In a whisper, he added, "I don't know how anyone in his poor condition could wreck everything in the water pavilion."

"Wreck?"

"The bench is in pieces, and the pallet torn." He swallowed roughly. "There was blood on the floor."

"Nils's?"

"Don't know. Can you come now, my lady?" Again he hesitated, shuffling his feet, then asked, "What did

Lord Sutherland have to say about Mr. Bjornsson?"

"I have not had a chance to speak with Papa."

"An alert should be sounded."

"Papa is on his way to town. I will speak to him after I come with you to see the pavilion. By then, he should have returned." She shivered, trying not to imagine what she might find there. She pulled on her broken bonnet, stuffing her hair beneath it. She glanced around the stillroom. Once she determined how Nils was hurt, she would come here and get what she must to ease his pain.

A fine mist was rolling in off the sea as she hurried with Jack toward the water garden. Skipping across the stones on the driveway, for she had left her other slipper in the parlor upstairs, she hurried after him. Jack's shoulders were still as rigid as the branches of the trees edging the steps down toward the pool.

Linnea did not pause as she went down the stone stairs to the garden or up the stone risers in the pavilion overlooking the water. Untying her bonnet ribbons, she grimaced when a piece of the brim fell off in her hands. She tossed it into her bonnet and set it on the newel post at the top of the steps.

In horror, she stared at the destruction. The bench was in pieces on the floor as if someone had taken an ax to it. Two of the shutters had broken slats. She tried not to think of how they looked as if someone had been shoved viciously against them. Feathers from the pallet rested everywhere, and two blankets were torn into shreds. The canisters had been burst, and water pooled in every low spot on the floor. Her stomach cramped when she saw the pinkish shade of one pool.

Olive rushed to her. "He just woke, my lady."

"Just woke?" She grasped Olive's hands. "Then who did this?"

"I am not sure."

"But how can he be awake already? I thought you put a tincture of opium in his water."

"I did, but I must have misjudged the amount. He is a brawny man." She sighed. "I was not certain he would wake when he seemed to be so lost in his own world."

"What do you mean?"

"He spoke strangely. I could not understand anything he said."

Linnea clasped her own taut hands together. "That is because English is not his customary language. He speaks another."

"Oh." Olive's eyes grew round, and Linnea guessed her maid had never given that idea even a thought.

"How long did you leave him alone?"

"Just moments, my lady. I went out to call after Jack to bring more bandaging from the stable. I don't know how anyone could have slipped past me. When I came back..." Olive shuddered and wrung her hands in her apron.

"Lady Linnea!" The command rang against the roof of the water pavilion. "I will speak with you now."

Sending Jack back to the stillroom with a list of supplies, including hops that she could put in a tea to bring sleep to Nils, Linnea skirted the puddles to go to where Nils was struggling to free himself from the blankets that had become tangled around him. "What happened?"

"Do you need to ask?" he spat back. Grasping the knife he had kept by his side, he held it up. The tip was stained crimson. "I told you Kortsson was near."

"But no one saw him enter the pavilion."

"He was here."

"Mayhap you *thought* you saw him here."

"And attacked a shadow of my mind?" He laughed coldly. "Do you think I could do this damage when you have me bound up like a swaddling babe with all these bandages?"

"You are badly hurt." She frowned as she tried to loosen the blanket from around his hurt shoulder. He must have been tossing about like a small ship on a wild sea. That suggested he had been in the midst of a brain fever. Yet, he seemed quite sane now. "Be still. You are making things worse."

"Things cannot be worse," he growled.

"You could be dead."

"Then I would not be here. I would be—" His hand fisted on the floor when she drew the blanket from around his broken arm.

"I am sorry. I do not mean to hurt you more."

Nils raised his head. "Why are you sorry?"

"I just said why. I did not want to hurt you more."

"Why not? You are my enemy, too."

"You are mistaken. I have no reason to be your enemy. You should concentrate on finding your true blood-enemy."

He flinched, then moaned.

"Do not worry about your enemies," she continued as he looked away. "I shall make certain that you are not left alone again until you can defend yourself. If you would agree to go to the house..."

"You see the damage here. Think what Kortsson would do in your father's house where there are no warriors. The blood I drew from him before he fled would become a river as he slew your family. At least he knows I am here and not within your father's house."

"I shall make every effort to see that you are safe. There will be someone with you always, and I shall make sure that Jack has a gun."

"A what?"

"A weapon that expels a ball of lead at a high speed."

He smiled grimly. "I would like to see this weapon, but I doubt you will trust me enough to do that before you turn me over to your king."

"Why would I do that?"

He locked eyes with her, and she nearly recoiled from his fury. "Because I am of the *Norrfoolk* and you are of Britannia."

"Norfolk is part of England. It is—"

"Not Norfolk. *Norrfoolk*."

Linnea frowned. His pronunciation of the two words was just about the same, but by straining she heard the slight difference. "What is *Norrfoolk*?"

"You don't know?" His laugh was taut. "Do you think me a *daari* that I would believe that?"

"What is a *daari*?"

"I told you before. It means a fool."

"Would you speak English, for heaven's sake?"

"I do not intend to make your interrogation of me simple, my lady. I will not be your way of gaining favor with your king." He arched one tawny brow. "Now I understand why you wish to safeguard me from my blood-enemy. The prestige you gain your clan by turning me over to the king will be great."

She laughed as icily as he had. "Keep talking like that, and I will believe you are as mad as the king."

"Do not compare me to that cur." He pushed himself up to sit, although his bronzed face became even grayer with pain. "Ask me what you will, my lady, but know that, as a *Norrfoolk*, I shall never bow my head to King Ethelred."

"Ethelred?" She gulped, for the first time believing he might be suffering from damage to his mind. "Mr. Bjornsson, the king's name is George, although his son, the Prince Regent, oversees England now."

"Do not attempt to baffle me with lies." His eyes narrowed. "I should have guessed no Englishman or woman would hold fast to a pledge to be honest. But I had guessed you would choose to lie about something that is harder to prove than who claims England's throne."

"I am not lying!"

"Ethelred has no son named George."

"No, of course not. Ethelred was king nearly a thousand years ago."

"Ethelred is king now."

"You are mistaken."

He tore back the sleeve on his left arm to reveal a gold amulet on the firm muscles above his bandaged elbow. "I swear by Thor's hammer that I speak the truth."

"Thor's hammer?" she whispered as she looked from his steady gaze to the amulet that was as broad as her palm. Swallowing hard, she reached out a trembling finger to touch the intricately carved gold band that must be worth as much as one of the fine race horses her brother Kenneth bred.

His hand clamped her finger against the gold. Although his face twisted with pain, he did not let her draw away from his splinted arm.

"Release me," she ordered.

"By Thor's hammer, I vow that I shall not until you tell me why you are being false about the truth you know as well as I do. Ethelred is Britannia's king."

She stared into his eyes. In horror, she realized he wholeheartedly believed what he was saying. Again she tore her gaze from his to look at the band on his arm and the embroidery on his blood-stained tunic.

She had seen such needlework in the oldest of the portraits of the family ancestors. That woman had a similar pattern on her otherwise simple gown. Intrigued by it, Linnea had read about medieval embroidery in one of her father's favorite books, which told the tales of the Norsemen who had been the terror of England.

When Ethelred was king.

No, there must be some other explanation! Nils might believe what he was saying, but it was impossible. Or was it? She stared at his tawny hair, his wind-scored face, his clothes, his words about a blood-enemy who had tracked him here and whom he had fought off with this knife with odd engraving, this spectacular gold band...

They all pointed to the same truth. It was a truth

she could not believe, but how could she accept that
Nils Bjornsson was a Viking who had somehow slipped
from his century to hers? He must be mad. Or mayhap
she had been right when she feared that his head had
been so badly hurt by his attackers that he saw truth in
what he was saying.

But she had not been hit upon the head. No one
could jump through time, but the undeniable facts were
in front of her. He was not like any man she had ever
met.

"Can it be true?" she asked, unsure of every word
she spoke. "Have you traveled nearly one thousand
years from the past?"

Five

"A thousand years?" Nils tried to ignore the memory of Loki's laugh that was playing through his head. Even this jest was too grand for the lying wizard. Lies! Had Loki put these words in Linnea's mouth? That made no sense. She was not of the *Norrfoolk*. The people of this island denounced the gods as myths which had no substance. "Why are you trying to fill my head with such a *lygi*?"

"A what?"

"A falsehood."

She rose. "I can see this conversation is going nowhere, and I wish to return to the house before the mist becomes rain. I need to discuss this with my father. I bid you a good afternoon, Mr. Bjornsson."

"Wait!"

She did not turn. By the straight line of her shoulders, he knew that she was furious. That was confirmed when she said, "I trust, by the time I return, you will have rid yourself of this outrageous assumption that you can order me around as if I am your slave."

"Lady Linnea, wait! Please."

"Please?" She paused as her honed laugh struck him like the blow that had landed him in the sand. "I did not guess you knew that word in English. Or even in your own language, whatever it might be."

She vanished down the stairs before he could find the words to answer. He wanted to push himself to his feet and follow, demanding answers to the questions taunting him, but he could not as much as sit. Blinking, he sought to clear eyes that blurred abruptly. Whatever had been in that cup of water still held him captive.

"Keep thrashing about," grumbled a voice behind him, "and you shall finish what your foe started."

Nils looked up at Olive. She was wearing the frown that never seemed far from her lips when Linnea was not here. Olive clearly wished him gone. Tempted to tell her that he would gladly be gone, he closed his eyes and ceded himself to sleep.

His dreams were formless, scattered images that made no sense. Yet, there was a sense of desperation, an unrelenting need that stalked him within that gray fog. Questions filled his head, repeating over and over. *What had happened to him, and what shape would Loki's ultimate revenge take on him? And why was that wizard plaguing him?*

***

"Give him this when he wakes."

Nils recognized that voice even through the pain that clouded his head as he came back to his senses. Linnea Sutherland's voice had the strength of wind against a sail, but was as light as a land-locked breeze. Never had he guessed that any Englishwoman would possess the powerful will that she did. She was uneasy around him, but she did not shrink with fear as others had on this island when he came here to serve his chieftain and his king.

His chieftain!

The thought of the vow he had made brought his eyes open like bed curtains thrown back on a new day. He had been asleep long enough for the sunshine to return. Was it another day, or the same one? A caustic laugh seared his throat. Why was he fretting about what day it was when he was not certain what year it was...or century. A shudder raced through him, and he moaned.

The hushed sound of silk came toward him, and he turned his head to see Linnea dropping to her knees beside him. Too often he had seen her thus, leaning over him, her eyes dim with worry and her lips ready to be kissed. He must be out of his mind, lost in some *saga* that had no basis in truth. No matter the year, she was an Englishwoman, and he was of the *Norrfoolk*. They were enemies. Even if she was helping him, Kortsson lurked not far from here, ready to strike again.

Her hand against his forehead was a sweet enchantment. Shutting his eyes again, he savored the delicious sensation of her touch. It offered a connection to something other than pain and the endless repetition of the questions he had no answers for.

"How do you feel?" she whispered.

He looked up at her, glad that she understood that the ache in his head leapt like a great fish from the sea at every sound. "Better."

"Really?" She smiled. "To own the truth, you look worse. Your bruises are becoming a very unflattering shade of dark blue."

Awkwardly, he pushed himself up to sit. She balanced back on her heels and watched him. That she said nothing pleased him, for she must understand that he had to test his limited strength. Smiling back at her, he needed to keep her from suspecting as well that he must know how much he could do so that he might flee this place and the unexpectedly kind captivity of his enemies.

"My arm may be broken, but my head aches nearly as much," he replied, watching her face closely.

"It appears someone was determined to knock some sense into your head, Mr. Bjornsson, but it appears that they have failed."

"Kortsson is the name of my blood-enemy."

"The name does not matter." She rested her hands on her knees. "You seem determined to risk your recovery with your impatience."

"I will risk whatever I must to do as I vowed."

"And what is that?"

He did not reply.

Her shoulders sagged as she sighed. "Mr. Bjornsson, you have no reason to distrust anyone at Sutherland Park. We have given you a haven here and excellent care."

"Yes."

"Very well." Her lips tightened as her eyes sparked with fury. "I will not intrude on your time any longer. Olive has a tray with your luncheon."

"Luncheon?"

"Your midday meal." She rose and went to get the tray she had left with her servant.

He looked past her to the window, ignoring the rumbles in his gut as his body reminded him how long he had been without food. Had it been three days, or more? He could not recall how long he had been lying on the beach waiting for death. If it had been so long, why was Kortsson here, too? His blood-enemy should have gone seeking other prey.

More immediate matters caught his attention when Linnea brought the tray to him. Grabbing an oddly-shaped piece of bread off the shining plate, he took a bite. It was almost tasteless and as pale as the foam on top of a wave. Although he had to struggle to swallow, he did. He dipped his finger into the bowl and sampled the broth. His eyes widened. Never had he heard that spices from beyond the land of the Rus were used here in Britannia.

Instead of giving voice to the questions, he tipped back the bowl and drank deeply of the beef broth. He set the bowl back on the tray. Wiping his mouth on his tattered sleeve, he smiled. "Is there more?"

"If you wish..." Linnea motioned to her servant.

"Send Jack to the kitchen to bring more soup for Mr. Bjornsson."

As the woman rushed down the steps, Nils put his finger against Linnea's cheek. Her dark eyes were wide when he tilted her face back toward him. Although he wished he could look deeply into them as he brought her mouth to his, he said, "I have many questions."

"So do I."

Her soft voice was an invitation to give life to his fantasies, but he must focus on finding out where the line was drawn between the truth and his battered brain's images. Shaking aside the longing to sample her lips, he said, "You tell me that Ethelred no longer reigns in England."

"Of course he doesn't. I told you. He died almost a thousand years ago."

"That is impossible. He was the king of Britannia when I sailed from the land of the *Norrfoolk*."

"That is impossible," she repeated back to him. "I told you that King George is our sovereign king, although his son serves as his Regent while he is ill."

He gauged her face. Her eyes met his evenly, and her voice was steadier than when he had touched her. She was speaking the truth. At least, *she* believed she was speaking the truth. There were no signs of madness about her. She seemed quite at ease here, as her servants did.

A pain throbbed through his head. Linnea Sutherland belonged here. Nils Bjornsson did not. Gazing up at the stone ceiling and along the walls, he noted as he should have from the beginning that this building was not made for withstanding an attack. The walls were of stone as few buildings were in Britannia. A lady should live within the wooden walls of a *burgh*, her bedchamber high in the tower on the hill within the walls. From the hushed sound of water below, he knew this building was set above a pond that would provide water in a siege. He could not recall if there were walls surrounding it.

He put his hand to his forehead. "Linnea, I am being honest with you when I say to you that when I set foot on these shores, Ethelred was the proclaimed king of this island. If this is not a dream, then..."

Her astonishment widened her dark eyes again. "Is that what you believe?" she whispered. "That this is a dream?"

"How can it be anything else?" He pushed himself to his feet. When he wobbled as he shifted all his weight to his right foot, she jumped up and stepped forward to steady him. He waved her away. It was time that she realized his pride allowed him to ask for no help, even when he desperately needed it. "I have never seen a building like this one nor clothes like you wear, in Britannia or anywhere else."

"You should not be standing. You will injure yourself more."

"I refuse to wait here for my blood-enemy to put an end to me."

When Linnea laughed tightly, he was astonished. She fisted her hands on her hips, giving him an enticing view of the splendid curves of her very feminine form. He pulled his eyes from that tantalizing sight to meet her gaze when she said, "Your enemies will have no need to put an end to you if you do them a favor and kill yourself by trying to do too much too soon. Yesterday, you were senseless, except for an apparent brain fever that drove you mad, and you..."

"I could not have destroyed that bench when I am bandaged like this." He frowned at his arm. "I could not raise an ax from the floor."

"And you shall not be able to for a long time when you risk your recovery by trying to walk across the room as if nothing had happened to you."

"Do not treat me like a witless child."

"Only a witless child would act so and risk recovery simply for pride's sake." She turned away when her servant rushed back up the stairs and to her side, an expression of anxiety and disbelief on her face.

Nils muttered a curse under his breath. Loki must be enjoying Linnea's arrogance when she treated him like a witless babe.

"It is fine, Olive," Linnea said. "I am fine."

"But he—"

Linnea glanced back at him, her face blank of any emotion. "He is excitable. Once he realizes where he is and that he is safe from his attacker, he will calm down."

"Attackers," Nils interjected quietly. "Kortsson was the last."

"More than one?" the woman named Olive asked. Her face became as gray as his must be beneath his bruises. "What if they come to the house, my lady? What if—?"

Firing him a furious scowl, Linnea steered her maid back to a chair next to the window by the stairs. "Sit here and watch for Jack to return with Mr. Bjornsson's soup."

"I would rather look out the window and see if anyone is approaching."

"I doubt if they will come up the road."

Nils was surprised when a laugh tickled the back of his throat. Linnea Sutherland had the clear eyes of a warrior, seeing the truth that others might choose to ignore in the midst of their panic. Keeping the laugh from escaping, he wore no expression as Linnea walked back to him. He struggled to focus his eyes on her face and not on the gentle sway of her hips.

"You should sit," she said, her tone still taut.

"How can I sit when I am filled with questions about what has happened to me?"

"You should sit, so you can recover from what happened to you." She motioned toward an iron bench by an open window.

When had that been brought here? Linnea and her

servants were determined that no other bench would be shattered to kindling.

Nils hopped on his good leg to it. When he glanced at her, she was not smiling. Was she sympathetic or hiding another emotion? He did not ask as he eased himself back onto the bench.

When she poured something into a goblet and brought it to him, he was pleased to sip the fragrant wine. He never had sampled anything so dulcet. Letting his shoulders ease back against the wall behind him, he watched as Linnea sat on a stool in front of him. She might be sitting below him, but there was nothing subservient in her pose.

"Thank you." He chuckled. "I assume that is another phrase you did not guess I knew in my language or yours."

A lovely color brightened her cheeks. "That was rude of me to say."

"When did the truth become considered rude?"

"You are a guest here at Sutherland Park, and it was inappropriate for me to say."

Swirling the wine in the bright blue glass, Nils regarded her closely as he lowered his voice. "I also recall you saying that Ethelred is no longer king of England."

"Not for almost a thousand years." She stiffened, and he knew she was as uneasy with this turn of the conversation as he was. "It is 1817."

"That term means nothing to me." Nils looked away from the abrupt compassion on her face. He did not want to be pitied. He was a warrior. Draining the goblet, he set it on the windowsill beside him.

"Ethelred was king of England around the year we would have called 990."

He clenched the fingers on his right hand into a fist. Slamming them into the arm of the bench, he ignored the shock on Linnea's face and how her servant whirled in her seat to stare at him, her eyes wide with terror. How could he have been so foolish? He had spoken of his need, hoping that Freya would heed his request to be left behind to finish his search when she had taken the other fallen warriors to *Valhalla*. She had heard him, but, for some reason he had yet to discover, had sent his plea to Loki. That wizard of mischief must have contrived this plan to keep him from both his reward in death and his hopes in life... and sent Kortsson with him into this time.

Slowly he glanced at the window. The very window where Loki had perched in his dream. But had that been as real as what was around him now? He resisted the taunting laugh that throbbed through his head. His voice or Loki's? The dream may have been real, and this truly might be the nightmare he could not flee. But he could not imagine that even a fevered dream brought on by the festering of his wounds would create such a journey to the future.

"Mr. Bjornsson, I am so sorry," Linnea whispered. "I know it makes no sense to you. It makes no sense to me, but I know what year it is. It is 1817. Search your mind. You will see that you know that, too."

"I know Ethelred is king of England."

"But I told you—"

He snarled a curse at her. Heaving himself again to his feet, he hopped to where a window opened on the sea side of this building. Ignoring the pain raging in his head, he fumbled as he tried to open the shutters on the window with a single hand. Several of the slats hung broken. When Linnea's slender fingers reached to unhook the stubborn latch, he caught her wrist.

Her servant shouted a warning, but Linnea did not make a sound as he tugged her closer, keeping her from undoing the latch. *Had Olive's warning been for Linnea or for him?* he wondered when the soft scent of whatever she used to clean her hair drifted toward him, as luscious as the first blossoms after a long winter. Her curves pressed against him were as seductive as the allure of the sea.

His lips were on hers before she had a chance to protest. They tasted sweet, just as he had imagined. A tempting invitation to further pleasure that they could find when—

The sound of her hand slapping his cheek resonated through Nils's aching head. With a growl, he released her. She motioned her servant away as Olive rushed to her side with a hushed cry.

"Mr. Bjornsson," Linnea said in that cold tone she seemed delighted to assume whenever she found fault with him, "I realize you are distressed at the facts that must seem as outrageous and unbelievable to you as they are to me."

"Facts?" asked Olive. "What do you speak of, my lady?"

Nils tensed, waiting for her answer. Among these English there was neither respect nor understanding of *Norrfoolk* beliefs. He had heard during his previous forays here mocking of Odin and Loki and Freya. Those who had dared to utter such words had no chance to repeat them, for his knife had put an end to their belittling of what he held dear.

Linnea continued to meet his gaze without flinching, but she said, "Olive, I wish to speak to Mr. Bjornsson alone. Will you go and see what is keeping Jack from returning from the house with that soup for Mr. Bjornsson?"

"And leave you with him and his beastly manners?"

"Mr. Bjornsson will not forget himself again." She gave Olive a tight grin. "Or you shall hear me slap him again."

"Yes, my lady." She shot Nils a fearsome frown before going to the stairs. At the top, she paused, her mouth moving with whatever she was mumbling. He waited, not sure if she would obey and leave her lady with him. She did, her head vanishing below the bannister.

"You may find," Linnea said, her voice still rigid with rage, "that you would do better not to vex everyone you meet, Mr. Bjornsson."

"You may find that you would do better to call me Nils, for your English tongue cannot speak my name correctly."

"Only if you realize that such informality does not allow you *carte blanche* to—"

"What?"

"It is French."

"French? What is that?"

"The French are the residents of the land on the other side of the Channel." When he continued to frown in bafflement, she added, "Where the sea narrows between this island and the continent."

"You speak of the Franks."

"Yes."

He nodded. "Many of the *Norrfoolk* live in the land of the Franks."

"As a child, I learned that the Vikings gave their name to Normandy, the section of France that reaches out toward England. The Normans won the English throne in 1066, and their descendants have held it since."

He laughed as he threw open the shutters on the window. "So it would seem that the *Norrfoolk* claim to this island was eventually won and long held."

"Indirectly." She faltered before a sigh sifted past her stiff lips. "Dash it! Can you stop playing a Viking lost in time?"

"I am being honest, my lady. All I have spoken to you about King Ethelred and Britannia is true." His brows lowered. "You think I am mad with an injury to my skull."

"You were struck viciously."

"True."

"You claim to have seen things that no one else has."

He cupped her chin as he had in the doorway below.

"My blood-enemy exists."

"You cannot be sure."

"I am." He reached under his tunic and tossed the knife to the floor at her feet. "I swear on the blood you saw on this that I drew it from my blood-enemy, not myself. You may not have seen him, but that does not change what I know is true."

"But..." She hesitated, then asked, "Do you realize what you are saying? That you have come forward in time from your millennium to mine?"

"It is not easy to believe." He touched the sill where Loki had laughed at him. "Yet I know it must be true." Leaning against the sill, he pointed to the ocean that was visible as a silver line through the trees. "If we were in my time, you would be watching from here and shivering in fear at the very idea that a *drakkar* and its crew of warriors would sail toward this shore."

"My ancestors fought to hold here, and they did."

"Are you so sure of that?"

"I know what I have been told." Her chin rose in a pride as enticing as her splendidly feminine body.

He laughed to conceal the longing that bounced through him. Kissing her had been foolish, for it had honed his craving for the delights he had denied himself in the months of his journeys on behalf of his chieftain. Months or centuries? He could not think of that now. He must learn more of this woman and this place and this time so he could defend himself—and her, for he owed her a life-debt—from Kortsson.

"But your very name denies what you believe," he said. "Sutherland is close to a *Norrfoolk* name. Suthrland."

"Close? They sound the same."

"To your English ears. Heed me. Sutherland is your name. Suthrland is the name I know."

She shook her head. "I cannot hear the difference."

"Because you are not listening closely enough."

"How can you say that? I tried to hear a difference,

but I did not."

He caught her chin in his hand once more and tilted her face away from his. When she stiffened, he bent to put his lips near her ear. He repeated the two names as he took a deep breath of her glorious fragrance. His fingers glided along her soft cheek. "Do you hear the difference, my lady?"

"Yes." Her voice quivered.

"Do you really?"

She pulled away from him, leaving his empty fingers cupping only air. He clenched them again as he cursed silently. No warrior should be so weak that a woman could break his hold on her with such little effort.

"I said I did," she replied tautly. "Why must you question everything I say and act as if I am lying?"

"You think I am lying when I speak of a time you tell me was a thousand years ago. You call me mad for being honest about seeing my blood-enemy."

"I do not know what to think." She rubbed her forehead. "Everything you do, everything you say tries to persuade me that you are being honest."

"But you cannot believe what I am saying."

"Can you?"

He did not hesitate. "I must, because I know what I speak is the truth. I am not of this time. I am of the days when Ethelred tried to keep my chieftain from claiming this part of this island." His gaze edged along her, and a smile curved his lips. "No woman in my time dresses as you do, either among the *Norrfoolk* or among the English. Silks are rare, coming from the lands far beyond the Rus."

"Rus?" She laughed shakily. "Oh, you mean Russia."

"The name survives nearly a millennium? It appears that my people made many contributions to your time, Linnea."

"Your time, too."

His eyes narrowed. "Do you still think I am plying

you with lies?"

"Even if you are not originally from this time, you are here in this time now." Linnea shook her head. Turning away, she kneaded her fingers together anxiously. "I cannot believe I am speaking so serenely of this. It is impossible that you and I can be having this conversation when you should be long dead."

"And forgotten." His hand on her shoulder kept her from walking away. When she looked back at him, he said, "I believe I know why I have been brought forward in time to this place where I should have died."

"Don't say that!"

"But you should know as well why I am here."

Shivering, she stepped away from his fingers that sent a heat through her that combated the iciness of her disbelief. "No, do not say that you should have died here."

"Everyone dies eventually. A warrior hopes for a courageous death, so that *Valhalla* might be his reward." His hand tightened into a fist. "That might still be mine if I do as I vowed when I first came to this accursed island almost a thousand years ago. I have to find the knife that belongs to my chieftain, the knife that was stolen from him by my brother. The shame is upon my family, and it is my duty and my honor to even this debt."

"A knife? You believe you survived for all these centuries simply to find a knife?"

"It was a blood-oath I swore, a blood-oath that Kortsson has vowed that I will not complete."

Linnea went to the window and looked out it. The familiar shapes and scents of the water garden seemed somehow different. "You are speaking nonsense," she whispered. "Even if you did swear such an oath, why would it bring you here? Why would it matter when the man you swore this oath to has been dead for so many centuries?"

"A blood-oath is binding on me as long as I

breathe." His hand on her shoulder turned her to face him. She wished she had resisted when she saw the obsession in his eyes as he whispered, "And I will see it fulfilled, no matter what I must do to complete it."

Six

"What are you looking for?"

Linnea spun away from the shelf, closing the heavy book and pressing it to her chest. She told herself she had no reason to act so guilty at the sound of her eldest brother's voice. She forced a smile for him.

Martin Sutherland appeared every inch his father's heir. In the past few years, the hair at his temples had taken on the silver shade of their mutual sire. He resembled Papa in other ways as well, for he was growing rounder with each passing year. A pair of eyeglasses were propped on his forehead, revealing dark eyes that often were focused on some financial report.

"You startled me," she said with a nervous laugh.

"I did not expect to see you hiding in here when your charming suitor just took his leave."

"Randolph was here?"

He frowned, looking even more like Papa when he was perplexed. "Yes, I thought you knew."

"No." She went to the door.

"Linny, what are you studying now?"

At the nickname he had given her when she was no more than a baby, her smile became more sincere, but it wavered at his question. Folding her arms over the book, she said, "You know how I love history."

"Yes, you always seem to be reading about some great past exploits with a dashing hero who is about to save England from destruction. What is it this time?" He reached toward the book.

"Can we talk later?" she asked, turning slightly to keep him from seeing the title. "I should—"

"Go and catch Tuthill before he leaves. I know he is as anxious to see you as he was to find out why Papa contacted the authorities about that cur you believe you saw attacking someone on the shore."

"I *did* see it."

"I hope you will not again."

"So do I."

" And I know you are eager to see Tuthill."

Linnea flashed him a grin before hurrying out of the book-room. She had not exactly lied to her brother, so she should not be suffering from these pangs of guilt. Silently she warned herself not to be so skittish. Even if Martin had seen the title of the book, he had no idea why she had developed a sudden interest in English history before the Norman Conquest. He would have simply shrugged off this new hobby, for he had no reason to suspect she had an actual Viking living in the pavilion's upper room.

Her steps faltered on the stairs. In the past three days while she had talked to Nils and tried to learn more about him, she had come to believe he truly was not of this time. Yet that was impossible. No one traveled in huge leaps from one century to another. Time took everyone along on a day-by-day journey into the future. No slower and certainly no faster.

But she could not deny that Nils Bjornsson seemed to be so lost. He watched everyone with the wariness of a man among his enemies...and his blood-enemy who, if she believe all of this moonshine, had traveled through time with Nils. Nothing she had done had persuaded him that he should trust her assertion that they wished only to help him heal and continue on his way. And nothing had persuaded *her* to trust her unexpected reaction to his brazen kiss. She had slapped his face, but she wondered if the resonance of that blow had lingered on his cheek as long as the heat from his lips on hers.

Linnea pushed those rebellious thoughts from her head when she stepped out of the house to see Randolph standing in the drive. His toe was tapping against the ground, and she knew he was impatient to be on his way.

"Randolph?" she called.

He looked over his shoulder. His vexed expression did not change as he said, "I thought you were out."

"Whoever told you that was mistaken." She tapped the book she held. "I was reading in Papa's book-room."

"You spend too much time reading such tomes."

"I enjoy it."

"How will any of that help you in your future duties?"

She could not keep from bristling. "My father values education for all his children, and I do not see any reason for my education to end simply because I am out of the schoolroom."

"But your education should take a different route now." He stepped closer to her. "An education in what you shall share with your husband." When his arm slipped around her waist, he pulled her closer.

The book bumped against his chest. He yanked it from her hands and dropped it onto the step. When she gasped as the binding creaked and the pages fluttered open, he growled something under his breath.

"Randolph, enough of this," she said, trying to pull away so she could be certain that the book was not damaged.

"Enough? I think not." His mouth pounced on hers.

She stiffened, shocked at his outrageous behavior...and by her lack of reaction to it. She was exasperated at his assumption that she would let him kiss her like this, but she felt nothing else. None of the surge of anticipation that had whirled through her like a storm when Nils kissed her.

He raised his mouth and frowned. If he had thought she would melt in his arms, he was mistaken, because she knew the limits of propriety, and he had overstepped them.

But you were ready to welcome more of Nils's kisses, until sanity returned.

Linnea edged out of Randolph's embrace as she silenced her rebellious thoughts. "I trust you are finished," she said as she bent and picked up the book, smoothing the pages back into place as she closed it. Looking past him to where a stableboy was bringing Randolph's horse, she added, "I bid you a good day, Randolph."

"Linnea, wait!"

"I must...I was on my way to..." She scowled at her own hesitation. It could doom her attempt to keep Nils hidden more swiftly than anything else. "I am already late." There! That was simple and almost the truth. Olive had work to do in the house, so they had arranged for Jack to stay with Nils. However, by this hour, Jack would be needed in the stables. If Nils was alone, he might—

She gasped when Randolph caught her by the arm, tearing her from her scattered thoughts. Nils had been this rude, but she had never guessed Randolph would forget his good manners. "Randolph, please release me at once."

"When you explain why you are treating me so coolly after you welcomed my calls with glee only a fortnight ago."

"You are being coarse."

He relinquished her arm and made a show of

straightening his coat. His red ears divulged his dismay at violating proper behavior. "Forgive me, Linnea," he mumbled. "I am not myself today."

"Is something amiss?"

"Nothing that you need concern yourself about." He gave her one of his smiles that suggested she should be thinking of nothing more important than which dress to wear to tea. The smile that threatened to send her up to the boughs with her annoyance. "Only some food and supplies stolen."

"By whom?"

"I don't know, but I suspect it may have been that vagabond you saw on the shore." He put his hands on her shoulders. "Do not be out alone again."

"I had Jack with me."

"Stay close to the house."

"I shall."

"Good." Going to his horse, he took the reins from the stableboy.

Linnea did not want to wait to see Randolph leave, but she stood by the steps until he was out of view along the drive leading away from the shore. The stableboy flashed her a smile. She was not sure why, and she pushed her disquiet from her mind as she walked toward the water garden. This was becoming more and more complicated with each passing day. How would she manage with Dinah's wedding approaching with such speed?

Opening the door to the water pavilion, she made certain it was closed tightly before she hurried up the stairs. She scanned the room. It was empty!

"Nils?" she called, hoping her voice did not carry out one of the two windows that were open.

She turned toward the shadows that had captured the back portion of the room. Blinking, she tried to make her eyes adjust to the dim light there.

"Nils?"

Again she got no answer. Mayhap he was asleep.

She shook her head. Even if he had been, any sound woke him, because he did not trust them enough to sleep deeply.

No one stood in the shadows. Baffled, she drew aside the shutters on the window on that side. Nils might have been able to get down the stairs, but how far could he go when he had to hop on one leg? She thought he understood that he was safer here than anywhere now.

A finger tapped her shoulder.

She shrieked.

Laughter added to the fire climbing her cheeks as she turned to see Nils standing behind her. In astonishment, she stared at the long branch that served as a crutch for him.

"Where did you get that?" she asked.

"Young Jack obtained it for me." He winced as he shifted his arm on the notch at its top. "I believe he tires of me hopping like a rabbit when I wish to move from one place to another."

"He does have a way of seeing the obvious solution." Setting the book on the bench by the open window, she asked, "Why were you hiding from me?"

He laughed, the bronzed skin beside his eyes crinkling. "Your surprise was an amusement for a man who has had nothing to amuse him for too long."

"I am glad I was able to provide that."

"Ah, sarcasm. You use it as a weapon when you wish to hide your true emotions." He curved a finger beneath her chin and tipped it up. "But your words are futile, Linnea, when your eyes expose the truth. Can it be that I saw anxiety on my behalf?"

"You are a guest at Sutherland Park. I should—"

"Be honest." His finger stroked her cheek lightly, the touch an invitation to explore the emotions in his eyes...if she dared to.

She wanted to fire back another quick answer, but she was imprisoned by the warmth of his gaze. This was outrageous! She had scurried away from Randolph's kiss like a churlish child. Now she was delighting like a strumpet in Nils's audacious caress.

"I thought you might have sneaked away," she whispered.

"And that thought upset you?"

"I feared you would injure yourself more. Kortsson seems to have paid a call at Randolph's house and stolen supplies from him. That means your blood-enemy is still near Sutherland Park."

"That was all you feared for on my behalf? And on yours?"

She shook her head. "Ask me nothing more. This conversation will lead to places we should not go."

"Because of your betrothal to another man?"

Linnea sank to the bench beside the book. "You would be wise not to heed all the gossip you hear."

"I do not, but this tidbit intrigued me." Moving the book to the other side of the bench, he lowered himself to the smooth slats. "You say so little about yourself, although you ask endless questions about me and my time." She must have flinched because he went on, "You can deny the truth all you wish, Linnea, but it does not change it. I have been brought to this time which is not mine, and I have been brought to you. There must be a reason."

"I found you on the beach. Anyone could have done the same."

"But *you* were the one who did find me when you wandered the strand alone." His hand curved along her nape as his fingers sifted up through her hair. "Just as you came here today knowing that we would be alone for the first time since that moment."

"I came here to show you what I had found in the house."

"For that reason alone?" He bent toward her, and she could look nowhere but into his eyes. "Did you, perchance, come here now knowing that we would be able to speak plainly?"

"I always try to speak plainly to you."

"Do you?" His mouth brushed her cheek as his palm cupped her nape, tilting her face toward his. "I speak not only of your words, but of the thoughts that glow in your eyes and wait upon your lips."

The quiver within her would not be smothered. It urged her to surrender to her longings and his. Then she was kissing him. Had he moved closer or had she? It did not matter as her hand swept up along his uninjured arm to his broad shoulder. This was madness and this was dangerous and this was a betrayal of her family which believed she longed to marry Randolph. But she ignored all that while she relished the bold warmth of his mouth.

When his lips left hers and coursed along her face, she closed her eyes and smiled. She wanted only to think of this delight. Why had no one told her how luscious a man's kisses could be? He moaned, and, for a moment, she thought he had hurt his broken arm that he held at an odd angle so he could press her closer. Then, his mouth found hers again, telling her that the desperate sound had come from his longing for this. Her fingers curled on his back when his tongue slipped between her lips, brushing hers in an invitation to far more intimate frolic.

He leaned her back on the bench, introducing her to his hard, masculine body as he slanted across her. A pain slashed the middle of her spine. When she yelped, he released her, amazement on his face.

Sliding away, she picked up the book she had brought from the house. She started to put it on the floor, then faltered. She set it on her lap. It was Papa's book. What would Papa think if he discovered her here in this stranger's arms? Fire flared through her again, but now an icy flame that swept away the sweetness of Nils's kisses.

"Linnea?" Nils touched her face gently.

"It would be better if we talked and did nothing else."

"Because you are promised to another?"

Linnea stood, holding the book in front of her like a shield. "Because of what you are and what I am."

"You are the daughter of Lord Sutherland."

"Yes."

"An English lord."

"Yes."

"And I am of the *Norrfoolk*."

"From a thousand years ago."

His eyes twinkled as he hoisted himself to lean on the crutch. "I can assure you that some things are unchanged no matter how many centuries have passed. Your kisses are sweet, whether in this time or if I had met you in mine."

"If you had met me in your time, you would not have stopped when I protested." When his eyes slitted as his mouth straightened, she looked away.

He caught her face in his broad hand and forced it up so her gaze met his. "I have never raped a woman. My blood-enemy never shows such restraint, but my duty here is—" He blinked and muttered something she could not understand. "My duty here *was* to serve my chieftain while he did our king's bidding to conquer this island." His voice grew husky. "So you do not think I could have persuaded you to kiss me if we had met in my time?"

"It is a moot question. If we were in your time, we never would have met. I would have been hidden by my family far from the Viking rampage."

"A true tragedy that would have been." His fingers against her cheek became a tantalizing caress.

When she was about to lean toward him and his captivating lips, Linnea stepped back. She must not show him how many more ways she could be foolish. Going to the table by the stairs, she set the book on it. She hoped Nils did not notice how her fingers trembled as she spread them across the cover. Until Olive could return here, Linnea must keep a distance between her and the temptation to sample just one more of his intriguing kisses.

She bit her lip when the uneven sound of Nils's crutch against the floor paused behind her. His warm breath brushed her back above her gown, twirling strands of hair about her in an invitation to a dance that needed no music except two rapidly beating hearts. Then he moved to stand beside her. She wanted to release her breath in a rush of relief, but that would disclose how deeply he unsettled her. She swallowed her terse laugh as she let the breath slide past her clenched teeth. If she thought he could not guess the course of her thoughts when she had opened her arms to him, she was a complete chucklehead.

"What is this?" Nils asked, curiosity once more woven through his voice.

"This is a book." She looked at him. "Do you know what a book is?"

"Of course. I have seen its like here in Britannia before. There was a monastery that stood on a small island not far from—"

She put her hands over her ears. "Do not think to enthrall me with tales of your comrades' bestial behavior when you overran that monastery and slew its residents."

Taking one of her hands in his, he frowned. "You again are assuming that you know what you cannot know."

"I know what you Vikings did to Lindisfarne. You sacked the monastery there and killed every living soul you could capture."

"The foray upon Lindisfarne took place in my grandsire's grandsire's grandsire's time."

"Oh."

His smile returned. "I wish I could have been part of that early foray, one of the first upon this island."

With a grumble, she pulled her hand out of his.

Dash it! This man gloried in killing. "It was your misfortune to be born too late."

"There is that sarcasm again. Linnea, you must not judge what you do not understand."

"I understand this." She flipped open the book to a page she had turned down. Pushing up the corner of the page, she pointed to the drawing in the middle of it.

He bent toward it and nearly toppled.

"Sit," she ordered. "You shall be able to see it more easily that way."

She thought he would refuse, then he nodded. Dropping heavily onto the nearest bench, he took a shuddering breath. Only now did she notice how pale his face was beneath his deep tan. He was trying to keep her from seeing that he still was weakened by his pain.

Sitting beside him, she balanced the book on her lap. "This is a book displaying what happened when the Vikings invaded England."

Linnea was silent as Nils stared at the picture. The Viking warriors were pouring off their dragon-prowed ship with its square sail. The buildings in the village were topped by flames. Bodies were scattered in every direction, and at the far left of the picture a Viking was dragging a woman by her hair toward the shore.

Looking from the horrendous portrayal of brutality to his face, she waited for him to say something. She wanted him to assure her that this was far worse than anything he had witnessed, that history had darkened the name of the Norse warriors, that he never would have been part of something like this.

"This picture is wrong," he said.

"Is it?" Her heart bounced within her, elated that he was not a beast like those depicted in this drawing.

He touched the helmet on a warrior stepping ashore. "This is not correct. No one among the *Norrfoolk* would wear horns protruding from a battle helmet. They would be knocked off with a single blow and make a warrior vulnerable to the jab of a blade."

"But otherwise?"

"Otherwise, the drawing of that man could be a portrait of Gyrd." He pointed to the man holding a handful of the woman's hair.

She swallowed her disgust as she asked, "Who is Gyrd?"

"My cousin." Tapping the center of the warrior's chest, he said, "Gyrd wears such an amulet with Thor's hammer, as I do."

"Like on your arm band?"

"And like this." He drew out the gold chain and pointed to the strange ornament. "This is Thor's hammer."

Linnea looked from the picture to the charm he wore. They were identical. "So you recognize this?"

"I just said so." He pulled the book from her lap and tipped it on its side. With a grimace, he handed it back to her. "I may speak your language, but I cannot read its swirls. What is the name of this book?"

The Vikings in Old England."

"So this is why you call me a Viking instead of a *Norrfoolk.*"

"The term is the one we are familiar with in this time."

"Viking is not what we called ourselves."

Linnea closed the book and set it back on the table. "I am sure you were called many other things by the English of that time."

"I have heard those names spoken in anger and in fear." His mouth tightened. "However, what is not shown in this book is the attacks made by Ethelred's men on the peace-loving people of the Danelaw."

"Danelaw?"

He picked up the book and paged through it. Pointing to a picture of a village where children played while the adults tended to their tasks, he said, "The Danelaw was the eastern half of this island that had been ceded to the *Norrfoolk*. There, English and *Norrfoolk* lived in peace for many years until the English broke that peace with raids that left many dead. Not just warriors, but women and oldsters and children. Only then was it determined that all of this island must be brought to its knees before our king. The English could not be trusted."

"They only were trying to get back what the Vikings had stolen."

"The Danelaw was created by treaty between the kings of the English and the *Norrfoolk*. The English broke that treaty and showed their dishonor. Our leader was a *daari* to trust them."

"*Daari*? You said that before, but I do not recall what it means."

"It means fool." He ran his fingers over the picture of the quiet village. The pain on his face was not from his broken arm or his ankle. Instead there was a dullness to his eyes, as if he were hurt in places no one but he could see. "All of us were fools. We did not expect Ethelred to denounce the treaty of his fathers. So many died."

"On both sides of the battle."

Raising his head, he met her eyes steadily. "Save for Nils Bjornsson for whom death has been denied."

"You think you can't die? That is the most absurd thing I have ever heard."

"I mean only that I was not granted a warrior's death in my own time, that I was brought here. If Kortsson finds me here before I am healed, I know he can slay me." He closed the book. As she set it on the table, he took her hand and drew her back to sit beside him. "I know you find this difficult to believe."

"As you do."

He nodded. "As I do. However, I cannot deny the truth that is before me. This is not the year I was in when I closed my eyes upon making my prayer to Freya."

"The goddess?"

"The one who takes the dying warriors to the *Valhalla* and their reward for their service and bravery. I asked her to help me complete my vow to my chieftain."

"To find a knife?"

"You remember?"

"How could I forget something so ludicrous?" Linnea asked, then wished she had not when his eyes became violet slits.

"There is nothing ludicrous about a blood-vow. I need to find the knife that belongs to my chieftain, so I can return it to him."

She put a hand on his arm. "It might not even exist any longer."

The hint of a smile tipped his lips as he touched her cheek lightly. "It must, or I would not have been brought here. Although I would like to think that you are my reward, *unnasta*, it—"

"What did you call me?"

He chuckled. "Some Norse words do not translate easily into your language."

Linnea ignored her curiosity. When his laugh took on that playful tone, she had learned that he would not give her a reasonable answer. He was enjoying teasing her.

Standing, she said, "I find it difficult to believe a knife would survive for a thousand years when it was lost to begin with."

"Not lost. Stolen. It is possible that Kortsson has it now." He held up his hands about eighteen inches apart. "The knife was this long, and it was made by a master. Its haft was gilded to accent the outline of Loki and a dragon that spiraled along it, its tail becoming the blade. Two red stones glistened for its eyes, and its tongue was painted a midnight black. Only when one looked closely could the tiny dwarves be seen holding up the coils of the serpent."

"Tiny dwarves? A trio of them on either side?"

"Yes!"

"I have seen that knife."

"You have?" His eyes brightened with anticipation and other emotions warning that anyone who had challenged this fearsome warrior had been a fool. "Where?"

"I am not sure."

"Linnea, I must know."

"In London it must have been. When we visited there during the Little Season before Dinah announced her plans to marry."

"We must go to London before Kortsson learns of this. I had thought he might have it, but if you have seen it, he does not."

She frowned. "You cannot travel now."

"I will heal. Then we shall go there. You will lead me to the knife before Kortsson can find it, and I shall take it to my chieftain as I have vowed."

"Back through time?"

His shoulders sagged as she never had seen them do before. "I had not considered that. There must be a way for me to satisfy my oath. Otherwise, there is no logical reason for me to be here." His jaw clenched. "Even Loki would not be so cruel."

"The god of mischief?"

"You are learning quickly, Linnea."

"I must if I wish to help you."

He looked up at her in amazement. "You wish to help me?"

"Yes."

"Why?"

She sat again beside him. To speak the truth of the obligations she had would only magnify this unbelievable situation. To speak of how she wished to see his eyes glitter with joy as they did when he drew her close would be foolhardy. To speak of how she could not trust herself when she was in his arms would be even more imprudent. The wisest choice she could make now was to believe they had been brought together so she could assist him in his quest.

"You must do what you vowed and be where you belong," she replied.

"So you will help me, even though the danger of the past may still be lurking here in this time?"

She did not hesitate. "Yes."

Seven

"So you think it will be that easy, Nils Bjornsson?"

Nils raised his head from the pillow that was more comfortable than any in his time. Too easily he recognized that voice. It belonged to Loki.

Sitting, he rested his splinted arm on his knee. He wiggled the toes of his other foot. Pain jabbed him, but not as savagely as it had even this afternoon. The crutch Jack had brought him was allowing him to stretch his cramped muscles without adding more injury to his ankle.

He met Loki's gaze evenly. As before, the wizard-god was perched on the windowsill. Moonlight washed him nearly into silhouette, but Nils could discern the sparkle of mischief in Loki's eyes. Or maybe Nils only thought he was able to see it, because that glitter was rumored to be omnipresent.

"No blood-oath is ever completed with ease," Nils replied.

"Yet you believe with the Englishwoman's assistance, you will succeed."

"I will succeed, and I will use whatever means I must."

"Does she realize that?" Loki laughed as he jumped down from the sill. "You have convinced her that you have the soul of a poet, not the heart of a warrior."

Nils snorted his disagreement. "She knows I am a warrior."

Loki squatted next to him and tapped his finger against his nose. "Do *you* know that when she is near, Nils Bjornsson? Freya was not pleased to hear you call an Englishwoman *unnasta*. That term is meant only for those among the *Norrfoolk*."

"It means sweetheart, as you well know. Nothing more, nothing less." Nils smiled. "And Linnea Sutherland is sweet."

"Odin himself has warned that a woman can dull your wits as well as your weapons."

"I know of the great god's advice. He counsels as well that a wise man recognizes his foes and uses them to his own advantage."

"So you intend to use her in your quest?"

"Of course. My oath is a blood-oath. I must do whatever is necessary to do as I pledged."

"Those are strong words from a mortal, Nils Bjornsson. Once already you have disdained your destiny." Loki stood and went back to the window. "Make sure you are ready to pay the price if you do so again."

"I have no choice. The vow is spoken."

"No choice?" Loki laughed as he jumped back up onto the sill. "You have choices now, Nils Bjornsson, but your path narrows ahead of you. Soon there will be only a single choice you may make. Right or wrong, it is all that will be left to you."

"I have made my choice."

"And Linnea Sutherland has made hers?"

Nils sat straighter. He had not expected Loki to speak of Linnea by name. The god had spoken of her only as "the Englishwoman," in the most disdainful tone.

"Yes," he answered, "Linnea has made hers."

"Without knowing what she has vowed?"

"What do you mean? She has vowed to help me."

Loki chuckled. "To share in your quest?"

"Yes."

"In its rewards if you succeed?"

Nils did not answer quickly. Linnea had said nothing of expecting a prize for helping him. Now that he had a chance to think of that conversation without her beguiling eyes teasing him to think of other things more delightful than his search for the knife, he realized she had not asked for anything. It might be that she was eager to be rid of him. He was an obstacle in her well-ordered life.

"A warrior," he said with slow caution, "always remembers to reward those who help him in his duties."

"True, and you will be generous, I am sure. But what if you fail?"

"I will not fail."

"Are you so sure of that, Nils Bjornsson? Do you have a god's far-seeing that you can know what the future holds for you?"

"Of course not."

Loki leaned his shoulder against the window's stone frame. "Answer me, Nils Bjornsson. You have asked a daughter of this green island to share in your quest."

"Yes."

"So she will share your rewards if you succeed."

Nils was sure his icy face had no more color than the moonlight as he whispered, "Are you saying that she will share my damnation if I fail?"

Loki's wild laugh erupted through the night like the crash of thunder. Something flashed, blinding Nils as if a thousand stars had erupted in his hand.

Blinking, Nils rubbed one eye, then the other. Slowly the bright glow waned, but the truth remained along with the echo of Loki's laughter. In his desperation to find his chieftain's stolen blade and return to the past where he belonged, Nils had entangled Linnea in his uncertain future. If *he* failed to achieve what he had vowed to do in his blood-oath, she would share his doom in the cold, ebony mists of Niflheim.

Forever.

Eight

"My lady, please wake up!"

Linnea tried to recapture the dream that vanished even as she fought to remember what it had been. Confusing images ricocheted through her head, none of them making sense.

Turning her head, she blinked as she saw Olive holding a lamp. Her maid reached out and shook Linnea's shoulder.

"My lady, please wake up!"

"I am awake," Linnea mumbled, pushing herself up to sit. She glanced toward the window. The stars were bright, so the moon must have set. It was still more than an hour before the first hints of dawn. "What is it?"

"'Tis *him*, my lady."

Linnea swung her legs over the side of the high bed. She recognized Olive's disgruntled tone. Clearly Nils had done something to unnerve Olive again. Even after a week had passed, the two continued to treat each other with open distrust.

"What has happened? If he is having nightmares again, you know you should just leave him alone." She rubbed her eyes and yawned. Last night's gathering had gone late, and her head ached with fatigue. "There was no need to rouse me, Olive."

Her maid affixed her most vexed expression on her face. "My lady, you know I would never wake you if the matter was not of the greatest importance."

"Yes, Olive, I know that." She eased her toes down from the bed onto the steps. Reaching for her wrapper, she pulled it over her shoulders, pausing when she heard a clock chiming somewhere in the house. Three chimes. She wanted to toss aside her wrapper and jump back beneath the covers.

"*He* refuses to heed sense."

"How?"

"*He* is insisting on taking his leave."

Linnea whirled to face her maid. "Leave? At this hour? In his condition?"

Olive nodded as she folded her arms in front of her.

Such a pose would not work with Nils, Linnea was tempted to say. She did not. Shoving her feet into the slippers she had worn to the dance last night, she rushed toward the door. She buttoned her wrapper as she hurried along the dimly lit corridor and toward the back stairs. Although it was unlikely she would meet any of her family at this hour, she did not want to chance it.

Jack was coming in the kitchen door just as she reached it. Anxiety lengthened his usually smiling face. "Thank heavens, my lady, you are here. He will not heed any sense."

"Where is he?"

"Trying to get down the stairs." Jack's grin returned for a moment. "I stole his crutch, so he is not finding it easy."

Linnea was tempted to smile, too, but she just patted Jack's shoulder before going out into the darkness. The grass was damp with dew and clung to the hem of her wrapper. Within steps, her toes were wet inside her slippers. She ignored her discomfort as she ran to the pavilion.

Light pulled her into the ground floor. A single lantern was set beside the door. Picking it up, she heard the swish of water against the doors on the side of the building that opened onto the pond. A thud came from above. She raised the lantern to chase back the shadows and saw Nils sitting on a step three down from the top.

"Where are you bound?" she asked, trying to keep her voice even.

"I must—" He muttered something else under his breath as he lowered himself down another step.

"How far do you think you will get when you cannot even walk down the stairs?" She pointed toward the door. "There are steps up from the pond in every direction. The front gate of Sutherland Park is nearly a quarter of a mile inland. Of course if you wish to travel along the strand, you need only clamber over the rocks that litter the shore." She put one foot on the lowest riser. "At the rate you seem to be going, you should reach there just about the time your arm knits and you can get rid of the splint."

Nils snarled, "That young *daari* took my crutch."

"Jack is not the fool. You are."

"I must continue on my quest. I have wasted too much time here."

Linnea laughed without humor. "You can wait until you heal, or you can chance hurting yourself worse. What is the point of risking your recovery with thoughtless impatience? I told you I would help you all I could."

When he winced as if she had struck his broken arm, her eyes narrowed. There was a desperation about him that she had never seen. Even when she had found him on the beach, he had possessed a cockiness that suggested he could do as he wished, with or without anyone's assistance.

"Nils, what is amiss?"

"I must be on my way. Alone."

She climbed the stairs and sat next to him on the cool stone riser. "Be sensible, Nils. You can barely walk with the crutch. How can you think of going all the way to London when I cannot even tell you which house to call at?"

"When I began this quest, I vowed nothing would halt me."

"Nils, be sensible!" Raising her chin, she asked, "Or did you lie to me? Are you like those warriors who cannot control themselves?"

"We spoke of men who become beasts when they smell the scent of battle."

She shook her head. "No, we spoke of men who think so much of the outcome that they do not consider the cost."

"I vowed a blood-oath to retrieve that knife for my chieftain."

"I know, but what good is trying to leave now when, if you wait a few more weeks, I may have recalled where I saw that knife? Then we can send to London for it, and you can be on your way."

"Waiting is wrong. I did not vow to bring that knife to my chieftain when it was convenient for me."

She put her fingers on his right arm. "But, Nils, what difference does it make *now*?"

"Nothing has changed my vow."

"But your chieftain has waited nearly a thousand years. What does it matter if you wait another few weeks before you go to London?"

At the sorrow in Linnea's voice, Nils did what he had promised himself he would not. He let his gaze be caught by hers. By Thor's hammer, he was witless to let her gentle warmth touch him again. He had been warned by Loki, who would not hesitate to make his threats real.

A sigh sifted through his tight lips. He was just fooling himself if he thought that the gods would let him remake his blood-oath now to keep Linnea from being a part of it. For some reason, he had been brought here to this place and this woman. To turn his back on this happenstance might bring on the very doom that he wished to avoid.

"Nils, let me take you to your bed," she murmured.

A thud of sensation seized him at the soft invitation in her voice. She did not mean it as his body was hearing it, for, while she was willing to let him steal a few kisses, she wanted him gone. He had never thought he would consider an Englishwoman wise, but Linnea Sutherland was.

"Nils?"

"Yes, yes." He sounded as short-tempered as an old man, and he doubted if she guessed his irritation was aimed at himself.

Hating that he had to depend on her to assist him, he said nothing while she helped him up the stairs and back to the area that was separated from the rest of the room by a trio of screens. The images on the screen were from the distant east, a place that apparently was as mysterious in this time as in his. Greatly exaggerated by the single lantern burning by the stairs, the dragons seemed ready to rise and devour them.

Nils heard his halting breaths. Not because the walking was difficult, for he had carried more than his own weight so many times on a *drakkar* as the deck rolled beneath him with the motion of the waves. The uneven sound came from his efforts to avoid the dulcet scent of her perfume that remained even in the depths of the night. Her arm was around his waist, so her breast—separated from him only by the thin layers of her garments and his— tantalized his side.

How much temptation could one man endure? The echo of laughter rang through his head. Was *this* torment what Loki intended to visit upon him? To have this luscious woman in his arms and know that he should be thinking solely of his quest? His only answer was the resonance of that taunting laugh.

He dropped heavily to the pallet where he slept. Beside him, Linnea knelt. Her exertion had added a pretty shade to her cheeks. When he reached up to brush a bead of sweat from her forehead, she slanted away from him, her eyes wide.

"You need to rest," she said, reaching for the blanket that he used.

He caught her hand, folding her fingers within his. The wool oozed between her fingers to brush his palm, but he could think only of her silken skin against his. Pushing that thought out of his head, he said, "I have rested so long. I need to consider how best to realize my vow."

"I have told you I will be happy to give you what help I can when the time comes for you to leave Sutherland Park."

He released her hand and swore under his breath.

"What is it, Nils?"

Knowing he should say nothing, he explained the vision that had increased his determination to continue on his bizarre journey. He watched her face closely. When he saw her disbelief, he wondered how he could blame her for her lack of faith. The old ways had not been part of England even during his time.

"It must have been a dream," she whispered when he was finished.

"A vision from the gods should not be belittled as a dream."

"True, but..."

He cradled her chin in his hand as he asked, "You think the blow to my skull has unsettled my mind?"

Pulling away, she came to her feet. "How can I suggest that when *my* mind believes you are here from a time long past? I was not struck, yet I face something that is impossible. I would be a hypocrite to suggest that you had not been visited here in my father's water pavilion by a Norse god."

"But you cannot believe." He sighed. "Nor does the rational part of my mind. Yet I am here in this impossible place."

"To complete your vow, and that is what you must

do."

He looked up at her. On the beach, he had wondered if she was some sort of dainty *Valkyrja*. Now he suspected she had the heart of one, for she spoke of honor and duty with the certainty of a warrior. "Yes," he said, waiting to see what scheme she had in mind.

"To do that, you must go to London." She counted on the fingers of one hand. "First, you must get well. Second, you must go to London where you will have the chance to search for the missing knife. For that, you will need to pass yourself off as someone who belongs in this time and in England." She shuddered. "Your accent is a liability in this time when we are at war."

"At war?"

"With the French."

He frowned. "But I thought you said that the descendants of the *Norrfoolk* on the continent won the English throne."

"Almost 800 years ago. Since then, there have been many wars between the French and the English. We have been battling Napoleon for years."

"*This* is the sort of thing I must know if you want someone to believe I am of this island in this year."

"Tomorrow..." Linnea glanced at the shuttered window where no hint of the sun's arrival could be seen. If Olive had not come to her to prevent Nils from leaving, it could have been hours before they were able to search for him. In that time, he might have been found by someone else who would have deemed him completely mad. "Today...Later today, we will devise a plan to help you do what you must. The first thing you must have is a name."

"I have a name of which I am proud."

"But Nils Bjornsson is not the name of a gentleman to whom the doors of the *ton* will be opened."

"The *ton*?"

"The upper classes who meet in London each spring

to arrange for business and marriages."

"Then I must have another name."

She nodded. "And a title. If you were to claim to be a baron or a viscount—"

"These words mean nothing to me."

"They are respected titles, and there are enough men who claim those titles that no one would take note of you never having come to London before. If you were a duke or a marquess—"

"Again, those are not titles I know."

"What do you know then?"

"In my time, your island had a king and his jarls."

"Jarls?"

Nils smiled at her bafflement, and she tried not to believe that he was enjoying betwattling her with his strange words. "Forgive me, Linnea. Jarls is the term the *Norrfoolk* use. Earl is what the English say."

"Earl? That title is still in use now, for my father is an earl. You can be the earl of...of..." She tapped her chin as she considered what title he should claim. "Barrington. That is close enough to Bjornsson, so you should notice when someone uses it."

"Earl of Barrington?" His nose wrinkled. "That name stinks of this island."

"Stinks?" She scowled at him. "You clearly need lessons on how to behave in polite company, Nils. On the morrow, your lessons will begin."

"Such lessons are certain to prove to be a waste of time."

"You have plenty of time to waste, Nils."

"A millennium's worth."

She started to reply, then drew the collar of her wrapper up as if a chill struck her. It had. Just the thought of how Nils had traveled through time unsettled her. Hurrying down the stairs and forcing a smile for Jack who was coming in the door, she did not slow as she went back toward the house.

A thousand years.

She could not imagine that length of time, yet Nils had traveled almost all of it to come here. His tales of speaking with half-forgotten Norse gods here in Sutherland Park bothered her almost as much as the idea that he had come so rapidly from the past.

And somehow he must find his way back to his own century to take the missing knife to his chieftain. She wondered if he had any idea how he would make such a journey.

***

Olive shook her head and scowled. This was an expression that was becoming habitual. "My lady, I do not know how you have the patience to deal with *him*."

"Nils is a guest here." Linnea took the tray her maid held out to her.

"No guest at Sutherland Park has ever been like *him*."

Wanting to agree, Linnea did not. She was unsure if either Olive or Jack guessed how Nils had come here or from where or when. She had taken great care not to say anything that would reveal the truth. Nils was certain to be as circumspect, because the greatest danger was to him and the completion of his vow.

Instead of saying what she was thinking, Linnea replied with, "Jack should be here any time now to get the list of items you need from the house."

"How much longer do you think *he* will be here?"

"It has been just over a week. His arm should take another four or five to heal, I would think."

"*He* does not need a healed arm to be on his way."

Linnea readjusted the heavy tray. "With a broken arm, he could not defend himself against any knights of the pad."

"What does *he* have that a highwayman would want?"

"Whatever he must have had before. Thieves would not know that he had been robbed of everything of value." She did not add that her real fear was that Nils would encounter Kortsson while still disabled by his broken arm.

Olive sniffed, but walked back toward the stairs.

Linnea sighed. Olive never had been so unforgiving of anyone, but her maid was furious that Nils did not show Linnea the respect Olive believed was her due. Under other circumstances, it would have been amusing to watch Olive stand nose-to-nose with Nils and insist on proper behavior. Nothing about this was amusing.

"Good afternoon, Nils," Linnea said, trying to put a lilt into her voice.

She did not receive an answer.

Puzzled, because usually at this hour Nils would be waiting impatiently for her arrival with his midday meal, she set the tray on the table and went to the screens set in the corner. She called his name in a near whisper, not wanting to wake him if he was asleep. Again she got no response.

She started to edge away, but heard a low groan. Was he in such pain? She stepped around the screen...and froze, save for her gaze which slipped along the undulating strength of his naked back as he stretched. She should turn around, look away from the bare skin above his waist, save for his sling that concealed his arm band and the gold chain that held the pendant he had called Thor's hammer. She should have gone back the way she had come, but she could only stare.

His bare skin was as bronzed as his face, so she guessed he had seldom worn his tattered shirt when he was aboard his Viking ship. The powerful motion of his muscles revealed that his work in the past had been rigorous. Her breath refused to sift past her lips as she admired his shoulders' breadth and how those sinews narrowed toward his hips encased in his tight breeches. She should look away. She should, but she continued to watch his easy motions as he stretched and compressed those enticing muscles.

Was the sheen on his skin perspiration or just its natural warmth? Her fingers rose before she could halt them, reaching out to touch him.

He faced her, his uninjured arm encircling her waist as he tugged her up against him. His mouth was on hers before she could react. When his hand stroked up her back, pressing her even closer, she was surrounded by his raw manliness. Its scent was in every ragged breath she took and on his lips and in the heat of his skin. When his tongue caressed hers, she heard another low groan. Was it his voice or hers? Lost in his embrace, she was not sure.

When he abruptly released her, Linnea wobbled back one step. Her heel tangled in his blanket, and she collapsed to sit on his bed. Her first inclination to laugh at her own clumsiness vanished when he knelt beside her, A flash of longing mixed with alarm fled through her when she saw the desire—as naked as his chest—in his eyes. She started to lean away, then gasped when she realized she was tilting back across his bed.

"Why do you look so put upon, *unnasta*?" he whispered. "You were watching me with avid interest."

"I came to tell you that your meal was here."

"And my lessons on how to be a proper English lord are about to begin?"

"Yes."

"And a proper English lord would not have a lovely and most proper English lady in his bed?"

"You are being ridiculous. Let me start your lessons, and you will understand why."

His fingers uncurled up into her hair. "I would rather teach you a few things that would show you what pleasure it gives me to think of doing something other than talking to you while you sit on my bed."

"Nils, you should not say such things."

"Just as you should not come here and stare at me with an invitation in your eyes."

Linnea inched away and stumbled to her feet.

Wrapping her arms around herself, so she did not give into her craving to touch him again, she said, "I came here to tell you that it is time for your lessons."

"Yes, my lessons." Standing, he smiled at her. "My lessons first, then yours?"

"You should not say such things."

"You have mentioned that already, but I had thought you wanted the truth from me."

"All I want is to teach you what you need to know to go to London and do what you must and leave. Now, put on your shirt, for no proper lord comes to the table without his shirt."

He seized her by the waist as she walked out from behind the screen. Herding her back to him, he held her with her back pressed to his chest. His lips coursed up the side of her neck, and a quiver raced deep within her. As his fingers splayed across her stomach, she could not fight the need to soften against him.

This time, she knew it was her voice when a soft moan drifted toward her ears at the same moment he gently nibbled on her earlobe. This was wondrous beyond anything she had ever imagined.

Imagined...

Linnea jerked herself away and rounded the end of the screen. Gripping the table, she sat on the bench beside it. She looked up as Nils hobbled around the screen, his shirt now on. Funny how she did not think of him as at all injured when he held her.

She was silent until he sat facing her across the table. Then, she said, "The first thing you must learn is the proper way to address the people you will meet. While you eat, I will teach you that."

"I will endeavor to learn."

"Good."

He stretched across the table and cupped her chin. "I shall be a good student, and I hope to be rewarded for my diligence in learning."

"You will be when you find what you seek."

"True."

She frowned. "Won't that be reward enough?"

"I had thought so." A beguiling smile tilted his lips even as it blazed in his eyes. "Even an hour ago, I would have thought finishing my quest was compensation for whatever I must do. Now I am not sure if I will be satisfied with only that as my reward."

"You must be." She looked down at the tray where his lunch was growing cold. A deep iciness tightened around her heart as she added, "I should not be in your arms."

"Because you are of this time and I am not? Or is it because of the man who held you by the road?"

Linnea gasped, "You saw me and Randolph?"

"It is very interesting that you speak of what is proper, but you are in his arms and then in mine." His smile became lopsided. "Or within my *arm*. Is that how a proper Englishwoman acts?"

Her hand rose, but Linnea forced it down to her side. How could she slap his face when he was right? She was letting Randolph kiss her and believe that she might be willing to be his wife. At the same time, she was welcoming Nils's kisses.

Quietly she said, "First we will begin with a discussion of how to address a peer and his wife and children."

"So you will avoid answering my question?"

"I can answer any question you have, but I thought you were eager to complete your quest and abide by your pledge to your chieftain. If that does not matter to you..."

"It matters greatly." The words were squeezed past his clenched jaw.

Hating herself for reminding him of the pain that was more vicious than that of his broken arm, she began listing what he needed to know. She might be able to hide from him how sorry she was for hurting him, but she could not conceal it from herself. Not that she had said those hateful words to keep him away...or how much it hurt to think that soon he would be leaving for good.

How had she become accustomed in such a short time to her anticipation of seeing him each day? How had she become so captivated by his touch that she could barely resist it? She had no answer for either question, or for how she would find a way to say good-bye to him when he recovered his chieftain's knife and returned to his own time.

Nine

Nils rubbed his aching ankle. He could now walk short distances on it, but he had not let anyone else know that. If Olive saw him, she would have reported back to Linnea before he could draw another breath. He had few advantages in this uncomfortable situation, so he wished to hold onto any he had.

Across the table, Linnea was selecting items off the tray that held his lunch. She was setting the various things in front of him. Although he knew he should be heeding her words, he could not keep from thinking how soft and beguiling those strands of hair had been when his fingers had loosened them to curve along her neck and drape across her breasts. She had a rare fire that she tried to conceal. Hiding it from him was no longer possible.

His hand fisted under the table. He must concentrate on why he was here. Not to enjoy the charms of this English lord's daughter, but to find his chieftain's knife. He had reminded himself of that over and over. If he could disregard Loki's taunts, he might be able to believe that there existed some connection between why he was here and the past.

"Nils, go ahead. Let's see how you do."

He forced a smile. "I suspect I shall do quite well. After all, I have been eating since I no longer depended upon breastmilk for my nutrition."

Linnea's hand halted him as he was about to pick up a slice of meat. "No, you must not use your fingers to eat. If you want to be welcome in a fine house in London—"

"I must appear to be one of you." He grimaced. "You need not repeat yourself endlessly on this, Linnea."

"I would not need to nag if you would pay more attention to your lessons."

"Paying attention would be far simpler if my tutor was not so distractingly lovely."

He had thought his words would vex her, but she said only, "If you wish, I shall find someone less distracting to give you your lessons. My oldest brother, mayhap, although I suspect he would not be willing to take over your tuition without an explanation of who you are and why you are here." Picking up a pronged instrument next to his plate, she said, "I suggest you use this."

He took it, tilting it one way, then another. "What is it?"

"A fork."

He continued to examine it, running his finger lightly across the top of the tines. They were blunt, so he could not guess what this instrument did. Looking past it to Linnea, he saw she wore a faint but superior smile. Was she trying to infuriate *him* now? He would not grant her that satisfaction.

Quietly, he asked, "What is this fork's purpose?"

"To hold food while you cut it and then to bring the food to your mouth."

"I have fingers for that purpose."

"Not in this time. It would be too improper to use your fingers, as I have told you already."

Dropping the fork onto the tray, he said, "This time has too many useless devices."

"Mayhap we do not consider them useless."

"Because you are too accustomed to them." He

put his finger on the fork's tines again and rocked it against the metal tray. "But who decided that such a tool was necessary when fingers serve as well? What a waste of time to invent this and then decree its use!"

"Mayhap its inventor had the luxury of time that was lacking...before." Linnea glanced at Olive who was talking with Jack. The two servants were spending more and more time together, because, Linnea suspected, they shared a common belief that Linnea was wasting her time trying to teach a vagabond the manners of a gentleman. If she could have revealed to them what she knew, they would understand. She must not do that. Jack had suspected right from the beginning that Nils was not exactly what he appeared. She was not sure what the stableboy believed, and she did not dare to ask because she might divulge something to let him guess the truth.

"What do you mean by that?" Nils asked.

Linnea had to search her mind to recall what she had last said. This deception was becoming more difficult as each day passed because she could find no time to relax. Even when she tried to sleep, her disquiet kept her awake.

Remembering what she had said, she answered, "I meant only that in times past, people did not have the luxury of time to have pleasant manners as we do now."

"Yes, you have come a long way since the days when the English lived in filthy huts with their pigs."

"No doubt so the swine were not stolen by Vikings who were raiding these shores in a crusade to gain some sort of despicable honor in killing whoever could not outrun them."

"I told you that the English broke the treaty and attacked our allies who lived in the Danelaw. We were fighting for our survival."

"And guaranteeing that others did not survive." She snatched the fork away from him to halt the vexing tap-tap-tapping. "You cannot whitewash such savagery."

"Whitewash? I do not understand."

"Pretend it did not exist, along with other brutal, unspeakable acts."

"You are speaking of them."

Linnea tossed the fork back onto the tray. "Just as you wished, but I have had enough of this conversation."

"Because you fear the truth?" Nils retorted as she stood.

"What truth? That you are a beast?"

He gripped her arm as tightly as he had on the beach. This time when she gasped, he loosened his hold. Surprised, she stared down at him. Her gaze was caught by his, as it was too often. She could not guess his thoughts because his eyes drilled her like whetted blades.

"I am no beast, Linnea. I am a man who was raised to defend what belonged to his chieftain and to honor the gods and my family. Do not belittle my ways that you do not understand."

"I would not if you would not belittle my ways which *you* do not understand."

Nils flinched as if she had dealt him a fierce blow to the jaw. Fury bristled from every inch of her, but with a regal dignity that was breathtaking. He doubted if he had ever seen a woman who was so courageous in defying a warrior. Or a woman who was so irresistible. But he must resist her and his escalating need for her. She was his sole ally during this unexpected journey.

"Forgive me, my lady," he said releasing her. "You are trying to help me. I should not be a *gaurr*."

"A what?"

"A rude fellow."

"'Tis most rude to keep talking in a language I do not understand."

He smiled. "But you will come to understand it if I use it often enough."

"And what good will it do me to learn a language that has not been spoken on this island for centuries?"

Nils looked away, and Linnea knew it was her turn to apologize for using words as weapons aimed at hurting him. When he came awkwardly to his feet, she gazed up at him. She had met a few other men who were more classically handsome. She had spent time with many other men who were dressed better, but she doubted if she had ever seen a man who had such a silent aura of strength as Nils Bjornsson. He was dangerous to his foes and unquestionably loyal to his allies. He was a warrior by choice...and his kisses thrilled her so much that the memory lingered like the impression of a flash of lightning on a stormy night.

Knowing she must say something—anything—to hide the no longer strange course of her thoughts, she whispered, "It gains us nothing to keep using words in an effort to hurt each other. We should remember we are allies."

His crooked finger brushed her cheek. "You give voice to my thoughts, *unnasta*, but you know that is not likely. There are too many aspects of our lives that are so different that we will never allow ourselves to trust each other."

"I trust you."

"You do?"

"Yes."

"Why?"

Stepping away before his questing finger could tease her into granting him the freedom to do more than caress her cheek, she said, "Because I know you need my help to keep you from betraying yourself when you are among others."

"That is why I should trust you, not why you should trust me."

"I know. I cannot explain it further." *I do not want to explain it further, for then I might divulge how much I long for your kisses.* Pretending to be oblivious to her own thoughts was foolish, but she must. "Shall we continue our lesson in how to eat with those of the

Polite World?"

As he nodded, she wondered if he was as anxious as she was to act as if there were nothing between them but the common goal of finding the missing knife. Mayhap that had been true at the beginning, but she no longer was sure.

She wondered if he was.

***

Linnea rolled her eyes as Martin finished the joke he was telling. When his wife, Minnie, slapped his arm playfully, Linnea's smile broadened. She had always liked Minnie, who was not as fancy as some of the ladies who had vied for Martin's attentions when he was an available bachelor. Minnie took her duties as the next Lady Sutherland seriously, but she did not flaunt her place in the household. Her dark brown hair was drawn back in a plain chignon, and her dress was simpler than the one Dinah had chosen to impress Lord Simmons.

Looking at her sister, sitting next to her betrothed on a gold settee in the small parlor, Linnea was astonished at a pinch of envy. She did not wish she was the one marrying Lord Simmons, that was for certain. Harvey Simmons was a pleasant fellow and had the wealth to afford an excellent tailor who made his coats to hide his bony form. Dinah seemed utterly taken with him, although Linnea was still waiting for him to speak of something other than wine or cards or horses.

Her envy was not of her sister's fiancé, but of the fact that her sister could openly admire a man who had caught her eye.

Was she out of her mind? She might not have changed her mind about marrying Randolph, but she would be insane to consider entangling her life with Nils's. Even if Nils was not determined to return to a time long past, he was the most overbearing and condescending and beastly man she had ever encountered.

"Martin," Minnie said with a laugh, "you should take care what jokes you relate when your younger sisters are in earshot."

"They are both husband-high," he returned as he refilled his glass from the bottle that still had dust on it from the cellars. Holding up the bottle, he smiled when Lord Simmons held out his own glass.

"Even so, you know Lady Sutherland would not be pleased to hear you speak so."

"That is why," Dinah interjected, "he saved the story until Mama went to Brighton to bring Great-Uncle Roger for the wedding." She wafted her lashes at Lord Simmons, who smiled broadly in her direction.

"Excuse me, my lord," said a footman by the door. "Lord Tuthill is calling."

Martin winked at Linnea as he stood. "By all means, bring him up without further delay." When the footman left to obey, Martin added, "It seems we shall be quite the party this evening."

Lord Simmons took a deep drink from his glass, his bright red hair gleaming in the lamplight with the motion. "I had noticed one was missing."

Linnea kept her smile from falling as they all looked at her. She wished she could please them by acting delighted that Randolph was calling, but the truth was that she had been glad he had not visited Sutherland Park for the past few days.

Even so, she rose to her feet when Randolph appeared in the doorway. She was aware of five pairs of eyes gauging every motion she made as she went to greet him. This requirement to act as if she were glad that he was intruding on her evening was absurd.

When she heard the echo of Nils's laughter, her feet suddenly seemed to weigh as much as Sutherland Park's gatehouse. How Nils would roar with laughter if he was privy to her rebellious thoughts! She had been careful not to let Nils discern—as she had taken care not to let anyone know—how often she found the constraints of the *ton* uncomfortable. She would not have been walking along the strand without her shoes and stockings the day she found him otherwise.

"Good evening, Randolph," she said, stopping far enough away from him that he could not kiss her as he had when she last saw him. She had to admit he looked handsome tonight, for his navy coat was unblemished by even a hint of dust, although his hair was tousled as if playful fingers had slipped through it.

He drew a bouquet of flowers from behind his back. "These are for you, Linnea." He lowered his voice. "I know they cannot atone for my crude behavior when last we spoke, but I wish you to know how sorry I am."

She looked from the bouquet to his earnest face. "Randolph, where have you been keeping yourself for the past few days?" She hoped her cheerfulness did not sound as false to the others as it did to her.

His brows lowered, and she knew he had noted to her brittle tone. "I am pleasantly surprised that you missed me."

"Of course she missed you when you did not call for almost a week." Martin, ever the genial host, came to stand behind her.

"I have been," Randolph replied in his most correct voice, "in London cleaning out my father's house there, so it can be sold."

"Tedious work, I would wager by your expression." Martin threw his arm around Randolph's shoulders and squeezed them companionably. "You know Simmons, I trust."

"Yes, we have met."

Linnea glanced at the others, but no one seemed to hear the edge in Randolph's voice. Was it simply because he was annoyed with her attempt to feign an effusive welcome or for some other reason? She was amazed to realize that she could not recall ever seeing Randolph and her sister's betrothed in the same room.

"Do sit down with us and enjoy a bit of the poker-talk that Simmons has brought with him from London," continued Martin, his smile far more genuine than Randolph's. "You may have more tales to add, if you are just back from Town."

"I had hoped to have a moment to speak with Linnea," Randolph said.

With a laugh and a slap on the back that sent Randolph forward a half-step, Martin winked at Lord Simmons. "You two will have time enough for whispering court-promises during another call. Come and sit with us and have some of this worthy port that Simmons brought."

Simmons chuckled as he snagged another glass and filled it with a generous serving. "I think the ladies were just about to excuse themselves so we might enjoy blowing a cloud." He reached under his coat and pulled out another cigar. "Let them fill their heads with all the details of the wedding to come at week's end."

"And toast Simmons while he is still free of the parson's mousetrap." Martin raised his glass. "To your last hours of your carefree bachelor days."

Linnea did not wait to hear the men's response. Going with Dinah and Minnie out into the hallway, she let her sister's chatter about the banquet to be held after the marriage ceremony ease her disquiet. Minnie gave her a sideways look, but Linnea was unsure what her sister-in-law was trying to say silently.

Whatever it was, Minnie did not take the opportunity to tell her while Linnea put the bouquet in a vase, or during the two hours they listened to Dinah prattle in another sitting room farther along the gallery overlooking the entry. Linnea waited until she heard the clock chime ten times. Then, rising, she excused herself. She needed to go and check on Olive before going to bed as she did each night now.

Check on *Olive*?

Linnea almost laughed out loud, but not with humor.

She might be able to fool others that nothing was different about her life in the past week, but she could not lie to herself. Going out to the pavilion to check that Olive was set for the night was only an excuse to see Nils again. She wanted to assure herself that he was not trying to sneak away, and she wanted any chance to be with him while she could. He had cast a spell over her like an alchemist, although she knew it was more likely that iron would be changed to gold than she could alter Nils from the outspoken warrior he was into the epitome of a fine gentleman.

A form wove toward her as she walked down the stairs. Her heart contracted sharply, then she realized it was not Randolph, but her brother Martin.

"Where are you off to at this hour?" he asked, his words blurred from the port.

"I have an errand I need to tend to before I go to bed."

"What has Dinah talked you into doing for her now?" He put his hand on the newel post. "She has run this whole family ragged with her requests for her wedding. I hope you are not going to be the same if you are witless enough to let your girlish dreams of catching yourself a husband lead you to marrying Tuthill."

Linnea gasped in amazement. "I did not realize that you disliked Randolph."

"Dislike him?" Martin shook his head as he sat on the bottommost riser. He must have been more foxed than Linnea had guessed. "I do not dislike the man. He is just the most boring creature I have ever met. Even with the conviviality of fine cigars and good drink this evening, he insisted on being dolorous."

"Mayhap," said Minnie, coming down the steps to stand beside him, "because he wished to call on Linnea tonight and not you old toads who were determined to sit and croak all evening."

"Is that a kind way to address your husband?" He

set himself on his feet and held out his hand.

When Minnie put her hand on his, Linnea could not mistake the love between her brother and his wife. She knew there had been much prattle about the earl's heir marrying the daughter of the vicar in the next parish, but no one had been able to persuade Martin not to have the wife of his heart. Somehow, past the lump in her throat, she bid them good night. She doubted if they heard her while they went up the stairs together, as engrossed in each other as they had been on the day they wed five years before.

This was the love she wanted. Not the quiet acceptance of Randolph as an inevitable part of her life. The thrill of Nils's touch was intoxicating, but was that what she wanted, either? She had seen her older siblings fall in and out of love with quicksilver speed.

She wanted this lasting love that brought a smile when loving gazes met. She wished she knew where to find it.

***

"Nils?" Linnea called as she did each time she came up the stairs since she had discovered him half-dressed. She glanced at where Olive was asleep on one of the stone benches. Olive would not rouse to less than the roof falling in.

"I am awake." Nils motioned for her to join him sitting where the moonlight draped across his chest like a luminescent cloak. When she hesitated, unable to see his face, as it was hidden in the shadows, he said, "Young Jack ran to the kitchen to get some cake for the two of us. He shall be returning any minute now, so you need not worry about being without a watch-dog."

She smiled and rounded the top of the stairs. "You are learning the cant of the Polite World with great speed."

"I never thought I would need to learn English a second time." He chuckled, and she saw the flash of the moonlight against his teeth. "Actually a third time because Jack has taught me some phrases that he has warned me not to speak in your hearing."

"Although he probably has."

"True, but he says a gentleman never speaks so to a lady."

"A gentleman?" She crossed the room slowly.

"He recognizes that once many men acknowledged my leadership."

She halted in midstep. "He knows the truth?"

Again Nils laughed. "No, but a servant learns young how to discern between his peers and those you would name the peerage."

Her lips twisted in a wry smile. That was true. Jack had shown respect to Nils from the day they rescued him on the shore.

"Are you going to stand there staring at me as if I had just come in on this beam of moonlight?" Nils continued. "Or will you come over here and sit with me?"

"I intended to ask Olive if she needed anything before I went to—before I went to sleep." She hoped the shadows hid the heat on her face and that he had not noticed her hesitation over the common saying. Yet every word they exchanged seemed somehow so intimate that she feared saying "bed."

"She seems quite set if her soft snores are any indication."

"Yes."

Nils held out his hand. She could not resist the offer to discover if this was the direction her heart wanted her to go. Putting her fingers on his wide palm, she let him seat her beside him in the puddle of moonlight. She leaned back against the bench behind them and gazed up at the moon as he did.

"The moon is one thing that is unchanged," he said quietly. "I have watched the moon from this shore, and it looked as it does tonight." Without a pause, he added,

"Did you enjoy your visit from your Randolph tonight?"

"Are you spying on me?"

He laughed, his breath brushing her hair like the whisper of a caress. "I amuse myself by watching the comings and goings on this estate. Once, I would have watched to gauge the strength of the defenses of this house. Now I simply watch to keep myself from going mad with boredom."

"Mayhap I can find something to entertain you."

"I doubt you mean that as you said it, Linnea."

His finger twisted in her hair.

"That is true." She unwound his finger from her hair. When his finger crooked over hers, she looked up into his eyes, but they were lost in the darkness.

He lifted her finger to his lips. When his tongue brushed its tip, she closed her eyes and swayed toward him. Being delighted by his bold ways was stupid, but she did not care. She wanted to enjoy this.

Footsteps pounded up the stairs.

Linnea pulled back as Jack came around the top of the steps. The lad's grin broadened when he saw her sitting beside Nils.

"'Tis good that I took an extra piece of this excellent chocolate cake," he said, setting a platter on the table. He handed Nils a piece of cake, then offered one to Linnea.

She shook her head. "I am not hungry. I will leave this dessert to the two of you."

Jack took a hefty bite of his serving as he went back and sat on the top step.

"What is that?" asked Nils, leaning forward. He pointed toward the window with his fork.

"It is a fork," Linnea replied.

He tapped her nose with his finger and laughed. "I am quite aware of that after our lesson. I meant *that*."

Looking out the window, she saw a flash of light close to the ground. "I suspect it is night owls on their illegal errands."

"Owls with illegal errands?"

"Night owls is the name given to the smugglers who bring brandy and other things from France."

"But England is at war with France!"

"Yes, that is true, but that makes the profits for the night owls even greater."

He scowled. "Those men have traded their honor and their obligation to their leaders for gold."

"I have seen their lights for as long as I can remember, although Papa tries to keep them from coming ashore here. When I was a child, I believed that the lights came from fairies dancing along this shore."

"Fairies?"

"They are but a legend. The stories describe them as small women with wings. They are tiny enough to hold in your hand, but they are exquisitely beautiful." She leaned back against the bench again and smiled up at the moon. "On nights like this, they come out from beneath the flowers and fronds where they have slept the day away. They dance on the moonlight and drink cups of sweet dew. Elusive, they must grant anyone who captures them one wish." Laughing, she added, "I used to hunt for them when I could sneak out of the nursery. I never caught one, needless to say, and Papa dressed me down for being out where I might have encountered a band of smugglers."

Nils took a bite of his cake, being careful to balance it on the fork. "But you still believe in the fairies?"

"Not as I used to. Then I was certain all I needed to do was lift the correct leaf, and a fairy would be waiting for me. Now I only hope one might be."

"So you could have a wish come true?"

"Mayhap." Linnea smiled. "To be honest, I would be so astonished simply to find one that I doubt if I could decide what to wish."

"I know what I would wish for."

"To go home?"

He nodded, his gaze growing distant. "Although I spent years in training in Jutland, I grew up along a fjord overlooking the northern sea. Those steep walls of stone were as much of a challenge to me as finding a fairy was to you."

"But I suspect you had better luck with achieving your goal than I did."

"I first climbed to the top of the cliffs when I was not quite eight years old."

"You must have been so proud."

"I was, but I also was not sure what I should do next to prove I deserved to be trained as a warrior. The summer days that far north lasted for more than a week. During that time, a boy could find all sorts of mischief to get into."

"As I nearly did here while searching for fairies."

"But now you know the lights on the shore are not dancing fairies, but smugglers." He sighed. "And I know what I must do next."

"Find the knife."

"Find the knife and return it to my chieftain. Nothing must deter me from doing that." His voice grew grim. "Nothing."

Ten

Linnea paused on the steps when she heard wheels on the drive leading up to the house. Setting her basket down, she rushed to embrace her mother as she alighted from the carriage. She wondered if she had ever been so happy to see her mother. Papa might be an expert on financial matters, but Linnea needed her mother's counsel now.

Lady Sutherland wore her iron-gray hair in a tight bun, but a few strands always fell down along her cheeks as if to acknowledge her warm heart. Raising a household of boisterous children and succeeding in finding matches for all of them had added lines to her face, but all those wrinkles were forgotten when she smiled. She nodded to the tiger and motioned for the packages to be carried into the house.

"Papa will be so glad you are back," Linnea said, laughing.

"I was gone but two days, and the staff know well how to handle all the preparations for your sister's wedding."

"But Dinah keeps asking Papa questions he deems beyond his knowledge."

Lady Sutherland laughed. "That sounds like your sister. She cannot believe that anyone would consider anything else as important as her coming nuptials, for it is the only thing filling her head. You are like your father, so you find it difficult to let one thing become so important that it outweighs everything else you are involved with."

"I try." She *did* try to think of other matters than Nils's quest, but usually succeeded only in thinking of how she delighted in his kisses that she should not be enjoying.

"I trust you will not be so witless when your turn comes to be wed."

"I hope not. Where is Great-Uncle Roger?"

"He would not be budged from his hearth for what he said was just another wedding." Her mother laughed. "That from a most confirmed bachelor who seems to be afraid that nuptials may be infectious."

Linnea chuckled a she picked up the basket she had been taking to the water pavilion. Olive had brought some clothes from the attics, so Nils would have something to wear when he went to London. They needed to be remade to fit him and updated so he would not look out of place.

Lady Sutherland climbed the steps. "Let me calm your sister. Once her wedding is past, I believe you and I should talk about matters of your future."

"Yes, Mama." Linnea did not let a frown form on her lips, although she had no interest in discussing any part of her future that might involve Randolph Denner. Her shoulders sagged as her mother went toward the door. Randolph had been pleasant enough to have as a friend, but she could not imagine him as her husband. To think of him kissing her with the fire that she had discovered on Nils's lips...No, she could not imagine it. Randolph was too restrained. Something about Nils's uninhibited determination to see his quest through to its conclusion was intoxicating.

Telling her mother that was impossible. Lying to Mama was just as appalling an idea, however. She started to follow her mother, then paused when the sound of a fast-moving horse came up the road.

"Will Martin ever learn any common sense? Riding neck-or-nothing is going to get someone hurt," Lady Sutherland grumbled. "Oh, my! 'Tis Lord Tuthill."

Linnea closed her eyes and took a deep breath. Having Randolph call at the same time her mother was talking about Linnea's future was not at all a good thing. Mama was as tenacious with her goal of finding all her children spouses as Papa was with his business dealings.

A not-so-gentle jab by Mama's elbow in her back sent Linnea forward a step as Randolph slowed his horse by the front steps. She waved away the dust that followed Randolph's wild ride and coughed.

"Ah, just the one I wished to see," Randolph crowed as he took her hand and squeezed it.

"Do speak with Mama while I—" She coughed again.

"Lady Sutherland," Randolph said in the same cheerful tone, "this is a double delight. I had not thought you were expected home until Tuesday."

"Today is Tuesday," Mama replied.

Randolph laughed. "So it is. I have quite lost track of time with these trips to and from London to finish the work on my father's estate. I have made what I am glad to report is my last trip to Town for a while." Turning to Linnea, he compressed her hand again. "I will be able to devote my time to other things now."

Wanting to tell him that she did not like being addressed as a "thing," she said only, "I am glad to hear that onerous task is done, Randolph. It must have been wrenching and so sad for you."

"Yes, it was not easy." He gave her a sideways glance. "It would have been much easier to bear if I had known my future was set as well as my past."

Linnea drew her hand out of his. How dare he speak so in front of Mama! "Your future might be settled for you in less time than you expect," she returned, furious.

"Linnea—"

"Do not lather me with excuses for your tasteless comment. I liked your father very much, Randolph, and I do not like hearing him dismissed so out of hand."

"I did not mean to suggest any disrespect to my father or to you."

"Then you would be wise to select your words with more care."

The ruddy tint of embarrassment climbed up from Randolph's stylishly high collar. He looked to her mother for assistance.

"My dear young man," Mama chided with a wag of her finger, and Linnea knew he had been wrong to try to get her mother to overrule her, "you should know by now that Linnea can be most stubborn when someone tries to back her into a corner. You would be wise to grant her some time to consider your suit." Kissing Linnea on the cheek, she added, "After you have finished speaking with your caller, do come in and have tea with me, my child. I am eager to hear how you have kept yourself busy while I was away."

The color in Randolph's face darkened to a shade that was not good for his well-being.

Linnea wanted to assure him that her mother liked to take tea alone with her children whenever possible, but that would make Randolph feel even more like an outsider in the Sutherlands' tight family circle. It must be lonely in his isolated house.

Instead, she handed her basket to Jack, who had come to get Randolph's horse. "Olive is waiting for this," she said, hoping Jack understood what she could not say in front of Randolph.

"Yes, my lady." He lowered his eyes, but his face was stained nearly as red as Randolph's. With guilt? Or was he simply trying not to chuckle about the secret they were keeping from the man everyone assumed would soon be her husband?

"What is wrong with everyone here today?"

Randolph grumbled as Jack led the horse toward the shade.

"Wrong today?" she asked, not sure how to answer his question. "I was not aware that anything was amiss."

"Mayhap because you are acting more strangely than anyone else."

"As I said, I was not aware of that."

"You could start by explaining why you are having a stableboy take something to your maid. Does he always run errands in the house? I thought you had footmen for such tasks."

"Olive isn't in the house. She is out in the garden." When his eyes slitted, she hurried to say, "We were going to take advantage of the sunny day to do some sewing."

"For Lady Dinah's wedding?"

She laughed. "It is a bit late for that. Her wedding is at the end of the week. Mama would be outraged if everything was not ready. I fear our sewing will be far more prosaic."

"Then you need not hurry away."

Linnea motioned toward the bench set by the driveway. "Shall we sit?"

"Here?"

"Or in the garden."

"Yes, that sounds better." He held out his arm, and she put her hand on it.

When he led her toward the water garden, her feet faltered. She shook her head when Randolph again asked if something was wrong. Searching her mind for any excuse to go to a different part of the gardens, she could not devise one before he led her down the steps toward the pavilion.

"This is nice," she said, sitting on a bench that had no view of the door into the pavilion.

"Closer to the pool—"

"Dinah is fond of taking Lord Simmons there."

That was an inspired response, she realized, when

he frowned and grumbled something under his breath. His irritation was not focused on her, but on Lord Simmons. Although she had seen that Randolph was not fond of her sister's fiancé, she had never guessed that he disliked the man so deeply.

When he sat on the bench, she edged farther along its length, keeping her hand between them. When he put his over it, she hoped he did not hear her sigh of relief. She would gladly let him hold her hand if it prevented him from drawing her closer.

"There are a few things I wish to speak of to you," Randolph said.

"Of course."

Those were the last two words she had a chance to say as Randolph launched into a list of all the reasons she should not delay the announcement of their plans for the future. She listened, hoping that he would go on long enough for Jack to slip in and out of the water pavilion without Randolph noticing. If Randolph became suspicious of what Jack was doing, the whole tapestry of unspoken lies could fall apart.

And then...

She did not know what would happen then.

***

"Lady Linnea asked me to give you this."

At Jack's voice, Nils looked up from the picture in the book that Linnea had brought from the house. He might not be able to read the words, but he could learn much from looking at the pictures of the city where his chieftain's knife might be. The strange buildings were so different from what he recalled from his single trip to London, although the winding streets appeared much the same. The river was unchanged, although when last he had seen the Thames, it had not been as crowded with such grand buildings made of stone. He wondered where the old Roman ruins had gone.

Jack was holding a basket. As Nils reached for it, he asked the young man, "Why did Lady Linnea not bring this herself?"

"She is not here to run errands for you, sir."

Nils closed the book and set it and the basket on the table. Jabbing the crutch under his arm, he stood. "I know that. However, I was asking only out of concern for her well-being."

"She looked fine when she gave me this basket and told me to bring it here." Jack rubbed one boot against the back of the other. "It may not be my place to say so, sir, but she has done more for you than anyone should expect."

"No, it is not your place to say so."

Jack's usually cheerful face tightened into a frown. "I don't know who you are, Mr. Bjornsson, but I do know one thing. You cannot guess how hard she has been working to make sure you are tended to. She hasn't told me why she didn't send you to the stables to recover as other vagabonds have been allowed to or why she wants no one else to know you are here. But I do know that those decisions have added to her burden to help you get well and on your way."

"Are you through?"

The lad flinched at Nils's cool, tranquil tone. "I guess so."

"Good, then maybe you will listen when I tell you that I appreciate wholeheartedly all that she has done for me. Just as I appreciate all that you and Olive have done for me as well. However, it is not your place nor mine to say what she should or should not do. That is Lady Linnea's right."

Jack's eyes grew saucer-wide with astonishment. "I thought...I mean...I'm sorry, Mr. Bjornsson."

"It would be easier if you would call me Nils, as Lady Linnea does." He did not add that he was tired of hearing how the English failed to speak his name correctly. His ears strained for the sounds of his own language when he was awake. During the time he slept, he hoped he would not hear it. He did not want another visit from Loki until he had learned more about what was going on here.

Shaking his head, Jack said, "I couldn't do that. It wouldn't be right." He walked toward the stairs.

"Jack, I need you to do something for me."

Nils watched Jack turn. The lad was totally loyal to Linnea and her father. Nils admired that fealty, but it would not suit his purposes now.

"Lady Linnea gave you my *sax*." Nils did not ask, for he had no doubts about who had ordered that the blade was to disappear. That she had brought Jack with her to carry him from the sand made it clear that she had asked the stableboy to hide it for her. The only question was where it was.

"Your what?"

"My knife. She gave it to you the day she came to ask your help in assisting me from the beach."

"Yes." The single word was reluctant.

"I want my knife back."

"I shouldn't." Jack squared his shoulders. "Not without Lady Linnea's say-so."

"I don't want her to know I have it."

"Is that so?" He walked again toward the stairs, halting once more when Nils called his name.

"Jack..." Nils cursed his leg that nearly folded beneath him on that single step. Locking his knee in place, he paid the devastating pain no mind as he went on, "I want to have it to defend her if the need arises. I do not want her to guess she is in peril."

"She knows." A sneer pulled back Jack's normally smiling lips. "How many times have you—?"

"I do not speak of me."

"Then whom?"

"The man she calls Randolph."

"Lord Tuthill?" Jack laughed. "He wants to marry her. Why would he wish to hurt her?"

Nils smiled coldly. "I did not say he would harm her. I said she was in peril."

Jack's expression hardened again.

Nils waited for the lad's answer which would reveal if Jack shared his disquiet over Tuthill. The fingers of his right hand flexed at ready by his side. He almost laughed. As battered as he was, he doubted he could keep Jack from doing anything he wanted. Yet Jack did not worry him. Tuthill did.

Not long ago, Nils had seen Tuthill ride toward the house at a reckless speed. It was not the first time he had observed the man's comings and goings here at Sutherland Park. What he had noted was that each time the man's chin had jutted farther. Tuthill was resolved to get what he had come here for, and Linnea's words had revealed it was her.

Just Linnea, or was Tuthill after a share of Lord Sutherland's wealth? Olive had suggested that might be so, but had refused to answer any questions after the one inadvertent comment.

That single comment had been the reason Nils had been trying to regain his strength with even more speed. It had spurred him to push his ankle until he could walk across this small room without having to pause to catch his breath. His arm was healing, and then...

To delay here and get more ensnared in the lives of these people would be stupid. He had his vow to complete. The visits from Loki were a reminder of his obligations and the honor that had not yet been restored. He swallowed his groan at that thought. Nearly a millennium of shame on his family because he had been ripped from his time and brought here for a reason that he could not understand.

If this was simply Loki's idea of a prank...Nils swore under his breath. This was too cruel even for that immortal trickster.

"Mr. Bjornsson, did you hear what I said?"

Again Jack's voice drew him away from his own dolorous thoughts. "No, I did not."

"I said that if I were to return the knife to you, I

would need your word along with the promise that I
could trust it," Jack said quietly.

"I never break any pledge." Nils fought not to smile.
The lad must despise Tuthill even more than Nils had
hoped. This might be the first good turn of luck he had
had since he awoke here. This and having Linnea find
him. He did not linger on that enticing thought, because
he must concentrate on this conversation. "However, I
can give you no reason to trust me other than that you
must."

Jack jabbed at one of the stones with the toe of his
boot. "I do not trust you."

"You are wise."

"But I do not trust Lord Tuthill, either." Jack
rubbed his sleeve against his cheek as he looked at the
window that had given Nils a view of the road. "He
seems to think that he is due the right to marry into this
family, that Lady Linnea should have no choice of her
own."

"Her father must be aware of Tuthill's plans."

Jack's vehement curse amazed Nils. "Lord
Sutherland agreed to let Tuthill court her. I heard that
Lady Linnea welcomed Tuthill's calls, but she is smarter
than that."

"Courting and marrying are two very different
things. I doubt if women's hearts have changed in a
thousand years."

"A thousand years? What do you mean?"

Nils chuckled. "Simply a turn of phrase. What I
meant is that I am certain a woman heeds her heart
now as she did a thousand years ago or two thousand
years ago or back to the beginning of time."

"But a lady's heart has no place in the negotiations
for her marriage. That is left to her father and her
suitors."

"True." He lowered himself back onto the bench
by the table. No matter how he tried, he could not
reconcile spirited Linnea Sutherland with a woman who

would docilely accept the man chosen for her by her father.

"Can I ask one question, sir?"

"Yes." He added nothing else, unsure what Jack was about to ask.

"When I bring you the knife, what do you intend to do with it?"

"I do not intend to use it to separate Tuthill's head from his throat, if that is what concerns you."

"It did not concern me."

Nils was amazed at what sounded like regret in the lad's voice. Maybe this time was not so different from his, after all. There had been those in his century, his brother included, who preferred such simple solutions to problems, but Nils had followed the lead of his chieftain who saw bloodshed as necessary only when fighting a blood-enemy or for honor. Yet he could not hesitate to do what he must to be certain Linnea, his only ally in this time, was able to help him find his chieftain's knife.

It was all that should matter to him.

He glanced toward the far window as he heard Jack speak Linnea's name. Going to it, he looked out to see her sitting beside the man she called Randolph.

All he should be thinking of now was recovering the knife. Yet his hand fisted on the sill when he saw the man next to Linnea take her fingers and kiss them fervently.

Listening for Loki's laugh, he suspected this was all another prank dreamed up by the wizard. Any other explanation was bound to create more problems.

"Loki?" he called lowly, so his voice would not reach the man who was coming to his feet and keeping Linnea's hand in his. "If this is your idea of a way to keep me from doing as I vowed, it will not work."

He hoped he was not lying.

Eleven

Nils took a tentative step, then reached for Linnea's hand. Bowing over it, he fought not to fall onto his nose as he heard Olive's superior sniff. The accursed ankle was bothering him more today than it had earlier in the week. Mayhap it was because of the rain rushing past the partially open shutters. The dampness had arrived with the morning, and the day had grown only more gray and dismal with each passing hour.

"This is stupid." Nils sat on a bench, glowering at Linnea.

"What is stupid?"

"Kissing a woman's hand when a man would rather kiss her lips."

"Nils!" She glanced away from him and toward Olive, who was sitting in her customary place by the window next to the stairs. Those windows were securely closed and locked, so Olive had to bend close to her knitting needles to watch the pattern of her stitches. Other than the one sniff, Olive had seemed to take no note of them.

"Oh, do not get huffy, Linnea." He bent and kneaded the aching skin along his ankle. "I was not speaking of you personally."

"I see."

He looked up. Her lips were pursed with

indignation. "You do? It seems to me that you are quite blind to the meaning of my words."

"I do not believe so. You clearly consider any woman yours to pursue as you wish."

"That is a man's prerogative."

She started to rise, but he reached across the table and grasped her hand, pinning it to the weatherworn boards. "Release me," she ordered.

"When you release your misconceptions."

"You were the one who spoke of kissing women."

"A merry pastime when one has the inclination." He watched her color rise as he eyed her up and down. "I do admit to having kissed other women before you, just as you have kissed other men. Maybe the only difference is that you are the only one I kiss now, and you cannot say the same."

"What are you talking about?"

"I have eyes." He gestured toward the shuttered windows and grimaced as raindrops left by a passing shower sprinkled through onto his hand.

"Jealous ones, it would seem, although I do not know why you would act so."

Slowly he pushed himself to his feet. "'Tis not jealousy that I feel. Nothing must halt me from doing as I must. For that, I need your attention focused on this quest."

"Olive," she said as she stood, "the rain is easing. Will you go back to the house and get our luncheon? Jack will be here any time now."

Her maid nodded. Picking up her knitting, she went down the stairs.

Linnea faced him again. "Speak of this without thought when others are listening, and you may find that you have more help on your quest than you wish."

"Finding my chieftain's knife matters only to me."

"That knife is nearly a thousand years old. I suspect there are many collectors who would be eager to find such a relic."

Nils frowned. "I had not given that idea any thought."

"Along with all the others you did not think clearly about." She walked back toward him. "I agreed to help you finish your quest, Nils. When you find your missing knife, you will be on your way back to your own time. Your life will go on as it has before you came here to Sutherland Park, and mine will do the same. It is something you should keep in mind."

His arm was around her waist, bringing her to him, as if it had a mind of its own. A mind which shared his thoughts, because the seductive caress of her breasts against his chest was the very posset he needed to ease the sickness within him when he had seen her with Tuthill.

She put up her hands to halt him as he tilted his mouth to kiss her. He refused to be stopped. She had not pushed Tuthill aside, and she would not do that to him. Her lips were intoxicating beneath his. Slowly, as he deepened the kiss, her hands unclenched against him. Her fingers spread across his chest, sending a savage need ripping through him, urging him to satisfy his craving with her.

She stiffened abruptly. Jerking herself away from him, she pulled aside his shirt. "How did you get that knife back?"

"Jack brought it to me."

"He should not have."

"Why not?" He stroked her arm and watched her eyes glow with the longing he suffered.

Then her gaze hardened. "Because you are most certain to do something stupid and ruin your recovery as well as your chance to do as you vowed."

"I will do nothing stupid."

"No? Kissing me just now was very stupid."

Nils scowled, but she did not look away. "I will try to remember that, and not be so stupid again. However, you shall not persuade me to return this knife to you."

"Have it your way." Linnea stamped to the top of the stairs. "I know I am a mere woman, and an English one at that, but you might—just once—acknowledge that I may know more about something than you do."

"Linnea!"

She squared her shoulders and went down the stairs.

He jammed the crutch under his arm, then tossed it aside as he hobbled toward the steps. When Jack stood at the bottom and looked at the door where Linnea's shadow was all that remained of her, Nils turned back toward the window. The white of Linnea's gown flitted like an earthbound cloud through the wet greenery of the garden.

The sweet flavor of her lips remained on his. He wanted her, and he wanted to finish his quest in a blaze of success. Why couldn't she understand that?

"She cannot because she is not like the women you have known, Nils Bjornsson. She is of this time and this place."

Nils slowly turned away from the window to stare at the woman in the middle of the room. Her hair was like plaited gold, catching its fire from the sunlight that was piercing the clouds. The embroidered silver and copper robes draping her voluptuous body emphasized every curve, drawing his eyes along them with their motion which suggested a gentle breeze was wafting through the pavilion. But the air was still.

The woman was exquisitely beautiful, so beautiful that he knew he was in the company of a goddess. Freya was desired by every god, every giant, every creature who lived in the earth, on it, or above it.

Save for Nils Bjornsson. Even the temptation of the greatest temptress ever known could not steal his mind from his quest...and from the woman who held the key to redeeming his vow.

Bowing his head, he said, "I am honored to greet you, Freya."

She laughed, the sound like the first precious trickle
of water freed from the ice with the coming of spring.
Bending, she put a pale gray cat on the floor. He had
not noticed the creature until now. Her fingers lingered
along it, and its purr filled the room.

"I was not so sure of that, Nils Bjornsson." She
ran her fingers along his shoulders as she had her cat.
"Why did you make such a vow and deny yourself the
amusements and glory of *Valhalla*? You would have
earned a place high at the table for your deeds that
were worthy of *saga*. Even Thor would be entertained
by the tales of what you have achieved in service to
your chieftain."

"I could not think of myself when my service to my
chieftain remains undone."

"But you do think of your pleasures." Her eyes
became as calculating as the cat she picked up again
and held to her full breasts. "Your thoughts are no
longer focused totally on that pledge."

"I think of getting hale once more."

"And you think of spending time with the woman
who found you by the sea."

Nils knew it was useless to argue with a goddess
who might know his thoughts before he did. "I cannot
travel far when my arm is broken and I know nothing
of this place. She professes to have seen the knife I
seek. I will use that knowledge she possesses to
complete my pledge to find my chieftain's knife."

"Broken arm? Is that and your sprained ankle all
that keep you here?" She laughed, the sound like water
rushing from beneath the ice with the coming of spring.
"Eira will attend to it." She glanced to her left.

As a form appeared as if stepping from a thick fog
into the clear, Nils bowed his head toward the woman
whose hair was as red as a wound. He recognized Eira,
the goddess who was also a healer. Unlike Freya, her
clothes were simple and without gaudy decoration. Her
gown hid her shape rather than accenting every sensual

curve.

"Nils Bjornsson, in this time and place," Eira said, her voice sounding as if it came from a distance, "your arm should not be broken."

He waited for Eira to say something else or wave her hands or do something. She turned and walked toward the steps. Whether she descended them or simply vanished he could not tell.

"Well?" asked Freya in a jeering tone. "For what do you wait, Nils Bjornsson?"

He opened and closed his hand, amazed that the pain was gone. "It appears you have done me a great favor this time, Freya."

"I have done you multiple favors, Nils Bjornsson." Her smile took on a predatory seductiveness.

Nils knew he must choose his words carefully. Freya had a share of every fault found among the gods, for she was greedy and covetous and sure of her power over mortals. He did not flatter himself that she wished to add him to her list of lovers that would stretch from *Asgard* to here and back. Toying with him was her aim, although he had no idea why she had chosen him to entertain her and Loki. If their intentions helped him do as he vowed, however, then he would play this dangerous game.

"For all of your help, I am grateful," he said, bowing his head to her more deeply than he had to Eira, for he knew Freya would demand a greater show of subservience from any mortal. "It is to gain your favor that all warriors aspire."

"Is that your aspiration, or is it another's favor you hope to obtain?"

"My chieftain—"

"I do not speak of a man, but of a woman." She opened the shutters on the window and gazed out. "There."

Nils went to stand beside Freya, although he knew what he would see. The satisfied curve of the goddess's lips warned that she was about to prove her point.

Linnea was walking toward the pavilion, a basket covered with a brightly colored cloth over her arm. How much time had passed since he turned to face Freya? Linnea now wore a gown of the pale pink of the rising sun reflecting off new snow. Her bonnet was lined with flowers as realistic as the ones growing on either side of the path.

He tore his gaze from her to gauge the height of the sun. He was no longer shocked at the discovery that the sun was far past its apex. For him, time had lost its steady rhythm, whirling forward in a floodtide and then slowing like waters eddying in a lazy stream.

Looking back at the verdant garden, he sucked in his breath as he fought the longing to rush down the stairs to show Linnea how he truly wished to hold her, feasting on her instead of the food she was bringing him for his evening meal. He no longer was restricted to a single hand to touch her soft skin.

When Linnea paused, Jack emerged from the part of the garden that was concealed from the water pavilion by the thick branches of the trees. She smiled at Jack, but what they spoke was lost in the distance. She laughed at something he had said. That sound reached Nils, tantalizing him with the yearning to have her in his arms.

"There is nothing to keep you from doing as you wish with her now," Freya murmured. "You need not worry about your broken arm."

"My arm, whether broken or sound, has nothing to do with any decision I make."

She laughed. "I could show you what you are missing with the Englishman's daughter, Nils Bjornsson." She lifted one gem hanging from her bracelet. Twirling the faceted green stone, she held it in front of his eyes. "Look within, son of the *Norrfoolk*, and you shall see the gratification the two of you could share."

"No."

"You do not believe it would be a delight to hold her even more intimately than you have?"

"It is not that. I do not wish to experience that only through watching." He put up his hand to keep from seeing whatever might be in the depths of the jewel.

Again she laughed. "Ah, it is as I thought. Your thoughts for her are lusty. Beware, Nils Bjornsson, for the price of satisfying all your desires in this place could be very high."

"The only desire I must think of satisfying is my blood-oath."

"So you *say*, but you look upon this Englishwoman with a craving that steals your thoughts as surely as the knife was stolen from your chieftain's hand. Will you give into your desire for something that should be denied you as one of the *Norrfoolk*?"

Nils's hands fisted. If a mortal stood before him, whether woman or not, he would demand retribution for such words. Freya was no mortal, and the words spoke of the shame he was trying to expunge with his vow.

"I will do as I must. Nothing will change that."

"Nils?"

Freya laughed as Linnea called from the lower floor as she always did. "Does this daughter of England fear discovering you with another?"

"She offers me respect and honor."

"Honor? You are a man who craves that, Nils Bjornsson. Is it all you crave?" She slunk around him, her fingers lingering along the bare skin at the neck of his shirt. "Be careful how you answer, for the words that cover your thoughts with others will not do so with me. I hear the truth of your longing for this woman. Take care that it does not waylay you from your goal."

"Nothing shall do that."

Freya laughed, but he could not mistake the anger in her eyes. "We shall see, Nils Bjornsson. We shall

see." She and her cat evaporated into nothing.
As Linnea came up the steps, Nils drew the sling
back over his elbow. To reveal the truth now might
convince her that he was mad. Maybe he was, or maybe
everything that had happened since he woke on the shore
was nothing more than a death-dream, the last thoughts
of a mind vanishing into oblivion. He was not certain
he wanted to determine which it truly was.

Twelve

Linnea rocked from one foot to the other, swaying with the melodies that were the perfect complement to the flowers erupting from pots on every table spread across the back terrace and down into the rose gardens. Here, in the shadow of an arbor, she smiled as she watched her sister being congratulated by her guests.

The wedding had been everything that Dinah had wished for. It had not been as grand as Martin's wedding five years before, but he was the heir, and Dinah was the next to the youngest in their large family. Only 300 guests mingled among the tables set in the perfectly trimmed garden.

Beside her sister, Lord Simmons was accepting the congratulations. Linnea would not speak to her sister of her suspicions that Harvey Simmons had offered for Dinah because he wanted Papa's business acumen to revitalize his shipping lines as much as Dinah for his wife. The war had cut deeply into the Simmons family's profits, and Lord Simmons made no secret of his hopes that his new father-in-law would open his own businesses so that Harvey Simmons might be able to invest in them.

Linnea smiled. This morning, when she had gone to the water pavilion to bring Nils his breakfast, she had seen the gardeners working to make sure not even a twig ruined the flawlessness of the grass. No drooping blossoms were left where any guest might view them. Chairs and tables were placed to be in the shade as the afternoon gathering began in the wake of the wedding ceremony.

All was as it should be.

Almost...

She glanced in the direction of the pavilion. Its roof was visible through the trees. She hoped no young couple would go there to have a tryst far from the eyes of their elders. Edging to her left a step, she was glad to see all the windows were shuttered. No chance motion would reveal that Nils was within the pavilion.

Forcing her tense shoulders to relax, she reminded herself that Nils would not want to be seen by anyone else. He had been sitting by the table, watching Jack shuffle some cards while Olive worked on the shirt she was remaking for Nils. Such a tranquil scene should keep her from worrying.

But she could not.

Since the harsh words she and Nils had traded when Jack returned the knife, Nils had been distant. Jack's apology to her had been less than heartfelt, and she wondered what reason Nils had given the good-hearted lad to bring the knife from the stable. It must have had something to do with her, because Jack had hemmed and hawed when she asked him to explain. The lad never lied, which had made keeping Nils's presence in the pavilion even more difficult for Jack. As she thought back on that troublesome conversation, she was not sure if Jack had given her an answer. All she knew for sure was that the lad had taken the knife back to Nils without asking her.

Having the two of them as allies would have been, under other circumstances, a wonderful solution to her problem of trying to assist Nils. Jack could easily escort Nils to London. She could send with them a letter of introduction which would open doors throughout Town.

That would grant Nils all the time he needed for his search, and she could...

Linnea wrapped her arms around herself as an icy shiver cut through her. The day was warm, but her thoughts were taking a decidedly cold turn. She hoped that Nils would heed her warning that doing anything with all these guests here could be perilous.

"Linnea! Linnea!" Dinah waved wildly to her.

Glad that she could escape her uneasy thoughts, she went to her sister. She took Dinah's hands and kissed her sister on the cheek. "You are glowing with happiness."

"I am so happy." Dinah hugged her. "I want to keep pinching myself to be certain this day is truly here and not just another dream."

"Don't pinch yourself. People will start to talk if you show up at your wedding breakfast all black and blue."

"Have you talked to Randolph?"

Linnea tensed, although she tried not to. "No, I have not seen him."

"He was looking for you." Dinah hugged her again. "Even if he had not had such ideas before, this wedding has clearly persuaded him that he wants a wife of his own."

"It would be wise to give Mama a few weeks to recover from all her planning for this one."

"Mama would love to plan your wedding soon. She told me so herself this morning."

But not to Randolph, Linnea wanted to argue. She held her tongue. It was possible that Mama had changed her mind, even though she had said nothing to Linnea about it. Letting her smile return and become more sincere, she told herself that she was worrying needlessly. "Dinah, I believe your devoted husband is eager to speak with you."

Dinah took one glance to where Lord Simmons was holding out his hand, then gathering up her skirt, ran to him.

In her wake, Linnea could not keep from sighing. Dinah truly had a *tendre* for her new husband, and he seemed to dote on her. Even if he had wed her foremost to obtain Papa's help with his investments, that did not detract from the kindness Lord Simmons showed her sister.

How Linnea wished for the same! In the midst of all the work for Dinah's wedding, Linnea wondered if anyone had paused to consider that Linnea did not even have a hint of calf love for Randolph. But did anyone comprehend how she longed to be truly loved by a man who set her heart to fluttering with every beat?

She refused to look toward the pavilion. Nils might set her heart beating faster, but more often than not, it was because he had infuriated her. His kisses were splendid, yet any woman who thought she would be first in Nils Bjornsson's life while he was upon his quest soon would discover how mistaken she was. If she had an ounce of wits left, she would send him with Jack to Town posthaste.

"That is a very serious expression for a wedding day," came her father's voice.

Linnea turned and smiled. Papa looked as elegant as any of the young men there. His hair was silvery and thinning, and his waistline was broader, but his happy expression hid the wrinkles except for the ones about his eyes. He held a glass that was filled nearly to the brim with wine.

"Weddings should be time for serious thoughts," she replied, her tone as playful as his. "Mama urged all of us to think deeply before we committed ourselves to walking to the altar to be wed."

"Your mother is a very wise woman. She married me, after all."

"Definite proof of her wisdom. Although I think she has questioned it several times during the past few days when she dealt with one matter or another of

Dinah's wedding."

Papa laughed. "I have grown accustomed to being either the father of the bride or the father of the groom. Your mother still frets herself endlessly that each ceremony will be less than perfect." He took another sip. "If you will not share this with your mother, I can tell you that the wine I drank before the ceremony eased any worries I had."

"Papa!"

"You are old enough to understand."

"I do understand." She chuckled. "I wish you had offered some to Mama."

"Or to you?"

"I am fine, Papa."

"Are you? It is not like you to linger on the edge of any gathering when there is music for dancing."

She patted his arm, but did not meet his eyes as she asked, "Did you ever consider that no one asked me to stand up with him?"

"Then the young lads are widgeons. If they had a single reasonable thought in their heads, they would be flocking around you like bees about a flower." Setting his glass on a nearby table, he said, "Then dance with me, Linnea."

"I would be delighted, Papa."

Linnea enjoyed a quadrille with her father, then another with her brother Martin. Wine was handed to her. The glass was refilled each time it was empty, and soon she was laughing along with the rest of her family. She had gotten so caught up in taking care of Nils that she had forgotten how much fun she had had at other family weddings. When Lord Simmons asked her to waltz with him, she twirled about on the trampled grass and waved to her sister who was now dancing with her husband's younger brother. If their steps were a bit uneven and did not match the tempo of the music, no one noticed.

As she thanked him at the dance's end, she turned

and almost stepped into Randolph. "Where have you been hiding?" she asked, weaving on her feet as if she still were dancing.

"I have been sitting with Lady Quinlan." Linnea laughed out loud. That dowager was well-known for knowing every bit of gossip from Dover to Penzance. "Your ears must be ringing, Randolph."

"She does enjoy her own prattle." He took her hand. "Stand up with me, and I shall share it all with you."

"I think not."

"Stand up with me, then, *or* I shall share it all with you."

Realizing that Randolph must have been sampling generous servings of her father's wine, Linnea chuckled again. "How can a lady resist such an invitation?"

"That had been my hope."

Deciding that Randolph was far more interesting when he was not being his usual arrogant self, she walked with him back to where the guests were dancing. She was amazed to hear the strains of a waltz. Randolph had denounced waltzing as barbaric at the assembly to announce Dinah's betrothal.

She wondered if he could hear her thoughts when he said, as they spun among the other dancers, "I think we should wed before summer's end."

"That is only a few weeks from now."

"It is time enough." He laughed. "After all, your father's household has garnered much practice in the preparation of a wedding. They need only do just what they did for your sister and her new husband."

Linnea wondered if the high spirits brought on by the wine could vanish between two heartbeats. She tried to keep her shudder from bursting forth. "Randolph, today is not the day to speak of this."

"But what better day to speak of our wedding than upon this day of your sister's wedding?"

"I want to enjoy Dinah's wedding."

He scowled, once again the Randolph she was familiar with. "Does that mean that you do not enjoy talking of our upcoming nuptials?"

"I need to remind you that I have not agreed to marry you."

He stopped in the middle of the dance. When someone hissed a warning at him, he ignored them.

"Your father—"

"Said it was my decision, and I have decided not—"

"Is there another?"

"Another what?" she asked.

"Another man you wish to wed. Is there another?"

Nils's image burst into her head. Arrogant and rough-edged, a single-minded warrior with a poet's soul, a man to fear and a man to respect. But was he a man she would wish to marry?

No! She was not sure whether that word had rung only through her mind or she had said it aloud. To be certain, she repeated more softly, "No. No, Randolph, there is no one else I wish to marry."

"So you will marry me?"

"I did not say that. I wish you would listen to what I say instead of what you want me to say. Will you stop being such a *gaurr*?"

"A what?"

Linnea knew she blanched, for her face was frigid. How could the words that Nils spoke be coming from her mouth? She was not of the *Norrfoolk*!

"Linnea? What is a *gaurr*?"

"You must have heard me wrong. I am certain I said boor."

His face flushed. "I hope I heard you wrong again, Linnea. It is unseemly of you to speak so to a man who has professed his devotion to you."

"And it is unseemly of you to try to force me into marriage like this."

"I am not trying to force you to do anything but be

reasonable. This has gone on long enough."

"You are correct. I am done with this conversation now."

"Linnea!"

Hearing the consternation in his voice, she did not pause. The only thing that would be proper for her to say now would be an apology. That she could not do, for to apologize could mean acquiescing to Randolph's demands that they wed. She wished he had not gotten serious. She had liked dancing merrily about with him, but that did not mean she wished to marry him.

Just as she had enjoyed his calls...until he decided to propose. The idea of romance had delighted her, for she had looked forward to the chance to share an evening with Dinah and Lord Simmons.

Walking into the house, she left the sounds of merriment behind her. Blast Randolph! Why couldn't he spend more than a few minutes with her without bringing up his wish to marry her? She so wanted to tell him the truth, but she feared that he would create a scene today that would ruin Dinah's wedding.

Linnea sat on the bottommost riser of the front stairs. All the footmen must be serving outside, because the entry was deserted.

She pressed her hands to her eyes. What was wrong with her? She had been rude, and she had no excuse for her behavior. Randolph might be acting with too much enthusiasm each time he broached the subject of marriage, but she could not allow Nils's rough diamond ways to become hers.

"Linnea?"

She looked toward the front door and slowly came to her feet. The man standing there was dressed in prime twig, as if he had recently enjoyed the attentions of a fine London tailor. His black coat was unmarred by even a mote of dust, and his breeches were of a remarkable gold that was nearly the shade of his hair. Those strands still brushed his shoulders, but the sling had vanished from his left arm. It was impossible, but the remarkable purple of his eyes told her the truth. This fine gentleman was...

"Nils!" she gasped. "What are you doing here?"

Thirteen

"What are you doing here?" Linnea repeated, wondering if she could hear Nils's answer through the clanging of alarms in her head.

"What I vowed to do."

"But I urged you to wait until after Dinah's wedding before you left the pavilion. Until things had gotten back to normal."

"Normal?" His laugh was barbed. "None of this is or can be normal for me."

"Where did you get these clothes?"

"Olive brought some from that trunk in your father's attics, if you will recall."

"But they did not fit you so well..." Heat scored her face.

He chuckled. "Any man who sails on the sea learns quickly the skill of using a needle and thread, because sails need constant attention. You sent Jack with the basket of sewing tools."

"For Olive."

"Jack delivered them to me."

"Along with your knife?"

He patted his side. "The boy has proven to be a worthy ally."

"That alliance may get you in hot water."

"Then my face will be about the same shade as

yours." He laughed. "Can I assume by the lovely color of your cheeks that I meet your high standards?"

Linnea looked away. She should not be staring at him like a common harlot seeking a customer. Yet her gaze shifted back to him.

He had exuded a raw maleness when he had been dressed in his rags on the beach. In the cast-offs Olive had brought from the house, he had appeared rather rakish, but now, he could have easily gained entrée to the Polite World. When he took her hand and bowed over it with a grace that astonished her, she knew he had been practicing every motion she had taught him.

He started to raise her hand to his lips, but her soft cry stopped him. "What is wrong, Linnea?"

"Your arm! It's healed."

"Yes."

"But how?"

"The bone is knit together, so I rid myself of that sling."

"It has been little more than a fortnight since I found you on the shore. A broken arm should not heal so readily."

His eyes became the shade of a stormy sky in the moment lightning flashed. "But you see the truth in front of you."

"Nils, please explain."

"I cannot."

"Cannot or will not?"

Before Nils could answer, she heard, "Ah, here is where you are."

Linnea stiffened at her father's voice. A curse that would have caused her mother to swoon rushed through her head and battered at her lips. She did not give it voice as she looked over her shoulder to see her father and mother behind her. Extricating her hand from Nils's and hoping that her parents had not seen how tightly Nils held it, she struggled to smile.

There was no need. Papa was looking past her to

Nils. A puzzled expression widened her father's eyes. "Sir," said Papa, as always the gracious host, "I do not recall us meeting before. If we have, I hope you will forgive my lack of memory."

"You have been very busy today with your daughter's wedding," Nils replied with a smile.

Linnea wondered if her parents realized his smile was a challenge to her. He was daring her to denounce him, knowing that if she did, she betrayed herself as well. Or would her folks consider him queer in the attic for believing he was a Viking from the distant past?

"Weddings are always a hectic time..." Papa paused.

"Niles Barrington," he supplied with a smile, "6th earl of that title."

"Barrington?" Mama frowned in confusion. "I do not recall such a name on our guest list."

"I was not invited."

Linnea drew in her breath, sure that all was about to unravel because Nils had chosen this moment to be honest. "Mama, let me explain how I found—"

"While in the midst of all the preparations for your daughter's wedding, Lady Linnea found me early this morning after I was set upon by thieves. They took everything I had, save for these clothes upon my back. She arranged for me to rest in one of your gardens while I took stock of my situation." His smile dared her to contradict this story he had devised without her.

"She found you?" Mama asked.

"Actually I chanced upon her while she was busy working in the gardens. I had seen the house from the road and thought I might find something to eat here before I continue on my way."

"Where?" Papa asked.

Linnea looked back at Nils. "Yes," she said. "Where?"

Nils's smile did not waver, but the good humor vanished from his eyes. "I am originally from Norfolk.

I have been traveling about England for several years now."

"For what reason?" asked Lord Sutherland.

"To enjoy my studies."

"Do your duties allow you so much time to wander about?" Linnea asked.

"My wanderings about *are* my duties. I have been making a study of the past, the times before William the Conqueror claimed the throne that had been won by Canute and his Jomsvikings."

She clasped her hands behind her back as she bit her bottom lip to keep from blurting out her questions. How had he learned so much about the English history that had happened after he should have been dead? Mayhap he had persuaded Olive or Jack to tell him that. He had not asked her any such questions, seeming to prefer instead to ask her about the quest...and to beguile her with fiery kisses.

"You are most fortunate, my lord," she said curtly, "to have the lack of other obligations that grants you the time to pursue your studies."

"Daughter," her father replied sharply, "it is not like you to be so discourteous."

Linnea had no answer. She had been acerbic to Nils. Not meeting her father's eyes because she did not want him to know she was lying, she said, "Forgive me, Papa."

"You know that the doors of Sutherland Park are always open to those in need." Papa put his hand on her shoulder and smiled. "It makes me proud that you have learned that lesson well, Linnea."

"Thank you, Papa."

She was not sure if he heard her mere whisper as he turned back to Nils. "Tell me," her father said, "what you are doing here in this part of England, Barrington. I fancy myself somewhat of a historian, but only as an avocation when I can take the time from my work."

"As I was starting to say, I have come in search of

the past." He arched a tawny brow in Linnea's direction as if to dare her to tell the truth.

She clenched her hands at her sides. He knew she could not speak it, for it would condemn her along with him. If her parents guessed that she had hidden a stranger in the pavilion in the water garden for the past fortnight, they would be horrified. The dark pall it might create over her sister's wedding with a recitation of her shameful actions might never be forgiven.

But how had he healed so quickly? As she watched him bow over her mother's hand, using his left hand to hold her mother's, Linnea could only stare. This was impossible! No one could recover from a broken arm with such speed.

Was she as mad as he must be? She was concerning herself about his arm when her father was conversing with a man who should have been dead centuries before.

"What specifically are you searching for?" Papa asked, drawing her attention back to what they were discussing. "There are ruins scattered across the downs, some that are believed go back to the era when the Romans conquered this island."

"Is that so?" Nils smiled at Lord Sutherland, although he would have preferred to continue to look at Linnea. She was undeniably an Englishwoman, but she possessed the heart of *a Norrfoolk* woman, brave and as willing as a warrior to do what she must to protect those she had a duty to. She had vowed not to reveal the truth to anyone, for he could not guess where his enemies might lie in wait. Now she had proven that she would not, although his appearance here clearly was trying her resolve.

But it was not just her courage that appealed to him. He had become accustomed to her ethereal beauty during her visits to him in that accursed building overlooking the lake, but he had not been prepared for how beautiful she would be when dressed in such a delicate silk gown. The white blossoms twisted through her hair were like stars in its midnight-dark glory.

He would gladly allow his eyes to feast on the way the gold lace followed the curve of her breasts while he imagined the beauty of her skin as he lowered her puffed sleeves along her arms. Then he would explore her with his fingers and his mouth, leaving no part of her untasted. The craving ached through him more fiercely than the pain when his arm had been broken.

"The Romans settled in this area and called it Britannia," Lord Sutherland said.

Nils started when the earl used the term Nils had known before he was swept forward into this century. Pulling his eyes from the ethereal Linnea, he replied to her father, "I am specifically interested in the journeys of the *Norrfoolk* through this area."

"The what?" asked another male voice.

Linnea's eyes widened. Her shock warned Nils of who must be standing behind him. Turning, he appraised the man he had seen only from a distance. Lord Tuthill's gaze, which was even with his, was the opposite of Sutherland's open and welcoming smile. Tuthill edged between Nils and Linnea, making it quite clear that he considered he had a claim on her.

Nils laughed, although he was irritated with Tuthill's posturing. It made Linnea very uncomfortable, if he was to judge by her now brittle smile. "Forgive me. I have become so accustomed to my studies that I let the terms I have learned slip into my everyday speech. I am speaking of the Norse." Without a pause, he said, "I am Niles Barrington."

Lord Sutherland said with a broad smile, "More properly, Lord Barrington. This is Randolph Denner, Lord Tuthill, a neighbor of ours here at Sutherland Park."

"Ah, yes," Niles replied. "I thought you looked familiar."

"Familiar?" asked Randolph. "Have we met before?"

"I know of you. Others have spoken of you in my hearing." He was rewarded for his comments with a hastily masked glower from Linnea.

"In Norfolk?"

"Not exactly."

"Didn't I hear you say you were from there?" Nils continued to smile. He had to admit that Tuthill was focused on finding out everything about him.

"Yes, but what I study is the *Norrfoolk*. The Norse who came to this island before the conquest."

Randolph did not lose his puzzled expression for a moment, then brightened. "Ah, you mean the Vikings." He grimaced. "I cannot understand why anyone would find such ill-mannered thieves interesting, but I suppose each man's interests are different." He put his arm around Linnea's shoulders. "Shall we go back outside and dance again, my dear?"

Linnea murmured, "Yes." She wondered how Randolph could not see the dangerous gleam in Nil's eyes when he had spoken with such contempt about the Vikings. It would have earned Randolph a torturous death if they were in Nils's time. Then, these two men would have faced each other with bare swords in their hands instead of glasses of Papa's best wine.

Papa continued to talk about the many historical sites near the house as Linnea went out into the sunshine with Randolph. As she followed the steps of the country dance, she wondered why Papa and Mama had come into the house. Had they seen her go inside? And Randolph? Why had he come into the house, too? Mayhap he had thought she was ready to apologize to him.

"Where did you find Barrington?" asked Randolph as she took his hand and curtseyed along with the other ladies.

"As he told Mama and Papa, he found *me*. He saw the house from the road and came here."

"Do you always welcome strangers to a Sutherland

Park wedding?"

Following the pattern of the dance, she stepped away from him. She smiled at Martin as he twirled her about with enthusiasm heightened by wine. Too quickly, she had to turn back to Randolph.

"Well?" he asked as if there had been no interruption.

"Papa taught us to help those in need."

"You are taking this stranger's side against me."

"Do not be silly. There are no sides to take." She stepped away and took her brother's hand to continue the pattern of the quadrille.

Martin glanced past her. "Are you and Tuthill having a lover's spat?"

"Of course not."

"He looks very unhappy."

Linnea frowned. "His unhappiness is all of his own making." She and Martin walked between the lines of dancers to the tempo of the music. Her steps faltered when she saw Nils standing in front of her. That he was next to a bench set beside the wall half the breadth of the garden away mattered little, for her heart lurched.

"What is amiss, Linnea?" Martin asked.

"Sorry. My slipper must have caught on something."

His eyes widened in puzzlement. "On this grass?"

"I said I was sorry." She wished she had remained silent when he frowned. Her tone had taken on a whetted edge.

By the time the set was complete, Linnea wished she had not agreed to come back outside. She had been wise to seek haven inside. Leaving Randolph in deep discussion with her older brother about the latest battle on the Continent, she slipped away toward the house.

A shriek froze her in midstep. There were more shouts and the sound of breaking wood. What was going on?

Linnea whirled and, gathering up her skirt, raced

around the corner of the house. She was struck by people running in the opposite direction. They shouted to her to flee. She ignored them as she heard another crash and a shout in words she did not understand. Coming around the corner, she pressed back against the wall as a gun fired. More cries answered it, from every direction.

Jack lowered the gun he held and turned, meeting her eyes. She rushed to him, then paused as she heard something crashing through the bushes in the garden. As she turned to follow, Jack grasped her arm.

"Stay here, my lady. I'll get some boys from the stables and halt the cur, I will."

She stared at the tables that were hacked into pieces. Food was scattered everywhere. Behind her, from the direction of the wedding gathering, shouted questions flew like birds scattered by a cat on the prowl.

"What happened?" she asked.

"A man popped out of the bushes. Started screeching like a madman. Grabbed for one of the kitchen maids. When she cried out for help, he went berserk. Started going after the table with a big ax."

"Ax?" She tried to swallow past the fear clogging her throat. "What did he look like?"

"Big man. Red hair." He faltered, then said, "Dressed in clothes just like we found Nils—"

"Lord Barrington," she corrected quickly.

"Really?" His surprise vanished as he said in a grim tone, "The clothes were the same. Do you think this could have been that Kortsson chap who attacked him?"

"I don't know, but we must be silent on that until we can be certain." Linnea had no time to say anything else as the guests poured around the side of the house to stare at the destruction.

Quickly she deflected their questions, speaking only of a crazy man who had apparently wandered onto the grounds of Sutherland Park. She looked among the guests to see where Nils might be. Why wasn't he here? Her heart slammed against her chest. Could Kortsson have found Nils already and slain him?

Her thoughts must have been clear on her face because Jack tapped her on the shoulder and said, "You may not have seen, my lady, but Lord Barrington has set off after that chap."

Linnea nodded, not sure if she was relieved or even more fearful. Nils was determined to stop this man who must have come forward in time with him. Neither man would rest until one of them was dead. Wishing she could go with Jack when he rounded up some of the stablemen and followed Nils, she hurried back to where her mother was trying to calm some of the women who had suffered from vapors.

She glanced toward the house. Nils would not have left without a better weapon than his small knife. Had she mentioned to him about the old weapons in the great hall? If so, he might have gone to get one. She ran through the nearest door. The cool twilight of the interior was welcome when her face was so flushed with fear. She turned toward the mansion's old section. As a child, she often had come back here with a book from her father's library and an apron weighted with apples, but she found no comfort today as she envisioned Nils facing his blood-enemy.

No elegant furniture or paintings of stiff-faced ancestors eased the stark stone walls here. Her footfalls, even in her soft slippers, echoed through the vacant corridor, but she found nothing forsaken about this place. As a child, she had thought the dusty corners carried the scents of ancient times. Not just of this house, but mayhap even from the sands of the pharaohs' Egypt or when the Greeks had debated philosophy in distant Athens.

Walking into the high-ceilinged room that had been part of the original keep, she paused when she saw someone else was here. For a moment, she feared it was Kortsson. Then she relaxed. She could not mistake those broad shoulders or the golden hair that claimed even the faint light from the windows near the roof. "Nils?"

He smiled as he walked toward her, a plate in his hand. "I thought Niles was the name we had decided upon for this deception."

"What are you doing *here*?" She stared at the cake on the plate. She had not guessed that the wedding cake had been sliced. Blast Randolph for vexing her so much that she missed it! And doubly blast Nils...Niles! Double blast him for intruding and bringing his blood-enemy here to interrupt the wedding.

"Your father was gracious enough to reveal where you would go when you wished to be alone."

"But why are you here? I thought you went after Kortsson with Jack and the other stablemen."

Nils took a deep breath and released it slowly. "Kortsson is too cunning to be found by them...or by me today. He had a good head start to find a place to hide where even I cannot trail him. I lost his tracks on the stones leading to the shore. I must wait for him to appear again."

"At least you know he is still nearby."

"Yes, and I will find him and put an end to his attempts to halt me." His mouth quirked in an abrupt smile. "That is, however, for another day. Now it is time for you and me to speak."

"About what?" she asked, although she already knew.

"I could see that you had questions when I greeted your father, Linnea. I thought it would be wise to come somewhere where we could speak of our *hyggja*."

"Will you speak English?"

"I meant to say that we could speak of what we are thinking."

She crossed her arms in front of her. "You know quite well what I am thinking. You should have told me you planned this little surprise for my sister's wedding."

"It would not be a surprise if you knew of it." Niles looked up at the high rafters. "This is amazing."

Linnea recognized that change in his tone. During the past fortnight, she had come to discover it was useless to continue to speak of a topic when he no longer wished to. "It is the oldest part of the house."

"When was it built?"

"Sometime at the beginning of the 12th century."

He handed her the plate and walked to the firepit in the center of the floor. "This is familiar. We had such places to heat our homes, unlike the odd hearths you have pressed against the walls."

"It is easier to build a chimney when the firebox is by the wall."

"Chimney? What is that?"

She pointed to the smoke-stained chimneypiece on the hearth between the two largest windows. "That is all that you can see from inside the house."

"The English stopped building good firepits simply so they could decorate the fronts of their hearths?"

Going to the thick doors that led outside, she set the plate on a table beside them. She put her shoulder against one and shoved. "Ouch!" she exclaimed when the door refused to move.

Nils laughed and went to help Linnea who was trying a second time to open the door. "Do you always act like a battering ram to get what you want?"

"No, not always."

"Odd, for it seems to me that you have since we first met."

"Mayhap," she said crisply as he pushed the door aside, "it is because you fail to heed me unless I am forceful."

"I have heard you seldom be mistaken, but you are about this."

She tried to push past where he stood in the

doorway. He clasped her shoulders and held her so that she could not escape him. In the delicate dress she wore for her sister's wedding, she might have donned strands of moonlight. The light fabric swirled around his legs like sea foam.

Her eyes widened when he edged forward to pin her back against the door frame. "Don't, Nils...Niles," she whispered.

"Don't touch you? You quiver when I touch you. I thought it was because you fancy my touch as I fancy touching you."

"Why are you making this more complicated?"

He smiled as he ran his finger along her shoulder. "You ask as if you believe that I have any choice."

"Of course, you have a choice. You could treat me as a gentleman should."

"Or I could kiss you."

She shook her head. "It is different now."

"Because we are in your father's house?"

"Yes, partly."

"And the other part?"

She slid out the door and took a deep breath. For a moment, he thought it was in relief at having escaped his embrace—a thought that sliced through him like a well-whetted blade—but then she said, "I love the scents in this back garden at this time of year. The pungent green of the earth mixes with the salt from the sea."

"Linnea, there is much we need to speak of." He resisted the compulsion to bring her back into his arms. Then he would be able to think only of her and how much he wanted her. Dressing up in an Englishman's finery to come to the house had not been to seduce her, but to show her that it was time to continue with their plans to recover the knife.

"That is the chimney." She clasped her hands behind her. "It draws the smoke from the fire up and out of the house. It is much preferable to living in a cloud of smoke as was done before chimneys were invented around the 13th century."

"Linnea, heed me. We must speak of our journey to London. Now that I am well, we must not delay."

Her eyes, as dark as freshly tilled soil, lowered from the roof to meet his. "You should go, Niles."

"I am ready to leave for London when you are willing to go with me."

"I cannot."

"Why not?"

"A woman does not travel with a man who is not her husband or related to her by blood."

"Another silly rule among all the rules you live under?"

Linnea walked back inside, pushing aside the door that had not completely closed. She paused by the table and said, "I tire of you telling me all that is wrong with my time and my life. Your time was not perfect, either. Or maybe you thought so when you were enjoying your barbaric raids on innocent villagers. People here lived in intolerable conditions."

"With their pigs." He grinned.

She wanted to be angry with him, but she smiled. "You are the most exasperating man I have ever met."

"You know that is not true." He let the door close, leaving them draped in shadow again. "I have met Tuthill now, too, do not forget."

"I daresay you could match him, count for count, on any scale of exasperation, and you would still be labeled the most exasperating."

Closing the distance between them with slow, studied steps, he said, "And I daresay that you like being exasperated, Linnea."

"You are mad!"

"Am I? I observed the wedding celebration before I made my presence known." His voice deepened to a husky roughness. "I observed *you*. Your eyes did not sparkle when you spoke to Tuthill as they do now."

"Mayhap even after a thousand years your head

was battered enough so that you do not recognize the difference between vexation and...and...and—"

"Satisfaction?" he whispered, taking her hand and lifting it to his lips. He brushed it with a light kiss. Raising his head, he smiled. "I trust that is the proper way to greet a lady whose attention a gentleman wishes to obtain."

"Yes." She could barely hear her own answer over her feverish heartbeat.

"And this?" He raised her hand again. With a motion as slow as his steps had been toward her, he slid his tongue along the inside of one finger, across the sensitive skin at its base, and up her other finger.

Something shimmered deep within her, something unfamiliar, yet something splendid. When he tipped her hand over and stroked her palm with the moist fire of his lips, she grasped the lapel of his coat, fearing that her knees would fail her. He closed her hand within his and drew her even closer.

"That is not proper," she whispered.

"However, neither is it exasperating."

"No."

"Share my quest with me, *unnasta*, and I will gladly share this with you." He bent toward her.

"No!" Linnea pushed against his chest. She could not free herself from the iron band of his arm around her waist, but he released her when her cry bounced off the walls of the great hall.

"Linnea, I need your help in London to fulfill my blood-oath." His hands framed her face. "And, now that I can hold you without that sling between us, I can admit that I need you in my bed to satisfy this desire that you cannot deny."

"I do not deny it." She stepped away from him again. "But I do not intend to cede my good sense to it. That is the difference between you and me."

He laughed coldly, even though his eyes continued to blaze with the need that resonated through her. "That is not the only difference between you and me, *unnasta.*"

"Will you stop calling me that or explain what it means?" She walked away.

"It means sweetheart," he called after her.

Linnea knew she should keep on walking. This conversation had crossed too many boundaries, leading her thoughts into intriguing places where they should not go. She closed her eyes, savoring the memory of his brazen caresses. Without looking back, she said, "I will leave you here to eat your wedding cake, Niles."

"Cake? Confound it, *feila!*"

"*Feila?*" She faced him. "What does *that* mean?"

"It means woman, and you are the most confounding one I have ever met. I—" Abruptly he laughed and picked up the plate. As he walked to where she was standing, he ran a finger through the frosting.

"Nils!"

"Niles," he corrected with another laugh.

"Whatever you call yourself, you should not be eating cake with your fingers. I thought I had explained that we do things differently in this time."

"So you did, but there are some things I hope will never change." He stopped in front of her, and his voice deepened to a low growl, "Such as this."

She gasped as he placed a sticky finger against her cheek. When he licked the sugary sweetness from her skin, a warmth burned in the very depths of her body. Gripping his coat, she swayed with the strength of her desire as he painted her lips with the frosting. Her breath came fast and shallow when he kissed away every bit of the glaze, teasing the flavor from her. His tongue darted into her mouth, daring her to tell him to stop.

Running her fingertip through the icing, she touched his lips as he had hers. He grasped her hand and licked the sweetness from her fingers. At her soft moan of yearning, he smiled with the gentleness that tugged on her heart.

So many questions remained in her mind, but she

forgot them while his lips caressed the curve of her ear. His finger moved along her face in a parade of sweet sensations coming from her heart.

"Come with me," he whispered.

"To London?" Her voice was breathless.

His laugh swirled through her like flotsam on the sea. "To London later. With *me* now."

"I can't."

"More stupid rules that keep you from doing what I know you want as I do?" His flaxen brows slashed down to match his scowl.

"Yes." She raised her chin as she added, "But you have rules that constrain your life, too, Niles. Rules I think are silly."

"Such as?"

She did not quail before the fury in his terse question. "Such as an oath that has ripped you from your own time and deposited you here."

"There is nothing silly about my oath. It is not a rule imposed on me. It is an obligation I take on freely."

"Just as I accept the obligations of my place in this family. I would no more shame my father than you would your chieftain."

"I will shame no one when I speak of my desire for you." He caught her shoulders and tugged her to him. "You are a beautiful woman, and I would gladly welcome you into my bed while I search for my chieftain's knife."

"And then?"

Again his brows lowered, but this time in puzzlement. "I do not understand why you are asking that. You know I shall return it to my chieftain after I have made the man who kept it from me sorry."

"What?" She pushed herself out of his arms. "You never mentioned anything about vengeance!"

"It is part of my vow."

"A rule of yours?"

He nodded slowly. "If you wish to call it that."

"I hope you do not come to regret making that rule."

"As you regret the rules that have been forced upon you?"

She knew she should laugh at his question and call it foolish, but she could not. Not when he was looking at her with unrestrained desire in his eyes.

"Yes," she whispered, then turned and walked away before her own longings persuaded her that she should give free rein to them with a man who could not wait to finish his quest and leave her...forever.

Fourteen

"Right fancy, isn't it?"

Nils smiled as Jack came into the large collection of rooms that were set aside for the use of Lord Sutherland's guests. This room alone was bigger than Nils's cottage back in the land of the *Norrfoolk*, and three other chambers opened from it. One held a wide bed that sat in the middle of the room.

He laughed to himself. Firepits had been moved into the walls away from the center of the room, and beds had come out of their cupboards. The winters here were not as unforgiving as those farther north, so there was no need to close doors to keep in the sparse heat.

Another room was littered with hooks and shelves and drawers. He guessed they were for clothes. The final room, much smaller than the others, held only a metal container. Stains on the stone floor suggested it sometimes contained water, but he was not sure what its purpose was. It might be for washing himself or his clothes or both. He would have to ask Linnea.

Linnea...

She was his hope for success and the very reason that he might fail. She distracted him from his search, but he needed her help as he did no other's.

"Lady Linnea suggested I serve as your valet, sir."

Jack gulped, then said, "I mean, my lord."

Nils was about to tease the lad, but realized that Linnea may have let her servants believe that he truly was an English lord who had been left bewildered by the attack upon him. Again she was proving that she would keep her vow not to reveal the truth.

He realized as well that he was unsure what a valet was or how one served. Something else he would need to ask Linnea.

As if his thoughts had reached out to her, he turned at a soft knock and saw Linnea standing in the doorway. Beside her, Olive stood, frowning. He might be here in the house, but that had not changed Linnea's maid's opinion of any of this.

"Jack," Linnea said quietly, "Olive has brought some clothes to replace those that were stolen from Lord Barrington during the attack upon him. She will show you how to arrange them in the closet."

Before he could answer, Olive grumbled, "It isn't right, my lady."

"What isn't right?" he asked.

Linnea took only a single step into the room as Olive motioned to someone else in the corridor. A parade of serving women came into the room carrying piles of clothing, and he was not sure what else. As soon as they went into the room with the hooks and shelves, he repeated his question.

"Olive feels you should have been given your *congé* instead of welcomed into the house," Linnea replied, her voice totally without emotion. "I reminded her that this house has always welcomed those who were traveling through the shire."

"I am glad you overruled her." His smile gained him only another blank stare in return.

"If you are set for the night, I shall—"

"I have a few questions."

If she sighed, he did not hear it, but her expression suggested that she was anxious to be gone and done with him. He wanted to ask her why when she had been sweeter than the cake frosting this afternoon.

"What are your questions?" she asked.

"Jack tells me he will be serving as my valet. What is that?"

"Your personal servant as Olive is for me." She faltered, and her cool expression did as well. "Jack has never done such work, for he has always worked in the stable. However, I believe, under the circumstances..."

"He will see my errors as a result of this so-called accident you devised for my past."

"Yes." She rubbed her hands together nervously. "Anything else?"

"The metal tub in the other room."

Color flashed up her face. "That is for bathing."

"Does this pretty shade of red suggest that you are thinking of washing my back for me?" He ran his finger along her cheek.

"I shall leave your personal needs to be handled by you and Jack."

Before he could ask another question, Olive came back into the room, trailed by the other servants. "*Lord* Barrington's things are all ready for him, my lady." She fired him a glare that divulged how little she believed the web of lies that he had spun with Linnea's help.

"Thank you, Olive," Linnea said. Stepping back out into the hallway, she added, "Sleep well, Niles."

The door closed behind her, and Nils smiled. He doubted he would find such a strange bed comfortable, but he had learned to fall asleep anywhere at anytime, for a warrior quickly discovered the importance of taking advantage of any chance to sleep.

Jack peered out of the clothes room. Slowly he edged out. His normally cheerful face was long. "What do you want me to do now, my lord?"

Tempted to tell the lad that he had been tempted to ask the same of him, Nils replied, "I think a good night's sleep would be the wisest thing for both of us."

"Before you confront Lord Tuthill tomorrow?"

"Tuthill?"

Jack frowned. "I thought that was why you were wanting your knife back. To show that blackguard he should not assume Lady Linnea was his."

"I thought I would learn more before I made my demands."

"Oh."

Nils chuckled. If he told the lad the truth, that he was a Viking who had come to avenge his chieftain, Jack would have been thrilled. However, even a Viking warrior knew there was a time for attacking and a time for reconnoitering. Patting Jack on the shoulder, he said, "The time will come. I vow that to you."

"Another vow, Nils Bjornsson?" asked the too familiar voice from behind him.

When Jack did not react, Nils knew the boy could not see Loki who was perched on a table by the window. Nils sent Jack to gather what he would need for the night. Waiting for the lad to leave, Nils faced the wizard.

"I did not know you were keeping count of my vows, Loki," he said quietly, hoping his voice did not carry to the clothes room.

"I am keeping a close eye on everything you do or say. At the moment, there is no mortal more intriguing to me than you."

"Because at this moment, there is no other one who believes in the old gods."

"True." Loki's eyes glistened with mischief. "But that will change. The time will come when we are feared once more."

"Do you bring me a message from Freya?"

His scowl was fearsome. "I am not her message carrier. I am here only to watch and enjoy the mistakes you make, Nils Bjornsson."

"The only mistake I am making now," he said, knowing that he chanced bringing Loki's fury upon him with his bold words, "is continuing this conversation when I wish to sleep."

"Sleep while you can."

"While I can?"

Loki laughed again. "Some things mortals cannot know until time unfolds for them. But I can tell you, Nils Bjornsson, that you need to be wary."

"Why?"

"If you knew, you might be willing to be more patient and enjoy this time of ignorance."

Nils's hands closed into fists as the wizard vanished, leaving only the sound of his exultant laughter. Nils knew better than to disregard Loki's taunts. Anyone who did learned the price of thinking that Loki had less pride than the other gods in *Asgard*.

"Did you say something to me, my lord?" asked Jack from the doorway.

"No." Without looking at the lad, he added, "Get yourself some sleep."

If Jack answered, Nils took no note of him. Trouble was coming. He had not needed Loki's warning of that. Too long he had lingered here. Walking into the bedchamber, he slammed his fist into the door frame. This luxury was not for a warrior. It was time to do what he had come here to do.

***

"There is only one solution." Linnea stood from the table.

Nils came to his feet at the same time she did. They were the only two remaining in the breakfast-parlor, because her family had finished their meal minutes ago and gone to see Dinah and her new husband on their way to their honeymoon on the Continent. Nils suspected Linnea had lingered over breakfast in order to speak privately with him. Having this chance to be alone with her should not please him so much. Last night, he had spent hours focusing his thoughts on his task. Yet, a single glance from her this morning had threatened to undo his resolve to think only of finding that knife and returning to his own time.

"And what solution is that?" he asked.

"We need to get you enough information so that you will not make a mistake in London."

"I have not made a mistake here."

"Yet."

"I have not made a mistake yet, so you should have more faith that I will not make one."

"But London will be different. The *ton* does not forgive any mistakes. If you give them even a hint that something is not as it appears with you, they will seek any chink in your armor."

He frowned. "I do not have any armor, not to wear or as a shield."

"It is only a saying, Nils...I mean, Niles." She glanced uneasily at the door.

"The mistakes may not be only mine."

"That is why you need to learn more about London and the Polite World that will be there for the Little Season."

"That makes good sense."

She motioned toward the door. "I think my father's book-room is where we can best speak without others listening."

"The room where he keeps the books like the ones you have shown me?"

"Yes." Linnea could not miss how Niles's eyes glistened at the prospect of viewing more of the books that had fascinated him during his recovery. Her fingers reached out to touch his left arm before she could halt them. She snatched them back.

"You cannot hurt it."

"I wish you would explain how your arm healed so swiftly."

"I know."

She waited for him to add more, but he walked to the door and looked back at her, clearly anxious for her to lead him to Papa's book-room. He knew how this distressed her, and yet he was not going to ease her curiosity. Blast this man!

Walking in silence with him along the hall did nothing to lighten her spirits. She should be glad that he was keeping this wall of half-truths between them. That gave her the very best excuse to ignore her yearning for his kisses, but she could not be unaware of the coiled strength in his easy walk by her side. Until yesterday, he had been injured. When he had appeared at Dinah's wedding, she had been overmastered by his virile strength that had been hinted at even when he could barely sit on the shore.

The book-room was deserted. Through an open window, she heard the cheerful voices from the road in front of the house. She went to the window and waved to her sister, who was getting into Lord Simmons's elegant carriage.

"Will they be gone for a full turn of the moon?" Niles asked.

"Longer actually. They are spending a month in Rome before going on to Zurich. Those plans, of course, are dependent upon events on the Continent. If Napoleon tries to grab more of it to add to his empire, they will return posthaste to England."

"Rome? I know of that city. Zurich, I do not know."

She pulled a large book from a nearby shelf and opened it on a book stand. Flipping through the pages, she pointed to a map. "This is where Zurich is. In the Alps north of Rome."

"I have never seen maps this well drawn." He sucked in his breath in astonishment as he ran his finger along the page. "And the ink stays on the page instead of smearing so that a navigator can be tricked into misjudging the shore."

"Most books are printed now rather than hand-drawn." Linnea turned a few more pages. "Here is England."

Again he brushed his fingertip against the map. "I

know this inlet and that one." His finger rounded the bottom of the island and moved west. "I had heard of this area—"

"Wales," she supplied with a smile.

"I had heard of it, but I never traveled that far. Do you have a map of the lands of the *Norrfoolk*?"

She nodded and found the pages showing Scandinavia. Stepping back as he bent to look more closely at his homeland, she was struck by a sudden sorrow. It was easy to forget her compassion when he was being tiresome. Could she have been as eager to learn all she could to survive if their situations had been reversed?

Instead of answering that difficult question, she pulled another book from a higher shelf. The massive book wobbled in her hands, and she cringed as she feared it would fall on her head. When broad hands steadied it, she whispered, "Thank you, Niles."

"My pleasure, *unnasta*." His breath warmed her nape.

"You should not call me that."

"I know."

"But you just did!"

"I know." When he laughed, she grimaced. He enjoyed hoaxing her far too much.

Trying to pay no mind to how close he continued to stand as she opened the second book, she found the picture she wished to show him. "Look here."

"What is it?" He leaned over her shoulder to look more closely.

In spite of her efforts to appear serene when he pressed so near, her voice was breathless. "It is a ship."

"The sails..." He traced the highest mast. "How tall is this?"

She paged through to another drawing that showed the tars scrambling across the sheets, their forms silhouetted against the broad sails. Handing it to him, she said, "This should offer you some comparison."

"By Thor's hammer!" He sat on the arm of the closest chair as he stared at the page. "This ship is huge. My ship could have sat in the midst of its deck and not touched either railing."

"The ship in the picture would be considered a medium-sized ship nowadays."

"Amazing! Where are the oars?"

"They use only sails now, although there has been some work with creating a boat that runs on a steam engine."

"A what?"

"I don't understand it totally myself, but it has to do with steam turning paddles that move the ship through the water."

His eyes widened. "So even if the wind is calm, the ship could continue on its way."

"Yes."

"Amazing," he said again, but with a sigh. Closing the book, he placed it back on the shelf. "This time of yours has many marvels, but it seems you have paid for all this comfort and those new inventions with a tranquil life that provides little flavor to a man who has been accustomed to many challenges in his life."

She set the other book on its shelf. "Your challenge now is to convince the Polite World that you are one of them."

"Polite World! Even the phrase reminds me how far I am from my own time."

"I never guessed."

"Guessed what?"

"How lonely you must be."

He laughed. "Lonely? In this house with all your family and all their servants?"

"I am not speaking of that." She sat on the chair beside where he stood. "I was speaking of how lonely you must be for your own time and your own world."

His smile vanished. "I try not to think of it."

She ran her hands along his sleeves, but drew them

back when she touched the arm band he still wore. "I see you standing here in this coat, looking like any man among the *ton*, but I cannot help thinking of you as one of the men in the picture I first showed you of the *Norrfoolk*."

"I was brought to this time to do what I have vowed to do."

"Leaving everyone you know a thousand years in the past." She blinked back sudden tears. "I have given that very little thought. I have preferred to think only of the jumble you have made of my life. To think of never seeing my family or my friends or..." Raising her eyes to meet his, she saw the depth of his sorrow. She put her fingers lightly on his sleeve again as she whispered something she had not dared to let herself think before, "Did you leave a wife in that time?"

"My *viigi maka*—"

"That means wife?"

"Yes." Nils put one hand over Linnea's on his sleeve, and he wondered if she needed that comforting touch as much as he did now. "My *viigi maka* died of a winter illness the year after we wed. With her died our unborn child, for it was not ready to be born."

"Niles—Nils, I am so sorry."

He ran his finger along her soft lips as she spoke his true name. Her odd accent held a musical charm in his ears that was sweeter than the first birdsong of spring. "I would say that her death was the choice of the gods, but I did not accept it well. I have carried the grief with me for the past five years."

"So it was easy for you to be willing to die for your chieftain."

"In hopes of joining Gudrun?" He shook his head. "I did not wish to die any sooner than I must. If I had wanted death, I would have given myself into the *Valkyrja's* hands when I was marked for death on the shore. Instead I fought for life to do what I was meant to do."

"Which was to come here to this time and place."

"Yes."

"This is all so peculiar."

"On that we can agree." He walked out onto the terrace beyond the book-room. "When I look across these downs, I can see what is now, but I also can see what was. There were more trees then, and the settlements were much closer to the shore."

"Closer to shore? I would have guessed that they would have moved inland to hide from the raiders."

"There were raiders from inland as well, and the sea provided food for the people living here and an easier way to travel than by foot across the marshes and bogs." Facing her, he smiled. "Then there were those who believed the forests were filled with evil beings. Better to face human foes than demons sent by ancient gods."

"Thank heavens we know better than to believe that nonsense now."

"It was not all nonsense." He knew his retort had been too harsh when she pulled back from him, consternation blanching her face.

"I did not mean to—That is, I am sorry if I offended you in any way."

He cupped her chin and smiled. "*You* cannot offend me, save when you deny the craving that has grown between us."

"Acknowledging it would be foolish."

"Acknowledging it would be luscious, *unnasta*."

"Don't call me that! I cannot be your sweetheart, not when you are what you are and I am what I am."

His fingers rose to curve along her cheek. "We would have been enemies in another time, but here and now—"

"There is no here and now that we share. Once you have completed your search for your chieftain's knife, you will be returning to your time, and I will remain here. We have no past to share and no future to share."

When she drew away, he entangled his fingers in hers. She looked up at him, and he saw tears she fought to keep from falling. Slowly he released her hand, amazed by her strength of will.

"Linnea..."

"I shall return as soon as I retrieve some *carte des visites* and gloves to teach you how to pay a call when we are in London." Her voice trembled, but her chin remained high. "There is much more for you to learn."

"And you, too."

He heard her breath catch, the sound tempting him to capture her lips. She spun on her heel and rushed out of the room, her skirt rising to reveal an enticing glimpse of her ankles.

Nils glanced toward the closest window as he waited for the sound of Loki's taunting laugh. If this was the lying wizard's vengeance on him for defying the plans the gods had made, he could imagine no worse torment than wanting this woman and knowing that she was right when she said they had no future...together.

***

"I should have guessed you could be found here." Lord Sutherland smiled as Nils looked up from a book that had pictures of the other ships that sailed English waters.

"Really?" He closed the book over his finger. "How so?"

"You have spoken of your research into the Vikings. A man who enjoys learning about the past often finds the answers he seeks in books."

"True."

Lord Sutherland went to a table and picked up a stack of pages there. "I am glad that you are availing yourself of the books here. They do not get enough use."

"Linnea seems to spend much time here."

"I wish I could have inspired her love of learning in my other children. She possesses a curiosity about so much of the world around her. As you do."

"It is so obvious?"

"I have taken note of you watching everyone around you as if you are trying to decipher the present instead of the past."

Nils kept his smile from vanishing. What a *daari* he had been. If this Lord Sutherland was even half as wise as the Suthrland in Nils's time, little would his escape attention.

"Making observations is a habit, I fear," Nils replied when he realized his host was waiting for an answer.

"You are not like other professors I have met." Lord Sutherland laughed heartily. "You are not so lost in the past that you are unaware of what is around you."

"I have learned not to be blinded by the past or the present, for I might miss the very clue I seek to give me insight into both."

"An excellent point of view." Shuffling through the papers, Lord Sutherland smiled as he rearranged them. He set them back on the table. Going to a sideboard, he drew out a bottle and two glasses. He filled each with pungent wine and held one out to Nils. "Please avail yourself of the books here, but do not miss the old ruins scattered throughout the estate."

"What sort of ruins? You spoke of Roman ones. Are there others?" He took a sip and smiled. The wine of this time was far superior to what he had known in the past. When Lord Sutherland gestured toward a chair, Nils sat and waited for his host to do the same.

"This estate has many mounds that have been unexplored, although I suspect my sons have investigated several of them as I did with my brothers when I was a child."

"The mounds predate the excursions of the Vikings to these shores."

Lord Sutherland's brows rose. "You sound very certain of that. There are those who believe great Viking ships are buried within the earthworks."

"It is possible, but unlikely. It was the way of the *Norrfoolk* to set their great chieftains' corpses into their ships and set them afire. Some were dragged ashore before being fired, but many were sent burning off to sea, for a *Norrfoolk's* heart belongs to the sea."

Lord Sutherland drank deeply before saying, "Your knowledge continues to impress me, Barrington. One would think you have lived with your subject." He chuckled. "Of course when one has studied the Vikings as many years as you seem to have, I guess it's the truth to say you've lived with your subject."

"Yes, I suppose one could say that."

"Then tell me—" He looked toward the door. "Ah, Linnea, do come in."

Nils came to his feet and offered her a bolstering smile. It was unnecessary, he realized, when she pushed past him to hug her father and laughed as he teased her about getting rid of yet another daughter. The affection in this house was something that he had almost forgotten since Gudrun died. Never before had he considered what he had given up when he took his sword-sworn oath to his chieftain.

Or, he thought as Linnea turned to bring him into the conversation and he saw her warm smile, how much he must give up again.

Fifteen

"My lady, you must put an end to this with every bit of haste." Olive reached for the hairbrush on Linnea's dressing table.

"An end to what?" Linnea asked, picking up the brush before her maid could. She already knew the answer, she suspected.

"An end to this flirtation with this stranger who has been welcomed into this house like a long-awaited guest."

"By all that's blue, Olive, you have taken a disagreeable dislike to Niles."

"Nils! His name is Nils Bjornsson. Giving him another name does not make him a fine lord."

"That is true. However, we should not speak of that where others can hear."

"Why not? When did the truth become the wrong thing to speak?"

"Olive!"

Her maid flushed, but Linnea guessed it was more with anger than with embarrassment for having spoken so. "Forgive me, my lady. I am deeply concerned for your well-being."

"You need not be." She sat and ran the brush through her hair. Seeing Olive's scowl reflected in the glass, she turned to face her maid. "You know he is staying here only until he can go to London and continue his work."

"Continue his mischief more likely." She sniffed in disagreement. "The man must have taken a knock to his head while in the cradle. Jack tells me that he has heard Mr. Bjornsson—"

"Please, Olive! You must not call him that!"

Olive sniffed again, but nodded. "Very well, but you cannot ignore that the man is crazy. Jack has told me he has heard *him* speaking to someone who is not there. More than once since *he* moved into the house after your sister's wedding, I might add."

"Niles was probably just talking to himself. We all do that at one time or another while seeking the answer to some problem."

"Talking to oneself is one thing. Waiting for a response from someone who is not there is another."

Linnea did not answer. Chiding Olive for gossiping with Jack would gain her only another sniff. She could not defend Nils from these accusations when she found so much strange about him herself. Was he crazy? If so, he had drawn her into his delusions, because she could no longer discern between what was possible and what was utterly fancy. The whole of Nils being here was impossible; yet he was here. She did not want to imagine how much more bizarre all of this could get.

A knock on the door kept Olive from adding anything else. Rising, Linnea smiled when she saw Minnie enter. She had not had much of a chance to speak to her sister-in-law since the wedding. Kissing Minnie on the cheek, she motioned toward a chair set into a sunny bay at one side of the bedchamber.

"Martin told me," Minnie began, then glanced at Olive.

"Will you see if Cook has any lemonade prepared?" Linnea asked. She was rewarded with another glower from Olive who clearly wished to say more, but her maid nodded and left.

"Olive seems to be in a most dolorous mood today."

"She still feels," Linnea replied, glad to speak the truth, "that she must look after me to make sure I do not make a single misstep."

"She no longer is your governess."

"Mayhap you can persuade her of that. I fear I have failed utterly."

Minnie laughed and leaned back in her chair. "Oh, it is so nice to have the house to ourselves again."

"Yes, the wedding guests have left."

"Save for one."

Linnea could not keep from noticing the sideways glance her sister-in-law aimed at her. "Papa has asked Lord Barrington to stay as long as he wishes."

"Or as long as you wish."

"Minnie!"

Wagging her finger, Minnie chuckled again. "Do not try to bamboozle me, Linnea. I have seen how you look at that good-looking man. Even though married women are supposed to take no notice of any man other than their husbands, I have to say you have chosen a fine one to look at."

"Minnie!"

"Are you shocked?"

"Yes...no." Linnea relaxed in the chair and smiled. "I should know you well enough by now to know that you always speak your mind."

"So return the favor, Linnea, and tell me what you think of this unexpected visitor."

"I think he is quite charming."

"Quite?"

"All right, *very* charming. He is also very focused on doing the work he came to this part of England to do."

Minnie's nose wrinkled. "Studying old books and looking for old things in the mud. It amazes me that a man of his obvious vitality would be interested in such a sedentary pursuit."

"He does not seem to find it sedentary, for he has traveled far in his search for answers."

"Aha!"

"Aha what?"

"Linnea, you cannot hide that this man intrigues you when you jump so readily to his defense. That is wise of you when your only other choice may be Lord Tuthill."

"It sounds as if you are seeking an excuse for me not to marry Randolph." Her voice trembled as she longed to confide in someone who would heed her...and understand that this flirtation had gotten out of hand, and she did not know how to fix it without hurting those she loved.

Minnie became abruptly somber. "As you should be."

"You don't even know Niles Barrington."

"But I do know Lord Tuthill." Minnie grasped Linnea's hands. "Take care in the choices you make now, for whatever you choose may change your life irrevocably."

***

Linnea shaded her eyes as she looked along the sand which reflected the brilliant sunlight. Clear days, when not even the wisp of a cloud marred the perfect blue sky, were so unusual. Most days, a low bank of clouds clung to the horizon as if trying to hide where the sea merged with the sky. Only a hint of a breeze ruffled the lace on the hem of her gown, but the waves surged up on the shore, crashing like a runaway cart.

Coming here was exciting but offered no escape from Minnie's words of caution. She had not expected Minnie to be so forthright. Yet it was no surprise. Minnie had already made very clear her opinion about a match between Linnea and Randolph. Also Minnie knew how difficult it was for Linnea to hurt anyone's feelings.

Linnea had not been much more than a toddler when

she first brought a broken-winged bird to the house to be healed. Minnie had been there that day, for she had spoken often of how her heart had been touched by Linnea's hope to save the bird and Martin's determination not to let his baby sister know that it was impossible. He had found another fledgling and brought it to the house so that Linnea did not learn until years later that the first bird had not survived.

Hearing a yip, Linnea bent to pet Scamp. The pup was happy to be with her today, for Scamp had been banished by Mama from the house for chewing a hole in the corner of a dining room rug.

The puppy raced from beneath her fingers and down off the rocks. Streaking across the sand, Scamp barked in wild excitement. The sound of a whistle floated along the shore. The pup stopped, ears up, then raced toward a broad-shouldered silhouette farther along the strand.

Jumping with care off the boulders, Linnea bounced from one foot to the other. The sand was hot, but she left her shoes tied together and hanging on either side of her shoulder. She moved closer to the water where the waves kept the beach cooler.

Hearing another bark, she laughed as Scamp raced back to her before wheeling about in a spray of sand to rush to where Nils was standing by the water. She followed the puppy more slowly, pulling her bonnet forward so that her nose would not be reddened from the sun.

Again Scamp ran back to her, paused only for a pat between his silky ears, then scurried back to Nils. The barking sent birds rising from among the rocks and along the cliffs that rose from the far end of the curved beach.

Nils did not move, but she knew he was aware of her because he said as she approached, "There must have been a storm in the deeper waters."

"The waves are higher today than usual." She watched him stare out at the sea. He had disdained his coat and waistcoat. His shirt was open at the collar, and its full sleeves caught even the slight breeze. His buckskin breeches accented the sturdy line of his legs. Sand covered his bare feet.

"Have you always lived here?" he asked.

"Yes. When we have gone to London, I miss the sweet songs of the sea. There is something so mesmerizing about it."

"Mesmerizing?" He faced her. "Another word I do not know."

She stepped forward to stand beside him. "It means something that is so compelling that one cannot pull one's gaze from it."

"Ah, now I understand. You find the sea mesmerizing?"

"Yes, for it is never the same two days in a row." She took a deep breath of the briny air. "The waves can be dark or a brilliant blue-green. They can be thunderous or whispering to the shore. Sometimes, they are topped by bubbles which they offer to the sand like a gift. Other times, the foam is flung up onto the rocks."

"We of the *Norrfoolk* are not so poetic about the sea. For us, it is..." He frowned for a moment. "It *was* a tool, much as our boats and our axes and our swords were tools. We used it to obtain what we needed to survive."

"And as a route to conquest."

"That is true, too." He turned to look at the rocks. "There is no sign here of the battle that took place so many years ago."

"That is good."

He arched a brow, then moved along the crescent-shaped cove toward the end where rocks were piled higher than his head. "If you had said that to me when we first met, I would have argued with you."

"But you have changed your mind?" she asked as she followed.

"I have." He leaned his elbow on one of the boulders

and stared out at the undulating waves flowing toward the shore. "The battles that were fought here were brought about because of a loss of honor among the English, but those who attacked the *Norrfoolk* in the Danelaw are forgotten here. Their names and their evil deeds have been banished from history which paints the *Norrfoolk* as the villains. It is appropriate that there is no memorial here to a betrayal of trust."

"I am glad that you see the futility of trying to resurrect the past that has been forgotten."

"Not all the past has been forgotten." His hand fisted on the stone. "I am here to remember what was left undone. It may be that I should keep some of those memories alive." His fingers uncurled as they slipped along her arm. "I have shared the truth with you, Linnea, so that you might share it with others."

"But who would believe me?"

"I would."

She laughed. "Of course, you would, for the tales are of your telling. I wonder if anyone else would."

"What of Tuthill?"

"Randolph?" She shook her head. "He only believes what he can see and judge for himself."

"Yet he believes you love him."

"I doubt he believes that."

Nils started to answer, then paused as Scamp ran to him and leapt up against his leg. With a laugh, Nils pulled a small stick from where some storm had driven it into a crevice among the rocks. He flung it along the shore, and the puppy gave chase.

"Why would a man wish to marry a woman who does not love him?" he asked quietly.

"Were all marriages in your time only for love?"

"Of course not. They created alliances between families and between chieftains, but you do not need to seek strength in numbers before going to battle. Your king has an army and a navy to fight for England."

Linnea sat on a boulder and drew on her slippers.

"You have learned much from talking to Papa and Martin."

"They enjoy talking, and I enjoy listening." He knelt beside her. "Now I am listening to how you are avoiding answering my question."

"I did not know you asked one."

"I asked why Tuthill would wish to marry a woman who does not love him."

She clasped her hands in her lap so she did not reach out to twist his golden hair around her fingers. "You have not been listening closely enough to Papa and Martin if you must ask that."

"I assume that you are speaking of the industries and trade that your father has invested in so profitably."

"Yes."

"Tuthill is in need of money?"

She looked up at clouds that were rising inland in a race toward the sea. They were darkening to dim the perfect sunshine, but she did not move as she replied, "His father was a good man, but had the bad habit of gambling unwisely with men far richer than he was. Randolph inherited many debts with his title. He has paid many of them, but he wishes to regain the prestige for his title that comes from having plump pockets."

Nils sat and leaned his head on her lap. When she gasped at his brazen motion, he smiled up at her. "Then Tuthill is a greater *gaurr* than I had guessed."

"Oh, don't use that word!"

"Why not?"

Linnea quickly explained how she had used it by accident while talking with Randolph. When Nils began to laugh, she could not help doing the same. "You are a bad influence on me, Nils Bjornsson."

"And you still cannot speak my name correctly." He put his finger against her lips to halt her reply. "Do not say that you will not speak it again, because I have come to enjoy the sound of it in your voice, *unnasta*."

She laughed again, hoping that it would hide the

pulse of delight that coursed through her each time he used that endearment. She was silly to let him entwine her life with his even a moment longer than necessary, but she would be even more foolish to throw aside this ephemeral joy simply because it was fleeting.

"When we are alone," she said, but she delighted in any chance to bring a smile to his lips. Or more importantly, to bring his lips to hers. "When we are alone, I shall use the name you first gave to me when I found you on this beach."

Linnea gasped when Nils stood and walked back toward the center of the cove. Jumping to her feet, she went after him. Sand coursed into her slippers, but she ignored it.

He raised his hand as she neared, and she stopped more than an arm's length from him. Why was he trying to keep her distant?

"It was here," he said.

She scanned the low cliffs burgeoning from the strand and recognized the pattern of colors in them. "Yes, it was right here that you were when I found you." Mayhap it was not her he was trying to keep away, but anything to do with this time that was not his.

"It was here that I was meant to die."

"No!" she cried. "If you had been meant to die, you would not be here alive now."

Turning to her, he grasped her shoulders. "It is not that simple."

"I know that. You shouldn't even be here, but you are! There must be a reason."

"My chieftain's knife—"

"Could have been returned to him by someone else."

Nils shook his head. "The duty was mine. It remains mine." His gaze drilled her as he added, "It was here that I asked Freya to send her *Valkyrja* to take me from the beach to *Valhalla* or..."

"But you are here, not in some paradise."

"Yes."

Linnea frowned. Nils was occasionally taciturn,
but never more so than when she brought up questions
about how he had been brought to this place and this
time. Mayhap it was simply that he did not know, and
he was bothered by what he could not understand.

"You are more accepting of your peculiar
circumstances than I would be," she said.

"I have no choice." His hands glided down her
arms until his fingers laced through hers. "But I did
give Freya a choice that day. I asked her to send me to
Valhalla or to send me help to find my chieftain's knife.
You see the results?"

"I have told you that I would help you, Nils."

His lips quirked as she used his real name, but his
voice lashed her. "How soon can we leave for London?"

"Papa has been talking about taking the family there
before summer's end. When he goes, we can go."

"That will be several more weeks from now."

"I am sorry. I explained why I could not go with
you." She drew her hands out of his. "I wish I could
recall when I had seen the knife like the one you have
described. I know it was at the home of someone we
know well, for I must have seen it more than once if I
remember it, so why can't I remember *where* I saw it?"

"Loki."

Linnea looked up in amazement. "Please, do not
muddle things more with nonsense."

"It is not nonsense. Loki seeks every opportunity
to trick us mortals for his own amusement."

"But me? Even if I believed in that silliness, which
I don't, I am not of the *Norrfoolk*."

Nils bit back his retort. Why should he expect
Linnea to believe in the old ways? He had seen that
what he considered true was now dismissed as
mythology. If he spoke of his conversations with the
gods which once had been worshiped here as well as in
the northern lands, he would be considered mad. Maybe
even by Linnea, and he could not risk her questioning

his story. She must be the guide Freya had sent to him. Otherwise, there was no reason why he had come to this time and this place.

Except...His gaze devoured the tempting curves that were revealed so lusciously when the rising breeze pressed her gown back against her. When he was with her, alone as they were now, he did not wish to think of anything but her. She could be both his guide and his betrayer, for she stole his thoughts from his quest.

Was this fascination with her another trick perpetrated by Loki? The wizard exulted in confusing mortals until they completely lost their way. Nils must not allow that to happen.

Linnea held out her hand to him. "Scamp is barking as if he found something interesting. Shall we see what it is?"

"Yes." He slipped his hand into hers. "After all, that is how you found me."

"I hope Scamp has not found anything that unexpected again."

Her smile caressed him, inviting him to sample her lips. She did not offer him the chance as she led him toward where the puppy barked excitedly. Maybe she had guessed Nils's thoughts, because she chattered on like a spring bird meeting the morning. She spoke of the days when she and her siblings had enjoyed playing on this beach while their governess and tutors watched.

She smiled as she drew her hand out of his and ran to where Scamp was still yelping at a crab that had been washed up onto shore. "Scamp, leave the poor beast alone." Picking up a branch, she tossed it along the edge of the water. The puppy took after it with glee.

"Your dog is not only a great hunter but offers you protection against such wild beasts." Nils squatted. He lifted the crab from the sand and flung it back into the waves. "You are fortunate to have grown up here."

"I am. As I told you, any time we have traveled

from home, I have always been delighted to come back here."

"As I was always glad to see my home whenever I went a-viking."

Her smile disappeared. "When you came here to attack England."

"This was to be my last trip to Britannia." Standing, Nils drew his knife from the waist of his breeches. "I made the vow to complete my search for my chieftain's blade and be done with the life I had taken as mine when I was little more than a boy."

She glanced uneasily at the long blade. If she had thrown it into the sea instead of giving it to Jack to hide in the stable...Berating herself was futile, because she knew Nils would have found some weapon to wear as had been his custom.

"I don't understand," she said as his words echoed through her head, forcing her to pay attention to them instead of the honed blade that glistened in the dimming sunlight. "Why weren't you going to go a-viking any longer?"

"I was hoping to go west to Iceland."

She shivered. "Iceland? I have never wanted to go there. It sounds dreadful."

"But it is not. My brother went to Iceland and returned to tell of the rolling meadows that were spread in valleys beneath smoking mountains, and the hordes of fish in the cold waters."

"Brother?" They had spoken of his dead wife, but Linnea wondered why she never had given much thought to the rest of the family he had left in the past. Family and friends and allies and enemies. Looking toward the chimneys of Sutherland Park, visible above the sea cliffs, she tried to imagine how it would be to lose all that was familiar and to know that she might be separated from her family forever. She could not imagine it.

"My brother Hastein told me wondrous stories of

the people who lived in Iceland. They were creating a government that was ruled by the freemen who lived there. They have no kings like the ones who fight to claim all of the lands of the *Norrfoolk*." His lips twisted as he put the knife back in his waistband. "I should say they *had* no kings. I thought I would be accustomed to this change by now."

"So why did you come to England this time? I know you were looking for your chieftain's knife, but why did you make that vow when you wanted to go to Iceland?"

"I had to atone for our family's disgrace before I could think of my future."

"Disgrace? What disgrace?"

"The disgrace that was put upon us when Hastein stole our chieftain's blade, embarrassing him."

Linnea sat on a nearby rock. "Your brother took the knife? You never mentioned that before."

"It is something that I wish I never had to say. Hastein believed that our chieftain was more concerned about his own grasping for power than leading our people." He lowered his eyes for the first time since she had met him. Shame rang through his voice when he added, "For his actions, my brother was outlawed. He took Kortsson as his friend, which is why it is possible that my blood-enemy has the knife that Hastein stole."

"So you vowed to recover the knife to restore your family's honor?"

"Yes."

Rising, she put her fingers against his cheek and turned his face toward hers. "I am so sorry that this has not come about as you had hoped, Nils. It seems that the Fates are determined to make your search more difficult than anyone could have imagined it would be."

"Not fate, but the gods. I know you do not believe in their powers, but they exist."

"Tell me more about Iceland." Linnea did not want

to change the subject, for she wanted to learn more about the private man he hid so often behind his blustery exterior. "Why did you want to go there?"

"It was a place where a man might be free to make a life for himself. The laws were few, and they were made by the people themselves at the annual meeting called an Althing where people came together and decided how the island should be governed."

"Like our Parliament?"

"Save that, from what your father has said, you send others to represent you. At the Althing, it is said that any free man can speak." He smiled at her as he walked to a nearby stone. He scooped out some dark material, and she realized it was his coat that he had set aside when he came to the beach. "Any free woman can speak as well. Even a slave might be heard if the claim was deemed worthy."

"A woman could be heard?"

"The ways of the *Norrfoolk* required women to make important decisions while their men were a-viking. Why should they be denied that privilege when their men came back home?"

She laughed. "That is so different from what I know. A woman might oversee her husband's estate while he is away on business or personal matters, but when he returns to that estate his wishes dominate."

"Your ways are different."

"*Your* ways are different."

"Isn't that the same as what I just said?"

She shook her head and chuckled. "I mean that your ways now are different from what they would have been if we had met in your time. If I had had the misfortune to stumble over you on the beach as I did, we would not speaking like this."

"No, for I would not have been restrained by your customs. I might have been weakened by my wounds, but not so weak that you could have slain me." His smile became predatory, and she backed away a half-step in spite of herself.

He matched her pace. Pulling off her bonnet, he loosened her hair. He caught her hands when she reached up to halt him. Twisting her arm behind her back, he tugged her to him. His grip was not painful until she tried to back away. She froze, and he eased his hold on her arm, but not enough so she could escape.

"Nils, are you out of your mind?" she gasped.

"You would not ask that if we stood here, face-to-face, in my time." His finger slid along her throat. "I would have seen you dead for standing in my way." His finger edged lower to settle over her heart. "This fierce pulse would have been from fear."

"Please stop this," she whispered, wondering if her heart pounded with fear now, or from something else altogether? The resonance of his touch pierced her even more savagely than a blade.

"Do you think I would have heeded such a request?"

"We are not in your time. We are in my time now."

"But I am not of this time. When I stand here on this beach where I faced English warriors and watched my comrades fall to mingle their blood with our enemies', I think of what might have happened if you had chanced upon me at that moment."

"You have already said. You would have killed me."

"I am not so certain of that. Maybe I would have taken you as my *traell* back to the land of the *Norrfoolk*."

"*Traell*? What is that?"

"A captive slave." His voice grew low and rough. "*Unnasta*, you have a word in your language now that I have heard others use. A word that is much like *traell*. Enthrall. It means captivated, doesn't it?"

She met his hungry gaze as she whispered, "Yes."

"Then you would have been my *traell* while I was enthralled with you." His finger swirled along her breast, and she gasped at the powerful need rising through her. She gripped his sleeve, knowing she should halt him, but unwilling to lose even a second of this bliss.

Again he swept her against the hard line of his body. He pressed his mouth against the sweaty stickiness along her neck. "You taste wondrous, *unnasta*."

"You should not...We should go back to the house." A rumble of thunder was nearly drowned out by her raging pulse as he bent to let his lips follow the path his finger had.

With a moan, she curved her hands up his back, only realizing he had released her arm when her fingers splayed across his hard muscles. She gasped his name when his mouth moved along her bodice. When he put his hand on her sleeve and began to lower it along her arm, she stared up into his fathomless eyes that blazed with savage, primitive emotions. Knowing she should look away, she could not. Being dishonest in his arms was something she could not conceive of. She wanted to be swept into this wild rhapsody of rapture. She closed her eyes when he pulled her even closer before bending to let his fiery tongue glide along the curve of her breast.

She clasped his face between her hands. Bringing his mouth to hers, she feasted on his lips. His fingers tangled in her hair, but she barely noticed. Every sense was centered on his kiss and the spot where his bare chest pressed against her skin that had been moistened by his kiss.

Light flashed. Thunder shook the shore so hard that the ground rumbled beneath Linnea's feet. With a gasp, she stepped away. Nils whirled her back against him as the storm swirled around them. No tempest flinging itself upon the sea could be as strong as the fired winds of passion surrounding them.

When lightning struck the water not far from where they stood, Nils whispered, "Where can we find shelter?"

"The house—"

"At the house, we cannot continue *this*." His fingers stroked her breast.

Rain slashed at them before she could answer. With a gasp, she ran along the shore to retrieve her bonnet as it skittered away before the wind. She laughed when Scamp caught it before she could. Taking it from the puppy, she put it on her already soaked hair.

She turned and discovered Nils just behind her. He said nothing. He did not move. The choice was all hers. He had made up his mind.

"My family will be anxious," she said, looking up at him through the rain.

"That you are out in this storm or that you are out in this storm with me?"

She grasped his strong forearms that were now covered with the dark wool of his coat sleeves. "You are here in order to preserve your family's honor. Would you have me dishonor my family?"

"There is no dishonor in wanting us to be one."

"In this time, there is for me."

He started to reply, then his arm slipped around her shoulders. She was startled when he set his coat over her drenched gown to protect her from the blustery wind swirling the rain. The odor of wet wool surrounded her, but it was not unpleasant because the coat also held his scent. He turned her toward the path leading back to the house.

"We will return to your father's house," he whispered. "We will reassure them that you are unharmed." His rakish smile returned as he climbed up on the rocks and offered his hand to assist her up. When she stood beside him, he said, "Once we have shown them you are safe, surely your father will feel obligated to repay me for protecting his daughter."

"Papa will be grateful." She watched her footing as she went from rock to rock. Stepping onto the path, she waited for Nils to do the same.

He jumped down from a boulder and swung her up against him. "I can think of no better way for him to repay me then by agreeing for you to stay with me tonight."

"I do not think he will be *that* grateful."

"And what of you, *unnasta?*"

Linnea pulled out of his arms again, although she wanted to remain there. "I did not think you would wish me to feel anything as tepid as gratitude."

"I want you to savor every emotion as I savor every bit of you." He captured her face in his hands and kissed her hard. "Come to my bed tonight, *unnasta.*"

"Tonight?"

"Why not?"

"Nils..." Her voice trailed away, as she could not tell him no when her heart shouted that she accept. "If it were possible..."

He laughed. "It is very possible."

"Not now. Not with me." She put her hand up to his face, then flinched as the lightning exploded across the sky again.

Without speaking, he took her hand and ran with her along the path toward the house. Scamp raced after them, barking with excitement. She faltered as she stepped into a puddle. Nils laughed again. Sweeping her up into his arms, he continued up the path.

"I can walk...or run," she protested.

"If you will not stay with me tonight, I shall not let this moment pass without taking advantage of every opportunity to hold you."

"You are insane."

"You are not the first in this house to think so."

She looked hastily away. If she did not know better, she would begin to think that he could hear through closed doors and read the thoughts that only she was privy to. She closed her eyes and leaned her head on his brawny shoulder. On this one thing, she had to agree with him. To let this chance pass unsavored would be wrong.

When the rain stopped striking the brim of her bonnet, Linnea opened her eyes. Voices came from every direction as Nils set her on her feet in the center of the foyer.

"Linnea!"

She looked up to see Papa coming down the stairs at a speed that would have earned her a reprimand.

"Linnea! My dear girl! Look at you!" Her father hugged her close. "We were so fearful for you when the storm blew up and no one knew where you were."

"Niles brought me home from the shore."

When Lord Sutherland grabbed Nils's hand with both hands, Linnea was amazed to see tears glistening in Papa's eyes. "I am so grateful to you, Barrington, for watching over my daughter. I thank whatever Providence that brought you to Sutherland Park now."

"It was my pleasure," Nils said, smiling.

Linnea avoided his eyes. Papa would be shocked to discover that the force that had swirled Nils forward in time had been created by Freya and Loki. She put her hand to her head. Was she beginning to deem all of this silliness to be the truth? She wondered how she could accept that Nils was from the past and still question what he believed was true.

"By Jove, you should have heeded your wife, Sutherland," said a man who was coming down the stairs at a much more sedate pace. "She said your daughter knew enough to come in out of the rain."

"Barely, I am afraid," Linnea replied.

Her father put his arm around her shoulders. "Linnea, this is Dr. Varian Foster, who has just arrived from York. Foster, my youngest."

Linnea held out her hand. Seeing water dripping from it, she shook it before offering it again, "May I add my belated welcome to Sutherland Park, Dr. Foster?"

"Thank you."

Her father grinned. "Dr. Foster, this is Niles, Lord Barrington. I know you have been waiting anxiously to talk with him."

"With me?" Nils asked, his eyes widening. "Why?"

"Dr. Foster is an expert in the study of the Vikings. He is very eager to speak with you about all you know."

Sixteen

Linnea stiffened as she glanced at Nils. An expert on Vikings? Here? Now? For the first time, she was tempted to believe that what Nils had told her about Loki was true. Only a vengeful god could have orchestrated Dr. Foster's arrival at this time.

She shook such thoughts out of her head. Indulging in such silliness would betray them more quickly than anything else. But the same question heckled her. How could she believe that Nils was from the past and yet discount the fact that any other aspects of his time might have slipped with him forward to her time.

Nils's smile did not waver, but she recognized the glint in his eyes. She had seen it on the shore when she found him injured. It had been there as well each time he spoke of the past and the battles he had fought and the vow he had made. Although she doubted if Papa or Dr. Foster took notice of that dangerous shimmer, she tensed.

"I would be honored to speak with you at your convenience," Nils said with a bow of his head toward Dr. Foster. "I am glad to meet someone who shares my interest in that subject." Smiling at Linnea as if there were nothing amiss, he added, "Linnea has proven to be an apt listener when I speak of that time in history."

Dr. Foster chuckled. "It is a unique woman who is

fascinated with such an intellectual subject."

"You will find that my daughter is quite unique." Papa gave her shoulders a squeeze.

"Thank you, Papa." She kissed his cheek, wishing she could confide in him. She had missed his good counsel in this puzzling situation, because she had always been able to ask for his insight before this. "If you will excuse me, gentlemen, I shall change from these soaked clothes before Mrs. Gerber grows more upset about me dripping on her freshly mopped floors."

"Do not fret about that," her father replied. "Go up to your rooms, and I will have hot water sent for you. You do not want to take a chill."

She nodded. Going to the foot of the stairs, she put her hand on the newel post and turned. "Papa—"

"Do not fret, child. I shall have Mrs. Gerber make sure there is enough hot water for Lord Barrington as well. You know that Sutherland Park treats our guests as family."

When Dr. Foster laughed and added something, Linnea paid no attention to his words. She tried to catch Nils's gaze. He seemed totally engrossed in the conversation. Knowing that she could not loiter here like a naughty child eavesdropping on her elders, she slowly put her foot on the first riser.

Its faint squeak, so commonplace that she had not noticed it in years, must have caught Nils's ear. He glanced toward her, and the memory left by the heat of his kisses surged through her anew even though he turned back to answer a question she had not heard Dr. Foster ask.

She took the glow of Nils's amethyst eyes with her as she climbed the stairs. Storing the memory in the most treasured section of her heart, she began to strip off Nils's coat as soon as she had closed her bedroom door.

Olive came forward to help. She said nothing, which warned Linnea that her maid was not at all pleased with the results of this afternoon's walk. When Olive stamped about the room as if she were trying to rid it of crawling insects, Linnea was as silent. Anything she said could be the wrong thing. If she showed too much interest in who Dr. Foster was and what he was doing here *now*, she would arouse Olive's curiosity.

Although she would have liked to linger in the warm bath, Linnea redressed quickly. She twisted her wet hair at her nape and nodded when Olive asked if she would like some hot chocolate to chase away any residual chill.

Linnea waited until her maid had left, then slipped out of her room. She clung to the shadows left by the storm as she walked along the corridor. Hearing Lady Sutherland's voice from the floor below, Linnea hurried toward the guest wing. She did not want her mother to guess where she was going.

Her own words to Nils on the shore returned to taunt her. If she was discovered sneaking to Nils's room, she would destroy the Sutherland family's reputation as well as her own. She knew that, but she must speak with Nils when no one else could hear.

Reaching his door, she knocked quietly. She waited, then knocked again. When Jack did not answer it, she looked both ways along the hall before opening it.

She froze when she heard a voice within. Nils was talking to someone. Jack? If so, why hadn't Jack come to the door when she knocked? Jack was taking his duties as Nils's valet very seriously. Mayhap Nils was giving him a list of instructions, and Jack was concentrating on that instead of her knock.

Her eyes widened when she realized Nils was not speaking English. He must be mad! If someone overheard him...

A finger tapped her shoulder.

Linnea nearly bumped into a table by the door as she whirled to see who was behind her. She pressed her hand over her frantic heart when she saw Jack's quizzical expression. "You startled me!" she said.

"Forgive me, my lady." He rubbed one foot against the back of his other leg. "I just wanted to give you a warning."

She looked past him, scanning the corridor. It appeared empty, but someone could have seen her skulking here.

"He does this often," Jack went on.

"He?"

"Lord Barrington. He talks to himself like that a lot. 'Tis strange, because he uses funny words that sometimes sound like English and sometimes sound like gibberish." He stared at the floor. "I watched one time, and he kept looking at the window and talking."

"All the time?"

"No."

"Jack!" She remembered what Olive had told her about how Jack was distressed that Nils was acting oddly. Mayhap it had not been just gossip. She had to know for sure. "Please tell me. It might be something left over from his injuries."

"Do you think so?" The lad's smile returned. "You may be right about that, my lady. He did take quite a blow to his head."

Linnea listened by the door. "Whatever it is, he has stopped now. While I speak with him, bring some wine to take away the chill."

"Olive said she was bringing hot chocolate." His eyes twinkled.

"For me. Lord Barrington will prefer something stronger," she replied with a smile. Olive might be reluctant to play a part in this charade, but Jack reveled in every minute of it.

Jack turned, then paused. "Almost forgot. This came for you." He pulled a crumpled page out of his pocket.

"Thank you." Linnea's smile tumbled away as she opened the folded sheet to see Randolph's scrawl. He would be calling soon. Blast! She did not need the problem of him pestering her for an answer as well.

"Anything I can do, my lady?"

She patted Jack's shoulder. He had been such a good ally through all this. "Get the wine for Lord Barrington."

Although she suspected he would have preferred her to ask him to slay some mighty dragon or take on some other great task, he nodded.

Linnea drew in a steadying breath as she knocked again on the door and pushed it a bit farther open. "Niles?"

"Come in."

Slipping past the door, she drew it closed behind her. She looked about but did not see him. "Niles?"

"Here," said Nils as he stepped out of the bathing room. He wore black breeches but nothing else. The dark color accented his bronzed skin and drew her eyes from his tawny hair. Her gaze swept down along his strong chest that had been so enticing against her skin. "I thought you would have been calling before now."

"We must talk." She clasped her hands behind her back. Did he know that the topmost button on his breeches remained undone? A flame coursed up her face, and she tried to submerge the myriad of emotions flooding her. She told herself that nothing mattered except Dr. Foster who might see the truth about Nils Bjornsson that no one else had.

"I suspected you would wish to."

"Now that you are done speaking with whomever you were talking to before."

His good humor vanished as his brows lowered in his most forbidding expression. Seizing her arm, he pulled her closer. "You heard that?"

"I heard you speaking."

"Did you see anything?"

She tried to pull her arm away. When he released her, she was amazed enough to blurt out, "I did not peek into your bathing room if that is what you are asking."

"I know that." His laugh was as stiff as his lips. "If that had been true, you would be that most alarming shade of a new sailor cooked red by the sun on his first voyage." He finished buttoning his breeches as casually as if he always dressed in her presence. "The color you are now, Linnea."

"Stop teasing me! Jack has heard you talking here in whatever tongue you use."

He whirled her back to him. His mouth slanted across hers, his tongue probing into her mouth. She fought the enchantment that lured her into softening in his arms as she explored the expanse of naked skin that was separated from her by only the breadth of the water clinging to it.

"That is the tongue I use," he whispered as he brushed her neck with eager kisses.

"You know that was not what I meant."

"It is the only one of which you must speak."

"Jack is bothered by your conversations with someone who is not here," she murmured, struggling for every word as he nibbled on her ear.

"Then he should pay them no mind."

"Olive is certain you are mad."

"She is right."

Pulling away, Linnea stared up at him. "She is?"

He herded her closer again. "I am mad. Mad for you, *unnasta*. I want you."

"Nils, not here."

"Ah, I have ruffled your English sensibilities again." He kissed the tip of her nose. "Give me one good reason why you should not come into the other room with me and be my lover."

"Jack will be returning soon with the wine I asked him to bring for you."

He laughed. "He will wait if the door is locked. That is not a good reason, *unnasta*."

"Then let me give you a truly good one." She put her hands up to keep him from kissing her. When her fingers brushed his bare skin, she moaned and brought his mouth to hers. She needed to be held like this. She needed the thrill of his touch and the joy of his soul-deep kisses.

His voice was unsteady as he whispered, "Are you arguing against or *for* becoming my lover?"

"I want..." She ran her fingertips along his stern brows. "I want what you want, Nils, but there is Dr. Foster to consider."

He trailed beguiling fire along her neck. "I do not want to consider anyone but you now that you are here where I had only dreamed you would be."

"Don't jest about this." She stepped back and turned away before the promise of passion in his eyes urged her to toss aside all good sense. "If I had not thought the situation was critical, I would not have..."

"You do not need me to tell you that you would not have come here otherwise." He ran a damp finger along her arm. "However, you are more than welcome to play valet for me while Jack is doing a few errands." When she looked at him, he gave her his most roguish smile. "I knew you would be calling on me as soon as you were done with your bath. Despite your English ways, you seem to find excuses to circumvent them when you feel a need to."

She sat on the chaise longue. She tried to keep her eyes aimed at his, instead of letting her gaze wander along his water-jeweled skin. Each drop accented his undeniable strength.

"I cannot stay long," she said.

"So say what you came here to say."

"You should leave Sutherland Park posthaste, Nils."

He reached for his shirt. Pulling it on, he said, "I know that. I have asked you to go with me to complete my quest."

"No, I mean you should go now. Today. Go to

London. I will try to join you there as soon as I can, but you should not stay here when you may say the wrong thing and create suspicions in Dr. Foster's mind."

He laughed, closing his shirt and reaching for his waistcoat. "What could I do that would cause any sane man to believe I had lived a thousand years ago and suddenly found myself in this time?"

"I don't know. There might be something. You will have to watch every word you say."

"As you will."

"Yes."

"Linnea, you should know by now that I do not back away from a challenge."

"This is more than a challenge."

"Do not let him worry you."

"But he is worrying *you*."

He paused in buttoning his waistcoat. Facing her, he said, "I thought I had hidden that well."

"Mayhap you have, but I know how I would feel in these circumstances."

"And how is that?"

"As if, suddenly, I were the prey of a woods-wise hunter."

Sitting beside her, he brushed a strand of damp hair back from her face. "*Unnasta*, one is always both the hunter and the prey."

"Mayhap in your time, but not in mine."

"No? I think Tuthill's attempts to court you would have persuaded you that you are the prey, even as you control the hunt."

She looked down at her hands, which were clenched so tightly that her knuckles had bleached. When he put his wide hand over them, she whispered, "I try not to think of it that way."

"But you are his prey."

"I know how to handle Randolph," she said more forcefully. "What worries me is Dr. Foster."

"He has no reason to suspect I am anything other

than what I say I am."

Linnea came to her feet. "Nils, you are making every effort to pass yourself off as a man of this time and this place." She put her hands on his shoulders. "You have betwattled my family and friends into believing you are what you say you are, passing off your so-called odd ways as idiosyncracies."

"But you fear this Dr. Foster will see my ways as what they are."

"Don't you?"

He slid his hands up her arms as he drew her down to sit on his knee. "I have thought about little else since the man was introduced to us." His grin returned. "Except for now when I can think only of how sweet you smell and how soft you are and how much I want you."

"Nils!"

He laughed. "Again you sound like the teacher who is disappointed in her recalcitrant student."

"You must realize the threat to you. Dr. Foster is going to ask questions about you and this information that you have been spouting."

"Spouting?"

"Papa has spoken to me of the interesting conversations you have shared."

"Your tone suggests I should have been more reticent. It might have been possible if your father's mind was less keen and his interests less varied."

"I know." She put her hand on his arm, not surprised that it was as rigid as it had been when she had found him on the shore.

Standing, he set her on her feet. "Don't you think I recognize that this situation is as dangerous as when I was lying on the beach waiting for death? If I am shown to be a liar in your father's eyes, I shall be banished from Sutherland Park. Then it will be impossible for you to help me in my quest."

"What has been said has been said," she replied

quietly.

"A wise way of summing up the situation."

"So what you must do, Nils, if you will not go by yourself to London—"

"Going is futile unless you come, too." He pounded his fist against his palm. "You are right. I have no place to begin the search in London without your guidance."

"You must be prepared to answer the questions Dr. Foster is bound to ask you."

"Questions?"

"About your research, about what intrigues you about this subject so much that you are willing to leave the comfort of your home to tramp across the marshes and fields to learn more about people who became a part of England so many centuries ago."

"Wise questions."

She smiled. "And he will expect intelligent answers from you."

"I do know a few things about the *Norrfoolk*." He chuckled.

"But you know too much about the *Norrfoolk*."

"What?" His brow furrowed.

She clasped his arm. "Nils, he will expect you to prove how you know what you know."

"I cannot do that."

"No, but..." She raised her fingers and began counting on them as she outlined the questions Dr. Foster might ask, along with the answers that might protect Nils. As Nils started to smile, she hoped he would heed her words.

A tentative knock on the door interrupted her. As Jack walked in, she mumbled something before she hurried out into the corridor. She released the breath she might have been holding from the moment she had come to Nils's door. Nils would heed her urging to be sensible, but she feared her heart would not any longer.

Seventeen

Linnea was pleased to come into the parlor and see her mother there. No one else was in the comfortable room where Mama was checking the flower arrangement set on the lyre table near the tallest window.

"Ah, Linnea, just the person I had hoped to see." Mama motioned for her to come to her side. "I trust I do not have to repeat the scold your father must have given you about failing to keep a close eye on the weather this time of year when we have so many thunderstorms brewing."

"No, Mama, you do not need to repeat that scold." She kissed her mother on the cheek, not wanting Mama to guess that Papa had been too eager to introduce Dr. Foster to Nils to think of anything else.

"Good." Wiping bits of leaves from her hands, she said, "I understand you were with Lord Barrington."

She flinched, then realized Mama was not talking of Linnea being in Nils's rooms. "Yes, we met on the shore. We were playing with Scamp when the storm crashed down upon us."

"With Scamp?" Mama's right brow rose sharply. "I would not like to hear that anything else untoward had been happening."

"I know, Mama." It was all she could say without resorting to falsehoods, and she already was being false with her family about Nils's origins. That dishonesty ate at her, twisting her stomach, each time she spoke with Mama or Papa.

Mama's smile returned. "I know you do, child. You have always been the most prettily-mannered of all the children. If it had been Dinah..." She shook her head and chuckled. "Your coquettish sister is now wed, so she is her husband's problem."

"Mama, when we came back from the shore, Papa introduced us to a friend of his."

"Actually Dr. Foster went to school with my brother," Mama said as she stepped aside while a maid set the tea tray on the table in the middle of the parlor.

"I never heard you speak of him before."

Lady Sutherland laughed merrily. "I doubt if I ever have had the need to speak of him. It was quite out of the blue that he sent a request to pay us a call at Sutherland Park. Your uncle has visited him at his home in Oxford on several occasions, but I have not seen Dr. Foster since your father and I wed."

"Did he say why he wanted to come here now?"

"I am sure that your father must have mentioned to you that Dr. Foster is in the midst of a project of some sort of historical research." Her mother's smile faltered. "Linnea, you sound disconcerted by Dr. Foster's visit. Is there something that bothers you about it?"

"Having a friend of my uncle's calling is no reason for disquiet, is it?" She tried to copy her mother's cheerful laugh.

"Then what is amiss?"

"I hope nothing is."

Sitting, Lady Sutherland patted the cushion beside her. "I believe you are more distressed than you wish anyone else to know. Olive told me that you had received a note from Lord Tuthill."

"Yes." She sat, but promised herself that she would speak to Olive as soon as possible. Olive needed to recall that she was no longer Linnea's governess, but her maid.

"Are you bothered because Lord Tuthill is pressing his suit?"

"It is not a comfortable situation." It was glorious to be able to be forthright at last.

"You have inherited your father's gift for minimizing your problems."

"Mama, if you were to speak to Papa about my uncertainty, he might listen."

Lady Sutherland's fingers grazed Linnea's cheek gently. "My dear child, if you were to share your uncertainty with your father on this, he will heed you. I think you have a greater problem."

"Getting Randolph to heed me when I speak of my mistake in letting him think I wish to marry him now?"

"No. I am speaking of—" She abruptly stood. "Lord Barrington, you are always so punctual."

Linnea's hands clasped more tightly in her lap as Nils gave Mama his most charming smile. The way her mother had reacted to Nils's arrival suggested that she had guessed quite rightly that Nils was the reason why Linnea was unsettled.

He bowed gracefully over Mama's hand. Again he was dressed in the perfectly tailored coat he had worn when he appeared at the house during Dinah's wedding. "It behooves a gentleman who is about to enjoy the company of two lovely ladies not to miss even a moment of any such opportunity."

"I suspect you are a man, Lord Barrington," Mama returned, "who seldom misses any opportunity that is to your favor."

"You are right, my lady." He looked past her and smiled more broadly. "You look much drier than when I last saw you, Linnea."

Although she knew Mama would not guess that he meant when they had parted ways in the foyer on their way to get their baths, fire slapped Linnea's face. How had she gotten so caught up in protecting Nils that she forgot to protect herself from ruin? Yet, as his smile warmed his eyes—and her—she knew she would gladly risk anything for the chance to taste his kiss once more and once more after that and once more after that...

"Lord Tuthill, my lady," came a footman's voice from near the doorway.

Linnea's stomach cramped, but she kept a smile on her face as Mama went to greet Randolph. As always, Randolph was in prime twig, although she considered the bright green stripes of his waistcoat a bit garish. She guessed he had assumed a preference for such colors during his last visit to London.

Rising, Linnea also went forward to greet him, pausing while he bowed over Mama's hand. His motions were even smoother than Nils's, but his greeting did not sound as sincere. That was absurd, for Nils was deluding everyone with his tales. Or was Randolph trying to hide his true emotions as well? That was a most unnerving thought.

Only when Randolph raised his head and scowled did she realize that she had stopped next to Nils. She started to step away, but Nils's hand at the back of her waist kept her beside him.

"He shows his determination to break your heart quite clearly," Nils murmured.

She did not answer him as she stepped forward and offered her hand to Randolph exactly as her mother had. When he grasped her shoulders and bent toward her, she turned her head at the last moment to keep him from kissing her on the mouth. She was almost certain she heard him mutter a very crude phrase under his breath as his lips brushed her cheek.

"Randolph!" she gasped, hoping she had misheard him. A strong odor of something more potent than wine came from him, and she wondered how much he had been drinking before he had called.

He ignored her scold as he turned to greet her father who was coming into the room. Randolph's cheerful smile would offer Lord Sutherland no hint that anything was bothering him, but Linnea knew only if Randolph was deeply distressed would he speak so in her hearing. Linnea started to label Randolph a hypocrite in her mind, but halted herself. She was no better than he was, for she played such a huge rôle in this lie that had taken over her life. When broad fingers touched her back, the sensation as light and fleeting as a butterfly's passage, she smiled.

Nils.

With no one else would she have been as aware of such a feathery caress, the mere passage of his fingers across her skin. She would have dismissed anyone else's touch as a chance contact. While Papa introduced Randolph to Dr. Foster, just entering the parlor, she savored Nils's touch. She was courting danger to let him be so bold, but she wanted to enjoy this for as long as she could.

Randolph held out his arm to her in a silent order. Knowing that any hesitation might create the very scene she wished to avoid, Linnea put her fingers on it. He clamped his hand over hers and gave Nils a cold smile. She did not look at Nils as she let Randolph lead her to where the tea waited. Her one effort to select a chair failed when Randolph seated her next to him on a small settee.

Nils crossed the room, chatting with Dr. Foster as if they already were the closest of tie-mates, and sat across from her. When the toe of his boot brushed her slipper beneath the table, she wanted to smile. He might be trying to fortify her for this disquieting gathering, or he might simply be attempting to disconcert her with the reminder of how much more intimately he wished to caress her.

"Linnea?" Her mother's tone suggested she was repeating herself.

"Yes, Mama?"

"Will you pour?"

"Thank you. I would be delighted to." Anything to keep her fingers busy so no one could see how they quivered with anxiety—and anticipation—of Nils's touch.

Linnea concentrated on serving the tea as she listened to the conversation around her. It was cordial, but careful. Randolph asked Dr. Foster about his journey to Sutherland Park and commented on the weather. Mama expressed her delight that a storm had not come during Dinah's wedding. Papa accepted Dr. Foster's congratulations on a good match for yet another daughter. It was all exactly as it should be.

She held out a tea cup to Nils, and he gave her the scintillating smile that always stirred something deep within her. The cup rattled against his saucer as her fingers trembled. When Mama gave her a disapproving glance, Linnea steadied the cup.

"Thank you," Nils said, his fingers stroking hers gently as he took the cup from her.

"You are welcome."

There was nothing out-of-the-ordinary about their words, but she heard Randolph grumble something under his breath. She stiffened. If he was going to react so to everything said between her and Nils, this gathering was going to be even more discomfiting than she had feared.

"Did you say something, Tuthill?" asked Nils, his smile tightening. "You must speak up if you wish all of us to hear."

"I—I—" Randolph's ears grew crimson as he turned to Dr. Foster, who was listening with a benevolent smile. "Lady Sutherland mentioned you were here for a very special reason, Dr. Foster. May I inquire as to what it is?"

"I am here to do some research out on the downs."

"Research for what?" asked Randolph.

Dr. Foster shot Nils a wide grin before replying, "Any traces I can find here of Viking settlement."

"Vikings?" Randolph laughed tersely. "Has everyone in Sutherland Park suddenly become obsessed with those ancient thieves?"

Linnea looked hastily at Nils, hoping he would endure yet another insult fired at him by Randolph. This one was not even intentional, but it could be more hurtful than any of the other remarks Randolph had made out of spite.

"Thieves?" asked Dr. Foster before she could think of words to ease the tension that her parents and Dr. Foster might not even be aware of. "I suppose you could call them that, my lord. Many of them were." He laughed, the sound showing that he enjoyed life in all its aspects, even arguing with Randolph. "However, you would have to say the same of many of the folks in our own century. Not just the pickpocket or the highwayman, but the businessman who cheats his partner and the bakery worker who absconds with an extra biscuit at day's end. I believe we would find unscrupulous sorts in every era." His smile broadened as he added, "Lord Sutherland has told me repeatedly, Lord Barrington, that you are a renowned expert in this field. Odd that I have not heard of you before now."

"My work has not yet been published." Nils smiled at Linnea, whose shoulders drooped with relief. Did she think he would not recall all she had told him upstairs? Or was she just pleased the conversation had taken this turn that she had anticipated?

"No?" Dr. Foster ran his fingers through his beard. "Why not?"

"I have been busy in recent years with the obligations that came to me when my uncle died and left me his title and his debts." Nils's laugh sounded sincere. "You understand that, don't you, Tuthill?"

"I prefer," Randolph said in his sternest tone, "not to speak of business in the presence of the ladies."

Lord Sutherland chuckled. "Then you fail to

understand the women of this family, my boy. I can assure you that Lady Sutherland has great insights into any discussion of the current economic situation in England. Her knowledge is superior to most men I have met." He patted his wife's hand with a rare public showing of affection. "A man is fortunate to have a helpmeet who shares his interests."

Not to be put off, Dr. Foster asked, "So you are planning to publish the results of your research, Lord Barrington?"

"As soon as I complete some other business." He looked again at Linnea.

When Tuthill bristled like a hedgehog, Nils wondered if Tuthill would have been so belligerent had they met a thousand years in the past. His fingers brushed the haft of the knife he kept hidden beneath his waistcoat. It was intriguing to see Tuthill squirm in this exchange of polite words, but there would have been greater gratification in meeting him across bare swords where the prize granted to the winner was Linnea.

Seeing distress blossom in her expressive eyes, Nils let his favorite curse rumble through his head. She was distressed. Why? Because he was playing Tuthill for the *daari* he was? She professed to have no interest in marrying this man; yet she was pained by his humiliation. This made no sense. Women in his own time had been straightforward, although oft-times baffling to a man. In this time, far too often, he could not comprehend why Linnea reacted as she did. Except when she was in his arms. Then there was an honesty in her innocent caresses that spoke plainly to him.

"Lord Barrington?"

Nils looked back at Dr. Foster. "Forgive me. What did you say?"

"I was asking what the hypothesis of your research is?"

He hesitated. *Hypothesis*? That was one word

that Linnea had failed to mention to him.

Linnea laughed and tapped his arm playfully. "Do not be anxious that Dr. Foster will appropriate your theories about the Vikings."

"Of course not!" huffed Dr. Foster. "My lord, if I gave you any idea that that was my intention, I beg you to accept my apology."

"No, no." Nils wanted to thank Linnea for saving him yet again, but knew that would have to wait. A quiver raced through him, reacting in every part of him, as he imagined them alone when he showed her just how grateful he was for her help, and for her alluring touch. Forcing himself to concentrate on the conversation here, he added, "That was never in my thoughts, Dr. Foster. I was simply trying to think best how to put this." He laughed. "Now you can see why my results have not yet been published. My thoughts are too scattered."

"I can understand why."

Nils wanted to snarl an oath when Dr. Foster smiled at Linnea. By Thor's hammer, setting off Tuthill again would only succeed in hurting her.

As if he had not discerned anything amiss about Dr. Foster's smile, he said, "One thing that is often overlooked in the annals of that time is that the *Norrfoolk* were following in the footsteps of the English."

"How so?"

He was able to smile more sincerely when he saw Linnea was listening as intently as Dr. Foster and her father. "Almost as many years before the time of the *Norrfoolk* excursions here as have passed since them, the Roman armies conquered this island and named it Britannia."

"That is true, but I do not see how that connects with your statement."

"Patience, Dr. Foster." Nils glanced at Linnea, and she was relieved to see amusement in his eyes. She hoped Tuthill would notice it as well, so he would realize that he should not read more into this conversation than the words spoken.

"I am simply very curious, my lord."

Nils's amusement was hidden when he looked back at the professor. "When the Romans were recalled to Rome to protect it from invaders, they did not have time to take all their valuables with them. Much gold and jewels were left in the retreat. The English took those items for their own use or remade them to fill their churches and homes. As they stole from the Romans, so the *Norrfoolk* stole from them."

"A most interesting theory." Dr. Foster grinned. "I would enjoy witnessing you sharing this with my colleagues. You must pay me a call in Oxford, so I might savor that moment."

"Oxford is not far from London," Linnea said. "When we next go to London—"

"Ah, that will not be possible," Dr. Foster said. "I will be going in the spring to oversee an excavation in Iceland." Again he released one of his enthusiastic laughs that shook his belly. "Let others be fascinated with what Napoleon's soldiers uncovered in Egypt. While they are arguing about ancient mysteries that may never reveal their secrets, I shall enjoy learning more about the *Norrfoolk* that traveled the northern seas from Scandinavia to the far reaches of the western Atlantic Ocean."

"Iceland?" Nils asked. "You are very fortunate, Dr. Foster."

Mama shook her head. "To go to a place filled with volcanoes and ice and cold winds? I doubt if I would say that anyone who goes there is fortunate."

"I have heard that Iceland is a very intriguing place," Linnea said.

"You are right, my dear young lady." Dr. Foster chuckled again and bowed his head toward her mother as he went on, "Your description of the bleak land better fits Greenland. My stop there will be brief before going on to Vinland."

"Vinland?" asked Linnea, seeing Nils's puzzlement, which he quickly hid. "Where is that?"

"We believe somewhere in Canada or the coast south of there." Locking his hands over his belly, he sighed. "Not that it is possible to go to the United States with the recent declaration of war between them and England. However, I hope to prove that the stories in the old *sagas* are true, and the Vikings reached the New World."

"The New World?" Nils asked quietly.

"America," Linnea murmured, hoping he had gotten that far in his study of the geography book she had seen him perusing several times in Papa's book-room. "You believe the *Norrfoolk* went that far?"

Dr. Foster tugged on his beard as his eyes narrowed. "I notice that both you and Lord Barrington speak that old Norse word in the way I have argued with other ancient history scholars is correct. Where did you learn to speak it so? Bradley at Cambridge refuses to acknowledge that my translation and pronunciation are correct."

"I am only pronouncing the word as I had guessed it would be pronounced," Linnea replied, making sure she still was smiling. Dr. Foster must not suspect that she had learned to speak the word from the only living Viking. "If it is wrong, Niles has been kind enough not to correct me."

"No, no," Dr. Foster said, "you are, in my opinion, quite accurate in the way you say it." He turned to Nils. "You would do well to heed exactly how she says it, Barrington. Your pronunciation is a bit different."

Nils chuckled. "I have noticed that as well, and I can assure you that I make it a practice to heed everything Lady Linnea has to say. She has proven very insightful about various matters of the past here at Sutherland Park."

Randolph quickly changed the subject to the various

events that would be held throughout the shire during the summer. When Mama enthusiastically discussed with him the upcoming fair at the parish church in the village just inland from Sutherland Park, Linnea relaxed back against the settee. She sipped her tea and hoped that the next discussion on this topic would end up as successfully. Dr. Foster seemingly accepted Nils as a colleague in the study of the Viking explorers.

When Mama announced that it was time for the gentlemen to enjoy some wine before dinner, Linnea was glad to come to her feet and bid them adieu. She said little more during dinner and the conversation that followed, again in the parlor, but this time with Martin and his wife present. Noting how Minnie avoided speaking to Randolph, Linnea promised herself that she would talk, on the first possible occasion, to her sister-in-law about her unexpected antipathy toward their neighbor.

It was nearly midnight when Randolph took his leave. Again he had to be satisfied with no more than a kiss on the cheek. She hurried up the stairs where her mother waited, watching to be certain nothing improper took place.

"What an interesting evening," Mama said as they climbed the stairs to the next floor. "I believe we should have another *conversazione* here soon. It is refreshing to speak of scientific discoveries and business matters."

"But you seemed so pleased to discuss the village fair with Randolph."

Lady Sutherland laughed. "You must learn to distinguish between being interested in something and being a good hostess."

"Mama!" She could not help laughing, too.

"You will learn the skills when you have a home and guests of your own." She paused where the hallway diverged toward Linnea's rooms. Putting her hand on Linnea's cheek, she said, "We shall speak more of this on the morrow, for I do not like how the light vanishes from your eyes at any mention of your future."

"Mama, if—"

"Do not fret, my dear child. All will come about as it is meant to be. For now, I must retire. I have accounts to review for your papa tomorrow morning, so I must be clear-eyed."

"Yes, Mama." She bid her mother good night, then turned down the quiet passage to her rooms. Once these hallways had been filled with conversation and laughter, but, one by one, her older siblings had left home, taking so much of the noise with them.

Opening her door, she was amazed to see only a single lamp was lit. Olive customarily had the room ablaze with light. She walked to light another, but halted when a tall silhouette rose from the windowseat.

"Nils," she breathed. She looked back at the closed door. "You should not be here."

"Jack is proving to be an excellent accomplice. He told me he would keep Olive busy in the kitchens for a few more minutes." He held out his hand. "Come, *unnasta.*"

She put her fingers on his wide palm and let him bring her to sit on the thick cushions of the windowseat. With only a single lamp unable to chase away all the shadows, there was no worry that someone would see that she was not sitting alone here.

"Nils—"

His finger against her lips slid down to her chin to tilt it toward him. "Let me look at your face in the moonlight. I have seen your smile in the sunshine, but now I want to see now how you would look beside me during the night."

She breathed his name in the moment before his lips stroked hers. He leaned her back onto the cushion, and she welcomed the pressure of his strong body pinning her beneath him. Sensations she could not name rushed through her when his motion introduced her to his undeniable desire. The hard lines urged her to cede herself to him.

With a groan, he drew back. Her protest was silenced by his mouth over hers before he whispered, "Jack cannot keep your maid away long enough for us to satisfy this craving."

"Then why are you here?"

His laugh was tinged with regret. "You know how to drive a man to desperation, *unnasta*. I wanted these stolen minutes to reassure you that you need not worry so much about him."

"Randolph?"

Linnea did not understand what Nils said, but she knew it was a curse. He released her and stood. When she feared he would walk out of the room, he faced her and spat, "Do not speak his name when you are in my arms."

"You know I do not love him." Swallowing roughly, she halted herself before she could let the words *as I love you* escape from her lips.

"But you have not told him to leave Sutherland Park with his futile dreams of marrying you."

"No."

When she added nothing more, he swore again. "I have no interest in speaking of Tuthill."

"So you must wish to speak of Dr. Foster. You are fascinated with him."

"As you would be fascinated by a poisonous snake."

An icy chill struck her as she rose and lit another lamp. "Do you think he is that dangerous for you?"

"All of you are." The back of his fingers grazed her cheek. "Dr. Foster has great interest about the past, and he is eager to learn more. However, the greatest danger comes from you, *unnasta*. You tempt me to forget my quest for anything but the sweetness that awaits me on your lips."

She was not certain if he or she was more surprised when she turned her face away from his. Leaning her hands on the wide window frame, she gazed out at the sea beyond the tamed gardens of Sutherland Park. "I do not know why you are staying here when Papa would give you a carriage to go to London."

"And where would I look? I need you to come with me to be my guide, Linnea." He stroked her hair. "There is much we could learn from one another."

"I told you I cannot travel alone with you to London."

"And I told you that I think that is an absurd restriction to put on a woman."

"Would you allow your sister to travel alone with a man who...a man who wants more than kisses from her? I think you would slay any man who suggested that to your sister." Linnea wanted to take back the words that reminded him too poignantly of the family that he had left behind so far back in time, but it was too late. In the windowpane, she could see the reflection of Nils's face as sorrow stole the rough edges from it. Whirling, she put her hands on his arms before he could walk away. "Forgive me for reminding you of your pain."

"You do not remind me of what I cannot forget." His shoulders squared as he looked past her to the shore. "I will never forget it. Never."

Eighteen

Nils heard the lighthearted voices from beyond the stable. Realizing that he had never explored in this direction, he walked around the paddock. The laughter grew louder as he approached a group of people clustered by another fenced area. There must be a half dozen people standing by the fence, but he could distinguish Linnea's musical laugh from all other sounds.

How long had it been since he had held her in her bedchamber? Six long days, but he would have guessed it was six years, for he had thought endlessly of that stolen moment when he had almost given into his longing for her. Since then, even when she had not been busy with tasks throughout the house, his time had been monopolized by Dr. Foster. Only Lady Sutherland's invitation for the professor to join her for a visit to her favorite roses had given Nils this chance to escape.

"Niles!" Linnea exclaimed as she turned to wave to him. "Do come and join *us*."

The slight emphasis she put on the last word was all the warning he needed. He had his smile firmly in place as he nodded to Tuthill, who was standing possessively close to Linnea. Trying not to glare at the hand Tuthill had on her arm, Nils added a greeting to Martin Sutherland and his wife.

"'Tis about time," Martin said, chuckling.

"For what?" Nils hoped his tone did not sound too cautious, but he did not want to assume the wrong thing from Linnea's brother's terse comment.

"For you to elude Dr. Foster's interrogation of you about everything Viking." Martin laughed again and slapped him companionably on the shoulder. "You are too blasted polite, man."

Nils looked at Linnea. How she had lamented that he would never learn what he needed to enter the Polite World unnoticed. Her gentle smile told him that his amazement was too visible. A jab of an elbow in his side forced his eyes away from hers.

Martin grinned broadly. "I was going to suggest that you tell him that not every thought you have is rooted in the distant past, but eventually his eyes are going to show him that, I would suspect."

"Martin, watch what you say," his wife hissed. "You are going to embarrass him."

Nils was not sure if she meant him or Tuthill, so he said nothing as Martin put his arm around his wife. Something unanticipated pinched Nils. Jealousy? Not of Tuthill, who was drawing Linnea closer to the fence to put some distance between them and Nils, but of Martin, who could be so open with his affection for his wife.

He went to stand by the fence as well and discovered it was a sheepfold. A wild bleating filled the air as a husky man tilted one of the sheep on its side and clipped the wool from it.

Leaning his elbows on the wooden rail, he let his hands drape over the side. "You might find it an easier chore if you sit the sheep back on its haunches and shear it that way," he called to the struggling man.

"You know how to shear a sheep?" asked Linnea, her eyes wide.

"I have...had—" He cleared his throat when he realized Linnea was not the only one listening. He could

not tell her now of how the sheep-filled meadows had
climbed the sides of the fjord where he had spent his
boyhood. Nor could he share the tales of the festivals
and how his father had taught him to take the wool
from a sheep in a single piece with a few slashes of a
sharp knife. The stories of that time must wait until
they were alone. Quietly, he added, "I have had
experience with many of the aspects of farming. When
I have not been traveling, I have enjoyed tending to the
husbandry on my lands."

"I did not realize that a *Norrfoolk*—"

"Linnea, despite what you and Dr. Foster think, I
have a life beyond my studies."

She stiffened, then smiled when Tuthill asked her
what was wrong. The expression was so brittle he
feared she would shatter. This subterfuge bothered her
more with every passing day. So accustomed was she
to being the pampered youngest child of her well-
respected father that she had never needed to learn to
hide her true thoughts from an enemy.

Now she must learn and learn well.

Tuthill asked, "Is something bothering you, Linnea?
You know this does not harm the sheep."

"Yes, I know." Her answer was meek, but her tone
was not.

Nils silenced his chuckle as Tuthill began to explain
in precise detail the whole process of shearing. No
wonder Tuthill was completely oblivious to her lack of
interest in becoming his wife. He ignored everything
she said and did, assuming she was more witless than a
child.

Linnea's smile returned when Minnie Sutherland
linked their arms, and the two women went to another
pen where the lambs were bleating as they waited for
the ewes to be returned.

Martin arched a dark brow. "I do wonder what the
two of them are plotting now. I hope it is nothing that
will require more dancing."

"Dancing is not horrible," Tuthill retorted. "There was plenty of it at your sister Dinah's wedding."

"Enough for me for a while."

Nils could not restrain this laugh.

Tuthill scowled at him and turned on his heel to go to where the women were stretching their hands through the fence to pet the lambs.

Rolling his eyes, Martin said, "He assumes every comment is aimed at him and Linnea's indecision."

"Rightly so, for she has been delaying that decision for some time it seems."

"That is a woman's way." He shrugged. "Tuthill is a fine man. I am not sure why she is hesitating. I know our father would be glad to be done with the whole of this marriage situation, so he can concentrate on the important concerns of his businesses."

Nils did not reply as Martin went to stand beside his wife. By Thor's hammer! He had not guessed that Linnea's brother was in favor of this match. The reasons Martin gave were practical, but the truth was that Linnea would be miserable with Tuthill.

Wandering in the opposite direction, for he wanted to compose his thoughts before he said the very thing that would worsen the whole of this, he realized he could not let her be forced into this marriage that would make her miserable. She had saved his life. For that, he owed her his help in saving her from becoming Tuthill's bride.

"You are a man of honor, Nils Bjornsson."

The words, in his own language, halted him in midstep. He stared at the form in front of him. The muscular man in his middle years was dressed in simple clothing of gray and blue. A dark bird sat on each shoulder, and two large dogs stood on either side of him. Not dogs. Wolves. Nils choked back his shock when he saw the man had only one eye.

"Odin?" he asked, not sure if he believed his own question. The greatest of all gods had traded one of his eyes at the well of wisdom for more knowledge.

"I had thought to see what so interested Loki and Freya." The god chuckled, the sound like a harsh winter wind in Nils's ears.

Nils started to kneel, but Odin's raised hand halted him.

"You can see and hear me, son of the *Norrfoolk*, but others cannot. They will question your mind's strength if you prostrate yourself in these sheep droppings."

"As you wish, so shall it be."

"It is not as I wish. I had expected to see you at the table of the heroes in *Valhalla*."

"The shame upon my family must be cleansed."

Odin nodded. "That is true."

"My brother's shame is mine and all my family's. When I have returned the knife to my chieftain, then the shame will be forgotten as if it never existed."

"And will you meet your brother in a *holmgänga*?"

Nils shook his head. He could not imagine slaying his own brother in the one-on-one duel to the death beyond the reach of the laws of the *Norrfoolk*. "He has joined the others who were outlawed in seeking a place to live in Greenland to the far west. To chase him there will bring only more disgrace on my family. My blood-enemy here is the son of Kort. He and I will meet in a *holmgänga* if I can find him."

"You are a man of honor, Nils Bjornsson. That is why I am here. Your success so far—"

"Success? I have done nothing." He bowed his head. "Forgive me, Allfather, for interrupting you."

"You are my child." Odin put his huge hand on Nils's shoulder, the weight nearly driving Nils to his knees. An icy chill flooded out from the god's fingers. "Your success so far is measured by the fact that you still breathe and that you are closing in on the treasure you seek. You should know that there are those in *Asgard* who believe you would fail. There are those who wish you to fail. There are those who wish to see the old battles fought once more, so that mortals know the old gods have not vanished, but only are waiting for the time to return. It is because of those many beliefs in how your quest should unravel that you remain alive. Loki dares not kill you when there are others intrigued by your experiences here in the land of the English. Be wary in all that you do, Nils Bjornsson."

"I shall."

Odin's single eye narrowed. "This is not my time or my place any longer. Fare well, Nils Bjornsson. I shall not see you again until you sup at my table...if that is to be."

He was gone.

Nils took a deep breath and released it slowly through his clenched teeth. Odin would not have brought him this warning as a jest. The Allfather, who ruled from his high throne, was not like Loki.

How had his quest become entangled with the halls of *Asgard*? None of this made any sense, but that did not matter. He must do as he had vowed.

His foot struck something that skittered across the ground. Picking it up, he saw it was a discarded ram's horn. He drew his knife and slashed the blade across the narrow end, smoothing it. He blew through it. The low, haunting sound rushed from the wider section of horn. Turning to face the north, he saw everyone around the sheepfold had paused. He paid them no mind as he blew in the horn again.

The sound rushed through him like the pounding of strength that filled a warrior's body in the moments before he entered battle. This was the call to rush to a ship that was waiting in the fjord. His comrades would scurry from their cottages, so the hillside was dotted with the light from a score of torches. With each man came his family to wish him good fortune and good hunting on this journey to distant shores.

It was the call to battle.

His battle.

In this place he had visited before but in this time he had never imagined.

***

"Do you want to raise a cloud with us, Niles?" Lord Sutherland held out an open box.

Nils reached for the odd article that he had seen the other men holding in their mouths while they burned one end of it. By Thor's hammer, he should have asked Linnea to explain what the purpose of the odious smoke was.

"It may not be as finely rolled a cigar as what the earl is accustomed to." Tuthill's cool voice held a challenge, although Nils was not sure what setting fire to a rolled collection of leaves was intended to prove.

Tuthill should not be pouting like a child. Through the afternoon and even at dinner, he had used every opportunity to turn the conversation to Dr. Foster's research. The professor had gleefully prattled on and on about his work and peppered Nils with questions. While he attempted to answer them without revealing the truth, Tuthill had ogled Linnea. Maybe Tuthill had expected Nils to retire for the evening when Dr. Foster had. Instead, Nils had joined their host and his son and Tuthill here in the book-room in the hope that Linnea might come to bid her father good night.

He needed to talk to her. Odin's words were a warning that there was little time left. They must go to London posthaste.

"I cannot say what an earl should or should not like, for I have not led an earl's life long," Nils said in response to Tuthill's sharp comment. Nils might as well be honest when he could. Even a hint of the truth might unnerve Tuthill enough to keep him from getting too close to the whole of Nils's past. "However, I assume that because Lord Sutherland is offering these to us they meet his standards."

Lord Sutherland's brows shot up. "You are only

recently in receipt of your title? Who held it before? Mayhap I knew the previous earl."

"I doubt that. My uncle was seldom anywhere but at his dirty acres." He chuckled as he recounted the story that Linnea had devised for him. Determined to stick to the simple facts, because anything intricate might trip him later, he said, "I fear I have inherited more than his title, for he also was fascinated by the past. He traveled often in pursuit of his studies, but only through books. In that way, we differ. I like to *see* the places I am studying, so I have been wandering throughout this part of the island in search of the sites I have read about."

Tuthill took a brand from the hearth and lit his cigar. Holding it out to Nils, he said, "You will find it smokes more easily if you clip off an end first."

"Here." Lord Sutherland took the cigar and snapped a small tool against its end. "You would need three hands otherwise, my boy."

Nils noticed how Tuthill stiffened when Linnea's father addressed Nils in such a friendly tone. "Thank you, Sutherland." He held the cigar between his fingers as Sutherland did.

The smoke was acrid. It twisted up and around his face like a savage cat trying to claw its way up through his nose and into his brain. He started to draw in a deep breath, then halted. The odor now was burning in his chest. Holding the cigar up to his lips as the other men did, he began to cough.

Tuthill sneered, "Too strong for you, Barrington?"

"A tickle...in my throat," he gasped, not wanting to admit the viscount was correct. He picked up his glass of wine and downed half of it in a single gulp. It eased the fire in his lungs, but the smoke still curled up and around him from the cigar. Setting it down beside his glass, he stood. "Pardon me."

"Are you all right, my boy?" Lord Sutherland asked.

"I am fine." That was a blatant lie. "I will return after a visit to the necessary."

His host chuckled and waved his hand to dismiss him. "Hurry back. I want your opinion on where best to direct Dr. Foster tomorrow to keep him out of what little hair I have left."

"Of course." Nils walked out of the room, closing the door behind him.

Retching, he rushed to the far end of the hall and threw open the doors that led to a balcony. Fresh air! He wanted fresh air. He gulped mouthfuls, then sat on the stones and looked out to sea. Leaning his head back against the wall of the house, he sighed. He must be more careful. Another mistake like that could divulge the truth.

"I shall close the door, Mama. I—Niles!" Linnea slipped out the door and, closing it, dropped to her knees beside him. "Are you all right?"

"Yes."

"You are a rather bilious shade of green."

"No doubt." He held up his sleeve and sniffed it. Choking, he offered it to her.

She sniffed and pulled back. "Cigar smoke! I hate its smell. It makes me nauseous.

"Apparently it does the same to me."

Linnea stared at Nils's strained face. Egad! She had not paused to guess that he never had smoked before. Tobacco would have been unknown in England in his time. No wonder he appeared such an odd shade.

She did not intend to, but she began to laugh. Once she started, she could not stop. She pressed her hands to her side as her laughter stitched a pain in it.

"Your compassion is touching," he said dryly.

"I am sorry." She sat back on her heels. "But I find it so amusing that a man who has fought incredible battles, sailed across the sea in a ship that is not much bigger than a carriage and four, and can make a ram's horn into a musical instrument is laid so low by the smell of a cigar."

"It is quite ironic, isn't it?"

"You will need to accustom yourself to the smell. Gentlemen often smoke cigars and pipes in London."

His eyes glittered strangely as he rose to his knees. Taking her hands, he pressed them to his chest. "*Unnasta*, let us leave for London tomorrow."

"Tomorrow?" She stared up into his eyes that burned with his obsession. "Nils, I told you why we must wait until Papa goes to Town."

"Bring Olive with you. Then you are not traveling alone."

"But—"

"Bring Jack as well. Between them, they will provide all the chaperones you require." He released her hands and gently clasped her face. "*Unnasta*, if you bring them with us—"

"Even if Mama and Papa would consider allowing us to travel so, it does not matter. I promised Randolph I would be by his side to greet his guests at an assembly he is having on Saturday evening." She drew his hands down from her cheeks. "That is only four days from now. Once I have done that, we can talk more about this."

"Are you so sure that we will be able to talk more about this then?"

"Of course. After the assembly—"

"Where Tuthill expects you to announce that you will marry him."

She hesitated, then nodded. "Yes, he expects that."

"He will not appreciate having his betrothed leaving for London with another man."

"I did not say that I would marry him."

"You did not say that you would not."

She gripped his hands tightly. "Nils, I must go to this assembly. Mayhap I will be able to find the way to tell Randolph the truth in a way that will not hurt him."

"Forget Tuthill. It is imperative that we leave posthaste."

"Nils, I *promised* him."

He slid his hands out of hers and sighed. "As you promised to help me?"

"It is a pledge I intend to keep."

"But, Linnea, you do not understand. We must leave without delay."

"Why? What has changed so much that we cannot wait a few more days?"

He stood. "You would not believe me if I told you, Linnea."

"You sound frightened." Coming to her feet, she clutched onto his arms. "I never thought I would see you frightened."

"Nor did I. I thought no one was braver than Nils Bjornsson, who was respected by his allies and feared by his enemies."

"But?"

He clasped her elbows, drawing her to him. "But what happened to me today, what I saw and heard, you will not believe."

"I am trying, Nils." She leaned her head against his chest. "I wish I could believe."

"It may not matter if you believe or not." He rested his head atop hers as he told her of Odin's words to him. He paused, then said, "If I do not complete my quest soon, all may be lost."

She stepped back. "But I promised Randolph."

"I know." He slanted his mouth across hers for only the length of one beat of her swift pulse. "I will not ask you to break any promise you make."

"I *will* help you. Let me think of a way to persuade Mama and Papa to let me escort you to London. There must be a way."

"I hope so." He turned and looked out at the sea rising and falling in its endless rhythm. "I hope there still is a way to complete my quest."

"And if you don't?" She tried not to let too much hope enter her voice. If he did not fulfill his vow, he would have to stay here...with her.

"I don't know."

Nineteen

"An outing? How wonderful!" Linnea tried to sound enthusiastic. It was not easy when all her thoughts were focused on how bleak Nils's face had been during their short conversation on the balcony the previous night.

Minnie smiled. "Yes, I thought it could be just Martin and me and Randolph and..." She hesitated, then said, "Niles."

"What?" Linnea realized Minnie was staring past her. Twisting to look over her shoulder, she saw Nils entering the room. She understood why her sister-in-law's mouth was open and her eyes wide.

Nils was dressed to take a ride about the countryside. His elegantly cut coat did not give any hints that it had been remade for him from one of Martin's. Somehow, the shoulders of the coat had been widened to accommodate his broader ones. His nankeen trousers that hooked beneath his brilliantly polished shoes accented the lean strength of his legs.

"Oh, my!" Minnie whispered.

"What is wrong?" Linnea asked.

Her sister-in-law shook herself, looked at Linnea and quickly away, but not before guilt flashed on her face.

Putting her hand on Minnie's arm, Linnea

murmured, "It is not a horrible thing to look at other men when you are wed. After all, men look at women all the time."

"Linnea!" Minnie giggled, then put her hand over her mouth to hide the sound as Nils came closer.

"Will you share the jest?" he asked.

That set Minnie off onto another round of giggles.

Linnea chuckled as she said, "It was something I doubt a man would understand."

"Or something he would be wise not to delve too deeply into?"

"Exactly." Putting her arm around her sister-in-law's quivering shoulders, she said, "Minnie was just speaking to me about an outing she thought we might enjoy."

"An outing? Where?"

Minnie composed herself enough to say, "An *al fresco* meal."

"By the shore," Linnea hurried to explain when she saw the confusion on Nils's face. "We would take the food there and eat on blankets."

"And this is something you enjoy?"

"Yes."

"Even when you get sand in your food?"

Linnea laughed. "The idea is to enjoy the sunshine and the water and to get away from the decorum of eating here in the house. We have the opportunity to set aside the napery and eat with our fingers."

"Ah, I understand," he said, although she was not sure if he did.

Minnie stood. "I shall let Cook know. Randolph should be here soon. He told Martin that he would be calling before midday today."

Nodding, Linnea waited until her sister-in-law was out of earshot before she asked, "Were you planning to go for a ride, Nils?"

"Yes."

"To London?"

"There is no reason to go without you."

"I have already spoken to Mama. She is willing to listen, suggesting that Minnie might like to go to Town to visit some friends. It is a wondrous idea. Minnie loves any chance to go to London to call on the friends she has made. Having Minnie with us will give countenance to the whole arrangement."

"Or I could simply abduct you from the spot where you stand." He stepped so close that his beguiling strength seemed to overmaster her. "I could sweep you up into my arms and run out of this house with you."

"You could," she whispered, losing herself in the mysterious depths of his glorious eyes.

"I would toss you into a carriage and shout the order to take us to London without delay."

"You could."

His finger traced an aimless path along her shoulder. "It is not a short journey, so we would have to find a way to spend the time."

"We could speak of how best to find the knife."

"Or we could become lovers." A roguish smile tilted his lips. "The motion of a carriage would not be as wondrous as making love with you on the deck of my ship, but it would do."

"Would do?" She laughed, trying to ignore the images his brazen words suggested.

"I would and so would you."

"You presume much, my lord Viking. I am no frightened lass hiding from your rapacious pursuits."

He laughed. "When I hold you, you would see that the pursuit is over and the prize has been won. Or I simply could toss you over my shoulder and take you to your room and show you there what you have denied us."

"You would not dare." When he smiled, she whispered, "You would not, would you?"

A devilish twinkle brightened his violet eyes as his arm crept around her waist. "You have changed me,

unnasta. In times past, no Englishwoman would have
dared deny me any request I made. Then, if we had
met, you would have gladly taken me to London to keep
me and my comrades away from your home and family."

"Then, if we had met, I would gladly have seen
you with a blade driven deep into you."

"True." He whispered against her ear, "A knife is
not what I would like to drive deep within you, *unnasta.*"

"Nils!"

His hushed laugh sifted through her, as electrifying
as if she had tried to capture a bolt of lightning in her
bare hands. "Be honest. Tell me, *unnasta,* that you
have not had thoughts of the ecstasy we could share,
and I will speak of them no more."

"I have had such thoughts." She stroked his wind-
scored cheek. "Many, many times."

"Then we should—"

Linnea heard the same footfalls Nils had. Stepping
away from him, she hoped no one detected her high
color as she went to speak with her brother and
Randolph, who must have just arrived because he was
smoothing wrinkles from his coat. She tried to heed
what they were saying and to answer, but she was too
aware of Nils. He was more than an arm's length from
her, but her skin tingled as if he held her. When he
spoke with her brother about whether to take horses or
to walk to the spot where they would be having their
meal, she could have sworn she was a marionette and
he was the puppeteer. She seemed somehow connected
to him with invisible strings that pulsed with all the
longing that she could no longer deny.

She wondered how much longer she would be able
to hide this desire for a man who should not even be
here with her. And what would happen if she did not
keep denying it...

***

Sunshine burnished the sand to brilliant off-white.
This cove was not the one where Linnea had found Nils,

for the walls of the cliffs were higher but not as steep. This cove was on the opposite side of the boulders that had not been by the sea in Nils's time. Two open carriages waited by the boulders. On the cove's far side, trees grew nearly to the tideline, offering some respite from the hot sunlight.

Linnea sat beside Minnie, her parasol knocking her sister-in-law's if she was careless. The wool blanket beneath them itched, and she would have preferred soft sand to dig her toes into. But Minnie came to the strand only when she could have these comforts, so Linnea acquiesced.

Farther along the shore, Martin and Randolph were fishing. She could not remember the last time her brother had caught any fish in this cove, but he relished the chance to try. She considered telling him that Jack regularly pulled fish from the next cove. She did not. Although Nils had been all alone on the deserted beach when they found him, something from his time might linger beneath the waters where a chance cast could find it.

Linnea laughed as Scamp ran past, showering her with sand. Calling the puppy's name, she was surprised when he trotted back to her. He usually paid her little attention. When he raced past her again, she heard a laugh behind her.

She smiled at Nils. No wonder Scamp had seemed to obey her. He adored Nils. Did Scamp believe in his puppyish brain that Nils was *his* pet because Scamp had found him on the shore?

"You are a troublemaker, pup," Nils said, holding out his fingers for Scamp to sniff.

Scamp's tail wagged so rapidly that it was a golden blur as the puppy stuck his head under Nils's hand in a plea to be petted.

"He makes his wants known, doesn't he?" Nils squatted beside the puppy which jumped up to put front paws on Nils's knee.

"He does." Linnea stretched to stroke Scamp's silken head.

Nils put his fingers over hers, caressing them as gently as she was the puppy. "We could learn a lesson from his honesty."

"A hazardous lesson." She glanced at Minnie, whose eyes were closed. Was her sister-in-law asleep?

"Nothing is gained without some peril," Nils whispered.

"Is that the creed of the *Norrfoolk*?"

His fingers entwined with hers as he leaned closer to her. "It is my creed." He yelped when Scamp began digging furiously in the sand, spraying it over him.

When he reached for the puppy, Scamp pulled Linnea's stockings from the blanket and fled with them.

Linnea laughed as Nils ran after the puppy to retrieve them. Scamp criss-crossed the sand, leading Nils on a wild chase. Nils almost caught the puppy, but Scamp squirmed away and sped under the line from Martin's fishing pole.

Cornering the puppy against the cliffs, Nils scooped him up and brought him back to Linnea. He dropped Scamp on her lap. "I will let you extract your stockings from him, so I cannot be accused of ruining them."

"Thank you."

"You could thank me more by..." He smiled at Minnie as she reached over to pat Scamp. As if there had been no pause, he added, "Telling me, Linnea, where that chilled wine is being kept."

Although she wished she could have offered him the kisses she guessed he wanted as his reward, she pointed toward the cliffs. "There is a small stream that runs beneath the overhang. Martin put the container in the water to keep it cool."

"Thank you." Setting himself on his feet, he said, "I will bring you ladies some wine, if that is your pleasure."

"Yes," Minnie said, although Linnea could barely

hear her through the thunder rushing through her head.

The pleasure she wanted with Nils had nothing to do with a glass of wine. It had everything to do with those strong fingers that could be so gentle and his lips that promised such delight.

"He is quite taken with you, Linnea," said Minnie as Nils walked toward the stream.

"I have noticed that."

"And you are as taken with him?"

She picked up a stick and hurled it so Scamp could chase after it.

"You are avoiding giving me any answer," Minnie said.

"Yes."

Minnie chuckled. "That single word speaks volumes."

"Niles is here to do his studies, and then he will be leaving." She picked up the stick that Scamp brought back to her. Flinging it toward a large tree to the left, she said, "He has made that clear from the beginning."

"Good intentions are often changed when love enters into the mix."

Linnea smiled at her sister-in-law. "His obligations are very important to him, and I doubt if anyone will waylay him from doing them. You need not waste your matchmaking on us." She hoped Minnie did not notice her shiver of delight when she spoke of Nils and her.

"I am not worried about matchmaking for the two of you. It seems you have begun on that road yourself." Minnie lowered her voice as she glanced at the men. "I know Martin very much believes that you should be settled in marriage with Lord Tuthill, but I would be glad to speak to Martin to ask him to talk to your father about—"

"You barely know Niles!"

"True, but I know Randolph Denner."

Linnea stared. She had guessed that Minnie disliked Randolph, but not so much that she was willing to try to persuade Martin to change his mind. "Speak plainly, Minnie," she begged.

"There is nothing I can say that you do not already know. Lord Tuthill is a fine man, and he would make someone a good husband. *Someone*, Linnea, but not you."

"I have not told him I will marry him."

"Good."

Linnea was astonished anew by Minnie's fervor, but she said, "Minnie, I need to ask a favor of you."

"Of course. You know you need only ask."

"It is...It is an important favor, and I do not want you to feel uncomfortable if you cannot agree."

"You appear to be uncomfortable just asking."

"I am."

Minnie giggled. "I have just the dandy. I will tell you a secret that you must keep to yourself. That way, you are doing *me* a favor, because I cannot keep this secret to myself any longer, and I should not tell anyone."

"If you should not tell anyone—"

"But I must!" She smiled as she grasped Linnea's hands. "Oh, do me this favor, Linnea, before I quite burst from having told no one. If you do me this favor, I shall gladly do whatever you wish."

Linnea nodded, again overwhelmed by Minnie's vehemence. "Of course. What is your secret?"

Putting her finger to her lips, Minnie leaned forward to whisper, "I am going to have a baby!"

"You are?" Linnea flung her arms around her sister-in-law. There had been so many whispered asides about the marriage that had not produced an heir. Now all the suppositions that Minnie Sutherland had been a poor choice as the wife of Lord Sutherland's heir would be silenced. "Oh, Minnie! I am so happy for you and Martin."

"But you must tell no one. Not even your parents. We want to be certain that nothing goes amiss."

"I believe they will begin to notice in short order that you are not the shape you have been."

"By then, I will have told them." She hesitated, then said, "There have been other times, Linnea, but something went wrong within weeks."

"I had no idea."

"No one knew but Martin, and we want to be sure before we let everyone else be excited. However, this is the longest I have been able to carry our child, so I just had to share with someone."

She hugged Minnie again. "You know I will tell no one until you and Martin decide to spread the joyous news. Papa will be so proud that I doubt he will be able to keep his waistcoat buttons from popping."

"I know." Minnie folded her hands in her lap. "Now, tell me what favor you want me to do for you."

Linnea blinked, torn from her joy by a sudden burst of disappointment. She could not ask Minnie to make the trip to London with her and Nils. That might put the unborn baby at risk. Patting her sister-in-law's hands, she smiled. "It will have to wait."

"Oh, Linnea!" Her eyes grew wide. "I promised you that I would do you a favor in return for keeping this secret. Now..."

"You will do me the very best favor possible by taking care of yourself and that baby."

"But—"

"I say that with all sincerity." Linnea looked past Minnie to where Nils was striding back toward them. Somehow, she would have to explain this to him without revealing the truth. A promise made was never broken. Ever.

Twenty

Nils tossed his cards to the blanket as he listened to Tuthill launch into another explanation of why investing in shipping at this time was foolhardy. Although he wanted to tell Tuthill that a sea-wise captain could elude any blockade or even a warship in pursuit, he did not. That would create questions he would find difficult to answer. If he had had more time, Linnea could have taught him to read the symbols that were in the books in her father's book-room.

He ignored the cards that should have won him this game as he stood. "Linnea, there is an old mound just inshore from here that I promised Dr. Foster I would visit today." When she winced, he clamped his lips closed. Something was bothering her. With the mound? Or the professor? He could not ask her when the others were listening.

She put her hand on the one he held out. "Yes, there is."

"Will you show me where it is?" He closed his fingers over her trembling ones. When she did not meet his gaze, he had to fight not to frown. What was bothering her was not a small thing.

Tuthill did not hesitate to scowl. "Linnea, I thought you were going to spend the afternoon at the shore."

"I had told Niles I would show him that small

mound near the spring just up this stream." Linnea glanced at Nils, and he saw her disquiet as she asked, "Would you like to come with us?"

"More Viking ruins?" Tuthill's nose wrinkled. "Do you ever think of anything else, Barrington?"

"I have been known to on occasion."

Minnie hid her face against her husband's shoulder. Nils almost laughed aloud as he saw how she quivered with silent laughter.

Linnea's voice was still quiet. "You are welcome to go with us up to the old mound, Randolph."

"I will meet you back here." Tuthill kept his gaze on the cards he held. "I have no interest in mucking about today, and, to own the truth, I am enjoying my best winning streak in years."

Nils did not give Linnea a chance to ask him again. If he did not know better, he would have thought she *wanted* Tuthill to come with them. She said nothing as they walked toward the path that led up from the beach. When she drew her hand out of his and again refused to meet his gaze, he knew something was amiss.

Terribly amiss.

"This way," Linnea said, her voice flat as she climbed the path.

He edged in front of her and turned to face her, walking slowly backward. "Do you need help?"

"I have been climbing up and down these cliffs since I was a small child."

"I did not mean that."

She looked back at the strand. "Can we speak of this later?"

"When we are out of earshot of the others?"

"And out of their view?"

His body tightened at the thought of being alone with her. Then, noting the despair in her eyes, he sighed. Whatever was troubling her was not inconsequential, so it must be dealt with before they gave themselves to rapture. How many more barricades would be placed in their way before they could savor the passion that should be theirs?

"Yes," he replied. "Past the top of the hill." His eyes narrowed as he saw Tuthill come to his feet. "Do you think your suitor will follow us?"

Linnea turned when she heard the frustration in Nils's voice. She waited, then realized Randolph was going only as far as the stream to refill his glass from the bottle of cooled wine there. Walking up the path, she looked back again to see him sitting with his cards in his hands.

"Odd," she murmured.

"I would ask what is odd, but everything is."

She smiled. Trust Nils to try to bolster her spirits! "It is not like Randolph to be so fixated on gambling."

He drew her up over the edge of the cliff. "You have mentioned to me more than once while you taught me how to survive in the Polite World that men of this time choose to gamble on the slightest matter."

"Papa told me of three men in his club when he was a young man who wagered heavily on which way a raindrop would slide down a windowpane."

"I would rather wager on my own skills than the laws of chance, which favor no man."

She smiled. "Papa would say it was because those men preferred the chance of a great loss to the work that would guarantee a strong victory."

"Your father is a very wise man." He did not release her hand as she led the way through the knee-high grass. "A millennium ago, he would have been well-respected as a great leader."

"The family history speaks of ancestors who have fought for England in every conflict since the Conquest." She chuckled. "Mayhap before."

"I am glad that I did not ever face your ancestor across bare blades." Whirling her into his arms, he kissed her lightly. "*Unnasta*, if I had, you might not have been here to help me."

She pushed away before he could kiss her again. She must explain to him what Minnie had told her. As she saw the warm glow in his eyes, she hesitated. The truth would destroy the pleasant afternoon for him. She would tell him later.

Coward! The word rang through her head in an unfamiliar voice. Not hers, for the voice was masculine, but it was not Nils's. She glanced behind her and saw no one nearby. *Coward!*

Shaking her head, Linnea continued along the path, almost invisible among the undergrowth. The mound was a bare spot among the trees growing more closely together away from the cliff's edge. Grass and wildflowers covered the top of the mound, but no trees had ever taken root in it, distinguishing it as different from other hills along the downs.

Hearing branches crash behind her, Linnea turned to see Nils pushing through the brush. "What are you doing?" she asked.

"There is a stone here."

"A stone?" She tried to follow him.

He held back the branches so she could slip through. He knelt by a gray stone. "I believe it is a marker stone." He brushed more of the undergrowth aside. "It is carved with writing."

"Writing?" She peered at the faded lines that resembled birds' legs and talons. "I cannot read it."

He ran his fingers along the lines and cursed.

"What is it?" she asked.

"The first letters here spell Kortsson's name."

"Why would he carve his name here?"

"As a warning to me."

"That makes no sense," she said. "He knows you know he is here. Why would he taunt you like this?"

"It is not a taunt, but a threat. See the rest of this? It says: *This stone was raised by Hardar Karlisson in the memory of his father Karli Mottulsson.*"

"It is a grave? Martin always has suspected this

was some sort of gravesite. Mayhap that is its tombstone." She looked at the mound, then whispered, "Did Kortsson carve those letters to tell you that he plans to kill you?"

"He knows I know of his plans. He chose this place, I would guess, because he wants to remind me of my tarnished honor."

"What do you mean?"

He tapped the stone. "It is unlikely there was ever a corpse beneath this soil. Not a body of any of the *Norrfoolk*. This is a tribute stone. The body would not be here. At his death, such a well-respected man usually is burned with his ship, horses, and slaves."

She recoiled, horror icing her face. "Horses and slaves are burned, too?"

"It is an honor to join one's master in *Valhalla*."

"That is barbaric. I shudder at the thought of innocent beasts and people being forced to die like that."

"It never has been by force. In my time, maidens offered themselves as sacrifices to join a chieftain in death. It was a great honor."

"It is—"

He stood. Gripping her shoulders, he pulled her closer. "Do not repeat that it was barbaric. Those women had the choice of offering themselves for such an honor. They were not like women now, who are traded like chattel to husbands who openly dishonor them by keeping mistresses. They are not docile like the women now, who are selected by their husbands only because they need an heir and the money a wife may bring to fill empty coffers."

"But at least the bride does not end up dead."

"She still breathes, but is she truly alive as she waits on a parade of callers whose existence is as miserable as hers?"

Linnea arched her shoulder to break Nils's hold on her. It was futile, for he was too strong. Instead she lashed out with, "You do not know what you are talking about!"

"No? I have closely watched those within your house and those who attended your sister's wedding. I have seen how wives and husbands act toward one another. They often treat each other with contempt."

"Not all of them. My parents have a happy life together, and Martin and Minnie..." She did not want to speak of Minnie now, because that reminded her too clearly about the truth she was hiding from Nils.

"They seem to be the exception, from what I have observed. It seems wrong to spend one's life being unhappy."

"Why are we arguing? I agree with you."

"Do you? With all your heart? Most women in my time had a voice in deciding which man they would wed."

"That was *your* time."

"And you think the ways of this time are right?" he asked as they went back to the path.

"These ways are the only ones I know."

"But do you think they are right?"

Linnea walked back to the edge of the cliff and looked out toward the sea. Perching on a rock, she said, "I think everyone should have the right to be happy, as long as their happiness does not cause pain to another."

"You are not answering my question." He sat beside her. His hand leaned on the rock behind her.

All she needed to do was rest back against his arm, which would be only slightly less unyielding than the boulder. Then his fingers would sweep up her as he pulled her up against his muscular chest. His mouth would brush hers with the question that became more intense each time they were together alone.

Beneath her fingers, the soft hair curling along his arm kept her from severing all connection with him. Then she wondered if that was even possible. All her thoughts centered on him, all her dreams included him, all her longings were for him.

"I cannot answer your question," she said as his arm curved around her. "I am thinking of your blood-enemy and how he might be watching us even now."

"No, he is not here."

"How do you know?"

"I would have seen him. I will deal with him when he is brave enough to show his face to me. Do not think of such a dreary subject on such a nice day."

She smiled. "You call this day merely nice? What could be more beautiful than a day that is sunny and warm?"

"A day that is sunny and warm upon the waves. Nothing is like being on the sea."

She bit her lip when she saw the longing in his eyes. There was a sadness she had never seen before. The intensity of it ached through her as if it were her own. Putting her hand on his shoulder, she remained as silent as he was. Tears burned in her eyes when he put his hand over hers. His gaze remained on the distant horizon where the sky fell into the water.

"If you were to go on one of the ships that are currently sailing," she whispered, then faltered for she did not want him to leave.

He looked at her. "*Unnasta*, I have seen pictures of the ships the English sail now. They are grand and glorious and separate a man almost completely from the sea. I want to feel the spray scouring my face and know that the stars are hanging above me when I sleep."

"On the main deck—"

"Which is twice a man's height above the waterline, mayhap even more." He sighed as his gaze turned back to the sea. "I need to feel the water only a board's breadth beneath my feet so that my ship and I are a part of the waves' mighty dance. Maybe I will change my mind when I step aboard one of the ships in the harbor in London."

"Nils, about London...I must tell you," she said

quietly, unable to be dishonest with him a moment longer and let him hope for something that had become unlikely, "that I asked Minnie, and she cannot go to London at the week's end with us."

Nils's arm clenched beneath her fingertips, but his voice remained tranquil. "If Minnie is unable to go after Tuthill's gathering, maybe your brother—"

"No, Martin will not be able to go, either." She blinked back tears. She did not want to hurt Nils like this, but she could not risk Minnie's baby, either.

"Have you spoken to him of this?"

She shook her head. "I do not need to. I know what his answer will be."

"You seemed so certain Minnie would be interested in paying calls on her friends."

"I thought she would be, but she cannot go now."

"Did she give you a good reason why not?"

"Yes."

"And?"

Taking a deep breath, she met his gaze evenly. "I cannot explain further. I promised."

His brow furrowed as he stood. "You promised what?"

"To say nothing of why Minnie cannot go."

"You are talking in circles."

Linnea reached out to take his hand. "I know it sounds that way, but I must ask you to trust me yet again. Let me talk to Mama and Papa and—"

He swore viciously in English, then with words she could not understand.

"Nils, it is not a frivolous reason that keeps Minnie from being able to travel with us." She reached for his hands again, but he locked them behind his back as he strode away along the cliff. She jumped down, running after him. "Why are you angry at me? I have done the best I can."

Nils fought his need to go back to Linnea and accept what he knew was her heartfelt apology. He could not.

Because of some silly vow she had given her sister-in-law, she was preventing him—*again*—from satisfying the blood-oath he had given his chieftain. "I have wasted weeks waiting for you to help me."

"Help you?" She caught up with him and grabbed his arm. Fury honed her voice and snapped in her eyes. "Nils Bjornsson, all I have done for the past month has been in an attempt to help you! I have made certain you had food and were tended to and learned what you needed to in order to survive here and—"

Seizing her shoulders, he pulled her to him, his mouth covering hers. He was hungry for every bit of her. That hunger threatened to make him forget everything but her. He must not. But as he feasted on her beauty, he longed to loosen her silken hair and let it flow against him as he tasted her mouth's sweetness until he was sated. Along her slender curves, outlined by the modest style of her lavender gown, his gaze wandered with the eagerness of a winter-weary man emerging to embrace the sun.

The whisper of his name in her beguiling voice resonated in his heart. Her fingers steered his hungry lips back over hers, and he tightened his arms around her. His hands reacquainted themselves with her supple body as he sampled the dulcet textures of her face—her brows, her eyelids, her nose, her cheek—before finding her welcoming mouth again.

When he raised his head to look down into her glazed eyes, he stroked her cheek. How often these eyes sought his in his dreams! His fingertips tingled as the rest of him reacted to the fantasy of her skin against his.

"*That* is what would help me now, *unnasta*. Having you and finding my knife."

"And then what?" she demanded. "You will take the knife back to your time and your chieftain."

"If I can." He smiled. "Come with me, *unnasta*."

"Back to the time of the *Norrfoolk*?"

"Why not? I have seen your time. Come with me, and live with me in mine."

"As what? Your *traell*?"

"You would not be my slave."

"Then what would I be? You know there is no place for me in your life in that time. Then we would be enemies."

His fingers curved along her face. "You can never be my enemy."

"And your allies? Will they accept me as one of them?"

Pulling out of his arms, Linnea ran down the path. She could not endure seeing the pain on Nils's face. As she reached the bottom, she realized she was in the cove on the far side of the rocks from where the others were sitting on the blanket beneath the trees. She whirled to return up the path and on to the other cove.

Nils stood a half dozen paces behind her. He said nothing as he edged toward her like a hunter sneaking up on his quarry. When she smiled, his stern expression did not change. Her laugh had a nervous edge as she backed away from him. She could imagine him prowling these shores, sending fear into every heart.

"Nils, what are you up to?" she asked with another uneasy laugh.

He burst into a run toward her. She fled in the opposite direction. She could not outrun him. Dodging his fingers, she sped across the beach. She reached the boulders, then spun and raced away. He caught her. She yanked herself away. He jumped forward. With a shriek, she fell backward into the water. She started to rise, but his arms around her waist tugged her back into the waves.

"Are you out of your mind?" she cried.

"This is the way we had fun."

"In the fjord?"

He splashed water at her. "Where the water is not much colder than this in the summer. This is refreshing.

We should have taken a swim together before this, *unnasta*." He slid his hand down along her drenched sleeve. "But without all these clothes."

"You are deranged," she retorted, but quivered at the thought of touching his sleek body.

"No, I wished only to show you that your customs are not so different from mine. You will find yourself at home in my time, if you will come with me."

Jumping to her feet, Linnea ran to shore. She shook water from her hands before wringing her hair out onto the small stones. She kicked off her shoes. Bending, she poured water out of them.

"Are they ruined?" Nils asked.

"I am afraid so."

"We always took our shoes off before we went into the water." His voice was as serious as a judge's exacting a sentence on a felon.

"Did you really?"

"Yes." Kneeling in front of her, he said, "Leather does not do well in the water. That is why we always oiled our boots before we went to sea."

"I will remember that."

He cupped her chin as he brought her mouth toward his. "Remember nothing but this, *unnasta*."

Linnea turned her head before he could kiss her and persuade her that he was right. Her heart already was pleading with her to heed him. What did it matter when she lived as long as it was with him? No! It was not that simple! She belonged here. Now.

With him...

Standing, she picked up her soaked shoes and went to the boulders that divided the coves. She might flee him, but she could not escape her thoughts that trailed her. She wanted to be with Nils. She wanted to tell him that she loved him. Both were impossible when he would be gone as soon as they found that accursed knife.

"Linnea!"

She was amazed when the shout came in front of

her rather than from behind. Looking into the next cove, she saw Randolph wildly waving to her. She waved back.

"We have been so worried!" he called as he ran toward the rocks. "I went up to the top of the cliff and you were gone. I—"

"Look out!" Linnea cried when Scamp ran in front of him.

Nils roared with laughter beside her as Randolph did an odd double-step. Randolph's arms windmilled. It was no use. He stumbled into a wave breaking onto the beach and fell.

"Niles, that is not funny!" Linnea chided, scrambling down off the rocks at the best pace she could manage.

"And what isn't funny about it?"

She rolled her eyes and tried not to laugh. He was right. Randolph's tumble had been comical.

Nils jumped down from the rocks as her brother came running. "Stay back, Martin," he shouted. "I am already wet. I'll help him as soon as I..." He reached up, grasping Linnea at the waist.

"You are asking for trouble," she murmured as he slowly, so very slowly, set her on the sand. "Randolph is not going to like this one bit."

"I hope you are right." He gave her a squeeze before walking out into the water and offering his hand. "Let me help you, Tuthill."

Randolph waved him aside as Scamp bounced through the water, splashing both of them again. "I can manage quite well by myself."

"Are you hurt?" Linnea asked as he wobbled while coming to his feet.

"I am fine." His tone suggested that his dignity had been bruised far more than any other part of him. He glanced at Nils who was wringing out his water-logged coat. "You will ruin that by crunching it like that."

"I fear it will be ruined anyhow. It is wool."

Linnea smiled, hoping to shove aside the edge of tension between the two men. "I have often wondered why sheep don't shrink when they are out in the rain."

Taking her arm, Randolph steered her away from Nils. Usually she would have protested his overbearing assumption that she would go with him, but just now she needed to put some distance between her and Nils.

Randolph eyed her up and down and asked, "How did *you* get wet? Not cavorting with Barrington, I hope."

"I fell in the water, and he helped me, as he offered to help you."

"I do not like how much time my future wife is spending with another man. I trust this behavior will end immediately. It would be embarrassing to have word of this being bandied about when we announce our plans at the gathering Saturday."

She stopped in midstep and faced him. "I think it would be for the best if you and I did not announce any plans to wed on Saturday."

"But if we wait..."

"I would not wish to keep you from finding the right bride, Randolph."

His mouth straightened. "I have found the right bride. Your father has agreed to this match. Your brother sees the good sense of it. Ask him, if you do not believe me."

"It is not that I disbelieve you, Randolph."

"I do not understand why you cannot see the good sense of a match between us."

"I see the good sense, but my heart doesn't."

"What does that have to do with it?"

Linnea stared at him as Nils's questions rang through her head. Randolph was not even pretending that he had a *tendre* for her. It was simply that he wanted to be a part of the Sutherland family and the prestige they possessed throughout England.

"Randolph," she said coolly, "I think it would be

better if we speak of this when we are not soaking wet."

"If—"

"I do not want to speak of it now." She crossed her arms in front of her and gave him the stubborn glower that he had aimed at her so often.

He started to retort, but Minnie said, "Linnea was quite clear, Randolph."

Linnea turned to smile at her sister-in-law. She had not heard Minnie come up behind her. When she saw Minnie standing beside Nils, her smile faltered. She stared up into his eyes, wishing she could give him the answer he wanted. The answer she wanted, even though what he asked might be so utterly impossible that even discussing it was a waste of time.

Minnie said something that Linnea did not catch as she went with her husband, following Randolph toward the two carriages that had brought them to the shore. Nils was silent.

"I should..." Linnea was unsure what she should do, and lying was inconceivable when she was enticed by his eager gaze.

"If easing your pity for Tuthill is more important to you than seeking a solution here with me," Nils replied, "then go."

"Pity? It isn't pity."

"Then what is it?" He cupped her elbows. "Do not lie and tell me it is affection that you feel for Tuthill. I heard what he said to you."

"No, it is not affection."

"Then what?"

She looked to where Randolph was stepping into his open carriage. "It is guilt."

"Why?"

"He believes I will willingly marry him. I let him think that I was falling in love with him, when I have come to see that I was falling in love with being in love. He has been courting me earnestly, but..."

He smiled and folded her hands between his. "But

you prefer to be in my arms."

"And that is wrong!"

"I do not see why. You are not pledged to him."

"No."

"I hear indecision in your voice."

She drew her fingers out of his and clenched them so she could not grasp his again. "I was wrong to let Randolph think I was falling in love with him, so now I must find a way to put an end to his expectations that I will wed him."

"Just tell him."

"It isn't that easy. My parents wish to have me settled."

"But they will never force you to wed a man you do not want to marry."

"No, they would not, but I have duties, too, Nils. You think foremost of your duties. Don't discount mine."

Nils opened his mouth to answer, but the call of her name interrupted him. He watched as Linnea turned and walked to where Tuthill held out his hand to assist her into the carriage.

Vows and obligations. Once they had guided his life. Once he had taken pride in taking on both. Once he had sought any opportunity to make them his.

Now all he wanted was Linnea.

"Hurry up!" Martin shouted.

"Go ahead," he called back. "I will walk and give my clothes a chance to dry."

If Martin yelled something to him, the breeze and the sound of the waves carried it away. Nils watched as the carriages were turned to make their way to where they could be driven to the house.

"It is not as you thought it would be, is it?" growled a voice behind him. "*Daari!* Fool and traitor to your oath."

Nils turned, his hand reaching for the blade hidden beneath his coat. He drew his fingers away when he stared at the form materializing out of the brilliant sunlight. "Loki, I thought you had given upfinding amusement with me."

"You speak boldly for a mortal." For the first time, Nils realized the god was shorter than Linnea, for his head did not reach Nils's shoulder. Loki walked around him as if appraising him from every side.

Spinning to match the wizard's steps so that his back was not to Loki, whom he could not trust, Nils said, "I see no reason not to speak the truth, for you shall discern it one way or the other."

"But a mortal should not speak to a god as if they are equals."

"I did not mean that." Nils bowed his head, but kept his eyes focused on Loki. "You know I hold all the gods in the greatest respect."

Loki laughed. "You are wise to do so, and you are right. I no longer find you amusing."

"Then..." He was not sure why Loki was here. The god who delighted in twisting words until the truth was impossible to recognize would not have come here simply to bid him farewell. To say that might enrage Loki.

"Then I must find someone else to amuse me. Maybe I will be amused by the woman who has amused you so much."

"No!"

Loki's smile vanished, his eyes becoming twin storms. "You dare to tell me what I cannot do?"

"Linnea does not even believe in you."

"She will believe in me by the time this is over." Loki released a wild laugh. "Believe in me and fear me."

Twenty-One

As she walked along the twilight-dusted hallway, Linnea heard laughter from Papa's favorite sitting room. He and Mama and Martin and Minnie must be playing cards tonight. She envied them their simple entertainments, because nothing seemed simple for her any longer.

Randolph had called again this afternoon to ask her once more to reconsider announcing their betrothal on Saturday. She had demurred. She suspected he would call tomorrow again and the day after and on Saturday. Every effort she had made to avoid hurting him had been for naught.

Going down the stairs, she drew her crocheted shawl over her shoulders. She slipped out a side door. If she was seen, someone might send Olive after her.

Or Nils.

She needed to be alone, so she could think. Everything was a complete muddle. She could not blame any of this on Nils because she had been simply letting life sweep her toward this inevitable clash between Randolph's plans and hers. She should have been honest with him right from the start.

With Randolph or with Nils?

Pulling the shawl more tightly about her, although the night was mild, she walked toward the water garden.

She had not been there since Nils had come to the house during Dinah's wedding.

She went down the steps, taking care that she did not miss one in the thickening darkness. This place had been her haven as it had been Nils's. Could she find that sanctuary again while she tried to sort through her thoughts?

The sounds of the night creatures were loud among the flower bushes. When a wisp of night breeze rippled across the pool, the light of the rising moon danced to its silent song. A plop and a widening circle was all that remained of the wake of a frog slipping into the water.

Linnea looked up at the pavilion. The shutters covered the windows, except for the ones that would have given Nils a view of the road and the house. She had known that he watched the comings and goings at Sutherland Park to make the hours pass more quickly and to learn more about life in this time. He had learned so much, but the one thing he needed to know still eluded him.

He needed to find that knife. A knife with a dragon crawling from its haft down onto the blade. She had seen it. She knew she had. Why couldn't she remember where?

"Mayhap because you do not want to," she whispered as she looked again at the pavilion. When she had first brought Nils here, she could not wait for the moment when he would leave Sutherland Park. Now she dreaded it, knowing he would take her heart with him.

Sitting on the bench, Linnea clasped her hands in her lap and tried to clear her mind. She had promised to help him, so she must try. So much whirled through her brain, she could believe a storm had erupted within her head. She wondered when she last had sat alone like this to sort out her thoughts.

She stared at the pool, which had become as smooth

as the looking glass in her room. Not even a leaf moved
on any of the bushes or the trees. The night sounds
were evaporating into silence. She stared about her.
Nothing seemed amiss, but why was everything so still?

A hand settled on her shoulder, and she jumped to
her feet. Whirling, she saw a woman standing behind
the bench. The woman's hair was the silver of a newly
minted coin. Not even the moonlight could dim its rich
sheen. Dressed in loose robes that were more suited
for private chambers than a garden, she was smiling.
In her hand, she held a round crystal globe. She let it
roll over her fingers and back and forth.

"Who are you?" Linnea asked.

"Do not be fearful. I mean you no harm." She
balanced the clear ball on her fingertips as she held up
her hands, which were a ghostly white in the moon's
glow. "I was walking this way and saw you sitting
here. I thought I might stop to speak with you."

"Are you lost?" It would be beyond ironic that
Linnea had created the story of Nils being set upon by
highwaymen and wandering—lost and seeking help—
onto Sutherland Park's lands when this woman might
have suffered the very same in truth.

"No, I am not lost, although this is far from my
home." She smiled. "You need not fear me, because I
wish you no harm."

"I did not mean to suggest that. I only meant to
offer you a place to rest and food to eat if you are lost
and in need of shelter."

"Your kindness to another stranger is laudable."

"Another stranger?" Linnea asked with studied
caution.

The woman's smile broadened. "It is well known
that you asked your father to open his home to a
wayfarer who had lost more than his way."

Linnea nodded. That fact was probably known in
every household throughout the shire by this time. Every
guest who had ever come to Sutherland Park was the

source of much interest among their tenants. "It has long been a tradition that Sutherland Park opens its doors to those in need."

"But it has been far longer that your guest has been lost."

Linnea stiffened. This woman's words were vague, but too close to the truth that no one knew, save she and Nils. "If you are not lost—"

The woman smiled. "There are many ways to be lost. One can lose one's way on a path or upon the sea or in the journey of life. The stranger who has come to you is not the only one lost."

"I do not understand you. You are making no sense."

"No?" She laughed. "Maybe I do not, but I do know one thing. You love him."

Linnea stared at the woman, whose hair glowed more brightly silver in the moonlight as she came around the end of the bench. Somehow, Linnea must have betrayed herself when someone was watching. Somehow? She almost laughed. Minnie had seen her affection for Nils. Randolph had, too, she feared. And Nils...Had he seen it? She closed her eyes and recreated the intensity on his face when he had asked her to come back in time with him. He must know as well.

Yet she could not speak of the truth in her heart to this woman. "How can you think that you know?"

"I know it as you know it." The woman smiled and put her hand in the center of her chest. "You know within you. Here."

"Even if I did love him, what does it matter? I cannot tell him."

"Because he must be free to seek what brought him here?"

Linnea took a step away from the pool. "Who are you that you have so much knowledge that no one else should have?"

"I am someone who wishes to see the pain within

two hearts eased."

"Thank you, but..." She backed away another step. "If you are hungry, go to the kitchen door, and someone will be there to give you something to eat. I bid you a good night."

Linnea whirled and bumped into a hard form. Nils put his arm around her to steady her. When he asked if she was all right, she nodded. She started to ask him what he was doing out here in the garden, then saw he was staring past her at the woman with the wondrous silver hair.

"Sit here, and I will be right back," Nils said, seating her on the bench.

"But—"

"Wait here, *unnasta*. I will...I will be right back." He went to where the woman was still standing by the shore of the pool.

The woman said something, but the only thing Linnea could understand was, "Nils Bjornsson."

Linnea gasped, horrified at the sound of his real name on someone else's lips. Both Jack and Olive had been careful not to use it when others might hear. How did this stranger know it?

Nils continued to stare at the woman before him. He had left the house, hoping to find a place to be alone. Something had drawn him to this garden by the pavilion that once he had despised as a prison. Then he had seen Linnea here, and he had guessed she was the reason he had found himself summoned here...until he saw she was not alone.

"Vjofn?" he asked.

"You recognize me, which bespeaks well of your knowledge of the ways that were yours." She held up the crystal globe, which reflected his face back to him. "I see your questions. I will answer one by telling you that I am here because it is as you have feared."

He bowed his head toward Vjofn as he asked, "Do you speak of Loki?"

"He is very angry that you have tried to gainsay him," she replied.

"I know that, for he has told me so himself."

"Loki is a *daari*, but a powerful one. Take care what you do, Nils Bjornsson. He believes that a mistake was made when Freya allowed you to survive. He has stated openly in *Asgard* that such a mistake must be rectified."

"Odin has spoken to me of—"

"There are ways that Loki can outsmart even Odin himself. You know well the old tales. You know Loki's vengeance is as horrific as his arrogance. He has been playing with you for his own enjoyment."

"But he has not slain me."

"No, but only because he suspects you have a powerful ally."

"Freya is not my ally."

"There are many in *Asgard* who have reasons to keep Loki from slaying you instantly. Maybe even Loki himself, for he knows you would be granted a seat at the highest table in *Valhalla*."

Nils sighed. "My quest to regain honor is not yet completed. That place at Odin's table might not be mine."

"Whether it is or not is for the Allfather to decide. However, Loki is wily, and he is determined to have his way. He cares little who suffers when he is determined to prove that he is right." She turned her icy blue gaze toward Linnea. "Take care with all decisions you make, Nils Bjornsson."

She put the crystal in his hands. It was not icy cold as he had expected. Instead, it was warm as if she had been holding it for a long time.

"What is this?"

"There are those who acknowledge your bravery and your sacrifice in denying yourself a hero's welcome in *Valhalla*. I was asked to bring this to you."

"By Frigga, Odin's wife?"

Vjofn smiled. "Your allies are as powerful as your enemies, Nils Bjornsson, but you cannot always depend on their help. That is why I have brought you this."

"What is it?"

"Whatever you want it to be. It has been sent to you as a reward."

"A glass ball?" He was confused. Searching his mind, he tried to recall when he had ever heard of one of Frigga's handmaidens carrying such a thing. He could not remember, and he wondered if there were stories that even mortals were not privy to about the world of the gods. "If Loki sent you with this—"

Her smile did not change, but he sensed her fury. "I do not come here for Loki. I never do his service."

"Forgive me."

"You have reason to be concerned, Nils Bjornsson, but you should know that the treasures Odin possesses are not only made of gold."

"Why are you talking about Loki and Odin?" Linnea asked, as she put her hand on his arm, startling him. "I don't know what else you are saying, but I recognize their names."

"Hush, Linnea." He patted her hand, but he continued to stare at the woman whose robes swirled around her even though the night breeze was gone. "I must think."

"About what? What can be more important than the fact that this woman knows your real name?"

"You can see her?" He stared at Linnea in disbelief. "You can hear her?"

"Of course." Linnea was tempted to put her hand up to discover if Nils was suffering from a fever. "Why shouldn't I see someone who is right there?" She gestured toward the woman, then gasped. The woman was gone! She looked both ways along the pool. "Where is she?"

"Not here." His voice was grim again.

"Niles!" she gasped, careful not to speak his true

name, although she was certain she had heard the woman use it.

"That is not my name." He gripped her arm and brought her to him. "By Thor's hammer, that is not my name. I tire of this charade of pretending to be someone I am not. When I saw Vjofn here..."

"Who?"

"Vjofn, one of Frigga's handmaidens."

Linnea struggled to speak past her shock. "Frigga? Odin's wife? Like in the myths?"

"How can you call the truth a myth when Vjofn was here speaking with you?"

"You are making no sense." Her vexation focused on him. Nothing had been the way it should be tonight. Mayhap he was frustrated with hiding the truth behind his façade of being an English peer, but she hated the lies, too.

His hand slid up from her shoulder to cup her cheek. He held it so his gaze locked with hers. "I want to know why you can see Vjofn when you do not believe in the old ways."

"I don't know. I was sitting on the bench, thinking, when she walked up to me and began talking."

"Thinking? Of what?"

She hoped the moonlight hid the flush climbing her cheeks. "Of all that has happened since I found you on the beach."

"So you called her."

"Called her? I told you. I was thinking. I did not call to anyone. I..." She stared up at him as he slowly nodded. "What you are suggesting is impossible. Even if the old gods ever existed, why would one of them come here to speak with me? I am not of the *Norrfoolk*."

He smiled. "Your accent is becoming less intolerable, Linnea."

"How kind of you to notice!" She walked away from him along the pool. Did its serene surface hide many raging storms like the ones whirling about inside her head?

"Are you going to ignore the truth?" Nils asked from behind her.

"I know I was sitting here, and I know a woman I did not recognize came to speak with me. The rest is skimble-skamble."

"Call it silly, if you wish, but the truth is before you." He paused, then said, "It *was* here before you."

"But what you are suggesting is simply impossible."

"As it is impossible for me to be here?"

Linnea walked back to where he was standing by the bench. "Yes," she whispered. "I still am not sure I believe you are here."

"Sometimes, I wonder about that myself."

"And other times?"

"Other times, I do this." His mouth captured hers as his hand holding the crystal globe swept around her waist, enfolding her to him. Her hands tightened on his back to keep from being swept away by the tempest of her longing.

He kissed her until she melted against him. He held her, teasing them both with the passion neither could deny. Without his arms around her, she doubted if her unsteady knees could have supported her. She wanted to touch him, to have him caress her.

With his lips grazing the skin along her neck, she admitted the truth she had been hiding from herself. She had let him lure her into his arms so she could encourage him to love her like this. No longer could she pretend to be oblivious to the need which had kept her from sleeping.

All yearning to push him away vanished along with her foolish belief that she could halt this love from devouring her in its need to be satisfied. So long she had hidden her longings behind the screen of propriety while she fought his easy assumption that their love was inevitable. She had not wanted to admit he was correct, but he was. In defeat, she found the sweetest victory she could imagine.

"Nils..."

"Do not speak, *unnasta*. Let me savor your lips against mine."

It took every bit of her strength to push him away when she wanted to pull him even closer. "I must. I must know. Why did she come here?"

"To give me a warning."

"About what?"

"Loki. He is angry with me."

"Why?"

Nils wanted to tell her that it was not important, that all he wanted now was to make love with her. He could not lie to her now, not when lying with her was what every inch of his body craved. "My blood-oath was heard by Freya, who would have sent the *Valkyrja* to carry me to *Valhalla*. It apparently was also heard by Loki."

"The god of mischief."

He smiled. "You have been studying the old stories, I see."

"But they are only stories."

"Maybe now that is all they are, but when I first stepped foot on this shore, the *Norrfoolk* knew well the names of their gods and feared what each of them could do to a careless mortal who did not respect their power." He stroked her back in slow circles. "Then the gods lived much closer to mankind."

"You have seen and spoken with them before now?"

"No, but that did not keep me from believing the *sagas* of those who had seen the gods." His fingers closed into a fist against her back. "Now I know why those who had seen the gods were frightened. The games played by those who live in *Asgard* are not for us here in this world."

"Nils," she whispered, "are you frightened, too? I cannot believe that some story would scare you."

"It is not a story when Loki is looking for someone

else to amuse him, because my adventures here in this century no longer do. He has had every chance to kill me with his magic, but he has not. I have been wondering why, but I suspect it is because he is enjoying the chance to taunt me and threaten those around me."

"You have seen him, too?"

"When Jack was worried that I was talking to myself—"

"You were talking to Loki?" She could not believe her own words. Shaking her head, she whispered, "This is all impossible."

"I believe it is possible, for Loki has visited me often since I awoke to see your face, *unnasta*." His voice grew hard. "Loki tires of my refusal to offer him the amusement he seeks."

She grasped his shoulders. "But that is good! He will not come back here to taunt you."

"You have learned the old *sagas* well." A reluctant smile could not ease his taut lips. "But the truth is, *unnasta*, that he has not left this time, either."

"So he wishes to cause trouble for someone else here?"

"Yes."

Her eyes widened. "Me?"

"I believe that is why Vjofn came to speak with you. There is no other reason that makes sense."

She clasped her hands in front of her. "None of this makes any sense, Nils. I am not of your time. I am not of the *Norrfoolk*. I am of my time and of this place. Why would Loki take an interest in me?"

"Because I have angered him."

"You seem to have the most intolerable luck with your journey here," she murmured.

"It has not all been intolerable." He tipped her face up and brushed her mouth with a gentle kiss.

"What is this?" she asked, pointing to the crystal globe that reflected the light as if it had pulled the moon within it.

"Vjofn gave it to me."

"But what is it?"

"She said it was a reward, and it was whatever I wished it to be."

Linnea laughed. "Your gods and goddesses are furtive about what information they will share."

"It may be simply that we mortals cannot understand what they know."

"Whichever it may be, this is very beautiful." Her hands rose toward his fingers that held the globe.

At the moment her fingers touched his, bright light flashed around her. She screamed his name. Had lightning struck right where they were standing? Out of a cloudless sky?

"Linnea, I am right here." He pulled her to him, and she pressed her face to his chest.

When scratchy wool scored her cheek, she put trembling fingers up to touch the intricate embroidery decorating the front of the gray tunic he wore. The pattern of the silk threads of brilliant reds and whites and golds were identical to what had been on the tunic that had been stained with blood when she had discovered him on the beach.

She pressed her hands over her mouth as she edged back to see his legs were encased in cross-gartered leggings and brightly polished boots. A sword that was more than half her height was lashed to his belt. Raising her gaze higher, she moaned when she saw the conical metal helmet with a nosepiece that gave his familiar face a savagery she had never imagined.

He put his hand up to his head, then scowled. "Linnea! What are you wearing?"

"Me?" In disbelief, she looked down at her simple gown. It was made of light brown wool. Belted at the waist, it had the same bright decoration at its neckline as his tunic. On her feet, soft slippers covered thick stockings. She touched an embroidered band tied across her forehead and over her hair, which fell past her shoulders.

This must be a dream. She must have fallen asleep in the garden. The woman, the crystal globe, this place...It must all be a dream.

Nils ran his hand along the hilt of the long sword at his waist. "This is my sword *Jagar*."

"It has a name?"

"Yes, it means the hunter." He looked around them. "I recognize *Jagar*. I know this is my sword. Just as I know this is not Britannia nor the land of the *Norrfoolk*."

"How do you know...?" Linnea slowly spun around, realizing that the flash of light was not from lightning, but from dazzling sunlight. Her eyes widened when she saw a huge rainbow touching the ground not far from where they stood. She never had seen the end of a rainbow, only its arc across the sky. When she saw the far end was visible as well, and dropped to the ground on the far side of a wide chasm, she whispered, "Where are we?"

"You will not believe me."

"I do not believe my own eyes."

Walking to the edge of the abyss, he looked across it. "This is *Bifröst*, the great *asabru*. The great rainbow that hangs above *Midgard*. It hangs over the earth, the place where mortals reside."

She stared at the crystal he still held. If this was a dream, she should know only what she knew. She had never heard the word the *Norrfoolk* used for rainbow. But if this was not a dream..."Did this globe kill us?"

"I am alive. My heart beats." He touched the center of her breast. "And yours does as well, *unnasta*. If we—" The words he murmured were in his own language before he said, "Look at that, and tell me that you see it, too."

Linnea could not even gasp. The huge building had been obscured by the sunlight, although she had no idea how. Resembling ruins of the old settlements left from before the Conquest, this castle glittered as if it had been raised from a single piece of gold. The walls were high, but the wide gate was thrown open. A path, as golden as the walls, reached toward the rainbow.

"What is it?" she breathed.

"It appears to be *Fensalir*, Frigga's palace."

"Frigga, the High Goddess? Frigga who sent Vjofn to give you that globe?"

"One and the same."

She wrapped her arms around herself, then let them fall to her sides as she touched the fabric of her unfamiliar gown. "Nils, this makes no sense."

"I think it does."

"How?"

He cupped the globe. "Put your hands over mine, Linnea."

She hastened to obey. When they both had touched the crystal before, they had been brought here. She took a deep breath and put her hands against his.

The bright light vanished. Linnea was about to crow with relief at the sight of stars in the sky above them, then realized she was seeing them through a gigantic window. This was not the water garden of Sutherland Park.

The room she stood in beside Nils was so tall she could not see the ceiling. No furniture was visible. A firepit was set in the middle of the floor, the flames making no smoke. She looked down. She still wore the strange clothing.

Nils smiled and held out his hand.

She put her fingers on his as she whispered, "What is this place?"

"We are within *Fensalir*. Stories are told by fires on cold wintry nights of the fires that burn here and give off no smoke, so none of the gods will be blinded when they decide to look upon *Midgard* from one of the windows here." He ran his finger over the ball in his hand. "Each time we both touch this, it takes us somewhere else." With a laugh, he set it on a stone by the firepit. "It is here that I wish to stay with you."

"Why here?"

"*Fensalir* is Frigga's castle." He whirled her into his arms. As he scattered kisses across her face and along her neck, he whispered, "And Frigga is the goddess of love."

"I thought..." She moaned as his tongue slid up behind the back of her ear. "I thought Freya was the goddess of love."

"She is the goddess of lust." His eyes glowed as fiercely as the light within the ball. "I want you, *unnasta*, for this time and as long as we can be together."

Her breath burst from her when the gentleness vanished from his lips, and she tasted his yearning. She wanted this now. It did not matter if Frigga or Freya lived here. She wanted his love and his lust, his most basic animal need. It made no sense, but nothing did. This was what she wanted. This was what she needed, had to have.

He scooped her up into his arms and walked toward the closest wall. His hands slid up under her skirt, caressing her legs. When her lips parted with an eager sigh, his tongue jabbed at hers. He set her on her feet and pressed her back against the wall as his fingers grasped her skirt, raising it higher. She gasped when she heard material snag on the wall behind her.

"Nils..." Speaking was almost impossible when her breath careened through her like the flames leaping on the firepit.

With a laugh, he reached behind her and lifted a latch. He drew her forward as he opened a pair of doors that revealed a cupboard in the wall. Her eyes widened when she saw that it was not a closet, but a bed.

"Be my reward, *unnasta*," he whispered. "Be mine in this time and in this place."

"Yes." Mayhap this was simply a dream. Even if it was not, it was a dream come true to be here with him. She wanted this. In this time and in this place, and in her time and in her place. The latter might not ever be possible, so she would grasp joy while she could.

He lifted her up to sit on the high bed. Unbuckling his sword, he leaned it against the wall, then set his metal helmet on it as he kicked off his boots. He knelt and drew off her shoes, his fingers stroking the arch of her foot. Slipping his fingers through hers, he sat beside her on the blanket. His fingers entwined through her hair, and an eager response flowed throughout her body. As his mouth moved along her neck, she drew him closer to her. She immediately sensed a difference. All the many times he had kissed her, he had held a part of himself back. She softened to him in answer to the invitation he had made so often. She shivered with unrestrainable hunger when his mouth moved along the curve of her breast.

He tilted her chin up with his fingertip, and she stared up into his eyes, unable to move, to blink, to breathe as he whispered, "I never thought we would have this chance."

"I know."

He silenced her with a fiery kiss. Sliding her arm around his shoulders, she sank into the rapture. He teased her ear with his tongue, and she knew this was where she wanted to be. She sifted through his hair and met his mouth eagerly. His arms brought her up against his chest. All thoughts evaporated into the heat of craving.

His lips coursed along her face as he leaned her back. The aroma of herbs surrounded her, but she paid it no attention as she drew him down with her. His eager fingers drew aside the band holding her hair in place. Tossing it away, he found her lips with all the longing so many sleepless nights had honed.

He kissed her. Only kissed her, until she groaned with the need that would no longer go unsated. She tugged open the lacing on the front of his tunic, then slipped her hand up beneath it along his smooth back. Her groan became a gasp of delight when he bent to taste the skin bared by her gown's modest neckline.

Sliding her hands from beneath his tunic, she framed his face. Slowly she drew his mouth to hers. In the instant before his lips covered hers, she whispered, "Be my reward, too. Be mine in this time and in this place."

The warmth of his laughter vanished into a ferocious flame as he tugged her into his arms. His hard muscles pressed her into the bed. His lips delighted her with a rapid shower of kisses across her face. Touching her eyelids, her cheek, the corners of her mouth which ached for his lips, he dared her to abandon herself to passion. When he captured her mouth, she moaned against his lips. His tongue jousted with hers as it explored every slick secret within her mouth.

He loosened her gown, pausing so his fingers brushed against the skin over her rapidly beating heart. She held his gaze with hers as she slid his hand beneath the front of her gown to cover his. With a wordless moan, he slid her sleeves down along her arm, freeing her breasts to the heat of his gaze.

Her fingers tightened on his arms as his tongue etched its flame into her skin. She gasped his name when it followed a twin pattern on one breast as his finger did on the other, trailing up to its very tip. The rough texture of his face burnished her skin with delight. Fumbling to pull off his tunic, she ached for the sensation of his skin on her.

She pulled his tunic off, and she brought his mouth to hers, arching her back so her breasts touched his chest. He murmured against her lips before he crushed them beneath his. Slowly, he pulled her gown off. His hands slipped under her shoulders as his lips brushed her neck. At the same time, he undid the laces on her undergarment, sliding it down with the same slow intensity he had her gown.

Pushing aside his hands, she rose to her knees and

let the garment fall to the bed. She tossed it atop her gown. Even if this was not a dream, she wanted to throw away all her constraints along with her clothes. When he reached to bring her back into his arms, she took his hands and rested them on the top of her stockings, just above her knees. She bent forward to meet his lips as she guided his hands down her legs. His palms, made hard by his work, stroked her eagerly. She moaned as his breath brushed her skin.

She knelt beside him, and he pulled her down to him. The sensation of her bare breasts on his chest weakened her. The craving for all of him against her dared her fingers to settle on the waistband of his leggings.

His hands framed her face, bringing her mouth to his, as she lowered them over his strong legs. The hardness of him pressed against her hand, and she wondered how they could have waited so long for this. When she pushed his clothes aside, he caught her trembling fingers and drew them to him. As she stared up into the purple fires of his eyes, he led her fingertips along the broad plane of his chest toward the narrowing of his hips and the sharp delineation between his sun-darkened skin and the paler areas below.

Her breath grew ragged when his mouth covered hers. Their breaths mingled, hot and pulsating to the rhythms taking control of her body. When he leaned her back again, the splendor of his naked skin against her was both savage and sweet. She wanted to savor it forever, but was sure she would go mad if it lasted another second.

Her sigh became a moan as his mouth twirled about the tip of her breast. The ache deep within her demanded satiation. Now. She must be freed from this exquisite ecstasy.

When her fingers moved along him, discovering every sensual angle of his male body, his quick gasp seared her skin. As she gripped his shoulders, he rose over her and brought them together. His mouth captured her gasp as they moved as one, wanting the same satisfaction. As his breath burned through her, she surrendered to the frenzy she never thought she would be able to find in his arms. The sudden, lightning-hot explosion severed her from everything but him.

***

Linnea opened her eyes to discover Nils sleeping beside her. His head was against her breast, his breath warming her skin and enticing her closer. She reached to draw him to her as she woke him with her kisses in hopes of leading him to more of the passion. Then she heard the distant sound of triumphant laughter.

Who was laughing? Who was here?

She edged away from Nils so as not to wake him. Sitting, she drew the covers up over her and stared out into darkness broken only by the firelight and the glow of the stars overhead. Not just from overhead, because a powerful glow blossomed near the fire.

The crystal globe!

She watched rise as if lifted by an invisible hand. It began to spin. She reached to wake Nils. Would he understand what was happening now?

The ball shattered, shards flying everywhere. She threw herself over Nils, screaming out his name. Fire seared her, then it was gone.

Linnea sat up again and gasped as she saw the familiar outlines of her own bedroom windows. Rain was falling against them. She reached for her wrapper at the foot of the bed. Flinging it over her shoulders, she realized she was wearing her favorite nightdress.

Had it been only a dream? No, because even in the faint light as she drew the collar of her nightdress back, she could see on her breast the marks left by the bristle of a day's growth of beard. Nil's beard. They had been lovers. It had not been just a dream.

She reached for the door. If loving Nils was a disease, she feared she was infected. More than that, she feared she would resist any cure, for she was beginning to believe she had found what she had been seeking forever.

Forever...

Nils threw open his door as soon as she knocked. He pulled her into his arms and kissed her with the passion they had found in another place. "*Unnasta*," he whispered, "praise Thor that you are safe."

"And you! I feared you had been hurt by the ball exploding."

"Is that what happened?" He combed his fingers through her hair. "Jack, you are not needed."

The lad, who was groggily peeking into the room, said, "Yes, my lord."

As soon as the door to the dressing room closed again, Nils said, "What happened does not matter. What matters is that you know the truth now. You belong with me. Once I find the knife, we can go back to—"

"To your time?" Shaking her head, she stepped out of his arms. "Nils, we have talked about this before. You know that is impossible. I do not belong there any more than—"

He interrupted her as she had him. "Than I belong here?"

"That was not what I was going to say. I was going to say that I belong there no more than I belong in Frigga's castle."

"That was my reward for putting honor first."

"Ahead of my dishonor?"

His eyes grew hard. "Is that what you believe? That I brought dishonor to you by showing you how much I wanted you?"

"No." Her shoulders sagged. "You did not bring me any dishonor. I did. I am the daughter of an English lord—a 19th century English lord. You are...you are a Viking! You do not belong here, and I do not belong in your arms."

With a gasp, she ran out of the room and along the

hall. How could she have been so foolish? He had been honest from the beginning that he had given up the glories of *Valhalla* to tend to his oath. He intended to find the knife and return to his time.

But why had she spoken so to him when she wanted to give him her heart? The words had spouted from her mouth, cruel and hateful.

She faltered when she heard the echo of distant laughter again. Victorious laughter. With a sob, she flung open her door and rushed to her bed. Her dream come true had become a never-ending nightmare.

Twenty-Two

Nils stormed into his room. When he saw Jack was nowhere to be found, he knew the lad had learned that it was wise to keep his distance just now.

Tossing his coat onto the closest chair, Nils dropped next to it. He opened the bottle of wine he carried and tilted it back. Bothering to get a glass was silly when he was tired of the affectations of this time.

He could not blame English customs for the mess he had made of everything. When Vjofn had appeared in the water garden, he had been suspicious of Loki manipulating all of them. He had let Frigga's handmaiden persuade him that Loki played no part in the reward that the Allfather's wife had sent to him. Maybe Loki had not been part of the gift, but the wizard had taken advantage of it.

Destroying the globe and sending Nils and Linnea back to Sutherland Park must have been Loki's work. Linnea had trusted him enough to become his lover when they were within Frigga's fortress, but, back in her own time and in her father's house, she believed what they had shared was a mistake. If they had had a chance to discuss this in the haven of Frigga's castle, it might have been possible to find a compromise.

Instead, for the past day, Linnea had avoided him. She had turned and walked the other way to keep from speaking to him.

He took another deep drink of the wine. He hoped it was more potent than what he had drunk in his own time. If he became intoxicated, he might be able to forget the pain and betrayal on Linnea's face when she had fled from his room last night.

Dishonor? How could anything so splendid cause dishonor for her?

His hand clenched on the neck of the bottle. She had explained to him again and again how closely a young woman must guard her virtue in this time. It was no different in his time. Freya could have an endless listing of lovers, but a mortal woman should be faithful to the man she wed.

If he offered Linnea marriage, it would not change anything. He could not remain in this time once his quest to find the knife was complete. She would not come with him to his time. The gods' favor would not extend to letting him come back here when he had returned the *sax* to his chieftain. There was no solution.

"It is time you realized that, Nils Bjornsson."

Hearing a self-satisfied chortle, Nils stood. He was not surprised to see Loki perched cross-legged on a stool by the hearth.

Nils set down the wine bottle and pressed the cork into it. "I thought you were done with giving me a look-in, Loki."

"How like an Englishman you sound."

"I must learn to be like those in this place if I hope to be successful in my search for that which was stolen from my chieftain." He put one foot on the low chair beside where Loki sat. "You have had your fun with destroying what was so wondrous between Linnea and me. You have hurt her as you vowed when you deemed me no longer amusing. Why are you back here again?"

Loki was abruptly frowning. "Once you would not have kept me waiting even the length of a heartbeat, Nils Bjornsson. Then you did whatever I wished of you." His voice became a sneer. "Or do you recall that Nils Bjornsson is your name now that you have become the spoiled pet of these English?"

"I know who I am." He held up his empty hand. "When Vjofn put Frigga's gift in my hand, I accepted it as a warrior of the *Norrfoolk*, not as an Englishman. When I shared it with Linnea, I brought her to the wellspring of my people's soul, so she could share it with me while she shared herself with me."

"Before choosing her father's honor over yours."

"It was her choice," Nils replied quietly, hoping his serenity masked his pain at speaking those simple words. His eyes narrowed. "Or was it? Have you put words into Linnea's mouth that do not come from her heart?"

"You may believe that as you wish. Or you may believe that some things will never change." Loki laughed. "Those who call this island home cannot be trusted by the *Norrfoolk*. You should be grateful that I have helped you see that."

"I did not need your interference to see the truth."

"No? Do you recall why you are here? It was not to make that Englishwoman your lover."

"I know why I am here."

"Do you? Have you become that Englishwoman's *traell*, willing to do her bidding in exchange for her feminine favors?"

"I am no one's slave. I call no one—neither man nor woman—master."

Loki stood. "Nor do you recall the obedience you are to show those of us whom once you feared."

"I still respect those who will reside in *Asgard* until the day the world ends."

With a wordless screech, Loki raised his fists. He could not deny the truth of the *sagas* of how he was banished from *Asgard* to wait for the end of time in a cave, a punishment for angering those gods who possessed more power than he could claim.

Nils lifted his hands as the room exploded with light. Behind him, the bottle of wine broke as it hit the floor. Something else hit the floor with a crash and the sound of more breaking glass. He was not sure what it was.

Silence.

Cursing, he tried to clear the fire from his eyes. He rubbed them, then groped for the chair. This was just as Linnea had described, so Loki must have invaded Frigga's castle and sent them back here.

"My lord! What happened here?" Jack's shocked voice rang through the room.

Nils turned toward him and opened his eyes wide. He could not see. The glare remained, blinding him to everything else. His hands fisted. Was this Loki's ultimate revenge, stealing his sight so he could not complete his quest? He would find his chieftain's knife, even if he had to examine everything in Britannia with his fingers.

"Lord Barrington, are you all right?" Jack must be closer now, because his voice was louder.

"Help me to a chair."

"Help you...?" Jack grasped Nils's arm. "This way, my lord."

Groping for the chair, Nils dropped into it. He struck one of its arms, sending a pain down his leg.

"Do you want me to send for Lady Linnea?" Jack asked.

He was about to say no, then nodded. Pride would gain him nothing now.

Hearing Jack rush to the door and out of the room, Nils leaned back. It might not be pride. It might be fear—there was no other word for it—that Linnea might not come to help him. She must know, as he did, that the hours they had stolen in Frigga's castle bound them together in a way that could not be explained.

A way that Loki was trying to destroy.

"Vjofn," he said quietly in his own language, "you were our friend in the water garden. Do not abandon us now."

He strained his ears for an answer from *Asgard*.

A gasp came from the doorway. Linnea! Once before, she had been sent to assist him. Was she the answer to his prayers again?

"Nils, what happened?" she asked as she rushed to his side.

"I cannot see."

"Jack told me that. What happened?" Her despair was as apparent in her voice as it must be on her face.

"Are we alone?"

He could tell she had turned by the difference in her voice as she said, "Jack, bring cool, wet cloths so we can ease the pain in Lord Barrington's eyes. Lots of them. Fetch a bottle of wine, and also bring some of that powder that Cook keeps in the stillroom for when someone has had too much to drink."

"I have not had too much to drink," Nils growled as Jack ran out of the room again.

The door closed, and Linnea's soft steps came back toward him as she said, "I know, but the powder eases headaches." Glass was pushed aside on the floor as she asked, "Can you see me?"

He gulped great lungfuls of fresh air. Leaning his head on his hands, he kneaded his anguished eyes with the heels of his palms.

"Nils?"

At Linnea's soft voice, he raised his head. They must be alone, for she used his real name. He could not be certain, for all he could see in front of him was a fiery red. His first fear that the flames were real vanished, because the air was cool and the smoke was just a lingering scent.

"Nils, please tell me. Can you see me?"

"No."

Her moan of despair seared him more fiercely than the embers from the fire that had burst from Loki's hands.

He reached for her. When her fingers clutched his hand and pressed it over her heart, he whispered, "I do not believe that I am blind. Simply blinded. Everything is a strange scarlet, as if I had stared too long into the rising sun."

Her finger against his lips halted him from saying more. He heard her rise and go to the door. She thanked someone and murmured more. The door closed, and she came back to him.

A damp, cool cloth covered his eyes as she whispered, "Tell me. Was it Loki?"

He caught her hand, better able now to gauge where she was by the direction of her voice. He pulled off the cloth and squinted in an effort to see her face. It was still nothing but a ruddy blob.

"How did you guess that?" he asked as quietly as she had spoken. He heard other footfalls in the room, so he guessed someone else was here.

She must have guessed his thoughts, because she replied, "Jack will remain here by your side in case you need anything tonight."

"Having you by my side would satisfy my greatest need."

Her hands clenched on his arm. "Do not speak of that."

"Why not? It was because of what we shared that this happened."

"Loki?" She raised her voice and called, "Jack, please bring more glasses from the sitting room downstairs."

"I can get more in—"

"The sitting room glasses are the ones Lord Barrington prefers."

Nils almost laughed. He did not need to see to guess Jack's face was twisted with frustration at what seemed to be a senseless request.

"Yes, my lady," the lad replied. "I hope you are doing better, my lord."

"I shall be fine," Nils said.

As soon as the door closed, Linnea asked, "Do you really think so? Do you really think you will be fine?"

"I must hope so." He readjusted the cloth over his burning eyes. "And to answer your question, yes, it was Loki. Both today and when we were at *Fensalir*. As I told you, he is furious with me for refusing to be the source of all kinds of jests for him."

"I am sorry, Nils."

He lifted the cloth and squinted. Although the colors still flowed together like wet paint in the rain, he was able to see a little. His arm gathered her to him. "'Tis not your doing, *unnasta*."

"But I thought Loki was going to bother someone else."

"This may be his way of bothering someone else. Who has been hurt by all that has happened since we saw Vjofn in the water garden?"

"Me?" she whispered. She rested her cheek against his chest. "The words I spoke to you when we woke back here...I do not know where they came from. I chose to be with you. There was no dishonor in what we shared."

"Loki tore us from *Fensalir*, then wanted to be certain we did not seek such a paradise again." He laughed, but there was no amusement in the sound. "He has selected an ingenious way to hurt both of us for failing to be in awe of what he has done to our lives."

"I *am* in awe of all of this." She hesitated, and he could hear her gown rustle. "Especially of this." Her fingers guided his mouth to hers.

He did not need to be able to see well to find her lips. Pain wrenched deep in his gut when he tasted the salt of tears she must have shed. Because he had been injured, or had she been crying when Jack called her here?

Suddenly she cried out in horror. She jerked herself out of his arms. No, she was pulled away from him.

What was going on? His fingers found his knife with the ease of years of practice. What was happening? Where was Linnea?

Shadows moved and thickened. To his left. He tried to react, but hesitated. Was that Linnea? No, the shadow was taller than hers. He raised his knife. Too late. Something struck him. Fire burned up his left arm. He swung the knife again and found nothing. Footsteps! Too heavy for Linnea. He whirled. His knife hit metal, then was knocked from his fingers. Instinct alone made him jump aside. The whoosh of a blade came within inches of his stomach.

Where was Linnea? He shouted to her to flee as he turned to find something else to fight with. He tripped over something on the floor. He heard victorious laughter. Kortsson! Rolling over, he started to stand. He was knocked from his feet back to the floor by something long and heavy. Trying to push it off, he felt dampness on his hands. Warm dampness...blood! Not his! Linnea!

He shouted her name in desperation. His fear for her strengthened him. Ignoring the agony in his left arm, he shoved the weight off him. He jumped to his feet and grasped the bottle that had been on the table. He raised it to fight off Kortsson. It was a paltry weapon, but his blood-enemy must be stopped from hurting her...again.

"No!" Linnea cried as her slender fingers gripped his wrist.

"Stay back. I—"

"It is over."

"Over?" He squinted, wishing he could see something other than flimsy shadows.

She took the bottle, and he heard her set it back on the table. Still holding his hand, she drew him forward and down toward the floor. His fingers recoiled when they touched blood again. The body was still. Not even a breath moved it.

298   J.A. Ferguson

"Kortsson?" he asked in disbelief.

"Yes." She shivered so hard he could feel it all along her as she knelt beside him.

"You killed him?"

"He would have killed you." She gulped and whispered with a half-sob, "I used your knife."

He gathered her to him. She might be as brave as a Viking woman, but she was of this time, when slaying a blood-enemy was not deemed proof of restored honor. As she wept against him, he smoothed her hair. His fingers delighted in what his eyes could not see. Quietly he said, "Linnea, I owe you my life once more."

"He would have killed both of us." She paused, then drew back. He knew she was gazing up at him. "He does not have the knife, Nils."

It was as if he had been slashed again with Kortsson's blade. Lifting his hand, he found Linnea's cheek with a sense that he could not name. She leaned her face against his palm. Even though he knew how unlikely it would that his blood-enemy still had the knife after a journey of a thousand years, he had hoped when he faced Kortsson, he would regain both the stolen knife and his honor.

"What happened here?" came Jack's shout from the doorway.

Nils stood, facing the area where the light was brighter. That must be the door. "An intruder attacked. Linnea—"

"Was saved by Niles's quick actions," she interrupted.

He wanted to ask her why she was giving him the credit for slaying his enemy. The honor all should be hers. As Jack and then others of the household surged into the room, everyone talking at once, Nils had no luck getting anyone to listen to the truth. They all— including a most grateful Lord Sutherland—were too busy thanking him and taking the body away and sending for the authorities.

While everyone discussed whether this was the same man who had disrupted Dinah's wedding, Linnea finished bandaging his arm. The wound was not deep, but it had to be cleaned so it did not fester. When she was done, she remained as silent as she had been since Jack had arrived at the door.

Nils waited for the others to follow the footmen who were taking Kortsson's corpse out to the stable. He stood as Linnea moved past him, the hint of her fragrance telling him just where she was. Taking her by the arms, he brought her close. Gently he kissed her. When her lips quivered beneath his, he whispered, "*Unnasta*, what is wrong?"

"What is wrong? That man almost killed you!"

"But you killed him first. You are as valiant as a *Valkyrja*." He closed his eyes, but still could see little when he opened them. He bent to kiss her again, but she turned her face away. He cursed. If he could see her expression, he might know why she was denying them the pleasure they had shared so seldom. He framed her cheeks with his hand and tipped her face toward him. Straining to see, he said, "Tell me the truth, *unnasta*. Was that a kiss farewell?"

"Farewell?"

"You are pulling away from me as completely as when Kortsson jerked you out of my arms."

"I promised to help you find that knife, and I will. Kortsson did not have it, so it must be in London as I had guessed. I will help you find it. A Sutherland never breaks a promise."

"And then?" He kissed her tenderly, although he wanted to hold her close and steal her breath with his caresses.

"You know what you are and what I am. You will go back to live your life in your own century, and I will stay here. Despite all that has happened, nothing has changed, has it?" She stepped away from him and was gone before he could reply.

Even if he had had a reply.

***

Nils readjusted his cravat, looking at the room reflected in the glass. He was grateful that his eyesight had returned, although it had taken almost two days and multiple visits from the village doctor. On the doctor's orders, during the day, he had sat in this room with the drapes closed so he did not strain his eyes. It was good that Tuthill's assembly was being held after dark, or else Nils would have been unable to attend, for the sunlight still sent pangs shooting through his skull.

He glanced over his shoulder again and again as he finished pulling on his coat and adjusted his sleeves. Only Linnea would understand why he was so edgy. Jack just tried to stay out of his way.

Hearing a noise, he turned, but saw no one behind him. Stepping away from the glass, he resisted rubbing his still itchy eyes. Loki may have intended to teach him a lesson, but it was one he had already known. Loki was as insane as some of the old stories had suggested.

Nils walked down the stairs toward the foyer. The buzz of excited voices met him. He was surprised to see Linnea standing off to one side with Dr. Foster. While her parents and Martin and Minnie waited by the door, she seemed to be in intense conversation with the professor.

"How do you fare?" Lady Sutherland asked as Nils stepped down from the lowest riser.

"Much better." He bowed over her kid glove-encased hand.

"Such a freak accident." She shook her head. "I have never heard of its like."

"Nor I."

Martin asked, "Has your eyesight fully returned? The doctor was hopeful that it would be restored completely by next week."

Lord Sutherland clapped his heir on the back and

laughed. "Haven't you seen how he keeps looking toward Linnea? Of course the man's eyesight has returned."

Nils smiled at his host, but walked to where Linnea was still talking with Dr. Foster. Although he could not hear her words, her expression held an earnest desperation. Was she seeking some way to prevent their inevitable farewell? He did not want to remind her that he was far more acquainted with the way of the *Norrfoolk* than Dr. Foster, because that might still the last wisps of hope.

He could not keep from admiring her beauty. Her ebony hair was woven with small white flowers that matched the ones on her gown. With her pink cheeks and enticing smile, she invited a man to come closer and explore every bit of her sensual warmth. Her eyes glittered, but that light dimmed when she glanced at him.

The now familiar ache twisted inside him. He should be making her ecstatic, not miserable. Were the gods laughing along with Loki that, in helping him as she had promised, she was sacrificing her happiness...and his?

"Ah, Barrington," said the professor with a broad smile. "Now I understand why Lady Linnea's attention has been wavering during my explanation."

"I am so very sorry, Dr. Foster." Her words sounded sincere, and maybe they were, but Nils could think only of having a chance to speak with her alone. "I think we are ready to leave now."

Linnea was not surprised when Nils's hand on her arm kept her from catching up with the rest of her family as they walked out of the house. He drew her to one side, away from the lanterns on the house and the pair of carriages that would take them to Randolph's estate.

"I must know one thing before we leave tonight," Nils said softly. "We have not spoken of Tuthill since...since the accident."

She looked at where her family remained in earshot and understood why Nils did not mention Loki by name. "No, we have not, but nothing has changed. Randolph expects to announce tonight that I will wed him."

"I thought you told him you would not."

"No matter what I say, no matter what I do, he refuses to acknowledge my words or my actions. His mind is so set on a single course, he will not be shaken from it."

"Only a fool will not heed the words of another, especially when they have been repeated over and over." His fingers swept up along her face. "But then, I can understand his reluctance to let you go. You do look like an *engill* tonight."

"*Engill*? You called me that the first day when you were in the pavilion. What does it mean?"

He smiled, and something quivered deep within her. "Your language and mine are not so different on many words. *Engill* and angel sound much the same, don't they?"

"Angel? I didn't think...that is, do the *Norrfoolk* have angels?"

"At least one of them does." He pulled her more deeply into the shadows, and his laugh warmed her mouth as his tongue glided along her lips, decorating them with liquid longing. When her fingers curved along his nape, his kiss deepened until her swift breaths thundered almost as fiercely as her heart.

"Linnea! Where did you go?" Her mother's question was impatient.

Linnea put her hand on Nils's cheek, then hurried to where her father was waiting to hand her into her brother and Minnie's coach. She wished she could shake this feeling that tonight she would be saying good-bye to all she had dreamed of.
***

The ballroom was filled with so many candles and lights that it could have been midday. As Linnea sipped on her wine and listened to the myriad conversations around her, she could not help worrying that this would hurt Nils's eyes. She might have asked him, if she had seen him. He had ridden here in the other carriage with Dr. Foster, and the professor had been talking enthusiastically to him when they entered Tuthill Hall. By the time she had finished greeting Randolph and extracted her fingers from his grip, the two men had disappeared into some other room while Nils was congratulated for saving her from a thief.

Did he understand why she had let him be lauded for the deed? She feared he did not. It had been a futile attempt to show him that he could have the glory and honor he craved in this time, too. But he knew the truth. She had killed Kortsson, and he could take no honor from that. The only way he could expunge the shame on his family would be to return with the knife to the past and present it to his chieftain.

Minnie was waving her fan in front of her face, which was, Linnea noticed with sudden alarm, a sickly shade. Taking her sister-in-law's arm, Linnea steered her to a chair near an open window.

"Thank you, Linnea," Minnie said. She waved her fan more quickly. "Is it extraordinarily hot in here, or is it me?"

"It is warm...and it is you." She sat next to Minnie. "Do you want me to have Martin come over?"

"No, he is too squeamish. I fear he will sicken before I do." The air from the fan wafted the curls on Minnie's forehead. "If I sit quietly, I am sure I will be fine."

"If you want me to call a carriage, I can."

She shook her head. "That would mean explaining to everyone about the baby."

"Mayhap it is time anyhow." She chuckled. "Randolph has wanted to have an announcement made tonight. Why not a happy one?"

Minnie did not smile. "You sound as if you expect

to be making a not-so-happy announcement as well."

"I would rather not speak of it."

Grasping Linnea's arm, Minnie said with rare intensity, "You must speak of it. With Lord Tuthill, and without a delay."

"He will not heed me."

"You must make him heed you."

"And then what?" The words slipped past her lips before she could halt them.

"Marry Lord Barrington. He clearly dotes on you. He could pay no mind to anything but you when he saw you at Sutherland Park tonight." She flung out her hands. "He saved you from that horrible interloper as well, risking his life and his eyesight to make sure you were unharmed."

"No, I cannot marry Nils...Niles." Linnea hoped Minnie did not notice her mistake.

"Why not?"

Coming to her feet, Linnea said, "There are many reasons."

"He loves you, Linnea." Minnie snapped her fan closed, halting Linnea's reply. "Do not argue with me and tell me that I am mistaken. I know I am not." She took Linnea's hand. "And I know you love him."

"Sometimes love is not the only reason to marry or not to marry."

"I agree. Not being in love is a reason *not* to marry, but, if you love him and he loves you, do not forfeit this one chance at true happiness." Tears filled her eyes. "Martin and I fought the opinions of others to wed, even our families who did not understand that we had more than a calf-love for each other. I have no idea what is standing in the way of you marrying Lord Barrington, but ask yourself if you will think, even a few years from now, if it was worth throwing away this chance for a lifetime together."

Linnea nodded, but said nothing as she went to where her father was gesturing at her. The tears that had glistened in Minnie's eyes now burned in hers. A lifetime together? She and Nils had had two lifetimes together, but not a single one they could share beyond these precious days.

She had a smile in place as she reached her father. "Yes, Papa?"

"Our host was looking for you." He stepped aside so she could see Randolph beside him.

"Forgive me," Randolph gushed, "for neglecting you for so long. A host's duties are unending."

"I understand that."

"Will you stand up with me, Linnea?"

She hesitated. She did not want to hurt him or her father who had thought he had chosen wisely in allowing Randolph to court her. Looking from Randolph's expectant face to Papa's smile, she nodded. She could not hurt both of them when they had done nothing wrong.

She was the one who had done something wrong...by falling in love with a man who should not be here now. While she had resisted Randolph's attempts to give her a chaste kiss, she had shared delicious love with Nils. She should not have listened to her heart, for it had betrayed her before she could betray Papa and Randolph.

"Thank you," she said quietly. "I would enjoy dancing with you, Randolph." She let him take her hand. A part of her wished that her heart would leap with excitement as it did when Nils touched her. How much simpler all of this would be if she could come to love Randolph as she did Nils! But her heart continued its steady rhythm, as indifferent to Randolph as always.

Randolph's fingers tightened around hers as they walked away from her father. When she tried to tug her hand away, he growled, "Have you no shame, Linnea? I will not get into a tugging match here in the middle of the ballroom floor."

"Then loosen your grip. That hurts."

"Oh." He did as she asked. "I thought...That is..."

"Randolph," she said with sudden sympathy, "mayhap we should talk instead of dancing. There are some things we need to discuss."

"I would prefer to dance."

Linnea kept her sigh silent. She might have been changed in recent weeks, but Randolph had not. She doubted if he ever would. And why should he? This was the life he had chosen for himself—the quiet, quite respectable life of country aristocracy.

As the music played, she matched her steps to his as she waited for him to say something. Even if they had been strangers, it was his responsibility as a gentleman to make conversation with her while they danced. She was amazed that he had asked her to waltz. If he did not want to talk with her, why had he chosen this time to dance with her?

Her heart sank further when she saw Nils sitting next to Minnie. She wanted to be in *his* arms, twirling to this beautiful music. She closed her eyes as she imagined moving with him to the serene song that became a crescendo when they were joined together as one in the need that overwhelmed them. Swallowing her moan of yearning, she tried to smile at Randolph.

He frowned at her and did not speak during what seemed to be the interminable length of the dance. Only when it was over did he ask her if she would like something cool to drink. She nodded, and he led her to a table where a wine fountain offered the choice of a dark red wine and a pale one. Taking a glass of one— she paid no attention to which—she sipped.

"The air is close in here," Randolph said abruptly.

Linnea glanced about the room. "There are so many candles. They make a room seem more close than it is."

"Then let us get some air."

"Randolph, I do not think we should. After all—"

He yanked on her arm, nearly pulling her off her

feet. By the time she had recovered, they were outside on a low terrace that was shadowed on both sides by huge trees.

"I shall not be treated so rudely," she said as she tried to twist her arm out of his grip.

"You? You are the one who is treating me rudely!"

"Me? I have done nothing."

Randolph took a sip of his wine, then tossed it and the glass toward one of the trees. As the glass splintered, he herded her toward him. "That is right, Linnea. You have done nothing."

"So why are you in a pelter?"

"Because you are going to be my betrothed! It would seem that you should show me a modicum of affection on the night we are to announce our betrothal."

She shook her head. "I am not going to announce my betrothal to you tonight."

"I have been patient with you, Linnea. I have courted you and paid you compliments, and I tire of waiting for you to make up your mind."

"Randolph, I have made up my mind. You simply will not heed me when I tell you that."

"You are a foolish child, pampered by your parents and your older sisters and brothers. It is time that you understood what a man expects from a woman."

"But I do not love you," she said, trying to turn her face away as he bent to kiss her.

"Love? Love is not important in a reasonable marriage. Marriage is for other things than love."

"What other things?"

He gave her a haughty smile. "Do not worry yourself with that, Linnea. If you want love, I would be glad to show you how I will make love with you."

She opened her mouth to scream, but a laugh from the shadows intruded. Tugging against Randolph's arms around her, she broke free. She stared at Nils who was leaning against the thick trunk of the tree at the other end of the terrace.

"What are you doing out here?" demanded Randolph.

"It is possible," Nils replied, walking casually toward them, "that I came out here to raise a cloud."

Randolph sneered. "You turned green last time you smoked a cigar."

"That is why I said it was only possible." He took Linnea's hand in her lacy glove and bowed over it. "It is also possible that I have the next dance with Linnea."

"As possible as you smoking a cigar out here?"

"Quite correct, Tuthill. These dances are not of my taste. I admit that I have become so lost in my studies that I am not as familiar with the dances that are *au courant*." He grinned at Linnea as he used the French cant that so often baffled him.

Her urge to smile back vanished when Randolph asked in a heated tone, "Maybe you should request that the orchestra play some ancient song. Or didn't the Vikings dance?"

Nils laughed, and, by the doorway, heads turned. Several people peered outside, curious about what was so funny. "The Vikings, as you persist in calling them, enjoyed many entertainments."

"Raping and burning and looting."

"Randolph!" Linnea gasped.

He grasped her hands. "My dear, forgive my coarse speech. Such words are not for your delicate ears."

"'Tis not your words that I find objectionable, but your constant unkind comments to Niles. He is my father's guest, and you treat him with endless insults."

Randolph's mouth worked, but no words emerged.

"I do not take insult," Nils replied, although his narrowed eyes suggested otherwise. "One cannot take insult when another speaks out of ignorance." He held out his arm. "Allow me to take you back inside, Linnea. I feel in the mood for a dance lesson."

Linnea put her hand on his arm, grateful for the chance to escape, but even more grateful for the excuse to touch him. Her fingers stroked his arm, and she was powerless to halt them. When he smiled, she was sure she could never be happier than when she was with him like this.

"I am sorry," Nils said.

"Sorry?"

"For the state of your toes when I step on them over and over."

At his words, she glanced back at the door where Randolph stood, watching them, rage twisting his face. "I do not think I want to dance now."

"If I was wrong in intruding on you and Tuthill—"

"No, Nils, you were not. I need to be alone with my thoughts. Your voice and Randolph's and Papa's and Martin's and Minnie's fill my head, and I cannot hear my own thoughts." Putting her other hand on his arm, she fought not to splay her fingers across his chest as he slipped his brawny arms around her. "Give me the time to think."

"It cannot be for long."

"I know." She walked out of the room before he could ask another question. When she looked back, he was not following. She should be pleased that he respected her request, but she was not. She did not understand her own desires any longer. At the very moment they urged her to be reckless and give in to her need to be held by him while she could, she knew that anything less than forever with him would not be enough.

Twenty-Three

Linnea followed the maze of corridors in Tuthill Hall until the music from the orchestra was silenced beyond the stone walls. When she reached a door opening to the gardens, she faltered. Rain was beginning to pelt the walkway, and a chill clung to the air. Mayhap the storm was her escape. Surely no one would follow her out into it.

But Nils would.

Averting her face from the rain, she went down another passage. There were no wings on this house as there were at Sutherland Park, and she had to find somewhere to hide, somewhere where she could have a chance to think.

She came around a corner and gasped. A soft glow floated along the passage in midair directly in front of her. It was like the light reflecting through the crystal globe that had taken her and Nils to *Fensalir*. What was it? She hurried forward, not sure what she would find. Fear trembled through her. When last she had seen such a glow, it had been accompanied by what Nils insisted was a Norse god. That made no sense, but neither did this light that seemed to be coming from nowhere.

As she got closer to the glow, she stopped, then inched forward. It vanished. Stepping back, she watched it reappear.

Her disappointed laugh was shaky as she raised her hand and moved it up and down. The glow appeared and vanished in the center of the passage. It was just lamplight reflecting in a looking glass on the wall. Letting her longing to be in Nils's arms betray her was stupid.

Nils...

Linnea saw a tufted settee just inside the door. Going in, she dropped onto it. She loved Nils. That was the only thing she was certain of as her life spun out of control.

Her eyes widened as she stared across the room and saw a glass case set between the two windows. It had three shelves. The uppermost one held only a single, ragged bag. Bits of embroidery clung to it, but most of it had been ripped away. The middle one was filled with stones marked with the strange sort of writing she had seen on the memory stone by the mound. She paid them no mind, for on the bottom shelf was a knife in an ancient, water-stained sheath.

She jumped to her feet and ran across the room. Although time had stolen much of the glorious color from the haft, she could see the dragon's open mouth and how its tail vanished beneath the sheath. She stood on tiptoe to see the knife better. A gasp burst from her when she noted the three small creatures holding up one part of the dragon's elongated, snake-like body. She stared at another figure carved within the dragon's mouth. Not a man, but a god. Loki!

This must be the knife Nils's brother had stolen, the knife that had compelled Nils to come to this time so he might find it and fulfill his oath to his chieftain. Why had she thought she had seen it in London instead of here on the neighboring estate? She frowned, then recalled how Randolph had spoken of cleaning out his father's house in Town before it was sold. She must have seen it there when she went with Papa to call on the late Lord Tuthill.

Why hadn't she recalled that? She had been at the
Tuthill house in London a score of times.

The sound of distant laughter was faint, but she
could not fail to recognize it. Loki! He had had a hand
in this from the very beginning. Somehow, he had
betwattled her memory, playing tricks on her mind as
he had with Nils.

It no longer mattered! The knife was here.

Looking back at the doorway to make sure no one
was there, Linnea lifted the hook closing the door of
the glass case. The hinges screeched as if to warn that
she was trespassing. She lifted out the knife and cradled
it in her hands. It was heavier than she had expected,
and it would take a strong man to wield it.

A man as strong as Nils.

A half-sob threatened to bubble past her lips as her
exultant smile faded. If this truly was the knife that
Nils sought—and it must be because she doubted if
there could be another— once he had it, he could be
returned to his time and the completion of his quest.
She stared at the open case. She could put the knife
back in there, blow out the lamp in this room, and leave,
closing the door behind her. Nils had no reason to
suspect the knife was here. They could go to London,
and he could search there. He could seek and seek and
seek the knife...and he would remain in this time with
her.

"Linnea?"

She whirled to face the door and Nils.

"I know you wished to be alone," he said, "but we
must talk about what has happened between us,
unnasta."

Without speaking, Linnea raised the knife in both
of her hands.

A gray sheen ruined Nils's healthy bronze
complexion. It was as if she were seeing him again
when he was lying battered and near death on the shore.

Taking the knife from her, he ran his fingers along the dragon's head. He drew it out of the sheath and touched the carving in the blade.

When he tilted it toward the light, she said, "Loki and the dwarfs are on there as well." She touched the haft. "Right here. Just as you described it."

"This is my chieftain's *sax*." He put it back into its sheath. "Thank you, *unnasta*."

"Now you can return it to your chieftain."

His lip curled with fury. "When I have repaid Tuthill for not telling me about this knife."

"No, you cannot blame Randolph for denying you that knife." She grasped his coat sleeve. "Nils, you must listen to me."

He whirled to face her. "How many times have I mentioned my search for anything of the *Norrfoolk*? He never spoke of this."

"Randolph may not even know it is of the *Norrfoolk*. He is not interested in old things. How many times have you heard him mention *that*?" She touched the knife. "He probably considers this nothing more than a useless trinket that was not worthy of his time, although he clearly considered it valuable enough to bring it from London."

"This? You believe he sees no value in my chieftain's blade?" He raised the sheathed blade between them. "*You* recognized its worth."

"Because you spoke candidly to me of it." She put her hands on his arm, lowering the knife so she could see past it to his eyes that were slitted with rage. They widened as she added, "To you, Nils, this knife is the reason you were denied the death you believed would be your reward as a loyal warrior. It is the symbol of an obligation you have taken upon yourself to redeem your brother's name and your family's honor in a way that slaying your blood-enemy never could.." She touched the jewels sewn into the embroidery on the fraying sheath. "For Randolph, it is only one of the many things collected by the Denner family during the past thousand years."

"My vow is my vow, Linnea. I told Freya that I would see the man who kept me from doing as I pledged would pay for that with his life." Gripping the knife, he drew it from the sheath. "Nothing Tuthill can say will persuade me to spare his life."

Linnea stepped between him and the door. "You cannot kill him."

"Do not get in my way. You cannot understand."

"Because I am a woman?" She folded her arms in front of her. "I thought you said a Viking woman had rights and knowledge to match a warrior's."

"You cannot understand because you are a part of this time when honor means so little."

"How can you say that?" she cried, her serenity severing to reveal her pain. "You know that I care as much about my family's honor as you do. That is why..." She hid her face in her hands.

"*Unnasta,*" he whispered.

When his hand stroked her hair, she looked up at him. "Nils, I love you." There. She had said it. The words that had filled her heart until she feared it would burst had been said.

She waited for him to smile, but he scowled. "You say that and yet you are willing to give yourself to a most dishonorable man and tarnish the name Sutherland."

"Do not change the subject."

"I thought Tuthill and his dishonor and the dishonor he will heap on you were the subjects."

Linnea shook her head slowly. "No, the subject is why you cannot kill Randolph. I beg you to heed me."

Sorrow dimmed his eyes. "I did not realize that you cared for Tuthill so much. You say that you love me, but do you love him, too?"

"'Tis not how I feel about Randolph that matters. 'Tis the fact that he is not your prey. He is not the one who kept you from finding this knife." She took a deep breath and raised her chin. "I am."

He held her chin in his broad hand, a smile returning to his expressive lips. "I know you wish me to heed your gentle heart, *unnasta*, but you, who have not denied me the secrets of your soul and the sweetness of your lips, would never deny me the chance to succeed in doing as I had pledged."

"But I have." Stepping away from him, but staying between him and the door, she whispered, "I told you the knife was in London."

"You said you believed it was there. It was nothing but a mistake in your efforts to aid me."

"Then I found it here. If you had not come here as you have to discover me with it here..." She wanted to close her eyes and escape the accusations in his.

"You would not have told me?" He spoke the words as if he could not believe them himself.

"I do not want you to return to your own time." She ran her fingers along his cheek as he had hers so often. "I love you, Nils Bjornsson. You are the one who makes me whole, the part of me that has been missing for a thousand years."

"But I cannot stay here. I must complete my vow. The only reason I am living now is that Freya heard my pledge and saw it as honorable."

She took the knife and drew it from its sheath. Handing it to him, haft first, she said, "Then do what you must."

Nils looked from the blade to Linnea's eyes that glowed with courage. And with love. She yearned for him to remain with her here in this time, but she loved him enough to let him go back to the life that should have been his.

"*Unnasta*, I vowed to slay the one who kept me from returning this to my chieftain."

"I know."

"Yet you aver that person is you."

"Yes."

His arm swept around her waist as he brought her
to him. She tensed, and he knew she expected him to
slay her. How could she not see the truth? His lips
over hers must tell her.

When she pressed closer, he held her, the flat of the
blade against her, so it would do her no harm. He looked
down into her eyes, her loving eyes, and saw the
resignation there. He had sacrificed his chance to join
the heroes in *Valhalla*, but he had found a new life.
She was willing to forfeit everything to give him his
final chance at honor and that seat in *Valhalla*.

He groaned as he dropped the knife onto the settee
and slanted his mouth across hers. Her arms tightened
around him, and he knew she was kissing him good-
bye. *No! I cannot repay you for all that you have
done for me by killing you.*

He must have spoken those words aloud, because
she whispered, "You have made a pledge, Nils. A blood-
oath."

"But the blood was not meant to be yours." He
swore and looked toward the north wall of the room.
"This is Loki's doing."

"Is it?" She tilted his face back toward her. "Or is
it nothing more than the cost of saving your family's
honor?"

He kissed her again and again and again, as if he
could memorize the shape of her mouth, the flavor of
her lips, the scent of her flesh. As her hair tumbled
down into his fingers, he buried his face in it. No
memory would be as magnificent as this woman who
enticed him as no other had.

"What in hell do you think you are doing?" came a
furious shout from the doorway.

Linnea gasped as Nils turned to face Randolph.
She started to answer, but Nils said, "I would think it
was quite obvious what we are doing."

Randolph stamped into the room. Trying to push

his way between her and Nils gained him nothing, because Nils refused to move. Randolph put his nose close to hers and snarled, "Whore!"

Nils's arm was around his throat, the dragon knife against Randolph's ear before Linnea could react. "Apologize now, Tuthill, or you will not hear her accept your apology."

"Nils, please don't," she begged.

Shoving Randolph aside, Nils lowered the knife. He handed it to Linnea. "Guard it well, *unnasta*, for I fear I shall be tempted to repay this cur for what he has said."

She nodded, knowing he would have slain Randolph right here if she had not halted him.

Randolph rubbed his ear and grimaced when his fingers came away dotted with blood. "Barrington, are you planning to steal from my exhibit case as well as from my bed?"

"Randolph!" she gasped again as Nils's hand reached for the knife he wore beneath his sedate coat. "You should not speak so."

"Why not? 'Tis the truth, isn't it?" He snatched the knife from her. "This knife belongs in the exhibit case over there."

"He did not steal it." She raised her chin as she had to Nils. "I took it out to look at it."

"So you will steal from me and give what you take to this man you have fallen in love with." Randolph's lip curled. He tossed the knife toward the settee, but it missed, falling to the floor. She saw Nils wince, but looked back at Randolph as he asked, "Do you think he will love you more than he does his studies of long dead folk?"

"Love?" she retorted, hurt that he had spoken first of the knife. Mayhap he *had* known it was here as he watched like a miser over every valuable he had inherited. "I thought you said less than an hour ago that love was of the least concern in a reasonable marriage."

Nils said quietly, "That is why he decided to court you after he missed his opportunity to marry your sister Dinah. It does not matter to him which one of you he wed. What matters is the connection he could have to your father and his brilliant acumen for making business investments."

"Is this true?" she asked, staring at Randolph.

"You would believe this stranger over a man you have known all your life?" Randolph fired back.

"Answer me!"

Randolph swore, for once not apologizing for his language. "I have known both you and your sister all your lives. Either of you would have made a good wife. When Simmons set his cap on Dinah, I saw no reason to contest him for her, because you were unwed, too." He glared at Nils. "Now you flounce about like a harlot with this man."

"I love him, Randolph."

"Love?" He sniffed. "What good is love? I could have given you a comfortable life here in Tuthill Hall. You would have been close to your family, and we would have joined them for dinner regularly."

Nils added in the same hushed tone, "So you could gain any information you could from her father and brother about their business ventures. It is unfortunate, Tuthill, that you wasted all your charm on Lord Sutherland and his heir. If you had saved a bit for Linnea, she might have been willing to forsake love to marry you because she so wanted to be in love as her sister was."

"All this talk of love. What good is it? Can it repair a roof? Can it pay the tailor? Can it fund a household?"

Pity flooded Linnea, and she glanced at Nils. He had been right. She had pitied Randolph. First for the debts left to him with his title, and then for the shallowness of his heart that held no love for anything but financial security.

"Love may not be able to do any of those things," she whispered, "but it can make the impossible possible. It can go anywhere—It can go any*when* to reach the other heart it wishes to share. That is what I want for you, Randolph." She put her hands over his. "I want you to find the one person who fills your every waking thought and walks through your dreams. I want you to have the joy of seeing someone's eyes light up for you as they don't for anyone else. You have always been a good friend to my family, and you have been patient with me, but you do not love me. Why would you deny yourself the happiness that should be yours?"

"The dowry your father promised—"

Nils said quietly, "The bridesprice Lord Sutherland would have given you is less than what you could receive if you sell these items to Dr. Foster." He pointed to the open case. "He would be very pleased to have these Viking artifacts in his collection, and I suspect he would gladly pay dear for them."

"Really?" Randolph picked up the ragged bag. "For this?"

"It is a *veski*, the pouch a Viking would have worn at his side. I doubt if many have survived until this time. Dr. Foster should consider it of great worth, for I doubt he has anything like it." He glanced at Linnea, then went on, "You should speak to him about it, Tuthill."

"I shall. Without delay." He bent toward the floor. "If this small bag is so valuable, think what this knife must be worth."

"Yes, think of it," came a deeper voice from the doorway.

"Papa!" Linnea cried.

Lord Sutherland picked up the blade before Randolph could. "It is clear that you have cared little about the value of this until now when you believe you might be able to get some of the realm's gold for it,

Randolph."

"I never suspected these old things my father kept in a box on top of the tea chest had any value but sentimental."

"Sentimental?" Lord Sutherland appeared about to explode, but released his breath and frowned. "If there is any sentiment attached to this knife, it comes from my family."

"Your family?" Nils asked. "Why yours?"

"Because this knife once belonged to our family. It was stolen from the Sutherlands during the upheaval of the Civil War nearly 150 years ago." He frowned at Randolph. "Do not look so shocked. You know as I do that it was a member of the Denner family who stole it."

Randolph stared at the floor like a naughty child. "Yes, but because—"

"The reasons why it was stolen and the reasons why the Sutherlands did not demand it back at the conclusion of the war mean nothing now," Lord Sutherland said in his sternest tone, the one that all his children had learned to heed.

Apparently Randolph recognized it as well. He hung his head farther and nodded. "That is true. King Charles I is long dead."

"As were those who rose against him. The past should be buried along with those who lived it."

Linnea grasped Nils's arm as he flinched. She wanted to reassure him that Papa was not speaking of him, but how could she comfort him without revealing the truth?

"And," her father continued, "we should be thinking of the future. It seems right to me that in the future this knife should be where it belongs. There are ancient Sutherland family legends that speak of this blade being stolen from our family once before. Centuries ago. When the Vikings were prowling these shores, but apparently it was found again after the Conquest." He looked at Nils. "I would like to speak to you and Dr. Foster about that, Barrington. You may be able to help me sort out the facts from the legend about the Viking chieftain who came here to attack, but fell in love with an Englishwoman and stayed."

"Yes...yes, I would be happy to," Nils replied.

Lord Sutherland put the knife beneath his coat. "I came to tell you that we are about to take our leave. Minnie is not feeling well." A smile nearly exploded across his face. "I should let her share the happy news, but it seems she is going to have a baby. She needs to be resting quietly."

"We will be right there, Papa," Linnea said.

While Randolph trotted after her father like an eager puppy aiming to please, Linnea faced Nils. "Now you know why," she said, "Minnie could not travel with us to London."

"*This* is the secret you were keeping?"

"It might not have been a vow as grand as a blood-oath, but it mattered to me. I did what I vowed to do."

He stroked her cheek. "As I did what I vowed I would do. I saw the knife that my brother stole in jealousy returned to my chieftain."

"What?"

"I told you that my chieftain was sometimes called *Suthrland.*"

"I do not remember that."

"You may not remember because it was when you were trying to save my life, and I was making yours miserable."

"And succeeding very well."

His smile broadened. "My chieftain's name was Suthrland, but it might have become Sutherland as the years unfolded. The names are almost the same, so, in playing a part in bringing the *sax* back into your father's possession, I have returned the knife to the man who has the closest claim to my chieftain in this time."

"I do not understand. Papa said the knife was

already returned to my family so many years ago."

"True, but then it was stolen again."

"By Randolph's ancestor."

"By a Denner." He rubbed his chin, then grinned when he realized he was copying Dr. Foster's pensive pose. "Denner may very well be a name that came from the word 'Dane,' which was what the *Norrfoolk* often were called by the English during the reign of Ethelred. If his family line comes from a wayward Viking who remained here to escape the fury of his countrymen..."

"You think one of Randolph's ancestors was your brother?" she asked, guessing the course of his thoughts.

He shrugged. "It is possible. Or even Kortsson's son's son, down through the centuries. I doubt if we will ever know for certain, but it would make sense that I was brought to this time rather than when the Normans came to claim the English throne. Then the knife was recovered, but it was destined to be taken again. Maybe by my brother's seed. It was not until this time that the knife could be found by me and returned to my chieftain, once and for all, to serve my oath."

"So now you can go back to your own year." Her eyes grew heavy with tears, and she did not wipe them away as they fell onto her cheeks. "Once I hoped your time here would be brief, Nils, but I wish you could stay."

"Linnea, I—" With a curse, he pushed her behind him as a flash of light filled the small room.

The light glittered off the glass case and threatened to blind them as Nils had been at Sutherland Park. When Linnea tried to move, he kept himself between her and the glow that was ebbing to reveal a woman she had never seen before.

"'Tis Freya," he whispered. "The light is coming from the splendid necklace about her neck. It is the Brisingamen, the necklace that she had bedded four dwarfs to possess."

"Your quest is complete." Freya held out her hand. "Your reward awaits you in *Valhalla*, Nils Bjornsson."

"No!" cried Linnea, for the goddess was speaking in English. To taunt her? Linnea did not care what Freya's reasons were. Not when Freya was offering to take Nils away to a place where Linnea would never see him again. "His reward for his fealty should not be death."

Freya's lip curled in derision. "Be silent! You are not of the *Norrfoolk*. You may have some of their blood, but your thoughts are those of an Englishwoman. You do not understand the honor done to him in offering him this seat at the right hand of Odin."

Hearing Nils's sharp intake of breath, Linnea bit her lip. She loved him. She had told him that she loved him, that she was willing to sacrifice herself to allow him to return to his time. How could she stand between him and this glory that he had aspired to from the moment he took his warrior's oath?

"Why do you say nothing, Nils Bjornsson?" asked Freya, her voice once more a satisfied purr. "*She* does not understand the honor awaiting you, but you do."

"Yes, I do."

Linnea glanced at him again, tearing her eyes away from Freya's unbelievable beauty. His voice was as unemotional as if he were speaking of the weather. Less, for he had exulted in the play of the wind around them, always aware of how a breeze could send his ship across the waves.

"So come with me, Nils Bjornsson." Again Freya offered her hand.

"I asked you to send me your handmaiden to help me complete my quest, Freya." He bowed deeply. "I thank you for heeding my plea. You have brought Linnea into my life, and I thank you for that as well."

"You thank the wrong one," said a warm voice.

Linnea stared as another form took shape beside

Freya. This woman was tall and had thick blond hair. She wore a simple gown that was decorated with the complex pattern of embroidery that belonged to the *Norrfoolk*. At her waist were a set of iron keys hooked to a simple chain, but she wore a necklace even more glorious than the one Freya had.

In amazement, Linnea realized she had seen this woman before...every time she climbed the stairs leading up from the front foyer of Sutherland Park. "You are the woman in the oldest portrait hanging in my father's house!"

The woman smiled. "Then I had another name, but, Nils Bjornsson, you know me as Frigga."

"We are honored that you are here." Nils dropped to his knees, bowing his head. He had seen the painting, but he had not connected it with anyone in *Asgard*. The carvings he had seen of Frigga had not resembled this woman.

"Frigga?" Linnea gripped his shoulder, not sure if her abruptly weak knees could hold her. "You are Frigga, Odin's wife? But you look just like the woman in my family's gallery."

Frigga stretched out her hand. When Linnea hesitated, the goddess said in her melodious voice, "Do not fear, child. You have long been drawn to learning more about me and the times before now."

"Yes." She placed her fingers on the goddess's and knelt.

Frigga put her hand on Linnea's head, and a gentle warmth radiated through her. "You are not Freya's handmaiden, daughter of Suthrland, for you bear within you the blood of one who served me well when the Nine Worlds were born. On that day, my handmaiden chose to surrender her immortality for the love of a mortal. The sons and daughters she gave him have proven to be fruitful." She smiled. "I have watched over my handmaiden's children, and I am not pleased to have others interfere with one of them."

Freya grumbled something, flouncing her robes. Vexation flitted through her eyes. "So it is as Loki warned me." She pointed to Nils who was coming to his feet. "You have many powerful allies beyond *Midgard*, Nils Bjornsson. I should have realized that when you were snatched from the *Valkyrja* to come to this time. When next I deal with this world, I shall ascertain what the will of the residents of *Asgard* is first."

"You might suggest the same to Loki," Nils said, bringing Linnea up to stand beside him.

Frigga laughed. "You are a daring mortal, Nils Bjornsson. I suspect you, too, have within you the blood of the gods."

"That would explain why you have gained such favor among them," added Freya, still pouting. "Your brave deeds are exemplary, but no other mortal man has been granted the wish you have or allowed to make the sacrifice you did."

"I shall thank Odin myself when I see him at his table in *Valhalla*," Nils replied.

"That time is not now," Frigga said, again putting her hand on Linnea's head. "It is pleasing to see that those who possess my handmaiden's blood still live in honor and still treasure the love that fills their hearts."

"Thank you," Linnea replied. "I know you have helped Nils in the completion of his quest."

Frigga smiled. "I only sent him to you, child. The rest was your doing. However, Nils, son of Bjorn, you gave up much rank to come here to see that the blemish upon your family's honor was erased. You should know that what you gave up is still yours."

"I do not understand," Nils said, glad to speak the words he had thought so often since he began the search for the knife.

"You are, in this time, *Lord* Barrington." Frigga smiled and touched Linnea's hair like a doting grandmother. "You will have the rank you deserve as a reward for your protection of the heart of my handmaiden's child."

"Can you create a title for him just like that?" Linnea blurted.

Nils steeled himself for Frigga's icy fury, but the goddess smiled. "You have only seen part of what I can do, child of my handmaiden, so believe what you have seen. A title and the lands to go with it on an island off the coast of what you know now as England are his, as they would have belonged to his descendants if he had remained in his own time. Come, Freya."

Linnea sank to sit on the settee as the two women vanished. When Nils knelt beside her, she pressed his head to her breast as he leaned his cheek on her hair.

"You are still here," she whispered.

"Yes."

"You could have asked them to take you back to Ethelred's reign. This is not your time or your place."

"It was not, but I would like to remain here...with you."

Her breath caught, and she could not speak.

"*Unnasta*, I love you."

Tears spilled from her eyes as he spoke the words she had feared he would never be able to speak. "I love you, Nils Bjornsson."

"So you know it is true that we belong together." He looked up at her. "In this time or any other. In this place or any other."

"Yes." She touched his rough cheek to assure herself he truly was here.

"Then let me stay with you here and now." He smiled. "Here, as Niles Barrington, I can have what I always hoped would be mine."

"But you wanted to go to Iceland, and—"

He took her hands and kissed first one, then the other. "Dr. Foster wishes for me to join him and his staff on a research trip to uncover Viking relics at a site in Iceland."

Her eyes widened. "Your dream come true."

"I had thought so." He brushed his mouth against hers. "No dream can come true without you being a part of it, Linnea. Come with me."

"To Iceland?"

"You taught me what I needed to know to survive in your Polite World. Come with me, and let me show you what remains of my world." His tongue played along her lips until she giggled with delight. "Let me show you the love we share for this time and all others. Come with me and be my *viigi maka*, my wife, Linnea."

She laughed. "Yes, I want to share my *viigjinn* with you."

"How did you learn the *Norrfoolk's* word for wedding?"

"I have been speaking with Dr. Foster, too." She smiled as he drew her to her feet and into his arms. "I want to spend...What is the word?" Looking up into his eyes that glistened with love, she said, "I want to spend *aevi* with you."

"Forever?"

She nodded. "Forever."

"That can be a very long time."

Slipping her hand up through his tawny hair, she murmured as she brought his mouth to hers, "I hope so.

ABOUT THE AUTHOR

J. A. Ferguson is the best-selling lead author of Regencies and historicals (Ballads, Precious Gems, and Splendors) for Kensington writing as Jo Ann Ferguson and Rebecca North, paranormals for ImaJinn (writing as J.A. Ferguson), and historicals for Berkley (writing as Joanna Hampton), Harper, New Concepts Publishing, and Tudor. She writes inspirational contemporaries for MountainView Publishing (writing as Jo Ann Brown). She sold a historical suspense to M. Evans and contributed to an encyclopedia published by Garland on the English Regency period. Her work has been honored with award nominations by ROMY, *Romantic Times,* Rom/Con, and *Affaire de Coeur,* and has been showcased on Amazon.com. *The Counterfeit Count,* May 1997 Zebra Regency, won the 1998 ARTemis Award for Regency from Romance Writers of America. She is the editor of *Now That You've Sold Your Book. . .What Next?* and wrote the clause by clause explanation of publishing contracts included in it.

She is the past national president of Romance Writers of America and is the recipient of the Emma Merritt National Service Award, the highest honor for volunteer work from Romance Writers of America. She also has received the first Goldrick Service Award from the New England Chapter/Romance Writers of America. She was awarded a Massachusetts Art Grant to teach creative writing, and she established the romance writing course at Brown University.

She lives in Massachusetts with her favorite hero— her husband Bill—her three children, one very arrogant cat and an outrageous kitten.

J. A. Ferguson enjoys hearing from her readers. You may contact her at:

J. A. Ferguson
PO Box 575
Rehoboth, MA 02769
email: jaferg@erols.com
http://www.joannferguson.com